THIRTY YEARS
OF RAIN

THIRTY YEARS OF RAIN
Edited by Elaine Gallagher, Cameron Johnston, Neil Williamson
Interior design, layout and typesetting by Hal Duncan
Published by Taverna Press, Glasgow, Scotland

ISBN 9781326753429

THIRTY YEARS
OF RAIN

EDITED BY ELAINE GALLAGHER,
CAMERON JOHNSTON, NEIL WILLIAMSON

Taverna Press

Contents

When You Say SF...

The question most asked by new members thinking about joining the Glasgow SF Writers' Circle is: do you guys *only* write Science Fiction? Of course, the answer is no. The SF in the Circle's title is a shorthand. A *hook*. Let's say the S stands for *Speculative* or *Strange*. Anything that encompasses the myriad, hard to define exotic flavours of creativity that quicken the hearts and fire up the imaginations of people like us. From space opera to cyberpunk, from heroic fantasy to magic realism, from horror to supernatural romance, one of the Circle's strengths, one of the reasons for its longevity, has always been the openness of its members to view every style, every mode, every trope on their own merits. And to encourage individualism and experimentation, always with an eye on the market but also with the understanding that selling your work isn't always ultimately what's important. What's important is conjuring dreams—*your dreams*—and discovering how to do that the way that only you can.

In this book you will find the weird and the fabulous, the adventuresome and the mundane, the subtle glimpse and the full out, downright strange. You will find short stories and long stories, flash fiction, vignettes and poetry. You will find work by authors whose names are familiar from bookstores and awards and you will discover new writers that you are going to love.

Every story in these pages is wildly different from the next, but all of the authors share one thing: for a few weeks or a few years or a few decades they've sat down and discussed what makes great fiction, then they've gone away and put that into practice.

We hope you enjoy the results.

That Was Then, This Is Now
Duncan Lunan

This book marks the 30th anniversary of the first 'Science Fiction and Writing' course which I set-up in 1986, and out of which came the Glasgow Science Fiction Writers' Circle workshops, which continue on a fortnightly basis to this day.

In the run-up to *The Glasgow Herald's* 200th anniversary Chris Boyce suggested an SF and fantasy short story competition for new writers. The judges were Chris, the late Professor Archie Roy, Alasdair Gray and myself; the prizes were an Amstrad word processor and an astronomical telescope, presented by Joe Haldeman and Keith Roberts at that year's Albacon III SF Convention in Glasgow.

The first story received was Richard Hammersley's "Big Fives", a terrific story, written in a redacted futuristic version of English, suggesting that the judging would be harder than we thought, especially when the numbers of entries climbed past 300. The final winner was "Spaced Out" by David Crooks.

At the end of the competition, Dr. Ann Karkalas, a member of an earlier SF Circle with myself and Chris in the 1970s and a course organiser at Glasgow University's Department of Adult and Continuing Education, suggested following the competition with a 10-week writing class. The Department mailed every competition entrant within 25 miles, and attracted enough students for the class to go ahead.

Participants included Richard Hammersley and Elsie Donald, both runners-up in the competition, and Michael Cobley, whom I knew through the SF conventions. Late in the first term I held a workshop—and when Anne Karkalas asked if we would like a second term, the class's reply was yes, provided that the emphasis was on workshops. At the end of the second term the group continued as the Glasgow SF Writers' Circle.

One major influence on it was a workshop on workshops which I attended during a two-day folk singing seminar led by Ewan MacColl and Peggy Seeger in 1966. But the big difference from their technique is that there is no place in the Glasgow SF Writers' Circle for a *leader*. Veronica Colin took on the role of organiser, because all groups need someone to administer and agitate, to answer queries and keep things moving, and she performed it wonderfully. However, there are no gurus; all voices in a critique group are equal. I learned that method in the mid-70s at the UK Milford SF Workshop (modelled on the US Milford Workshops led by Damon Knight), founded at Milford on Sea by James Blish, and chaired by John Brunner in the four years for which I attended. I learned a great deal from it and GSFWC's format follows its principles.

In our version of the Milford formula, the story for discussion is read beforehand, and while the critics speak in turn around the room, the speaker may not reply except to a direct question—forcing attention to all that's said before agreeing, rebutting or arguing. There may then be a second open round of discussion, which often continues in the pub, but generally we feel the first round's enough stress for one evening. Wide berths have been given in many Glasgow pubs to the group in the back corner engaged in animated discussion of something truly arcane, but we do buy a lot of beer.

In the classes, adapting MacColl's techniques, I first let the members critique one of my own stories, to show that I could take it as well as dish it out, but also to demonstrate that criticism should be constructive, and, where negative, should be specific and suggest remedies. To paraphrase MacColl: *"To say 'this scene is rubbish' is not criticism, it's abuse. What I think you meant to say was, 'The character's motivation here isn't consistent with his earlier actions, and that could be fixed by...'"*

The group format allows a potentially painful process to become impersonal, and although (as a psychologist once pointed out) it has elements in common with both group therapy and with Chairman's Mao's group criticism, the object is not to score points but to help one another achieve professional publication. Pretty well everyone who has stuck with the group has achieved publication in one field or another and some, like Louise Welsh, William King, Michael Cobley, Gary Gibson and Hal Duncan, have made it their careers.

The workshop method isn't everyone's cup of tea, however. The professional writers around in the 80s (Chris Boyce, Gus McAllister, Archie Roy, Alasdair Gray) all declined to be involved except as competition judges, and by coming to talk to the class about their own approaches and experience. At the celebration of the group's 21st anniversary, I said that the GSFWC writers had made it by application of their own talents and effort, and would almost certainly have made it anyway, by one means or another; it was just very gratifying that they'd chosen to do so by this particular route, and thereby helped so many others along the way.

This is far from the first anthology to showcase work by the group's members. In 1989, I edited "Starfield, Science Fiction by Scottish Writers", with a cover by Sydney Jordan and an introduction by Angus MacVicar, honouring the two Scots who first got me into SF, and featuring all of the winners and several of the runners-up from the five years of The Herald competitions. "Shipbuilding", launched at the 1995 Glasgow Worldcon, was a joint effort by GSFWC and the East Coast SF Writers' Group, and "Nova Scotia: New Scottish Speculative Fiction" celebrated the same event in 2005. But three books in over 25 years hardly do justice to all the talent out there.

GSFWC continues, as belligerently as ever, to help new writers into print. Having moved back to my home town of Troon and turned 70, to some extent I'm now watching from the sidelines. But as new opportunities open up in the Scottish SF scene, and the GSFWC takes on a welcome international character—as always, I wish the new writers herein every success.

The Freedom of Above
TJ Berg

Alex blamed his inability to sleep on the absence of her hair tickling against his neck, on the fading of her scent—night sour and lavender—from the sheets, on the lack of the occasional jostle of foot or elbow. These things represented the void that was June more than the empty body lying in the coma ward. No brain activity, they told him. There was no question. It wasn't like a hundred years ago, when there was room for doubt.

"Lights," he muttered, giving up. The room gradually illuminated. He made a cutting gesture with his hand when it had reached a gentle light. As usual, it responded too slowly. The house always seemed better tuned to June. He reached for his earp on the end table, wrapped the thin wire behind his ear and tapped the retinal projector into place. The RP flashed a brief green, signaling a sound connection. Then he picked his t-shirt up off the floor and slipped it on, padded barefoot down the stairs and tripped the Vwall. "Yosemite," he said, before it had a chance to bring up the news. The footage of their week backpacking and climbing in Yosemite began. They'd climbed the face of Half Dome together. And how many other crazy things?

On the Vwall, she was lying on her back staring up at the night sky. The perspective was his, leaned on his side to take in her face as she took in the stars. "I can't help it," she said. "All that endless universe." She'd been too young for the competition to go to Mars. She'd hoped there'd be another. That they could go together. He'd never told her how frightening it was, the thought of flying through space with nothing but a bit of human engineering between him and an endless vacuum. But he'd overcome his fear of heights for her. He would have overcome that, too. Until wet leaves killed her. Not even Crash Aversion could stop a car fast enough when someone falls into the road almost under the wheels. The car swerved, but hit her head with the bumper. She would never go to Mars. She would never do anything again.

Tomorrow would be even more terrible if he didn't get some sleep. They'd allowed him the full, standard one month safety margin before pulling the plug. That expired tomorrow. *These days,* the doctor had said. *Everything is replaceable but the brain.* She'd been very sympathetic. *She might look whole, but she's gone. Just take some time and find your way to saying goodbye.*

Like that was ever going to work.

But if he could only get some sleep. If she was just there, beside him, like she'd been for the last seven years, then maybe. In their video, his helmet cam caught her hiking ahead of him, bounding toward a boulder at the edge of a cliff or hill, silky black ponytail bouncing at the back of her head. If he could have that again, her hair in bed with him, her weight.

Alex booted up his 3D printer. He'd booted it up almost every night for the past two weeks, thinking the same thing, but not quite daring. He knew it was common enough. Hell, people used to go to stores before they had the privacy of a 3DP to download things like this to. And it wasn't as if he was going to use it for sex. Just the weight of it, some hair, something to have on the other side of the bed. All the ready lights glowed green. He activated his earp and searched one of the bodymap sites for an appropriate size and shape and plugged in her hair type. He downloaded it, but couldn't bring himself to print it. He shut down and sat on his couch, watched the Yosemite trip until he half dozed, startled awake to the sound of bombs, no, something heavy hitting metal, bonging.

It was from the Yosemite feed. Squirrels chucking giant sugar pine cones down to crash from a hundred feet up against the metal bear bins by their camp site. It had started like some kind of bombardment at dawn, terrifying them, then leaving them laughing and recording the chaos. He turned off the video. Today was his last day with her body.

They allowed him to hold her hand through to the last moments. It was too soft, like an old woman's, not the rough-skinned hand he remembered. He nuzzled his face in her neck, but she smelled of hospital soap and alcohol wipes. Even her hair didn't feel right.

Sun streamed in, hot on his back. A nurse started to close the shades. "No," he said, his words mushed by the crush of his cheek against her chest. "No, let her see the sun. She always liked to see the sky." Any adventure but underground, she would do. He remembered her utter panic the one time he'd convinced her to try caving. She'd scratched his face trying to push past him. *Even when I die. Even when I die, don't bury me,* she'd wept later that day. She liked the freedom of emptiness above and below her.

Alex's head rested on her chest as it drew its last machine assisted breath. Something shuddered inside. The wet pounding lurch of her heart slowed. At some point they left him alone. He assumed that meant the silent machines they'd been watching confirmed her death—her body's death.

Moments later a drawn out squeal stirred him. "I'm very sorry, sir," a young man in a lab coat said. "But we need to collect the body." He leaned against a large silvery container, digital readouts all along the side.

Alex knew it was coming—another consequence of their caving adventure. June had been very clear in her living will that she wanted her body donated to research. He just hadn't realized quite how quickly they were going to come for her.

"Sir?"

"I'm going," he said. He didn't want to see her handled like a corpse.

✧   ✧   ✧

Four more days without sleep. The doctor had given him pills but they didn't really help. He would fall unconscious for a few hours, but wake into restless half-sleep. He gave in and printed the body. He tried not to think about what other men used these for when he laid it out on the bed. It had a heat generator, was pliant and soft, and he even rubbed a little of her soap on it to make it smell more like her. But in the end, it wasn't her. It was a weight on the other side of the bed. He threw it in the recycler.

He was making mistakes at work, dangerous mistakes that might get someone hurt. His boss, Lyssa, was sympathetic, but that didn't mean she could let him stay on the job. She walked outside with him, sat him on a bench with her in the park across the street while she smoked a cigarette.

"I'm just not sleeping," he told her. "I haven't slept alone in a long time."

"My sister went through this, too," she said. "Last year."

"It's just not right, her not being there."

"Take a few days," she told him. "We'll be okay." She slipped him a business card when she was done with her cigarette. A shrink, he supposed, jamming it in his pocket, but it had already uploaded to his earp when she'd pressed it into his hand. He thought about taking it off before the card could fully load, but it was only a short audio file, no visuals.

Dreaming of sex with Miranda Phoenix? Marilyn Monroe? How about the President's wife? We've got the maps. You've got the printer. If we don't already have it, we can map it. Any body, any time. The site link saved itself to his cloud.

Alex crinkled his face. What the fuck was wrong with Lyssa? Not only was unauthorized body-mapping illegal—and he really didn't want to know how she got access to this site—but did she think he was some kind of desperate pervert? His wife dies and suddenly he wants a celebrity sex doll? He pulled the card from his pocket. The RFID tag had burnt itself out. The only evidence left was the link saved in his private files. He crumpled the card and threw it into the nearest recycler.

He slept fitfully, dreamed of sex with June, dreamed of falling down Half Dome, crawled out of bed and watched movies until dawn. He wasn't sure he was the man in the movies anymore, the one that laughed and talked and lived with June. He stumbled to the bath-room but saw her toothbrush, the cinnamon toothpaste she liked. He backed out, dizzy with exhaustion, tripped on an end table and fell to the floor. He curled up on his side. Nestled in the pile of the throw rug was one of her hairs.

Alex crushed his eyes closed.

He awoke, shivering, to his mom and dad bent over him. No, not them. They'd died. They'd always been dead. No, his sister, Hanny. And his brother-in-law, June's brother,

Quincy. Hanny hauled Alex up, but he fought her until she let him sit on the couch. He wouldn't go back up to his bed. "Alex," she said. He shook his head.

She made him breakfast, talked about funeral plans. Quincy was silent. He hadn't come to see her body off at the hospital. He hadn't wanted to see her die. He pushed a coffee cup around on the table. Hanny was in charge.

The slurry of days spilled across each other. Relatives and cards and flowers and phone calls and even awkward neighbors like winter slush, mucking things up when he wanted to freeze beneath a nice, pure white snow of grief. At night he lay in his bed, sweating or cold, drenched in desire or missing the warmth of her body. He piled some of her dirty clothes on the bed. He put a pair of her panties on his pillow, stared at a tear in the elastic.

He had one of her bras in his lap when he finally linked to the contact on the card that Lyssa had given him. A stream of protocols flashed across his RP then a private chat opened up. He had no doubt the face that appeared was a skin, but it was well made and listened with realistic facial expressions as Alex awkwardly explained about the death of his wife. "I, uh, I just want her body," he said. "Not for anything, you know, perverted. Just, something to sleep with. For a while."

A thin-lipped frown of sympathy and a tight nod. "Not an uncommon request. It can be very therapeutic. It is a shame that it's illegal."

"She'd have authorized it, I'm sure, if she'd known…"

Another tight nod, as if it grieved the skin. "Of course. That's one reason we have this service." Alex let himself believe that, ignoring the tickling memory of advertisements that had previously flashed up for sex with various celebrities.

"I, but—" He collected himself. "I don't have a scan, of course."

"No, but there will be plenty from her stay in the hospital. We have resources."

Then they talked about price. It wasn't cheap, but shockingly, within an hour, he had all the data files necessary for his 3D printer to create a high quality body. He'd paid extra for their secret recipe for "the most flesh-like material science had to offer." That took longer to print, but by the next morning, he had a body that he could drag up to his bed.

The first night with the June body he slept some. He awoke the next morning hard, pressing painfully against its flesh-like buttocks. He was massaging its breasts before he even quite realized what he was doing. He pushed the body away, heat burning his cheeks, then feeling doubly embarrassed that he was blushing at an empty room with only a sex doll replica of his wife to judge him. He almost threw it in the recycler. But it was so like her, so exact in every detail—the three moles on her left hip, the slightly larger left breast, the scars on her knees, and even her stretch marks faintly etched on breasts and hips—that recycling it almost seemed like murder. And, he had slept, felt calmer, less blurred. He left her under the covers. *Just something to fill her side of the bed,* he told himself. He wouldn't spoil her memory.

But each night, he woke, aching for her, aching to be inside her. He woke more and more until he was laying in sweat soaked sheets, awake through the night, thinking about her. They'd given the copy a hole. He closed it out of his mind. The days became, again, the grey of half-melted snow, sticky and slippery and dangerous.

Then one night he spread its legs and gazed down at the soft part, the gap that had always been so welcoming, and couldn't help it. He was so hard it hurt. He entered it, the gap, he let himself go.

It wasn't right. Not that it was wrong, as in he felt it immoral. Maybe a little weird, and he didn't like that this thing had her face, but it didn't talk, it didn't tease him or tell him what it wanted. There were no friendly nips from its mouth against neck or shoulders. It looked exactly like her, but it just wasn't quite right. He played with her hair, reminisced about a camping trip when he was a kid, tried to just talk like he might normally do after. But it wasn't working. It didn't feel like her. Not when he was inside, and not now. He slept lightly dreaming of how it used to be.

He linked again the next night and talked to the skin.

He was glad that his own skin was not so emotive, for he felt the red splotch his cheeks and neck as he explained his dilemma. At first, he was vague, using words like "inside" to describe the problem.

The skin smiled a sad sort of smile. The sympathy-face it generated was incredibly convincing. Alex almost felt like the man behind it really did feel for him.

"What you're describing is not easily remedied," he said. "I can't give you your wife back. I can adjust certain physical aspects. Is there something specific you'd like altered?" Was he teasing him now? Is that what kind of smile the skin wore? "Is there a way we can make it feel more right? To help you… get through your grief?" Alex felt his mouth go dry, thinking of what he wanted. He wanted her back, of course, that was what he wanted, to talk to her and climb mountains and go swimming, and eat a boring dinner of grilled cheese sandwiches, but he couldn't have that. He could have something though, something to help him get past the worst of this, couldn't he? Like the skin said, something to help him get through his grief.

Alex, clearing his throat to get past the lump of dryness, switched to more clinical terms. "Her vagina," he said. "It isn't right."

"A special scan is needed for that," the skin said. "Not standard medical practice. If she had died only today, we could probably arrange a scan, but you say weeks have passed. Her body would be too far decayed. It is not something you would like."

"No," Alex said. "No, actually, she might be well-preserved. She donated her body to research."

There was a long pause, the skin still and expressionless momentarily.

"We can locate the body, if you wish. But you'd have to gain access to it."

Alex leaned back in his chair, a wave of panic prickling his skin. "How could I do that? I don't know how to break in to—I don't know, wherever they have her."

Another long pause. He realized his jaw was clenched, his breath shallow. He tried to force himself to relax.

"She has been donated to a university. It is possible I can connect you with someone who specializes in such things, for a fee."

Alex didn't haggle, but did demand one thing. "I go with. I'll do the scan."

"He may not accept those terms."

"I go with," he said. He wasn't having some stranger scanning his wife's vagina.

He met the man named Clyde at a pub. The man dashed off the remains of his pint within moments of Alex walking in, then shifted his bulk off the stool. "Right then," he said. "You're the one wants his wife's vag?" A few people turned to stare at the loud, crude Englishman. Alex's cheeks burned. Clyde left two dollars on the bar and strode away, whacking Alex on the back to encourage him to follow.

They walked through a park and eventually onto the university campus. Clyde carried a large case, swinging it easily in his meaty fist. "Done weirder," he said. Alex spared a glance, not sure if the man thought they'd been having a conversation. "Just saying, wanting your wife's vag. Not exactly mad." Before Alex could object, Clyde said, "Here we are." The building said it was the Department of Physics.

"Here?"

He nodded, then continued around the back to a garage door.

"So, what do you do? Override the electronics or something?" Alex asked.

"No, I knock." He gave a couple solid thuds to demonstrate. A moment later, the door started rattling upward. "Universities." He shook his head. "Always a poorly paid post-doc around to bribe."

Light flooded the alley. A head poked out. A rather scrappy young man waved them in. The door closed. They stood among large boxes and crates while the young man handed out guest badges. The names said "John Brown" and "Mike Wood." The post-doc wore a photo identity card that said "Benjamin Blight."

"You have a comic book name," Alex said, then wondered at his own inanity.

"Can we hurry?" Benjamin said. "If my boss finds out about this she'll kill me."

"She should pay you more," Alex said, following.

Benjamin scrinched his face up. "She doesn't choose. The grants tell us what we get paid." He used his badge to go through a secure door that led to a poorly lit stairwell. "Don't want to use the elevator. There's probably other people around," he explained as they wound down. And down. And down. Alex lost count of flights.

"Christ, where are we going? The dungeon?" He ran a hand over the wall, expecting to feel damp.

"Oh, a lot of physics goes on underground. For safety, or sometimes for physics reasons."

"What the hell are you doing with June's body down here?" A cold sweat prickled across Alex's skin. They'd put her underground, in a cave, in a dungeon, away from the sky. To do physics on her.

"Hey man." Benjamin stopped. "Should we turn around and go back up?"

Alex muttered something. He knew it wasn't words but he did it anyway. June would have cut the scrawny physicist in two with some well selected words. Alex remembered the time that they'd been walking their friend's dog for her at her apartment complex, and some woman had accosted them, berating them for walking their dog on private property. After threats of police and reporting that met with only a blank stare from June, the woman had snorted and glanced at June with her clearly Mexican heritage and Alex with his mixed background. "Figures, you people don't even speak English."

"No," June said. "We just don't speak bitch." Then she'd continued calmly walking the dog. Alex would have muttered an apology and fled. He realized he was smiling and quickly squelched it. These two probably already thought he was a weird pervert. *June would have faced this,* Alex thought.

"No, let's go," he said. They continued down.

Finally they exited the stairwell and entered a hallway. Above, only every third light was on. Everything was dark and gloomy and even though he knew it was just where they were storing her body, he felt horrible that June was trapped down here.

"The clinic is this way," Benjamin said. Alex scrambled after him with Clyde trailing behind.

"Clinic?" Alex ducked in the door after Benjamin then stumbled backward into Clyde. He wasn't sure anymore where he was, when he was. What he saw wasn't right. Alex felt his knees go weak. Clyde steadied him with a surprisingly gentle hand.

June was stretched out on a hospital bed. Life support equipment trailed off of her just as it had when last he saw her. Her chest rose and fell. A heart monitor traced across the screen. Two other bodies lay on beds next to hers. The room was cluttered with shining equipment of metal and glass.

"What is this? What have you done?"

He pushed past Benjamin and ran to June, not quite sure what he was going to do. Clyde's hand wrapped around his arm and pulled him away from her. Benjamin held out his hands.

"She's dead, man. Remember? Dead. Just a body."

"This isn't—this isn't what you're supposed to be—" Alex stopped and sagged against Clyde, realized he smelled of beer and wasn't really someone he wanted to lean on, then straightened up and shook his arm away.

"She donated her body to research. No one said its heart couldn't be beating."

"Shit, that's cold," Clyde said.

Benjamin shrugged. "I let him come down here to do *that*." He nodded toward the case Clyde carried. "At least we have permission to use her body."

"That's my *wife!*" Alex grabbed June's hand. It was soft, too soft, hands that hadn't been used in too long. "I just wanted—and you—you guys lock her up in a dungeon and do, and do, I don't know what? What the hell are you doing with her?"

"We're preparing her for space travel."

"You're—what?" Alex clenched June's hand tighter.

"Space travel. These three will be part of the research probes."

"Space?"

Benjamin nodded. It was a tight, tense nod. He glanced at the door. "Can we hurry this up?"

Clyde set down the case and undid the clasps.

"Tell me about it," Alex said. "Please?"

Benjamin sighed. "I'm not a biologist. I'm working on the engineering stuff. But we were just waiting for a third body. They needed to die in a coma *and* want their body donated to research." He fiddled with his badge. "What we'll be doing is testing the effects of long term space travel in this experimental hibernation on muscle wasting and a bunch of other biological parameters. DNA damage and all that stuff." He had clearly become excited. His voice rose. "The mission will be three parts. It starts off heading for Europa. Then it divides. One will land on Europa and stay there, monitoring the environment and the body. The second will go into orbit then head home after six months. The last one will continue out of the solar system, sending back data on the condition of the body inside it, as well as all kinds of other data. It's never coming back."

"Which one?"

"Excuse me?" Benjamin's badge bounced down on his chest.

"Which one will she be?"

"Oh, it hasn't been decided yet which body will go where."

"Send her to space. I mean, send her on the one that goes away forever."

"Listen, I don't get to make the call. The biologists are in charge of the bodies."

"Send her to space. Send her off into the universe."

"Come on, I can't—"

"She was a mechanic, you know. Really good at it. Kept people safe, got people to work, made things run efficiently. Grease would stain the cracks in her fingernails." Alex stroked her hair. And what was he? A systems analyst for the Department of Defense. Every day she did real things, made real things happen, fixed real things. He mired himself in data. He hadn't liked it but she'd told him, over and over, that data was real. Data was important, too. Now, she could go to space. They'd send back data. Data about her. *Data affects the world, too,* she said.

He had to get them to send her. "She wanted to go to space," he said.

Benjamin had come up to her at some point, was staring down at her face. He touched her hand briefly, shuddered, backed away. "Okay," he said. "I'll try. I'll try to make sure she goes all the way out."

"Thank you."

"So," Clyde said. "Can we get this done?" He held up a shiny black scanner. It made Alex's stomach feel suddenly twisted and hollow. June was going to space. Should he really keep any part of her back? He wanted her, wanted everything of her, and wanted her body, wanted the excitement of her touch and the way she felt. And this was his only chance to keep any of her before she was gone. Her chest rose and fell.

She was already gone.

"Never mind," Alex said. He could never get back the parts of her that mattered. "Never mind about that."

"You sure?" Benjamin asked. Alex nodded.

"I still get paid for this," Clyde said. Then he put the scanner away.

"I'll, uh, let you know, and you can come to the launch," Benjamin said.

Alex nodded. He bent and gave June a kiss on the cheek. He put his mouth against her ear, so his words would be only for her. "I'll be watching for you in the sky."

Skyrider
William King

After the crash he was finished. One night he went over the wall and fare-jumped the first mag-lev out of Paris. He sat with a group of Workfree headed south to find a place in the state Pensions.

In a seat across from him sat a small dark-haired girl. Her name was Rosa. She had failed to find work in the theatre and was returning to Marseilles. She did most of the talking. There was little he could tell her.

He was on the run and wired for combat in an aircraft he would never fly again. He had just turned twenty-three.

The Wing carried him out over the bay towards Chateau d'If. Below he could see the tourist hovercraft. All around a flock of flyers banked and wheeled, crucified on the skeletal struts of their harnesses.

He pulled himself into a shallow bank, watching the digital readouts on the inside of his visor climb into the danger zones, feeling the cold tug of the wind on his body. It was a clumsy way to fly, a pale shadow of being integrated into an aircraft, but it was the only thing he had. The government provided a complement of recreational Wings to all Pensions.

On the roof of the arcology he could see Rosa. She was talking with someone. She seemed to be pointing at him.

He was at the wrong angle to use the normal approach to the Pension's landing ramp. Rather than try for a long, slow arc around the building he decided on the more direct method of descent.

He came in at a steep angle, bringing the Wing into stall configuration. The memory plastic of the harness whipped around until the Wing was almost a parachute. He absorbed the impact of landing with a flex of his knees, feeling the shock through the cushioned soles of his boots. A quick glance showed Rosa and another woman approaching.

The woman was tall and thin; taut muscles rippled under her tiger-stripe skinpaint. The only thing she wore was a Braun wrist-tag.

Her name was Monica. She was Rosa's supplier on the odd days that Rosa supplemented her government money with a little dealing. Rosa said she was an old friend, moving up in the world. She didn't seem to like her very much.

"Rosa said you were a pilot," said Monica. "I can believe it."

He shot Rosa an angry glance. She looked away guiltily. Her movements had an electric energy, her pupils were the size of pin points.

"What's it matter to you?" he said.

She stared at him. Their glances locked. "Do you really want to discuss it out here?" she asked.

He looked into her cold, blue eyes and then shook his head. "Let's go downstairs."

Discreetly, Rosa stayed on the roof. She was staring in fascination at the empty sky overhead.

The apartment was small but it had the basic amenities. The Tube clicked on as they entered, showing scenes from a Front National rally. The right wing alliance were getting a lot of media coverage. They were expected to hold the balance of power in Euro-Parliament after the elections. He hit the off switch on the console and the wall went blank.

He pulled the duvet over the futon then began to empty the ashtrays. After years of barracks living, Rosa's untidiness made him uncomfortable.

Monica swept the room with her tag. She was checking for bugs.

"My, aren't we the paranoid one?" he said.

She continued to sweep as if she hadn't heard. With a quick jerk she yanked out the fibre-optic cable connecting the tube console to the wall.

"Fibre-optics are virtually untappable," he said.

"Can't be too careful."

"Get to the point."

"Right. You don't officially exist, yet you're living in state housing reserved for the Workfree."

"So what? I live with Rosa. I've dropped out of the social security network. I'm not unusual. There must be thousands of invisible people in Marseilles."

"But you're a pilot."

His sockets were like Rosa's scars. They could not be hidden in the intimacy of the bedroom. She kept asking about them and one drunken night he had told her. He had never asked about the scars.

"It's strange that a man who can fly lives in a Pension. You have a skill. You could have a well-paid job if you wanted."

"Maybe I can't fly. Maybe I only told Rosa that to impress her."

"No. You can fly. We checked." She told him his real name, his squadron, the name of the hospital where the motor and perceptual centres of his brain had been modified. While she spoke, he gazed past her.

"What do you want?" he asked, still not meeting her eyes.

"We want to give you a job. Pay you for what you were trained to do."

He could see her striped back reflected in the wallscreen. She was offering him a chance to fly again in a proper aircraft. He had been remade by the military into a human component for a flying machine. He could only ever function fully in the air.

"You were trained to fly helicopters?" said Monica.

"Anything I can be hooked into."

"You didn't get this in an army surplus store," he told Monica, running his hands along the cool carbon-fibre flank of the Mitsubishi Skyrider. She laughed and turned to look up at the green slopes of the Atlas Mountains.

His respect for Monica's connections had increased greatly. In its day, the Skyrider had been very near state-of-the-art. Probably some Third World dictator had boosted his coffers by selling this one.

"It's fucking beautiful." He felt exultation well up in him as he gazed at his idea of perfection: the sleek propfan jet with reinforced rotors for near supersonic flight, streamlined as a shark, ominous bulges of weapons pods under each wing and a turret on its underbelly.

"It's radar invisible. We have the latest electronic counter measures systems on board. It's fuelled and ready to go."

He looked back at the white painted mansion. Men in Bedouin robes and heavy, insulated gauntlets were carrying crates out from the house. They held them at arm's length. The metal boxes glistened with moisture, condensation from the cool of their cryogenic interiors. Men with sub-machine guns watched from the roof.

"What are they?" he asked.

"Spare parts." She studied him closely. "Do you have a problem with that?"

He shivered a little.

"No," he said, at last. "No. They've got to come from somewhere."

Overhead, the fixed stars of the orbital factory halo gleamed in the night sky. He climbed into the cockpit. Monica clambered in beside him. He noticed the bulge of a holster under her cutaway jacket. She was wearing the baroque multi-layered skirts and jackets fashionable with the Nova Rich this season.

She pulled on a mike and headset. "Ready?"

He spooled out the fibre-optic cable, felt the click as he connected its jack-plug with his spinal socket. He leaned back and closed his eyes, feeling awareness of the onboard systems sweep over him in a familiar rush.

The Skyrider became his body, he became its brain. The engine throb was his heartbeat, complex detection systems were his senses.

After long abstinence, the sudden flow of information was almost too much, an ecstatic experience more intense than any drug. He could perceive a new and larger universe through senses better and faster than human. His body was no longer a weak, pulpy envelope of flesh but a sleek, hard thing, knowing neither weakness nor desire. In that moment, he felt like a god, ready to leap into the sky and hurtle through the vast African night.

With an effort, he regained control, forced himself to monitor the incoming data-flow and begin the pre-flight checks. There came a thrill of recognition as he spotted what he had missed in the initial confusion of jacking in.

"New systems," he said.

"Very new. But you should be used to them."

The hardware was highly classified, cutting edge military gear, the kind he'd been trained to use.

He reached out with radar fingers to probe the distant mountains. He took a deep breath. The readouts for fuel, airflow and temperature were superimposed on his sight. They all looked correct.

"You love this, don't you?" Monica said.

"Flying is better than anything."

"You'll have to teach me sometime."

He swivelled a microwave antenna, bringing it to bear on a comsat, unobtrusively patching himself into the air traffic control net. Reality melted into computer simulation, pumped directly into his brain through his modified nervous system. The land became a gunmetal grey sculpture in filled 3-D graphics.

He became a small point on a vast grid. Overhead passed the blue pulses of incoming planes, the white images of outgoing aircraft from Marrakech airport. Somewhere over Gibraltar, the flashing red arc of an emergency descent hurtled towards an ice-blue sea.

He added weather patterns and watched the dark lines of depressions sweep across the infinite plain of his awareness.

I'm adding the co-ordinates of our destination. Over the intercom circuit, Monica's voice sounded as though it came from light years away. The white tower representing their destination rose in the distance.

He asked the computer for the flight plan. Lines of light flashed out, weaving across the grid linking him to the distant tower. He merged into the systems until the Skyrider once more became an extension of his own body.

He fed fuel to the engines, feeling power build within his body. He rose over the simulated landscape as the Skyrider rose into the air.

He jacked into the weapons system and wheeled the belly turret through 360 degrees. Through its camera, he saw the mansion retreat and watched the fields scroll by below him. If anyone looked up, they would only see a dark shadow against the black and hear the whisper of muted engines.

Carrying a cargo of stolen eyes, he arced towards the Mediterranean.

❖   ❖   ❖

"It's immoral," said Rosa. Her speech was slightly slurred, her pupils were contracted. She had become her own best customer for Haze, the latest designer drug. "How can you do it?"

"It's money and a new ID."

"Do you know how they get those parts?" she said.

"No. And I don't care."

"Harvesting, they call it. They find parents who are too poor to feed their children. They pay them for spare parts. An eye, a kidney. You know what the going rate was for a kidney, when I was a kid here in Marseilles?"

His eyes wandered to the wallscreen. On it was an advertisement for Oui, a new perfume. An idealized Rosa strolled on a beach with a handsome man. It was tailored advertising, personalized for each tube subscriber from their data-files, a blend of computer generated graphics and real footage.

Rosa failed to notice his lack of interest.

"Three hundred Euromarks. They sell them to private clinics because there's always a shortage of voluntary donors. Police came down on it here, so now they import."

"I didn't make the world," he said. "I've got to live in it."

"Sometimes they don't bother to bring the kids back, just break them for spare parts. Who's going to complain?"

"What's that to you?"

She ran her finger over the scar on her back. It was a deep trench in the sea of blue bodypaint.

"I used to have a sister. She wasn't as lucky as I was. They let me go." She stared at him expectantly. He touched the tube console, began cycling through the channels.

"You can't do this thing, you just can't." She was almost crying. Behind her, images flickered: a soccer match, a soft drink, Charlie Chaplin.

"Who says I can't?"

"When they altered your brain to let you fly those copters, I think you lost something. Some part that lets you feel."

She said it slowly, as if she were piecing it together as she spoke, as if she were seeing him truly for the first time.

"I don't think you're human any more." Her voice was chill and a little afraid.

"That's not true," he said, moving towards her.

"Keep away from me," she said, the edge of drug induced hysteria clear in her voice. "I don't want you near me."

Fifteen minutes later he was carrying his bag through the foyer of the Pension. He was surprised to see Monica waiting for him. How had she known? Then he remembered her sweeping the room for bugs during the first meeting. She had reconnected the tube cable afterwards.

"Bitch," he said, as she moved to greet him.

The tiger mask formed a smile. "Now who's the paranoid one," she said. "You've passed, by the way. You're into the big time. Next trip you fly solo, carry real weight."

From the balcony of Monica's flat he could see the crowds on the promenade, a current of waxed paper umbrellas. Rosa had hated those parasols. She said skinpaint provided all the shielding needed from the ultraviolet rays flooding through the trashed ozone layer.

She wasn't answering his calls. A filter program blocked out all his attempts to contact her.

Restlessly, he prowled back into the living room. The angular Nova-Modernist furniture, grown from self-replicating crystal, contrasted starkly with the uniform fixtures of the Pension. It was a badge of wealth, like the private Intelligence who monitored the building, or the uniformed guards at the doors.

Monica lay on a cushioned couch that resembled a block of onyx, an inhaler on the table in front of her. She offered it to him. He shook his head. She took a hit and turned her attention back to the tube. He closed the glass doors to the balcony.

The huge head of Juan Delgado, leader of the Spanish Socialist movement, filled the wall. He was talking about law and order; a linguistic Intelligence provided simultaneous translation. He referred to the growing drug problem among the Workfree on the south coast. He called for more action by the police. Monica seemed to find it all amusing.

"What will I be carrying?" he asked her.

"Haze. Several million tabs of it. We have the local concession. You'll bring it in from our Moroccan labs."

"Who are we?"

"Local business. Marseilles has always been good for smuggling."

"Organized crime, as Delgado calls it."

She laughed. "More like disorganized crime. This is the age of decentralization. There are lots of different gangs. Most of the time we're at war. Why do you think you're flying a gunship?"

"You're worried about being ripped."

"It's dog eat dog. The big ones eat the little ones. So-called friends will sell you out to the law just to be rid of the competition."

Behind Delgado, computer graphics displayed the drug routes out of Marseilles to the Riviera and the north.

That night he made the first of many trips. That summer, he became a regular visitor to Monica's.

❖   ❖   ❖

Outside, the streets of Vieux-Port were hot. In Giraud's, everything was cool. Huge rotating fans swirled the air. People danced to Eurobeat synthesized by House Intelligence. Giant images of patrons were projected on wall and ceiling screens. Giraud's computers distorted the images, mixed them against hallucinatory backgrounds, fragmented them and edited the pieces into new patterns. The dancers watched hypnotized, locked in the high energy promise of Haze.

On the floor a girl collapsed. Two bouncers went over to her. One had a bionic arm, long and skeletal, from which the carapace had been removed.

He watched as the exposed motors and cables moved silkily, lifting the girl with ease. At a nearby table, a man muttered about a bad batch of Haze, said people were going down across the city.

He looked across at Monica. She was back in skinpaint, local colour, camouflage. The paint contained some luminescent micro-organism which highlighted her bone structure, made her look skeletal. She sipped the drink.

"It's been a long and profitable summer. You've done well," she said.

The House Intelligence picked the image of the girl as the most interesting thing on the dance floor. A splintered pattern of images showed beads of sweat glisten on her crimson face-paint. One wall displayed only her eyes with their shrunken pupils.

He watched the twitching girl. She was back on her feet but starting to fall again. She couldn't seem to balance.

Monica noticed his interest. "It sometimes happens. Haze affects the motor and speech sectors of the brain, produces a condition like Parkinson's disease. Long term exposure can do it, but a bad batch is the worst."

"Our last batch was bad?"

She shrugged, looking meaningfully at the girl on the dance floor then turned back to him.

"This offends you?" she asked.

He sensed the subtle challenge in her voice. He stared at her for a long time. He could not match the vacuum coldness of her gaze. Eventually, he shook his head.

"Good boy," she said. She fell silent for a time.

"You know, you and I are very alike," she said.

"I'm beginning to see that," he said.

On the floor, the girl continued to try and rise, limbs twitching uncoordinatedly, like a spider sprayed with insecticide. Her image filled the walls, sculpted in zoom and slo-mo.

That night, he returned to the Pension for the first time in months. Many of the people he used to know looked ill. He made his way to the flat he had shared with Rosa.

An Arab answered. He could hear the blare of the tube from within.

"Where is Rosa?" he asked.

"Who?"

"Rosa. She used to live here. Small dark girl."

The Arab turned and shouted something into the room, and the noise from the tube descended. He turned back and said: "She's gone."

"Where?"

He shrugged and closed the door.

"I must warn you," said the tired looking doctor, "she is one of the worst cases. Her motor functions are so impaired that we had to operate, wire her into her wheel chair."

"It's okay. I'd like to see her."

"Very well."

They moved through over-warm corridors. They had the empty, understaffed look of most Federal hospitals.

"Rosa," said the doctor, ushering him in. "We have a visitor for you."

At first, he thought she was ignoring him, then he made out the tiny movements as she tried to turn her head. She was shockingly wasted and her hair had thinned. Fibre-optic cable ran from the chair to the top of her spine. Her face was lined. She looked like a woman of sixty. There was a whine of servo motors as the chair swivelled to face him.

"Hello," she said, in a voice that was barely a whisper.

He looked round the room. It was utterly neat. "Hello, Rosa. How are you doing?"

"Gettin' betta." The words were slurred. Her hands were twitching slightly in her lap as if she were struggling to move them. He reached out and took one. She looked at him gratefully. It was disorientating to see the intelligence in those eyes, trapped in that shrivelled body.

"Not fair," she whispered. "Not this. Wanted fun. Not this."

"Christ, Rosa," he said. "I'm sorry."

The silence in the room was like an accusation. He began to talk simply to fill it. He told her that she would soon be better and then they could get out of Marseilles, now that he had money. He could tell by her eyes that she didn't believe him. The quiet seemed to swallow his words, reduce them to meaningless babble.

"I have to go," he said, finally.

"Come back?" she asked with a hint of desperation. "No visitors."

"Yes," he lied. "I'll be back."

At the door, he turned for a last look. Her right hand was twitching. He thought she was trying to wave.

❖   ❖   ❖

He lay in bed and watched the desert sky. The stars gleamed frostily overhead; the air was cold. He could see dunes rolling away into the distance.

The illusion was spoiled by Monica's entrance. Light from the open door flooded into the room. She seemed to step out of a dune. Behind her he could see the hall. Warm air hit him.

She was naked. Without paint, her flesh gleamed whitely. She strolled across and climbed into the bed. Her skin was still warm from the hot-air dryer in the shower.

"This is the last job," she said. "We're moving out of Haze. Since the Parkinson's scare it's not selling."

Political pressure over the casualties was making the police hungry for arrests. Monica probably wanted the money from this last consignment to make a run for it.

"What about me?"

She smiled, revealing small sharp teeth. She reached over to the side of the bed to touch the console. The walls returned to normal, the ceiling went dark. He felt the warm weight of her body press down as she moved to straddle him.

"Don't worry," she said. "You'll be taken care of."

They were waiting for him at the rendezvous point.

In the clearing were two men and a Hyundai 4x4. They stood outside the circle of bio-luminescent tubing that marked the landing site. He hovered overhead, surveying the scene through the starlight scope of the turret camera, looking for Monica. He could see no sign of her. Everything appeared normal, but somehow the pattern was wrong.

One of the men beckoned for him to come down.

He trained the guns of the belly turret on them. He monitored the radio bands closely.

"He suspects something," he heard someone say. "Take him."

There was a crackle of static and then a message came at him over the radio. "This is the police! We have you covered with ground-to-air missiles. Land now or we open fire!"

He tensed. He had been set up. With several hundred kilos of Haze in the back, they would have enough evidence to mindwipe him.

Information from the combat systems of the Skyrider pulsed through his mind. He hovered over the grey plain, suspended under the falling stars of civil airflights. He had already pinpointed the source of the radio call. In the distance, he could make out three insect-like shapes moving towards him. They skimmed over the radar map of the local terrain.

He fed the engine fuel and lifted off, drifted sideways into an evasive pattern and released a mix of chaff and incendiary flares from the tailgate of the Skyrider. He aimed the cannon of the belly turret at the source of the radio call and sent heavy slugs ripping through the trees towards it.

Bright diamonds of Nightowl missiles rose towards him from below. They flew into the glowing particles of chaff. One detonated, another arced away pursuing the red glow of the flares.

He arched himself back into the sky, ignited the afterburners. He watched the fuel readouts sink as he pulled into a high G turn. More missile-diamonds leapt at him. He released more chaff, set his ECM systems for maximum coverage. The warning dots were resolving into three Firedrake gunships. The police must have known about the armament of the Skyrider. They were taking no chances.

"Surrender now!" came the command from a nearby gunship. He sensed the command programs from the radio link attempt to over-ride his controls. Protective software countered that.

He rocketed towards them. The perfect, crystal calm of being integrated in the ship's systems swept over him.

His swift mental impulse released two missiles at the leading enemy chopper. He felt the Skyrider shudder as they were unleashed. The target peeled off upwards, blanketing the area with chaff and flares and broadband static.

One Firedrake swept by below him, while the other veered above and to the right. He altered the pitch of the blades and swung leftward and downward on his rotor axis.

He willed a stream of bullets towards his victim. Tracer crackled through the night. The pilot realised what was happening and tried to turn. His flight path intersected with the cannon shells.

For a second, the armoured hull of the craft reflected the heavy slugs, until they sought out the weak joint where rotor protruded from cowling. Sparks flew then the Firedrake yawed wildly and began wobbling earthwards.

He became aware of the impact of shells on his own body and moved to avoid the irritation, pulling the nose up until he was flying backwards towards a long valley yawning darkly on his display.

Diamonds erupted from a pursuer. He swung the helicopter and sprayed chaff. A warning bleep reminded him that his supply was running low. He power-dived into the radar shadow of the valley. The Firedrake blips vanished, replaced by ghost images of their projected flight paths. He swept over the corrugated grey of the valley.

He was below line of sight and radar, flying using nape-of-the-Earth tactics. He tried to calculate where they would do an overfly, fed the details into the computer.

It was most likely that one would enter from each end of the valley. He moved towards the left and hovered there just above the trees. He heard someone break the radio silence to request back-up. This gave away their position, but lent new urgency to his situation. He was wired faster than the police pilots, but could not cope with the reinforcements they could command.

For a long tense moment, he waited then the monstrous insect image of the Firedrake moved over the edge of the valley. He let fly with his last two rockets. The distance was too short for evasive action or chaff release. The chopper disintegrated in a ball of flame.

Too late, he became aware of the other enemy moving across the edge of the valley. It had not come from the far end, but raced in at an angle from where the other one had been.

Slugs hammered into the body of the Skyrider. He felt searing pain as systems crashed. The grey graphics blurred and faded, the data-flow through the system diminished from a flood to a trickle. A shell had smashed through the scanners. He writhed to avoid a hail of bullets, not caring how dangerous a manoeuvre this was so close to the ground.

Without the data provided by the Skyrider's external sensors, he was like a blind man. He cut in the backup systems and dropped back into his human body. He was momentarily disorientated by the blazing night sky seen through his visor.

Twin lines of tracer fire arced towards him. He knew that the Skyrider's armour was being chipped away. He brought his own guns to bear, willing them to fire. There was no response. The fire control systems were down.

He was going to die, but he intended to take the other craft with him. He opened up the engines and raced forward into the tracer. He watched his enemy loom larger in the darkness as he rocketed towards it. This was the way he wanted to die, hurtling like a meteor through the sky.

The Firedrake began to veer off, ducking sideways and down out of reach. Howling with frustrated rage, he turned around ready for another mad race towards collision.

Then he noticed the inferno below. The Firedrake had been too close to the ground. It had hit a tree and gone tumbling down the side of the valley. He could see its blazing carapace.

He turned the helicopter towards Marseilles, struggling to control a craft now barely airworthy. Nursing the crippled Skyrider home was a constant battle, the integration between human mind and airframe no longer complete. Parts of his extended awareness winked out as the systems went down. Soon he was reduced to flying on manual, by sight. Losing control of the helicopter was worse than losing control of his own body; it was a descent from Godhood.

Monica would have to pay for this betrayal, even if he had to crash the Skyrider into her apartment block.

He could see the distant glow of light from Monica's apartment window. He made final adjustments to the Wing harness, pulling the straps tight, testing the hand controls for responsiveness.

He launched himself from the roof of the Pension, catching the updraft it created. He flew in low under the arc of the rooftop security cameras. His reflection loomed raptor-like in the darkened windows. He was buffeted by the turbulent air close to the building. He fought to keep control, balancing finely on currents that threatened to send him tumbling into the street, thirty storeys below.

He brought the Wing to a stall directly over Monica's balcony.

He fell, watching his visor readouts race into the red zones. The balcony grew rapidly in his field of vision. Waiting till the last possible moment, he snapped open the wings to break his descent. Impact jarred through his legs and he began to fall away from the balcony. Frantically, he fought to regain his balance, clutching at the railing with his gloved hands.

Heart pounding, he righted himself, removed the Wing and slipped over to the window. He peered inside. The walls were covered in soothing kaleidoscopic patterns of light. Monica lay slumped on the couch, On the table near her sat a drug inhaler. He tried the handle of the sliding glass door. It was unlocked. With a savage motion, he jerked it open and leapt into the room.

"What?" she said, staring at him uncomprehendingly.

He caught her by the hair and raised her to her feet, grabbed her arm and forced it up behind her back. He began to push her towards the window. She struggled weakly.

"What are you doing? Let me go!"

He levered her arm further up her back until she moaned. On the balcony, he twisted her head around. She looked up at him. One side of her face was still illuminated by the lights from within.

"You shouldn't have set me up," he said. "Did they give you immunity for turning me and the others in?"

She shook her head. "I don't know what you're talking about."

He jerked her arm viciously. "Don't lie."

She took a deep breath, seemed to relax. Her eyes were bright and cold. "It was business. Nothing personal."

He laughed. "It was very personal for me."

"What do you want? Money? Negotiables? I could make you wealthy." She fixed him with a hard stare.

He thought about his loss as the Skyrider crashed. He held her gaze then slowly shook his head.

"What are you going to do?"

"Teach you to fly," he said.

He lifted her up. She screamed and kicked wildly as he threw her over the balcony. He watched her tumble down into the lighted street. He stood there until a crowd gathered and he could hear the distant wail of sirens.

He strapped himself back into the Wing and flung himself out into the sky. As he drifted upwards, he watched the tiny people below, his eyes as wild and predatory as a hawk's.

The Ranch
Gary Gibson

The room in which I spend my existence is five metres long, four wide. The floor is thickly carpeted, and a television sits in one corner, tuned permanently to a sex channel. At the moment, however, it has been switched off, as per my latest client's request. Opposite the only exit from the room is a bed: a mirror is mounted on the ceiling above, a second on an adjacent wall. The bed is styled after the kind of four-poster favoured by Southern dames in old black and white films set in the days of slavery. A cabinet stands nearby, in which can be found the many implements of my enforced trade, as well as a variety of costumes none of which, mercifully, I have yet been required to use. My clothing is simple: plain black slacks, low-heeled Italian shoes, and a black shirt open at the neck.

There are three cameras in the room—one mounted and visible in the corner above the wall mirror, another concealed within the ceiling light panels, while a third can be found lurking behind the ceiling mirror. Both mirrors are two-way.

The door is locked. There are no windows. This room is my cell, my purgatory.

I pace, feeling weak, dizzy with hunger. I catch sight of myself in the wall mirror: sallow cheeks, a light spattering of stubble, the cast of my face perhaps betraying a distant Italian ancestry. My name for the past few decades has been Carl Mencken. Before that, I remember little beyond a colourless mishmash of vague images and sensations that no longer have any meaning to me. I know only that that for seven months and nine days I have been a prisoner in this place.

A metallic rattle emerges from a speaker mounted just below the main, visible camera: Josie, clearing her wrinkled throat from somewhere at the other end of the Ranch. I can almost smell the unfiltered cigarette gripped between her polished finger-nails, her hair a tight nightmare tangle of tired peroxide curls.

"Mencken, honey?" The voice brittle, old, tired. "Got your next client on the way."

I can easily picture the roadhouses where Josie would have spent her formative years working behind a bar, the drive-ins where video store employees and truckers would have struggled to impregnate her in the back of their pick-ups. Now all that is left is a rancid, over-perfumed shell, a dozen carcinomas no doubt fruiting in the choked black soil of her lungs. In the vast boredom of my cell, I have constructed an entire life history for this woman.

"I want you to treat her real good, okay?" the voice continues. "She's watched you through the mirror coupla times, now she wants to ride the Mencken train." The voice fractures into a laugh that sounds like a series of seizures. I feel my knuckles whiten at my sides.

"You there, Mencken? Better say somethin'. Wouldn't want to send in the boys with the tasers, now, would I?"

No, I wouldn't want that. Not at all. "I hear you, Josie," I reply, gazing in the direction of the microphone.

"Good boy. Comin' through in just a minute or so. No special requests, just wants a good time. Bet you're glad of that."

I nod tightly, forcing a thin smile on my face. I imagine Josie's life pouring from her, from the great red raw wound I would make of her throat.

A minute passes. I know what lies beyond the locked door: a corridor, its walls decorated with flocked red wallpaper, leading to other rooms occupied by creatures of whom I know little except that they are like me. At the far end of this corridor is the security room, occupied by beings of an entirely different nature, working in shifts around the clock: men wearing concealing black Kevlar, their faces hidden behind visors and helmets, feet shod with heavy boots that lace up to the knees, powerful and deadly weaponry within easy reach—deadly even to the likes of me. I fear them more than anything, and the things they might do to me if I gave them reason.

Because of this I am obedient.

A knock on the door: small knuckles against wood panelling. I step over, and gently turn the handle, finding the electronic lock has now been deactivated. My client is standing there, small, like me: a little over five and a half feet in height, although some ancient fragment of memory tells me I was once considered tall, even imposing.

Her hair is expensively streaked Texas blonde, and in my imagination her story opens up to me: a life lacking excitement or danger, with only the common rituals of graduation and marriage and perhaps motherhood to alleviate the dullness eating at the heart of her. In her eyes I read the desire for something more, something to satisfy the secret needs that lurk deep within her heart.

To learn of the Ranch's existence, she would have had to become part of certain exclusive circles: perhaps, like so many, a boyfriend or a husband took her to a wife-swapping party or a club catering to certain erotic tastes. As time passed, and her little perversions and games took on a particular flavour, the Ranch might be mentioned: a word here, a word there. She would have expressed curiosity, and would have laughed in disbelief when the truth was finally revealed to her. Eventually, given time, she would have believed, or at least dared to hope.

And now she stands before me, several thousand dollars out of pocket. At least I don't come cheap.

"My name is Carl," I tell her, pulling the door wider. I smile gently, ever conscious of the watching cameras and the guards in the security room. "Would you like to come in?"

I watch doubt flit over her features; she's thinking of turning back. Blonde, but not so pretty. Lovers would not have been a given in her formative years. She has, no doubt, developed a rich fantasy life to compensate.

Then she steps into the room and smiles nervously. She eyes the bed behind me. In one delicate hand I see that she grips a tiny, useless crucifix with which, Josie will have informed her, she will be able to control me. This is nonsense, of course, but to suggest anything else would bring days of torture upon me, followed by much worse weeks or even months without sustenance. I have once before made this mistake, when I was first brought to the Ranch. Never again.

"Would you like something to drink?" I ask, waving one hand towards the tiny mobile bar that sits in one corner. Sometimes alcohol helps them, if they aren't already drunk or high. "Don't worry if you're apprehensive, most are. You'll be fine."

Doubt and desire war across her face: I can see the lust is winning. "You're not real," she tells me.

"I am entirely real," I assure her. "I can show you," I add, lowering my voice.

"You'd better." I can hear her heart hammering in her chest: her breathing is sharp and shallow. I know what to do. I take both her hands and gently draw her closer to me. I smile and draw a hand through her hair; she gasps in response. I am filled only with loathing.

I study her clothes. She wears expensive black jeans, and her demeanour and way of speaking would make it clear to all who encountered her that she comes from money. She would have to, to afford the Ranch's prices. I could tell you in that instant of the books that occupy her bookshelves, of the movies she watches late at night, dreaming of her vampire lover. I could tell you how little she truly lives in the here and now.

Her tension doesn't fade, but she's no longer as frightened: instead, she's allowing herself to believe. She glances towards the main camera, the only one they would have told her about. She's enjoying the frisson of danger gained from being alone, in a locked room, with a killer.

"Show me," she says.

I lean down and kiss her. The harsh light of the ceiling panels leaches the colour from her skin. I gaze past her, at my own, entirely visible reflection, with pale blank eyes. Remembering.

I do not know how I came to be, or where I am from. Sometimes I dream of places that might be Rome, or might be Paris, or Berlin, or London: that might be a few years or half a millennia in the past. I have no way of telling, for I never kept records. To do so would have been to provide a surfeit of willing executioners the means to find me. Unfortunately, my memories fade quickly.

There is no romance or pleasure in my life: I am driven only to survive. I can last for weeks, even months, without sustenance, but for all that time I carry a raging hunger worse than any of my victims could possibly imagine, because they at least can look forward to the peace of death. Perhaps I also have that option, but having always survived, I cannot know.

Here in the Ranch, they bring dead down-and-outs washed up in canals or business rivals with bullet holes neatly drilled in their foreheads for us to feed upon. It is not enough, never enough.

When the hunger has hold of you, it slams you to the ground, makes you scream night after night after night, reducing your thoughts and your existence to an unquenchable, devouring misery. In order to survive, you learn to stalk your victims over days, then weeks and even months: and when you know the time is right, when you know there are no witnesses, you strike. Often your victim is a woman, simply because it is easier to disguise your assault as a sexual one: and if those investigating notice a remarkable lack of blood, well, hopefully you are long gone by then.

But the time after feeding is the weakest: then you are so filled with all the joy of creation that you cannot move, cannot walk, instead merely lie wriggling on the ground like a piss-drenched drunkard. Or else you stumble incoherently, vomiting red because you have gorged yourself too much. And when that wonderful, heaven-blessed rush fades, you are left only with the hollowness of your existence, and the desperate need to escape.

Before the Ranch, I believe I came across those like me only twice. This I do remember: I killed them both, immediately. Their bodies rotted like any other.

My last memory before the Ranch is of San Francisco. I had arrived there by Greyhound. My first—and last—victim there had been a sailor, living in a houseboat in San Francisco Bay. I had answered his lonely-hearts advert. We had enjoyed a few drinks in a bar near the sea, while I sat consumed with such terrible agonising hunger I wanted to shriek until my lungs were raw. We retired to his home and I tore his neck open with a knife taken from the galley. I wept and moaned and shuddered with orgasms of pleasure as his blood gushed against my tongue.

That was when they caught me, as I lay supine in the night, the cabin walls around me drenched with scarlet. I heard their boots approaching across the pontoon, and knew I was done. I expected to die. Instead, they sprayed a gas in my face that made my skin boil and lesion.

When they brought me to the Ranch a few days later, I learned my first lessons quickly. Tasers, whips, sprays and rubber bullets made sure of that.

"Show me," she repeats. I stare at her, waiting for her to elaborate.

"Your..." she points hesitantly at my face.

I smile obligingly, trying not to look too menacing. I open my lips slightly, and feel the emerging canines press against my upper lips as they push down. She shudders and pales at the sight, and for a moment I think she might run. I don't care one way or the other: I have performed as required, and the money is not refundable. But she holds her ground.

Now the important part. I again lower my head towards her, watching her lips open in unconscious response. She stiffens again, and I stop for a moment, before continuing. She's been briefed on the rules, which had been long ago drilled into me. She can stop me at any time: it only requires a word.

She remains silent. I touch my lips, very gently, to her neck. She jerks away at first, and then holds her place. She whimpers with fright and desire. I lick her neck, very softly, just allowing the tip of one sharpened canine to barely contact the taut pink flesh. Her tiny fingers grip my upper arms, still holding onto the ridiculous crucifix.

And then I pull back, aware as always of the cameras, the guards.

"There's no hurry," I tell her, conscious that every word is part of the game. I gaze into her eyes, ignoring the dull pain that has been building in my bones and my flesh for days now, soon to become a soul-crushing festival of agony. I think of Josie, and of how she would laugh if she could see into my thoughts.

"My name's Susie," she tells me, as I draw her slowly over towards the bed.

"Susie," I repeat, as if savouring the name.

"You know what I want, right?" Her voice is lowered, hesitant. I nod. The instructions, run off on a desktop printer, were slipped under the door a half hour before Susie's arrival. I step backwards towards the bed, drawing her along with my hands, maintaining the illusion that I am the one in charge.

I feel her fingers draw sharply across my chest as I lie back. How many times has she stood on the other side of the two-way mirror with the wealthy select audiences who pay so much for their seats, letting her fantasy grow of when her own time in this room would come?

My arms are outstretched, as if about to embrace her. She is, in fact, safe from my all-vanquishing hunger: I could no sooner allow myself to cause her harm than she could imagine the sordid reality of my existence. I am her whore, her fuck-puppet. I am less than nothing.

I remove my shirt at the prearranged time, as specified in the instructions detailing the intricate course of Suzie's fantasy. I have already unbuttoned my trousers, and they have been pushed down to my hips. I lie, exposed, upon the bed. She kneels half-naked upon my prostrate form and grasps my cock with clumsy hands, her breath ragged.

I become hard, not out of desire, but out of fear of what might happen to me if I do not respond as expected.

Sunlight does not greatly affect us. Pale skin is more a symptom of lurking in hiding places far from the light of the sun. We are visible in mirrors. Garlic, for some reason unknown to me, burns us greatly. Stakes kill us, but so do bullets and knives, though we can survive far greater physical trauma than the likes of Suzie or Josie.

Once, they set an example.

A few short months before, I was manacled, chained and marched under guard into an atrium deep within the sprawling vastness of the Ranch. The atrium was open to the skies, and for the first time in many long weeks I saw real sunlight and tasted fresh air.

There were a dozen others already there, similarly chained and manacled and under guard, whom I instantly knew to be the same as myself. I ignored them, knowing I could not kill them at that time. I saw a man—his body wasted beyond belief—chained to a tall steel pole driven into a block of concrete in the centre of the atrium. I knew immediately he was also of my own kind. Certainly, no ordinary human could have remained alive with his body in so desiccated a state.

Wil is the owner of the Ranch, a tall, rangy Texan who always carries a hunting knife on his hip. I have heard whispered stories from a few of my clients that he owns and runs most of the whorehouses in this part of the country as well as operating websites and organising paid parties for the rich and sexually jaded. He also carried a bullwhip on that particular day, and strutted around us, eyeing us one by one.

"I want you to know what happens when you try to hurt one of my clients," Wil bellowed, his voice strident and self-assured, his potbelly pushing at his shirt buttons. "I want you to know I can be real fucking mean when my orders don't get obeyed. I want you to see what happens."

I learned later that the individual chained to the steel post—I never found out his name, not that I would have cared—had been carefully starved for the better part of six months following some unspecified transgression. I can only imagine he tried to attack one of his clients while in the despair of hunger. He was, quite literally, a walking skeleton. What happened next was appalling beyond measure, and I cannot deny I learned my lesson well.

They sprayed him with hoses, twice: the first time with a mixture of garlic, water and sand at high pressure, which simultaneously burned his skin with the effect of the garlic and near flayed him alive with the sand. He was, quite literally, scoured half to death.

But it didn't end there. Next, they sprayed him with corrosive acids. I watched his skeleton melt: and towards the end, even then, I knew there was something still alive in that melting ruin. What was left, they shovelled into a hole in the ground and covered over.

Always I dream of freedom: yet I cannot countenance the thought of what happened in that courtyard happening to me.

And so I obey every client's whim to the letter.

I lie back and let her take me. She manoeuvres me between her legs, while I try to appear as if I am enjoying myself. She leans down and whispers to me, "Don't worry, nobody's watching."

I glance towards the two-way mirror, an involuntary motion. I open my mouth, then close it again before I can tell her what an idiotic proposition this is.

"It's okay, sweetie," she says, cupping my jaw with one hand and turning my head back towards her. "I paid extra so we'd be left alone. Ain't nobody on the other side of that glass. Now, I want you to kiss me."

Not so shy, after all. My lips part, and she leans down. I know what she wants: I push my lips back until my extended canines are fully visible.

She leans down, her hips beginning to move rhythmically now I'm inside her. I feel sure she'll come quite soon. Perhaps I once took pleasure from this act, but instead of pleasure I only ever feel a kind of dull tingle between my thighs.

One thing I have learned in my time here. Male vampires, myself included, all have unusually small genitals. Perhaps there is a reason for this. If we truly evolved from some common human ancestor, as some apparently speculate, perhaps we have some other means of reproduction and the penis has become an evolutionary dead-end for our kind. Or perhaps we truly rise from the grave, but our lack of sexual interest causes the organ to wither over time. For all I know, we reproduce by splitting down the middle every thousand years. I have no way of knowing or remembering, and care less.

Her lips touch my cheek, and I can hear the frantic rush of her every breath. "I want you to bite me," she says.

I feel my penis begin to shrivel rapidly.

"Bite me," she repeats, laying soft kisses across my chin and other cheek. This was not in the instructions.

"It's against the rules," I croak. "They would…"

I can taste her life, she's so close: she's a bag of blood, and the hunger is a whirling maelstrom in my guts.

She twists suddenly to one side, and slaps me, hard, and then again. Does the little bitch actually want me to kill her?

"I can do worse to you," she hisses, her irises wide and black. I wonder what she's sniffed or swallowed for courage in a washroom before walking down the corridor to me. She shows me a small perfume bottle, carefully palmed so it is visible neither to the main camera nor to the one-way mirror on the wall. I can only speculate as to how she smuggled it into my cell, since all are searched before coming to me.

She slides the bottle between our bodies, moving it down towards my crotch. I feel a sudden cool moist pressure against the inside of my thigh: the pain comes a moment later and my back arches violently in response. I try to scream, but she's clamped her other hand firmly over my mouth. I feel the crucifix press hard against my gums and cheek.

Garlic spray. My eyes fill with tears, and a keening sound escapes between her fingers. I'm lost in animal panic. What does she intend?

"Bite me," she repeats again, her voice harsh. "Make me like you."

No, I want to scream. Make her like me? Impossible. I don't even know what makes me like me. My panicked eyes dart again towards the watching camera: but now I'm seeking aid rather than the opportunity of escape.

"Listen to me," I mumble through her fingers. She's stronger than she looks.

"One wrong word, and I'll spray you again," she loudly whispers, madness in her eyes. I can picture my skin bubbling under the effect of the spray, and hold back the desire to release the agony in a shriek. Whatever happens to Suzie, it won't be half as bad as what will happen to me. She releases her hold slightly.

It's hard to speak through the pain, but my existence depends on it. "I can't make you like me," I tell her, forcing the words out.

She presses the bulb of the spray against my crotch once more and I convulse. "You're a vampire! You can turn me. You're lying! Make me like you!"

"You would die," I beg. "And then they would kill me."

"I don't believe you. Do it."

I shake my head. "I have never made anyone a vampire. I don't know if they can be made."

She reaches down and grabs me by the hair. "I am telling you to turn me," she hisses in a half-shriek; I can hear the growing desperation in her voice.

She slaps me several times again. The blows sting. And then I laugh. It's so ridiculous: after so long, trapped in a room like some pathetic Hollywood wet dream of a vampire's boudoir, with some idiot Texas housewife so addled by her deranged fantasies she thinks I can turn her into something she could only ever dream of in her worst nightmares.

She becomes furious at my laughter, but I can't stop. She slaps me again, but I only laugh harder.

"They're going to kill you, you stupid bastard!" she screams at me. "So you might as well do it anyway!" She sobs then, muttered curses spilling out of her mouth. The desire for death and oblivion is written in her eyes. She throws herself over me, the smooth curve of her neck next to my face, and begs me yet again.

"What do you mean, they're going to kill me?" I ask, my own blood thundering in my ears.

"That's what I heard. There's too many people heard about this place, so they're gonna shut it down real soon. Won't want you round in case anyone figures out what's going on here." Her expression becomes vicious, and I see her plan unravelling: she came here intending to force me to 'turn' her into a vampire so she can no doubt lurk on moonlit rooftops, perhaps wearing the impractical black velvet dresses I can easily picture hanging in her wardrobe.

"You're lying," I stutter.

She shakes her head rapidly. "So turn me now, and we can escape together."

By now I'm completely incredulous. But for some reason, I believe her: I've learned to read people over all those long, long years, to know when they are or aren't lying.

And she's telling the truth, as far as she knows it. The Ranch will close: and I will die. Suddenly any other possibility seems absurd. How long, after all, could an entity like the Ranch continue to exist, before rumour and hearsay spread too far? Before it came under investigation? And when the time came, could any of its unwilling whores truly expect to survive?

"I'll do it," I tell her. Terror and the desire to believe again war with each other across her face. I lift myself carefully, trying to gauge how many seconds I have left. Is Josie listening in to our conversation? Of course she is, sitting there no doubt in some little cupboard surrounded by screens and microphones and speakers. How many seconds do I have before the guards come and drag this idiotic child away, and punish me? Very few.

Necessity can make anyone a great actor. I look up at her, putting on the brave, noble face so many of them seem to like, and beckon to her.

She's trembling. I still her, and bring my incisors close to her neck. Perhaps, if I do nothing, they will let me live regardless. Perhaps I am wrong, and she is indeed lying about the future of the Ranch. But if she's telling the truth, I can defy their authority with Suzie's death.

I touch incisors to flesh, and pause, indecisive.

In the distance, I hear shouts, and boots slamming against soft carpet, coming closer.

Her Choice
Elsie WK Donald

She walks briskly along the street. She has left her friends in the pub, pleading an early start at work, and because the theatres are busy she has a longer walk back to her car than usual. Still, in this bustling, brightly-lit town centre a woman on her own can feel secure.

She turns right on to a side street and walks uphill. There are fewer pedestrians here. Her car is parked in what used to be the city's red light district, until it reinvented itself with boutique hotels and chic little restaurants. She has not yet reached it when she hears footsteps coming up behind her. A male voice says, "Excuse me, do you have the time?"

Automatically glancing at her watch, she turns and says, "It's just after ten."

She looks up in time to note the disappointment when he sees her face. She has kept her body trim and fit, but her face is that of a middle-aged woman. Middle-aged by today's standards, anyway. Once it would have been called old.

Nevertheless he presses on. "No, do you have the time?" Putting great emphasis on the last two words, and with an attempt at a smile. So he is looking for a prostitute and would have preferred a younger one, but is willing to make do with her.

She looks him up and down. Past the first flush of youth, and he has obviously been drinking, but still quite presentable. Alone. Vulnerable, though he does not know it. She feels the stir of an appetite she hasn't satisfied for some time. He is not wearing a wedding ring. Should she engage him in conversation, find out if he is committed to another? No, she will do him the courtesy of assuming his integrity—and allow herself the luxury of a little sex without the minefield of emotional entanglement. She smiles back. "I believe I do."

He says, "I have a hotel room." Then he pauses and looks at her a bit doubtfully. "If they ask at the front desk, you're my aunt and we're going to my room to… to…"

What a charmer. "To reminisce," she supplies and he nods, relieved. She nearly leaves then, but she is more amused by his rudeness than annoyed by his vanity, and it has been a long time. They go to the hotel.

Afterwards she lies beside him for a few minutes. The bed is comfortable, but she really does have to go to work in the morning, so she starts to get up. He stirs beside her—she had thought him asleep—and says, "How much do I owe you?"

"Nothing, I enjoyed it too."

"No, I need to pay you." He gets out of bed and starts fumbling for his wallet. By the time he has found it she is half dressed.

"Here," he says, holding out some notes. "Will a hundred do?"

She looks at him silently, not sure if he is joking. He seems to take it for censure and pulls out more notes.

"Two hundred, then, but that's it."

She says gently, "Thank you, but I really don't want your money."

To her surprise he becomes furious. "Take it, you whore! That's what you are, a whore!"

She turns her back on him to continue dressing, but he pulls her around and slaps her hard. Her lip splits and she tastes her own blood. An old, almost forgotten hunger starts to rise. She breathes deeply, striving to keep calm. For a moment he looks appalled by his own brutality; then he throws the money at her.

He says, with an edge of hysteria in his tone, "You have to take it. I won't commit adultery; I won't have you do that to my wife."

She almost laughs, but he seems to be serious. So it's not cheating if he does it with a prostitute? What kind of lunatic morality is that? She is beginning to get angry, and that is not good.

Now he is the one to turn away. He sits down on the opposite side of the bed, not looking at her. A vein throbs in his neck. She focuses on it with longing, remembering another man. In those days, society's norms had dictated that to be an unmarried woman was to be celibate, and she had been happy enough. Until that fascinating man had decided—on a whim, because he had never had an old woman—to introduce her to the joys of sex. Then, for his amusement, he had tried to turn her into a monster and had left her, thinking he had succeeded, that she had no choice in the matter. But there is always a choice.

She takes a step closer to the man sitting on the bed, to his soft skin and pounding blood. The smells of sex still linger about the bed. Her arousal now is not sexual, but it is oh so potent. Another step and she can see him from the side, see that his fists are clenched and his face screwed up: though whether in anger or shame she cannot tell. She could end his pain, end it permanently. Would that not be better for his wife, than to have this creature for a husband?

Yet in his own pathetic way he must love her. He wanted not to be an adulterer for her sake, not his own. A small point in his favour, but enough. She will have compassion on him.

She steps back silently, picks up the money and puts it in a neat pile on the bed. He will have to come to terms with his infidelity, that much pain she will allow herself to give him. He must be listening for what she will do next, but she can make no noise at all when she wants. She is dressed and out of the room before he can react, and she knows he is too worried about appearances to come after her.

She walks back to her car. *I will not be defined by your expectations*, she thinks, meaning the man in the hotel, *or by yours*, meaning the man who turned her into what she is, *or by folklore or tradition*. She briefly touches the cross at her neck and smiles to herself. *I choose another way. I choose love.* The hunger ebbs. Her fangs sink back into their sockets as she relaxes.

Picture, of a Winter Afternoon
Ruth EJ Booth

She could have taught trees
to stand against concrete—
concrete to stand against time.

Could have shown the living
statues in the park
a thing, or three.

A bastion of wonder
in a sea of indifference;

a bright leaf
in a gale of litterfall;

a single word
she said:

look.

❖   ❖   ❖

It had been a day of inurements,
but grey banality now broke
to a sky split by constituents:
blues, bruised indigos—inky swells
that rumbled violent delight
and future joys of netherhours.

Before the dusk that gathered on—
before the storm, ahead: bright gold,
fringed grey—as we'd not seen
these seeming years of jollity—
flared, in unabashed joy,
in Light,

the last fire before darkness:
eternal engines burning.

        ✧   ✧   ✧

Feeds filled with its likeness:
smartphones held to weary eyes—
not from fear of prophecy,
but like a glass to an eclipse
they might have witnessed with their own,
so then testament with tears.

Yet she stood there as I watched,
and gazed through unashamed eyes.
That one should love their city so
their heart should break with its skies.

My Last Love
Heather Valentine

He has long stopped seeing me, my last love. At first, when I would brush his cheek, he would shiver and swear I was there. And when I would call for him, he might turn. It has been too long now, and he is so sure that he is mad that he no longer hears the real me, though he still jumps at sounds and embraces the breeze. I suppose he should. The creak and draft from the broken window in the third floor guest room can at least be heard, felt, experienced, while I cannot.

There is a new person in the house today, a plain young woman with a serious brow that suggests experience beyond her years. She is to replace the last governess, who left. I am not sure what hand I had in that. I have often watched Adaline in her room, but I did not think it troubled her last tutor. She said she was leaving to be married, and perhaps that is true. My husband is showing the new governess to her room now, and carries her case for her.

"It is simple, but I hope it is to your liking," he says, gesturing her into the suite down the corridor from Adaline's.

"Very much so," the woman replies promptly. He sets down her case and leaves her to settle in, warning her before he goes not to disturb the third floor guest room. He does not tell her it is because he believes I reside there. Does not tell her that he used to keep the room empty so he could not be caught telling his woes to me, of his loneliness in this great empty house and the friends he could not bear to visit because of how they remind him of me.

The governess flips open the lid of her case and begins to remove her dresses to the wardrobe, but then stops, shakily, her hands braced against the open trunk. She sobs too quietly to be heard outside the room, not even if my husband were still waiting by the door. But I am here, and so I hear.

I am not sure what is wrong, and unable to ask—but I cannot simply leave her like this. I extend a hand and hold it against her shoulder. I do not know if she feels it, but her quivering chest begins to still.

When she returns to unpacking her case I drift down the corridor to Adaline's room. I kiss her on the forehead as she snores in her cot. She does not wake. It is already dark outside, and the child shall likely lie peacefully until morning. Though I do not sleep, I find myself falling into torpor when the majority of the house is in slumber. Sometimes I rest in my husband's bed, sometimes another, in the attic or the servants' quarters.

Only rarely do I rest in my tomb. Tonight, however, I shall rest beside my daughter. In my hazy, scattered state I can almost believe that I am truly asleep, dozing in the armchair next to where she dreams.

The governess takes Adaline down to breakfast, and I follow. She is terse but not un-loving, though Adaline is wary of her, as she is of every new companion. My husband sternly guides the governess away from sitting in my old seat at the opposite end of the table.

"Miss Aitkin," he calls her, "how is your room?"

She thinks for a moment, and from the look on her face I think she is going to talk about what happened while she was opening her case, but her expression quickly changes. Whatever her sorrows and whatever she sensed of me, neither are for my husband's consumption.

"There is plenty of storage," she replies reassuringly.

I follow my husband until the clock strikes noon, when he leaves for town. Unable to stray too far from my tomb, I cannot follow him there. He is in a cheerful mood, and plays music in the drawing room while I recline in an unused chair. He does not play music as frequently he did when I first passed, and what he chooses to entertain himself with now is far less sombre. I sink back to the sound of spring melodies, the blissful tune drawing me into an almost restful state, as if I am being carried away in a breeze particle by particle. I snap back to alertness with the shut of the piano lid, and silence.

After he has left, I flit up to the schoolroom where Miss Aitkin is testing Adaline's French with a chalk and slate. Adaline's fingers rest on a neatly-drawn cat as she tries to recall le chat to her tongue. They pay no notice to me, as I suppose they shouldn't. A young girl bonding with her new governess should not be distracted by shades and shapes in the wallpaper. But as I am about to leave them be, the governess looks up and catches my eye. All colour drains from her face.

Tonight I find myself in a dream, though not my own. I play the role of some spectre, and am in Adaline's room, as before. My hair in this guise is lighter, my skin more tan than my own.

"Catherine," the governess murmurs, kneeling and shaking on the floor.

I feel I should say something, but I find myself simply shaking my head.

Miss Aitkin is quieter than usual this morning. I am careful to stay out of sight as I watch Adaline's lessons, in case I should frighten her. The child has finally remembered le chat, and the governess smiles at her genuinely, though not without a distracted glaze in her eye. My husband does not notice, instead busying himself with a notebook.

Her sorrow does not lighten after breakfast. I remove myself to the third floor guest room, this time to hide rather than to be needed. It is quite empty. It has a lamp, a shelf, and a bed, of course, but as it has not truly been a room for guests in years, it has been slowly emptied of its other contents; the books, the rugs, the toys borrowed to other parts of the house and never returned.

Not that these things are of use to me. When one cannot read a book or hold a cross-stitch, one becomes adept at living in one's own head, and so when I am alone I pass my time absorbed in the imagined melodrama of a fictional medieval court. I am brought out only as I hear footsteps, then quiet voices, and look towards the door.

"That's where father says mother lives," I hear Adaline say faintly, before the footsteps pass and continue on along the corridor.

I can usually tell when someone is speaking about me and, much as I may sometimes wish otherwise, my instinct is to be drawn towards them. I imagine I should have little purpose as a ghost were I to ignore those who think of me. As I sneak into the dining room, I catch the tail end of my husband recounting the story of my passing, looking mournfully towards my vacant chair as he speaks of still hearing my voice on occasion. He tells the tale a little differently each time. It still pains him to tell it, but it will never again burn with the rawness and hurt of a fresh wound. I do not let the governess see me as I slip out.

Though I have been trying not to disturb her further, I find myself entangled in the governess' restless mind again this night. This time, the blonde spectre is separate from myself, and pursues her. She runs to me for aid and I pull her close, but my black hair turns light before her eyes, and she screams, and screams, and wakes.

The governess is white-faced throughout breakfast. My husband asks if she was disturbed during the night, and she brushes him off with a terse smile and pleasant talk of the comfort of the mattress he has provided for her. Adaline asks of her also, as they go to her room, but Miss Aitkin shushes her, settling her for her nap. She turns to walk upstairs. I take myself to where I need to be.

I am in the armchair of the third floor room when she opens the door and looks straight to me. She appears relieved, almost, and crosses to sit on the bed. This is the closest I have been to her since that first day, and I can make out in better detail the point of her nose and the press of her thin, sensible lips.

"Who is Catherine?" I ask.

The governess's gaze drops. "She was a scullery girl around my age at the first house I was employed at, till she passed of pneumonia in the winter."

"You were close," I say. It has been so long since I had a conversation that I struggle with where to put my eyes, where to focus.

The governess pauses. "Closer than friends," she eventually replies.

"I understand." I turn my head to find that she is studying me, and attempt to observe her in return. Her blouse is embroidered with floral details that trace and loop and twirl onwards across her shoulder, and I follow them.

"As she was passing, I told her I wished she would never leave my side. And so she didn't. Or at least, something which appeared to be she didn't."

I suppose her hair was lighter, and her skin more tan than mine. "And you thought I was that imitation of she, returned?" I suggest.

I break my gaze from her clothing, and settle on her face for long enough to catch her nodding. "Though I gather you are someone else's spectre," she adds. Her water-blue eyes glisten with what I can only describe as longing.

"None but yours, today," I reply, in a way I hope is pleasant. When alive, it would be a careful choice to unburden myself to a stranger such as Miss Aitkin. Now that I can scarcely be heard, any connection is one I must trust. "My husband sees me less and less these days. I seem no longer to pain him this way, so I suppose it is for the best."

"I see." She places her palms together in her lap, fingers pointing to the floor. "Can you be touched?" she asks hesitantly.

"You are welcome to try," I reply, holding out a hand. She rises slowly, then tentatively reaches out. She is not truly solid to me, as I must not be to her, but I feel a vague warmth as she probes with her fingertips where she likely feels a cold.

"It was you that was in my room the first night," she says matter-of-factly.

I nod.

"Thank you for what you did," she says, her hand lingering in mine. "It is good to be cared for."

Before I can respond, her eyes dart away.

"Adaline will be waking soon."

"Then go to her," I reply. She looks back to me as she leaves, holding my gaze, then departs. I touch my hand where she felt it, now cold on cold, but the warmth in my chest lingers for a few minutes longer.

My husband takes Adaline into town in the morning. I expect Miss Aitkin to have gone with him, but I find her sitting at the breakfast table.

"Was that your seat?" she asks, nodding at the chair I'm now resting my hands on. I nod in reply. She quietly returns to her porridge and book, and does not stir again until she has finished eating.

"Do you have plans for the day?" I ask her.

"I suppose not," she replies.

"Would you like to visit my tomb?"

She looks at me warily, then nods.

"He said it has been two years," she comments as we wind through our gardens. I considered them beautiful at one time, but I have been drawn along this path so many times that I now barely notice them.

"Has it?" I have trouble telling a week from a month, which is perhaps a sign that it has indeed been that long. I can scarcely even remember my passing. I rested in bed for a while, and the next time I walked I was not alive.

My tomb lies within the family mausoleum, a squat cylinder with a domed roof, built of cool granite. I am drawn to hover by my body, and from my niche I watch the governess. She turns her head from side to side in wonder, examining the pillars and peering at the light filtering in through the twin windows; the stately, illuminated dance of dust motes and dandelion spores.

"It's beautiful," she says as she joins me, and glances down at my coffin.

"You have not changed," she adds, gesturing at the miniature; a circular profile of myself built into the lid as if it were a window. I am unsure if she is simply saying this to be polite. I feel more a vague blur than a person, most days.

"Was it Catherine you were upset over on your first night here?" I ask.

She nods. "It was hard to leave that place. Each time I thought things were changing, she returned to me in some way."

"As in your dreams," I note. She does not seem disturbed by this comment, merely accepts it with a dip of her head as she has all things concerning my existence.

"Perhaps it is as with yourself and your husband," she replies, "and I was jumping at shadows by the end. Or perhaps not." She pauses, and leans against the mausoleum wall. "The days we had together when she was alive, I shall never forget. But by the end, I feared her shade more than I loved it, and even that was beginning to wear. One can only cower so much before collapsing."

Miss Aitkin looks up and meets my eye, smiling faintly. "With you here...well, I do not believe a house can hold more than one spirit, especially if the second has never visited the place in question. I am remembering what it feels like to be comfortable."

Her eyes travel further, to examine the inscriptions on the ceiling. I explain a little of my family tree to her, surprising myself with my memory of it, and she seems delighted to learn. It is only when we hear clattering hooves at the front gate that we decide it is time to leave. We wind down the path to the house at a gentle pace, and I try to observe as she does, to watch the freshly blooming wildflowers and admire the statues.

Miss Aitkin is teaching Adaline numbers this afternoon, and I am invited to lounge on the armchair in her room and observe. Sometimes, when I was alive, I would watch her like this, with some embroidery or a book in my lap, and she would look up to me with a smile when she wanted me to note a particularly clever answer.

While practicing her multiplication, Adaline knocks over a block that tumbles to my feet. I reach down as if I might hope to retrieve it, but my hand passes through. Adaline scurries to the foot of the armchair to take it back without a glance at me. I lower my eyes from them and gaze into the folds of my imaginary dress until Miss Aitkin sends Adaline to ask when my husband wishes them down for dinner. I hear pacing, and Miss Aitkin shutting the door.

"Does Adaline usually respond to you?" she asks.

My eyes remain lowered. Miss Aitkin does not prompt. She simply waits, her deft hands clearing away the clutter of the lesson.

I sigh as if I had lungs, as if putting off what I must say will hide it. "In truth, Adaline has never responded to me in a way that cannot be mistaken for some other distraction."

Miss Aitkin pauses her tidying, and moves to kneel at my feet. "She speaks of you with fondness," she says firmly.

As thoughts come to my mind, I find myself sharing them. "I fear that perhaps she speaks of the idea of me rather than the person." I pause, but Miss Aitkin's bright eyes encourage me onwards. "She may even be too young to remember me. When I am near her, she simply looks to the window, or the chair, and I happen to be between her and the object of her gaze."

Miss Aitkin takes only a moment to think. "Even if she cannot see you, I do not doubt that she still loves you, in the way the living do. As your husband does you, or I Catherine—with true warmth and care when they think of you, even if you are not present to them every day." She takes hold of my palm again, and I move my second hand to cup hers in gratitude.

I do not wish Adaline to be forever chasing my shadow, but still I want to be with her, to speak with her and see her grow. I know why Miss Aitkin probes me. I cannot be a mother to this child any longer, and that I cannot bear. "Thank you," I reply. "I—"

Adaline returns as I am about to continue, and I am comforted that Miss Aitkin does not throw my hand from hers in guilt. Instead, she lowers it carefully and makes a motion as if to fool the child that she is adjusting the chair. Adaline informs Miss Aitkin that her father would like them down in an hour, and Miss Aitkin smooths the front of her pinafore and takes the opportunity to grill Adaline on her telling of the time. I slide through the wall, and know that even if Adaline does not see me, Miss Aitkin's eyes follow me keenly. I retreat to the guest room, and my mind takes me away. Lady Veritus has come to court again, bringing scandal and intrigue…

It is dark when Miss Aitkin comes to me next. I did not notice the sun setting, or indeed perhaps the days passing. She is wearing an outfit I have not seen her in before, a rare blue dress among the greys, and brings the sound of spring melodies drifting through the door with her.

"I am glad you are here tonight," she whispers, "though I cannot speak for long, lest your husband notice I have escaped the gathering in the drawing room." She glances behind her, face illuminated by the lamp she holds. "I wanted you to know that I care for you. Not as a memory, but as… a companion." She meets my eyes briefly. "As if you were alive, or I were dead."

Words do not spring to me, but I feel my way to producing a smile across my questionably visible mouth. She nods in acknowledgement and slips away into the corridor, the door batting shut in the draft.

In my loneliness I am as if asleep, and as if asleep I dream, and though the vision is mine it feels much less real than the dreams I have seen of Miss Aitkin's. It is a pink and red dream, and in it I am sure I dream in senses, of real hands on my waist and the smell of the garden after the rain and the sharp, acrid tang of lemon and ginger. When I stir, I know I must see her again.

I stumble through the corridors, not stopping and barely seeing until I find my hands upon a door and know that it is hers.

The governess sits on her bed, though she is now wearing a night-gown rather than her blue dress. She acknowledges me with a glance, and I set myself down next to her.

"Do you want me to tell you of how the gathering went?" she asks, releasing her hair from its pins.

"You don't need to," I reply. I feel as if I am shaking, as if I am coming apart. I must keep myself together with the concrete, with speech. "I came to see you, to thank you for visiting me earlier."

"I'm glad," she says, face flushing in gratitude. I feel the heady physical pull of the red dream, and avert my eyes from her. I am afraid she would think me like Catherine, another ghost that will not let her live. We are in silence, though I am not sure what kind, until I feel her warm hand turn my face and kiss me with all the vagaries of her mouth. I put my hands on her shoulders and feel her, more firm, more real, the warmth of her skin through her gown and the lavender scent of her perfume. I can be seen. I can be touched. I can be heard.

I am not sure if torpor takes me that night. In lying awake, or dreaming as if I am, I feel the scratchiness of the thick winter sheets, smell the once familiar mustiness of the house, can reach out with my cold hand and feel the expanding and contracting of Miss Aitkin's lungs through her back. Only in the morning am I dead again.

Miss Aitkin is not there when I stir. I flit to the window and see her in the garden, playing with Adaline in the freshly cut grass. Smiling, I drift down the corridor, heading for the ground floor study, where as expected I find my husband sitting at his desk, spindly hands smudged with ink from letter-writing. I perch on the rickety chair by the bookcase and observe him as he works.

"I shall always love you," I say, "in the way the dead do. With a love caught in my heart of you as you were when last I was alive. I have found my way to love another, and perhaps you shall too. But know that should you ever need me, I shall be here to listen."

He pauses, scratches out a word then pulls another sheaf of paper to begin his letter anew. He does not respond, but in my heart I feel he understands.

✧ ✧ ✧

I think I am in the garden again. Miss Aitkin is running with Adaline, and when she looks to me I feel like I am becoming a sunbeam, lovely and translucent. She sends Adaline to hide, and informs the girl that she will count to a hundred. As the child disappears into the wildflowers, Miss Aitkin draws me close. For a hundred beats.

"How do you feel?" she asks.

I realise I do not know.

"I feel…" I begin. I feel as I should not feel. I have found another love, and made my peace with my husband, but I still feel a sickness.

"It's a beautiful day," I respond. "And I am here with you."

She smiles acceptingly, and kisses my forehead as if it is real to her. I feel a faint clamminess, which I can only connect to her touch from seeing it.

"Seventy-six," she announces.

"Seventy-seven, seventy-eight, seventy-nine," I continue.

I know what that feeling is now. I have bid farewell to being a mother to my daughter, accepted that my husband will move on, and brought comfort and joy to the governess' sad heart.

All my tasks are done.

There is no sorrow holding me here.

I am loose and free as the housebird, flitting through the garden trees without a flock.

I dream again, or perhaps experience a different kind of sense. To say I was in the darkness, hearing voices, would be to impose my imagination upon what occurs. I simply am, and know that words are occurring. My husband wonders if there was some purpose he missed in my visits to him. The governess knows I am a good person. I am not sure if this is said aloud, if this is some conversation, or only their feelings, imaginary or otherwise. The words fade, and I am alone for some time.

I am in Miss Aitkin's room, sitting on the bed, and snap awake as she enters, becoming aware that I have been waiting for her to return.

"I was beginning to worry I would not see you again," she says, but with joviality rather than hurt. "It has been weeks since I saw you last.

"I'm afraid it has only been hours for me." I take her hands. "I am not as youngly dead as I used to be."

"I miss you when you are gone," Miss Aitkin says, quietly, and in that moment I almost feel her again, a sorrowful warmth pressing into my palm. "But I am glad you returned today," she says, her eyes raising and the pain passing. "It has been quite a week, and I could not imagine speaking of it with anyone else."

I grip her as best I can, unsure how long I will be able to hold her. I take a deep pause, and try to assemble my voice in its coyest, warmest tone. "Oh, please share…"

I can scarcely pay attention as she speaks, saying something about Adelaide and a party and the new cleaner. My hands shake in hers, fearing that each sentence will be her last, that some disturbance will take her from me and in doing so remove me from being needed here.

"…Are you well?" she asks, words drawing me into solid shapes again. I watch the blush of her cheeks, the soft quivering of breath passing her lips.

"I feel faint," I reply.

In her expression I do see love, I do see some kind of need. But still I am slipping. Perhaps I have strained myself too much, being there for her in the way I have. Perhaps I just need to rest.

I close my eyes. In the grey, she reaches out, and repeats my name. Her tears are a lighthouse, guiding me home. And I am anchored, for now.

Lady Veritus clings to her chambermaid's hand as she dangles above the vast, empty ocean. Do not let me go, she asks, the storm whipping beneath her. The chambermaid swears that she won't. They strain in pendulum until their hearts both accept—if she does not let go, they both will drown.

Watching the Watchers
Anya Penfold

Gregor stuck his bespectacled face round the door just as I was printing off the weekly report. "Spot of overtime, Dietrich?" he enquired, with mild disapproval. "Fancy a pre-weekend beer instead?"

Time had indeed ticked on. I smiled apologetically. "Sorry, boss. Raincheck. You know how it is. Gotta make it home for Curfew."

I fumed silently for the entire chugging, clanking bus ride home, but tried not to show it because I knew that every other commuter was in the same boat… or whatever overcrowded, maddeningly-slow form of transportation they had gambled on getting them home before they fell foul of the law. Instead, I smiled politely at my fellow passengers and made room where I could.

My worries about being late were unfounded. I made it to the front door with time to spare, my mood lifting enough for a genuine smile of greeting to my neighbour as we both fumbled with our keys. Although, I noticed he was on his way out.

"Missing the curfew, comrade?" I called cheerfully.

Mr Androvich snorted. "An oppression which should not have to be borne. It is an affront to my humanity and to my religious beliefs." He pocketed his keys and stepped back into the road, hesitating.

I beckoned conspiratorially. "I know of an old air raid shelter on Primrose, nice place to wait it out. The iced buns are to be recommended. The tea urn is a genuine antique."

My neighbour's glum expression turned a greyer shade of dour. "Tried that last time, it turned into a bit of a knees-up. No, I know of an old fallout shelter two blocks further over. The chessboards are ancient enough to be genuine antiques and the coffee is terrible."

Each To Their Own, as it is written. I wished him luck, but didn't wait to watch him hurry away.

I was still in the shower when the curfew bells started to peal. I swore under my breath, as is my habit, and towelled off in record time. I grabbed my chronically crumpled Hawaiian shirt off the top of the laundry basket and raced downstairs two at a time. The bells were still making their cacophony, at least, so I wasn't yet late.

❖   ❖   ❖

It was a pretty good curfew. Someone had gone to the trouble of hanging new bunting up and down the street, and the Chanahkas next-door-the-other-way had some sort of religious celebration of their own going, judging by the pennants waving languidly from their drainpipes. A small group of fundamentalists were shaking placards at them in a practiced manner, taking care not to obstruct the foot traffic in the process. I decided I liked the carefully-scripted 'We Object To The Ways In Which You Spend Your Time, For They Are Not Our Ways' sign best.

By the time I had thumped my own trestle table into good order, most of the placard wavers had succumbed to the lure of Mrs Chanahka's home cooking. The bearer of my favourite sign stood resolutely aloof, his expression reminiscent of Moses descending the Mount and getting his first eyeful of the Golden Calf. I strolled over to ask him how things were going.

"Terrible," he sighed. "Every curfew, it is the same. The heathens and infidels do as they please and the young people, they have no discipline." He gestured in disdain at his munching associates.

"You should try her mango chutney, it's really very good," I advised.

A wan smile crossed his face. "Ah, excellent. The very good mango chutney of the heathen and infidel is the temptation that is most worth resisting."

I left the old-timer to his steadfast vigil and returned to my doorstep. The unintentional overtime had put paid to the more elaborate of my plans, as usual, but I'd managed to scrounge up sugar and lime juice enough to pacify half a gallon of moonshine. It seemed to go down well despite having to serve it with an antique ladle and recyclable cups, and I handed it out to the thronging curfew-goers until I got bored and just left them to help themselves. I waved encouragingly to the solitary placard-bearer, but apparently distilled liquor was also a temptation most worth resisting.

As the strains of accordion music lifted above the throng in the street, I decided to spend the rest of curfew in the pub.

The first boozer I came to was too packed to even get in and look for anyone I knew. I had more luck in the second, mainly because Rogov is a head taller than everyone I know, as well as most people I don't. He was giving forth at the bar, arms wind-milling in the loud body language of the terminal extrovert. I waved for a pint of Worker's Hard ('The Hard-working Beer For When You've Worked Too Hard') and gave a sympathetic smile to Rogov's victim, currently pinned against the bar by my friend's flailing arms.

"Dietrich!" Rogov boomed, releasing the smaller man by dint of flinging one massive limb across my shoulders. "You should meet my new friend! He is interested in history and I was just explaining that the word curfew—"

"—didn't always mean the curtailment of the working month," we finished in three-part harmony. Like many amiable drinkers, Rogov tends to belabour the obvious after a few beers. I extended my hand to his companion, who gave his name as Lenn. With his angular features and air of harassment, he put me in mind of a weasel being subjected to the bonhomerie of a bear. I recognised the signs of one who has borne the brunt of Rogov's friendship.

"Do you have a particular historical interest?" I asked.

Lenn opened his mouth, but Rogov got in first. "*Political* history, my friend!" He thumped the counter. "Ah, he should have met Petrov, God bless him. He should be talking to Petrov now. But alas!"

The emotion was too much for him to bear on an empty glass.

"What happened to Petrov?" Lenn leaned forward, eyes alert.

"He hijacked a microphone on the bandstand last week," I explained quickly, while Rogov's attention was on the barmaid. "Gave an impromptu yet stirring speech about the evils inherent in a government that deliberately inverts the meanings of words."

"The Powers That Be were most upset," Rogov added, simultaneously beckoning for another round. "Quite hurt, in fact. They sent a car for him. It was a nice car." He nodded in appreciation. "One of those tinted-window jobs with the high-clearance chassis."

"And they just… took him away?"

Rogov thrust a pint into his hands and looked surprised. "Well, yes. They wanted to hear what he had to say. And here you are in town for only a week and who knows when he will return, and the tragedy of it is, you may *not* hear what he has to say! It is an evil chance, evil, that lets such ships pass in the night!"

Whatever Lenn was going to reply was rendered inaudible by a commotion from the doorway. It was a shame, as his expression indicated it might have been quite interesting, but we turned to watch with everyone else as a blond and chiselled youth pushed his way through the crowd revealing, as he approached, his reproduction SS-uniform. He leapt onto a table, nearly upsetting the drinks already standing there, and proceeded to harangue the onlookers about the supremacy of the Aryan race and the manner in which the evils of homosexuality would bring it to its knees. After only a few minutes he was driven forth by a torrent of appreciative comments and solicitations of a personal nature, and fled into the dwindling early evening sunlight.

One of the drinkers, the one who had pinched the demagogue's arse, seemed quite upset by the whole thing, and as it turned out he was a personal friend of Rogov's, Rogov spent some time patting his shoulder paternally. This had the happy chance of affording Lenn and I some time for our ears to stop ringing.

"It is always the same, always." Rogov sighed theatrically. "Every curfew, that boy returns and gives his same speech."

I felt I should make some gesture of sympathy. "Those who do not learn from history are condemned to repeat it?" I hazarded.

"Alas," Rogov confirmed, with one final, tumultuous clap to the shoulder of his tear-stained friend. "But Andrey here does so have this thing for the uniform of the oppressor."

❖   ❖   ❖

By closing time Lenn appeared to have attached himself to me. As we spilled out onto the street, I felt some small talk was in order.

"Are you in town on business?" I enquired, skirting a whole family cheerfully picking bunting out of the gutter.

Lenn's expression became furtive. "I am on a mission, which I perhaps should not explain to just anyone."

"A gay bar is probably the best place for fulfilling such a mission," I said. "Although I should caution you that neither myself nor my friend Rogov are that way inclined. You may be well-advised to follow one of the other punters home."

"I myself am not gay either," Lenn frowned. "I merely…but wait. Why do you frequent a gay bar if neither of you is a homosexual?"

"My local was crowded out," I shrugged. The bells heralding the end of curfew were sounding now, but very softly in case anyone who was already sleeping might be unduly disturbed. "And that bar is the one place Rogov's wife will not go."

"Because she hates homosexuals?"

"No, because it is the one place he goes when he does not want her to go with him."

"Because he is a latent homosexual and does not want her to witness this side of his life?"

"No, because Rogov wants one place where his wife will not go."

"Because Rogov hates his wife?"

I sighed inwardly. "I do not have the good fortune to be married, but if I was, I would want one place where my wife, dearly beloved as she would be, would not go. That bar is Rogov's such a place. Rogov's wife, dearly as she loves him, also has one place where Rogov will not go."

"The jewellery store," Lenn hazarded.

"No, it is a gay wine-bar down on Cherry Blossom."

"But Rogov goes to the gay pub," Lenn protested. "Why would he not go to a gay wine-bar?"

"Because he thinks wine-bars are bourgoise, and because his wife does not want him to," I explained. "And also he went there once and spilled a very expensive bottle of wine over the manager while explaining the economy."

"And was barred?"

"No, he was embarrassed because the stain would not come out. Now the manager wears that shirt so that people will ask what happened to it, and he can say, 'economics'. It makes Rogov wince," I said. "It is a terrible thing to see a proud man wince."

Lenn's expression became thoughtful as we trudged on through the darkened and emptying streets. "I believe you may be a man I can entrust with the secret of my mission," he declared at last. "You have an open and honest face, and to be frank, I do not believe your story of why two straight men would frequent a gay bar."

I did my best to assume an expression worthy of his trust.

"For two years now, I have been attempting to uncover the dark secret at the heart of our government," Lenn continued, his eyes now peering sharply over first his shoulder, then mine. I followed his gaze, but saw nothing of note.

"What dark secret at the heart of our government?"

"Aha!" Lenn replied. "You dissemble. It is fair enough. But a gay bar, surely, if anywhere, will be the place for those in the know to meet clandestinely and pass on pertinent information. As to the nature of the dark secret? That is exactly the question. All governments have a dark secret at their hearts. The road to power is paved with the broken backs of the oppressed, and the degree of oppression is reflected in the degree of secrecy surrounding it!"

I sensed from the rehearsed manner of speech he had fallen into that mine was not the first honest and trustworthy face he had encountered on his mission.

"Take this for an example," he continued, pulling a tattered paper from his pocket. "The front page of our state-sponsored newssheet! Have you ever read the byline? Really read it? *The Daily Propaganda: Don't believe everything you read just because it looks official!*" What government would print something like that if it has nothing to hide?"

I murmured words to the effect that an exceptionally honest government might encourage its citizens to seek vigilantly for the truth, and perhaps the Party In Favour Of Helping People To Do What They Like, As Long As They Don't Hurt Anyone (And Don't Take Too Many Sickies) was just the government to aspire to this.

"Ah!" Lenn exhaled bitterly. "And what of your friend Petrov, who has been so mysteriously disappeared? No doubt they seek the truth from him at this very moment! Informers and government spies and the secret police seek the truth vigilantly."

"There is no such thing as the secret police!" I laughed.

Lenn turned and caught me by the shoulders. The streetlights gave his rodent-like squint a decidedly disappointed cast. "*Everyone* says that, comrade," he sighed. "But if there are no secret police or informers, how did your Petrov's little speech come to the attention of the Powers That Be?"

"Well, he did make the local evening news," I confessed. "The band play-offs are a popular spectacle, and our journalists seem very keen to present dissident points of view. No doubt he can clear this all up on his return."

"And you think your old friend will ever return?"

"No doubt." I hesitated. "Tell me, my new friend, do you have a hotel to go to?" On seeing his expression, I sighed. "In that case, I think you had better follow me home after all."

By Tuesday, I had developed quite an amused affection for Lenn's daring mission. He seemed so serious about it all. I threw a two-day sickie in order to give him a tour of our fair city; in every bunker and den of disrepute he held earnest, furtive conversations with anyone who seemed remotely dissatisfied with their lot in life. We interviewed religious practitioners who resented the state's tolerance of the practice of other religions, pensioners who complained bitterly that the youth of today had nothing to complain about, and therefore seldom did, and one ancient teetotaller who abhorred the licence for licentiousness that the curfew and liquor laws provided.

"If he is teetotal, why does he hang out in a pub?" Lenn whispered as we wobbled into the street.

"I imagine he can't abhor alcohol half as well in a tea-shop," I observed. "But tell me, we seem to be having so little success with your mission. Is this the norm in the other cities you have visited? Have you tried asking the government directly?"

Lenn snorted. "I tried accessing the official documents as soon as my suspicions were first raised. It was useless, the archives were thrown immediately open at my request. Clearly the evil I seek is buried deep. Perhaps all records of it have been purged."

"You require hard evidence then, the actual testimonies of victims of oppression?"

"Precisely. Or better yet, the discovery and rescue of the victims themselves." Lenn grew thoughtful, and glum with it. "Who knows in what gulag, what oubliette, the poor souls like your friend Petrov may be wasting away, all hope lost?"

"I do not believe our government condones the use of gulags," I frowned. "And Petrov will be back soon enough."

Lenn waved his hand at me absently, his eyes misty with memory. "I thought I had stumbled on such a place once," he whispered. "Deep in the bowels of the government capital building. A windowless, dungeon chamber, where ranks of pale souls sat in dispirited silence. The door was not even locked to impede their escape, did they only realise it. Alas, it was the technical support office and they shouted at me to get out before I disrupted an important phase of their fantasy football campaign."

"I myself do not play fantasy football in the office," I offered soothingly. "But I understand it offers an outlet for competitive spirit, as well as—"

From the way Lenn glared at me, I realised he needed another drink to dull the memory of this trauma.

Feeling a pang of sympathy for my companion, whose incessant quest for the truth had driven him ever onward for more than two years, I guided him back to the bar in which we had first met. Surely the sight of familiar surroundings would be a welcome change for this lonely, if gregarious, traveller.

It was a happy coincidence, for as soon as we entered I spotted a familiar figure seated at the bar. It was Petrov, freshly released from his interview with the Powers That Be. He sat clutching a half-drained pint of Worker's Hard, his hands shaking and his face wan. His voice, when he spoke, was hoarse almost to non-existence.

"I talked," he wheezed, once we had refreshed his glass. "I talked for three days. I told them everything."

"And how did they take it?" I asked gently.

Petrov shook his head. "Not well. They said that all my ideas sprang from the desire to stop people from doing as they pleased, and as the Party In Favour Of Helping People To Do What They Like, As Long As They Don't Hurt Anyone (And Don't Take Too Many Sickies), it was unethical for them to implement a single one."

"Petrov has issues with the number of sickies taken by his colleagues," I murmured to Lenn, whose expression seemed to have frozen over during this speech. "He has been employed in the same position for twenty years now, a fine record, and has kept meticulous charts of the office malingering trends. He himself has not had a sick day in nearly a decade!"

Petrov seemed galvanised by my words, and required another pint to wet his throat enough to continue. "I told them!" he hacked, his tremors shaking a large puddle of beer onto the counter. "As all companies are owned by the state, it is the government's duty to curb malingering! Do you know what they said? That that sounded suspiciously like micro-management!"

I patted his shoulder.

Petrov hung his head in bitter defeat. "They also told me to take more sickies."

It took several more drinks to show proper sympathy for Petrov's humiliation. By the time Lenn and I regained the street, we had nearly missed the dusk.

"I am sorry for your disappointment," I told my companion. "Although I am glad to prove to you that my comrade Petrov is not languishing in a gulag."

Lenn waved his hand dismissively. "A clear case of brainwashing!" he snorted. "God rest his cruelly tattered soul and grant him healing. In the meantime, my mission continues. I *will* uncover the truth, and I sense that tonight I am closer than I have ever been to a revelation. But alas for the tinted glass! If I could just find out where they had taken him, if I could gain access... but wait. What is that?"

Across the narrow street, a grey, unmarked van had idled to the kerb. Two men in dark, unmarked uniforms were disgorged from it as we watched, and moved into the deeper night of an alley mouth. They returned seconds later, each with a hand supporting the elbow of what appeared to be an elderly tramp.

"What horror is this?" Lenn hissed, as the tramp was escorted to the rear of the van. The doors were firmly shut behind him, and his abductors climbed back into the cab and drove slowly on.

"Oh, that." I shrugged. "They are rounding up those who choose a vagrant style of life."

"What?" Lenn exclaimed. "And yet you have the effrontery to tell me there are no secret police! I cannot believe that a man such as yourself can turn a blind eye to such crimes! At least tell me, if you know and care, where are they taking the poor soul?"

I had to think for a moment. "Well, it's Tuesday. So they are taking them to the bowling."

❖   ❖   ❖

"Now you did tell a bit of a fib there, Dietrich," Gregor cautioned as he read my report. He raised his eyebrows at me over his spectacles, lips pursed in mild rebuke.

"Forgive me, boss," I replied, "but I am a traditionalist and believe that the secret police should indeed be a secret. Otherwise the title is rather a misnomer."

"'Each To Their Own'," Gregor quoted with a sigh. He flipped to the last page. "And this is the sum total of the dissent you have winkled out this week? People complaining about the way in which other people choose to spend their free time?"

I winced. "There does seem to be a distinct lack of radical opposition around, these days," I confessed. "What about the incident of the Aryan supremacist? He could be worth following up."

"Andrey and his lover had a falling-out again?" Gregor's eyes rolled briefly. "That boy certainly knows the way back into his heart. No, I'm afraid we can count that one out. It's a shame Petrov made it to the news before we had an in-depth file. We would have gotten the credit."

"What *are* we going to do about Petrov?" I asked, with concern for my old friend.

My boss looked distant for a moment. "Give him an attendance award, I suppose. I do hope he takes the state's advice after that and throws a few sickies. Otherwise we'll have to send him to a camp."

I nodded understandingly. "I daresay he'll be the better for it. I went to a very nice camp in the lakes a couple of years ago. Breath-taking scenery, despite the rain."

"I remember your postcard," Gregor smiled. "But I'm afraid I recommended Petrov for the one I take my wife to every summer. I caught a trout *this* big last year."

He frowned. "There was a better class of dissent when I was young. And people were against practically *anything* a government could do, back in the old days. I have read about it; on my own time, as well as during Orientation. It isn't natural for people to be so silent on the matter. Are the wellsprings of sedition so meticulously hidden that we cannot uncover them? Do people just not care anymore whether their government is good or evil?"

I felt a degree of optimism was required. "But what of my friend, Lenn?"

Gregor pursed his lips, blew through them, then shook his head. "Not really what I'd call dissent," he replied, not without regret. "Your knight errant is *seeking* to dissent, to call us to account for our crimes, and yet I couldn't in honesty concur that the desire to find something to be at odds with is identical with the state of *being* at odds with Policy. And you say he has been pursuing this mission for two years, and yet found nothing?" He shook his head again. "Shame you let him give you the slip, really. Perhaps he might have led us to something."

"Oh, Lenn hasn't given me the slip!" I exclaimed. "He had a flash of inspiration and went to pose as a voluntary vagrant in order to infiltrate the next round-up."

Gregor sat up sharply and lowered his spectacles to the very tip of his nose. "Your man is actually determined to pursue this course? Despite the avowed danger to his person, his mind, his very soul?" Mild as all my boss's emotions are, there was no mistaking the admiration in his voice.

I was pleased to be able to assent. "Lenn believes that his will, and the sanctity of his mission, shall enable him to withstand the horrors of brainwashing and torture. Thus he will return, shaken yet triumphant, to warn the world of the evil that lurks at the heart of their government."

"Oh dear." Gregor looked mildly concerned for a moment. "Well, what a very brave man. I hope he enjoys bowling."

The Lodger
Brian M. Milton

12th April

Dear Glasgow City Council,

I wish to complain about the giant alien hermit crab that has taken up residence in my conservatory.

When I agreed to take in a refugee from the fleet that had arrived over Earth I did so on the understanding I would be getting one of those more human looking aliens. Perhaps the nice one who appears on the news all the time as their spokesperson and was so funny when they appeared in that Children In Need charity sketch. Instead, I have been assigned K Fat (I think, I will admit I'm not clear on the spelling) who, while I am sure they are a lovely thing, what ever they are, is just simply not practical.

Firstly there is the question of living space. While the weather is mild it is no problem to leave the doors open but, with its more fleshy parts inside the conservatory and its pincers and head outside, they cannot be shut. This will not be good for K Fat come the winter, or for my heating bills. Secondly, the contraption it is currently "spinning" out of the window will soon interfere with my strawberry patch. I am told that this tube is to be thought of as its own plumbing but why the council cannot simply send round a man to build something less unsightly I do not know. This is being constructed across the most productive part of my garden and I will be very unhappy if anything affects that.

Please do not think that I am being racist in any way. I just feel my house is not best suited to its needs and perhaps a large hall in one of those amusement places the youth visit by the seaside might be better.

Yours sincerely,
Marjorie McFadden

27th April

Dear Sir,

I take great offence at your response to my earlier enquiry and I assure you that I will be making my dissatisfaction with your response known at the highest levels of the University. I am well aware that the alien refugees are people and not animals. That does not mean you are not best placed to answer my queries about their feeding habits and the safe disposal of their excreta. After all, you do cover a larger range of species than a doctor.

Yours,

Marjorie McFadden

28th April

Dear Glasgow City Council,

I would like to thank you for your swift response to my earlier mail. I am not entirely happy with the tone of it, but I will address your points in order:

1) Yes, I am aware that there are multiple species onboard the fleet and that they are fleeing from a terrible fate. This does not excuse council staff from doing a better vetting job.

2) I am now aware that her race is K'farr and that she is called Calaane. Perhaps your placement officer should have made that more clear on day one.

I was so embarrassed. It reminded me of my time in Prague when I confused the word beer for please.

3) It is true that we have a septic tank and I am glad that our unusual waste disposal situation has been useful. However, it was built by the Victorians and I do not believe they had K'farr, or any other type of alien crustacean, in mind when they designed it. At the very least I would like to know what the Scottish Environmental Protection Agency have to say about it.

4) I thank you for the offer to move my strawberries. While not the best time of year to do so I would like this done as soon as possible or I will be in no position to make my most popular jam in time for the Barrhead club show. I cannot let this visitor allow Mrs. MacArthur to get the top prize. I would not hear the end of it. Please advise when this can be done.

5) I was not aware of the possibility of a visit by an itinerant language tutor. Calaane's English is almost non-existent and I must admit to having trouble working out what of the noises she makes are language and what are intestinal. Please do arrange a visit and hopefully she can learn to speak properly.

Yours sincerely,

Marjorie McFadden

3rd May

My dear ladies of the Women's Institute,

I am writing to thank you all for attending my little event on Tuesday last to welcome Calaane to our small corner of the world. I am pleased to say that it has been noticed at national level in Edinburgh that we have been so forward in accepting refugees here and, despite Muriel's most unfortunate misunderstanding which I'm sure could have happened to anyone if they did not fully understand their lodger's requirements, I have been told there may be more formal recognition soon.

I am sure you will all agree that Calaane is the most interesting refugee that we have. She may not be the most pleasant to look at but, unlike some, I do believe that it is the personality that counts and I look forward to helping her become a useful member of society.

Yours sincerely,
Marjorie McFadden

21st May

Dear Glasgow City Council,

I am writing to express my annoyance at the implication that I am unable to feed Calaane, my K'farr lodger, and also to request the uplift of the crate of K'farr ships rations you delivered last Wednesday.

I would never have volunteered to take her on if I had felt I would need to rely on charity food donations. Would these resources not be best used on more deserving cases? Also on cases who are more able to withstand the smell?

I am sure that these ship rations were essential for Calaane and her people as they fled persecution but now that she is here I see no reason why Calaane can not eat human food. It is much easier to keep and does not cause passing dogs to cross the street.

Poor Calaane has suffered many indignities and was telling me recently of the struggles for food she had when initially escaping from her own planetary system during the later stages of the civil war and purges. Are you even aware that certain of her race's traditional foods were banned by the Junta? The food may have been horrible, it certainly sounds like it, but the experience has made Calaane a fussy eater and I am having enough problems convincing her to enjoy a good sausage casserole without you reminding her of the rations she used to have.

I hate to think what these rations would do to Calaane's digestion and then my septic tank.

Please arrange for their immediate removal.

Yours sincerely,
Marjorie McFadden

23rd May

Dear Glasgow City Council,

I wish to complain about the workmen you sent round last Tuesday to move my strawberries. While they have been successfully moved to the front border and look rather jolly in the sun there, I was not happy with the language they used.

I recently learned that K'farr live much longer than us and so poor Calaane is only a child, even if she is over seventy of our years old, and as such I feel that the use of swearing and demotic Scots is wholly inappropriate. We should be endeavouring to teach her the best of the English language, as she is educating me in the ways of her language. Since the lessons with your tutor began I feel we have both been making progress and I would not like to see that diminished.

I have been spending the warmer evenings reading to her from Shakespeare and Rowling and while she has been struggling over concepts such as boarding schools or witches, I feel we are getting somewhere. She is able to explain the fundamental problems with the rules of quidditch as a sport, for instance.

The K'farr have some lovely songs which, if I could only click my fingers to mimic her claw snaps, I would love to learn and I would not like to see that heritage diluted by slang and foul language. Please see that these workmen are disciplined.

Please also note that I have still not received assurances about the suitability of the septic tank for K'farr effluent and the man who visited last week to empty it has given me to believe there may be some issues there.

Yours sincerely,
Marjorie McFadden

2nd June

Dear Glasgow City Council,

I would like to thank you for the invitation to the reception at the City Chambers this weekend. Calaane is particularly looking forward to it as we have been practising a duet featuring the songs of her people and she would very much like to perform them.

She has also been rehearsing a short monologue on her journey here and the reason for it which, now that I have persuaded her to remove the section on the antennae mutilation that the Junta forced on her people in the internment hives, will hopefully be informative and suitably emotional.

Please send the flatbed round between 10 and 12 to avoid her ablutions.

On this subject, I have still not had a visit about the septic tank. As the temperature has risen a definite smell has begun to emanate from that part of the garden and it is playing havoc with my roses. This, along with the discomfort that poor Calaane is finding in an increasingly hot conservatory with limited shelter on her outside portions is making her life difficult.

I look forward to your suggestions,
Marjorie McFadden

13th September

Dear Councillor El-Amin,

I know that we have talked many times over the last couple of weeks but I would like to thank you and your community centre formally for all the help that you have provided to Calaane and I at this difficult time.

Your offer of a marquee during the initial heatwave was a godsend. The tarpaulins that the councilmen rigged up did a fair job of protecting Calaane from the worst of the sun but it was only a temporary solution and flapped loudly in even the slightest wind. This, combined with the fact that she has spent most of her life on board a spaceship, meant that she suffered badly from sunburn and I had to constantly apply the closest that we could find to a K'farr equivalent of Aloe Vera. Who would have imagined it would have been WD-40?

So it was with great relief that those young men came down after prayers and erected the marquee to give her some respite.

Calaane had been reading up on human religions and been learning some rudimentary Arabic, she is so much better at languages than I, so that she could come see what you get up to and thank you personally. In fact, it was doing this that probably saved her from serious injury. We were inside the tent as the water main in the road burst, but Calaane had disconnected herself from her "plumbing" and we were just about to move outside when the flash flood came down the road and through the garden. It was a hideous black wave of water, boiling round my car and then rushing towards us.

The marquee then began to collapse, as much from the water forcing the poles out of position as from Calaane struggling to be out of it, and for a second I thought it would collapse on top us. Calaane fought her way out of the tent and up on to the drive, moving out of the path of the water where I joined her.

It was at this point that your caretaker, drawn by the noise, came to see what had happened. He was wonderful, immediately taking us in, getting me a pot of tea and Calaane a couple of kippers from the freezer. Since then you have all been most helpful, offering us food and lodgings, despite the only room big enough for Calaane being where you hold your prayer meetings. This has been in such marked contrast to my insurers who are still delaying payment as they insist my septic tank was not rated for a K'farr and so, when the flood caused it to overtop, they feel they are not liable for the damage this has caused.

Your offer of accommodation for as long as we like is much appreciated but I believe that the interview I have given to the Herald should help to focus the minds of the insurers and get us out of your hair soon.

Once again, thank you very much,

Yours with heartfelt gratitude,

Marjorie McFadden

21st December

Dear Glasgow City Council,

I have just received your letter of the 20th on the subject of Calaane's resettlement. I cannot believe you are suggesting this. After the year we have had, we finally have our home repaired and were expecting to move back in on Wednesday, just in time for us to celebrate Calaane's first Christmas. I have been telling her all about it and, after the great time she had celebrating Eid while we were lodging at the local Islamic Centre, she was very much looking forward to it. Then we were going to have a proper Scottish Hogmanay, I'd even bought a Scotch and Wry DVD for that.

How, just as all this is scheduled can you turn around and say that she should move to somewhere more suitable for her? Who ever gave you the impression that my house was not suitable? I have been constantly supportive of having Calaane here and at no point have I felt this was not a viable situation. Indeed, as part of the flood repairs, I have expended a considerable sum of my own money to have the conservatory expanded so she can fit better. We have also acquired a new septic tank that even SEPA are happy meets the requirements put on it.

I am going to assume this is a mistake and continue with my efforts to give Calaane the best Christmas and New Year possible. I know she will do similar during the K'farr holiday in the New Year that she is planning to educate me in.

Yours sincerely,
Marjorie McFadden

30th January

Dear Glasgow City Council,

Today I received a letter purporting to be from your lawyers stating that Calaane would be removed from my house this coming Friday. This despite my last letter to you to say how happy she was here getting no response at all.

I am aware of the London Government's change of policy with regards to funding our refugees but I do not believe that moving them all into a camp is the correct answer. Yes they will be with their own kind, but Calaane is perfectly free to visit her K'farr friends at any point if she wishes.

Surely I do not need to remind you that her people were held in camps, or hives as Calaane insists on calling them, before being forced to leave their home system in the fleet. Returning them to a camp, no matter how humane, will only bring back those terrible memories. Just discussing it with Calaane yesterday the stress caused her to vibrate her shell at such a pitch it set my teeth on edge.

With this you have forced my hand and I shall be contacting the Herald today to see what the light of publicity can do.

With all the problems in the world, and clearly beyond it, surely it is not your intention to make things worse.

I am aware that certain parts of the media are complaining about our refugee friends but those are exactly the parts that your own councillors are so voluble about fighting. Glasgow is not an anti-immigrant city and I can't see what benefit you would think there would be in pandering to the few idiots in the city who are.

Yours in hope that you see sense,
Marjorie McFadden

3rd March

Dear Editor,

I am writing today to thank the good people of Glasgow who came out on Friday and supported myself and Calaane, my lodger. Once I thought of her as a poor, destitute refugee who had travelled across countless miles of space to arrive on Earth and who deserved the basics of human compassion.

Now, after almost a year of ups and downs she is much more than just a refugee. She is my friend. I have learned so much from her and grown so much as a person since meeting her that I cannot imagine going back to living on my own. To not be able to go into my garden, sit by her and talk over all that is growing, explaining what each plant is for, vegetables, fruit or flowers, and planning how we will replant it all after the flood, is something I cannot imagine. Even if she does still insist that foxgloves make a tasty snack.

It is this friendship that has made me fight so much to keep her in my house and not forced to move to the old council estate that has been designated for all the K'farr who have settled in Scotland.

It was most heartening to see so many come to support our fight on Friday, especially the councillors and MSP, but also the ordinary members of the public who showed the true, friendly spirit of Glasgow.

Calaane's case is now to be re-examined before the end of the month and I believe I can answer all concerns at that time.

Thank you all for your support.

Yours in gratitude,
Marjorie McFadden

17th April

Dear Sir/Madam,

In preparation for the hearing on Calaane of K'farr this coming Friday, please find enclosed the report I commissioned on my septic tank. You will find that the tank is operating correctly and while it needs to be emptied more often than it was originally designed for, it nonetheless is coping well.

Also, please find a report from the Food Standards Agency labs in Edinburgh who have tested the apples that the tree at the bottom of the garden produces. This shows no increased levels of anything that could be harmful in the fruit and, in fact, a slight increase in beneficial vitamins.

I can assure you that Calaane's effluent does not pose any form of threat to the environment surrounding my garden and may, in fact be leading to a bumper crop in the field next door.

Yours sincerely,

Marjorie McFadden

3rd June / Phase 3 of the Green Moon

Dearest People of Glasgow,

My friend Marjorie is a writer of many letters and electronic mails and she has told me that they are the best of all ways to get things done in Human Society. We K'farr would most normally petition our ruling councillors through the weekly audiences and so I have struggled to understand how all these small pieces of paper will help, but Marjorie said they would and it seems she spoke the truth.

Marjorie has just told me that it is now agreed that I may stay with her for the foreseeable future. This is good and makes me very happy. I am very comfortable in her conservatory, a perfect glass shell that protects me from the elements. She has made it larger and more constant of temperature since I first arrived and now that she has arranged an expanded secretion containment pit I feel sure that I can live here for years to come.

It is because of this good news that I wish to write to you all today to say thank you. All you people of Glasgow have been most accommodating and friendly to all of us refugees who arrived here two years ago. You have fed us and educated us and we can only be hugely humbled by your generosity.

To all you Marjories in Glasgow, I thank you from the very centre of my vestigial carapace.

I sign off with pleasure,

Calaane, K'Farrie of the Lost Fleet

10 Things to Know
About Staple Removers

Ian Hunter

(after Carolyn Clink)

1. The staple remover was invented by someone who bit their fingernails.
2. They are excellent for picking up small children by the ears.
3. Correctly applied, when the planets align, they can be used to extract the soul of a virgin.
4. They are excellent for picking up small children by the nose.
5. If the ends should stick together, you will die.
6. When applied to the neck they can be incorrectly assumed to be the bite of a vampire.
7. They make a good noise for scaring victims when chasing them through the woods.
8. They are excellent for making small children cry at parties.
9. Toothless old people who like to bite flesh always carry them.
10. Balloons fear them.

HEADKILLER
Michael Cobley

Bodies are… bodies are like cars. Some are run-of-the-mill, standard issue flab-jalopies, some are bad-luck-mobiles prone to random breakdowns, some are wheezing clunkers ready to come apart at the seams. And some, just a few, are fine, sleek vehicles, all physical fire and flash, with a well-tuned musculature and an immaculately-curated countenance. I could feel how good it was even before I pushed myself up on my elbows to gaze into the mirror that was fixed at the foot of the gurney. I smiled at the reflection. I grinned, I snarled, I frowned, I pouted, I put my features through their paces, amused as hell at the rubbery, twisty bulginess of the human face.

"So Crypto gets a pretty-pretty boy," came a voice from nearby. "Too pretty for you."

"I know how to take care of it, Mantle," I said. "And I have the charm, the skills and the memes, and that makes me…"

"Yeah, we know—the tip of the spear, the spark in the dark, the edge of the edge… oh, and the pain in the ass!"

An assortment of laughs, sniggers and dry chuckling came from the others. I nodded, smiling a tolerant killer smile as I swung my legs round to face Mantle, already sitting up on his stretcher trolley.

"Interesting rig you got there, Mantle," I said. "D'you think it was born or bolted together?"

More laughter and a forced grin from Mantle, all bared teeth and animosity. Such banter is normal for us, getting it out of our systems. Rivalries, quarrels, dustups—call them what you like—all the petty feuds we pursue while residing in SimHalla are firmly put aside when we're out in the field.

"All right, cut the jabber!" said the Colonel's face on the side of the little blimp-drone as it floated past the line of gurneys and down the full length of our converted freight container; AKA, the Deployer. "Time to suit up. Our employers are paying top dollar for your very special services and we have a tight schedule ahead."

A pair of technicians, garbed in onepieces and data goggles, began handing out bundles of clothing. Mantle and me exchanged half-smiles of the hate-on-hold variety then busied ourselves with getting dressed. The others were doing the same, unpacking the bundles and looking them over before putting them on. With a sidelong glance I fixed their appearances in my new, though temporary, brain-cockpit: Mantle's vehicle was a beefy, bearded male in its mid-40s, which suited his blunt, uncomplicated nature; 3Cuts was steering a young female, blonde, 20s, dovetailing nicely with that guns and knives fixation; Blokchain (explosives) and Embers (hacking) had a neatly-matched couple from Gatedville, USA; and Needler (electricals and security) was at the controls of a tall, whiskery male in a long, grubby trench coat. We were like wolves clothed in sheep.

"First things first—today's trigger phrase is 'Albedo Incarnadine'," said the Colonel from his blimp-screen. "Commit it to memory. Now, we shall recap the salient points of the mission. Our target is billionaire politician, Dan Thresher. Tonight, he will be giving a keynote speech at a rally in a sizeable mid-Western city, the second-last date on a 10-city tour cementing his candidature for next year's primaries. Your job is to kill him and his entourage and make it look like the work of deranged fundamentalists."

Not for the first time, I wondered if our handler, the Colonel (AKA Colonel Silvertop, AKA Colonel No-Name), was an actual, flesh-and-blood, realworld effective or if, like us, he'd been transmapped from meat-life into the meta-life of SimHalla, a quantentity persona assembled from the transmap datafracts, a sustainable weave of thought, whim and mind. We are Headkillers, downloadable assassins, guns for hire, yet the Colonel seems...different. One of the others thought that he might be an AI, but I've had a few private chats with the Colonel and I'm pretty sure that he's not one of those clockworkers so beloved of the bot engineers. I've encountered a few and I've never felt that hallmark hollowness in any dealings with him.

"Now, Crypto will use his cunning talents to gain a private audience with Thresher," the Colonel went on. "When they're alone, he will grapnel the target and engage the depattern-overwrite. Then Crypto-as-Thresher will call in Thresher's confidantes, one by one, sending them off, on a pretext, to meet the rest of the team at pre-arranged secluded locations. Depattern-overwrites again, then the team will gather the new hosts in the VIP hospitality suite, bringing the shells with them..."

Each of us is equipped with a clever device that the techs call a grapnel. All you do is peel off the cap to expose the microbarbs then slap it against the back of the target's head. At this point you've either immobilised the target so that physical reactions don't enter the picture, or not—in which case they'll be treating you as hostile while fumbling around the back of their head to find out what you did. But since the grapnel microbarbs immediately deliver a fast-acting paralytic on skin contact rowdiness quickly ceases to be an issue.

After that the nanobuilders go to work, spreading a conductive web throughout the target's cortex, hijacking the synapses and ganglia, channelling all that bio-electricity. Then comes the depatterning phase, which takes about a minute and a half for a thorough personality wipe. At this point you're already cabled up, so switching your inputs over to the target's sensorium is a cakewalk: first vision, then hearing, taste and smell, in that order, ending with touch once the nervous system is fully integrated.

It's all such a smooth, seamless process. During the overwrite, your awareness doesn't even drop out, not for an instant. From start to finish it's usually about four and a half minutes, five tops, and there you are, at the wheel of your new meat-machine, complete with all its uses and defects. And there, at your side, is a motionless shell—

your previous host body. The transitioning overwrite stage erases your own datafracts and leaves behind a cluster of basic action routines, so that it'll nod, smile, sit, stand and do as its told. Way back at the start, I used to get uneasy at the emptiness in those eyes which had been mine, but SimHalla training and a few missions of body-swapping soon cured me of any nerves. When we're out in the world, the experience is an exhilarating skindance from one shell to the next, a pleasure of the flesh unique in itself.

"...so once you have Thresher, his coterie and your shells together in the hospitality suite, you'll find a holdall containing six loaded handguns. You can do the killing in any order you like, as long as all the guns are fired and the scene plausibly looks as if Thresher and his people were offed by these six individuals. Their back-stories have already been modified, along with phone, net and bank records tying them to the Excelsior Tabernacle of Sacred Deeds, a rural fundamentalist grouping.

"Your trigger phrases will burst-cast your cogstates to our receivers and once everyone's dead, the grapnels will initiate the neural cleanup. I know that you will all perform to the best of your abilities but, as you do, keep this in mind—this is our first mission in this kind of low-security environment and the outcome will directly influence our chances of similar contracts in the future.

"Now, if you've finished gearing up, prep for insertion."

Mantle shot me a reptilian smile that said, *wait till we get back to SimHalla, sucker.* Before I could conjure up an *as-if-I-care* shrug, he was moving towards the exit, jostling and joking with the others. In that moment I couldn't help but recall *that* mission ten months ago in the jungle with the lab, the exploding chemicals and the escaped test animals. We were at the final stage and I had to hijack one of the lab techs to place and prime the charges. But in my haste I damaged the grapnel cable and found that I'd duplicated myself into the lab tech without erasing my previous host. Lab-tech-me had grinned then strolled off to the chemical store with a pocketful of charges, but being a careless asshole he got the timing wrong and Mantle was still in the menagerie when it all went up.

Luckily my asshole copy perished in the inferno while a char-grilled Mantle only just managed to speak the trigger phrase. Since then he never misses a chance to grind that axe, keeping his grudge fresh. At least I learned something important—when the meat is disposable, you start taking it for granted, no matter who's inside.

Save me from the sump of ancient history, I thought. So I shoved the old memories aside, switched into mission-mode, and went to join my fellow Headkillers.

Persuasion and a facility with language are my specialties. Memes, similes and metaphors, words, terms, phrases, alluding to one thing with linguistic constructs that supposedly reveal an inner truth. To me this moment, when we're standing patiently in line, chaperoned from his blimp by the Colonel, always makes me think of a specific metaphor. Right back at the beginning I used to imagine that we were paratroopers gliding over enemy territory by night, waiting for the signal to jump, and I later learned that Embers sees it as getting ready for a demented WW1 infantry charge across No-Man's Land. Now, though, I view it all through a more sardonic lens, as if the Deployer, our converted shipping container, was some kind of huge box magazine, jammed into the head of an ignorant world, firing us off, like rounds, eager ammunition for the Colonel's master plan.

And a masterly plan it was too, well-conceived, superbly balanced between the necessary stages and the overall timing and playing to the strengths of everyone in the Headkiller team.

Shame it never turned out that way.

We left the container truck at ninety-second intervals. I was last out, blinking up a street map on my ocular display, identifying the parking garage then the conference centre two blocks away, as I headed for the exit.

Transitioning from SimHalla into a meatsuit in base reality, was always a testing process, getting the feel right, acquiring the habit. In SimHalla, all the inputs for one's sensorium are synthesised and blended into a smooth holistic impression. The garage's rich miasma of burnt petrocarbons and oily metal could be modelled, even to include that whiff of vomit near the foot of the up-ramp and the pungent stink of dog crap as you emerge into the brightness at street level. Reality, though, possesses a certain horrible, gritty detail that simulations just cannot match. I've always felt that authentically organic filth is something to be cherished.

Out on the streets the air was urban, carrying taints of fried food, tyre rubber and a beery waft from some spillage outside a nearby shuttered saloon bar. It was late in the afternoon and employees were draining from the office blocks and flowing towards local metro stations and bus stops. As I neared the conference centre, I realised that many of them were heading that way too. Looked as if Thresher would have no shortage of appreciative followers.

I paused at an intersection and distributed my prep-pack's contents amongst various pockets. Included was a clip-on ID badge which went on my coat lapel, completing the necessary profile. Then I hurried across and joined one of the lines snaking through the conference centre's wide, canopied entrance. I found myself standing behind a broad-shouldered male in working clothes, while in front of him two silver-haired older women chattered like gossiping birds. A family of four took up position behind me, with the wife mouthing her devotion to Thresher like an artless prayer while herding her offspring (bored) and hubby (bored but trying to sound upbeat).

Ordinary people, down-home folk, the average undistinguished middle of the nation. Before my conversion to digital personhood, before my time in the military, my early life was spent around people like these. If I really tried I could dig down to those old, old memories, but they felt like outgrown clothes, dusty keepsakes without meaning. Vestiges of a discarded life, effectless, blank, dead.

By contrast the sight, just then, of Mantle nearing the front of the queue entering from the other side was sufficient to focus my thoughts, firing up the animosity that I'd grown to cherish. Everyone should have a hobby, after all. Mantle spared me only a flicking glance as he shuffled along in line and disappeared into the foyer. Less than a minute later, I too reached the doors where my face and ID were scanned before I was allowed through. Stairs led up to where a succession of Thresher workers gave me a flag, a cap, badges, stickers, coasters, pamphlets, pens, and a brightly-coloured bag adorned with the face of their demigod for me to carry it all in.

Channelled along the foyer, I went with the flow like an obedient supplicant. I climbed more stairs and pushed through heavy burgundy drapes... and suddenly I was engulfed in shadows, music, voices, a carnival excitement. Surrounded and carried forward a dark-sided passageway by a press of jostling people, I began to notice features in the surf of conversations and chatter that swirled all about me, ripples and repetitions washing down the line. Which meant there had to be a source.

The passage opened out above an immense horseshoe of seating, eager supporters filtering down the aisles, seeking good views of the waiting stage. But it was the back wall which caught my attention, its alcoves, its knots of onlookers. As I said before, my specialty is persuasion, interpersonal engineering, the ability to deduce the mainsprings of motivation, the scars that offer leverage. I have a hyper-perception when it comes to words that are more than they seem, phrases, sayings and slogans which alter minds as they pass through them. Receptivity is the key trait, which everyone shares to one degree or another, and repetition fits it like a key. The rear of the auditorium was a soupy fog of memes emanating from the alcoves where screens replayed clips from Thresher's old speeches. All the sins of political power were there: pride, arrogance, self-righteous hypocrisy, avarice, flattery for the powerful, an iron fist for the powerless and the scapegoats.

I smiled widely as I went from alcove to alcove. It felt like a banquet, yet I knew that this was only the appetiser. Thresher's greatest hits were being served up to the congregation in the full and open understanding that they would be hearing them all again from the mouth of the Man Himself—and they knew, with the intoxicated fervour of the irredeemably beguiled, that still it would be as if they were hearing it all for the first time.

It was a galvanising spectacle. I'd studied the theory of viralinguistics, coped with all the permutation puzzles, trained well, long and hard in the scenario suites back in SimHalla, but none of that had prepared me for the spectacle of upper level multiplexity creating unanimity at the lower level. Thresher was not a trained memetician, just a gifted amateur, but what gifts and what organisation! I looked around me. Nearly three thousand had arrived by now—they were like a horde of little meme-boxes, getting jolts from the playbacks as they moved from alcove to alcove, or from the pamphlets and posters, or from each other.

Thresher was connecting, in that he was connecting them to him. No wonder someone wanted him stopped in his tracks.

And that was when an insight struck me with the dazzling impact of revelation. Suddenly I could see not just the thousands gathering here, but also in the streets and buildings beyond the conference centre, the city and its tributary towns and the cities further out, and the roads and cables and satellite and internet that stitched it all together... I could see a far-off goal, which seemed suddenly, tantalisingly within reach. The delights of SimHalla are immeasurably varied, but only reality can provide prizes which are really worth the struggle and the risk. The Colonel's masterplan was a marvel of economy, but now I could see how to modify it. Step One was still getting close to Thresher, but after that...the thrills of improvisation beckoned!

I studied the positioning of the venue staff and Thresher's own people. I blinked up a display map and noted that the stage-left access door was chained shut. The right-side door was manned by two uniformed Thresher goons who were checking backstage passes against lists, so my clip-on, Joe-Average-Flagwaver ID wasn't going to cut it. I was going to need a new ride.

In my ocular display I called up a list of Dan Thresher's full retinue, excluded the driving, catering and security personnel, leaving behind the inner circle with their support teams...and even as I was scanning the profiles one of them strolled past. Female, 40s, brunette, sharply-suited, equipped with an ear-jewel/lip-bead combo into which she was murmuring while thumbing through entries on a palm-tab. In a mo-ment, I had her data—Rachel Miller, PA to Thresher's head of PR. I ruffled my hair, loosened my tie then I glanced at her as if in surprise and said:

"Sorry, but are you on Mr Thresher's staff? It's just that..." (quickly I scanned for a Customer Liaison name) "...Mr Kirby asked me to go and find someone..."

"Kirby?" she said. "Justin Kirby?"

I nodded. "There was an altercation in the foyer," I went on breathlessly. "A pro-tester, with a banner! He started shouting, and there was shoving, so Mr Kirby marched the guy into a side office..."

Miller shook her head. "Not another of these pests...I've heard nothing about this. Why didn't Kirby contact me over the comnet?"

I shrugged. "Could have been damaged in the scuffle..."

"Scuffle?"

"...so Mr Kirby sent me to get someone senior, urgently..."

Because even personal assistants like to feel important, that urgent matters can actually require their personal attention, especially when it might give them the chance to shine. So, it wasn't hard to steer her with a mixture of bluff and assertion into an empty corridor then an office ('Mr Kirby said the guy had to be kept away from the foyer...just through here, Ms Miller'), and that was where I slapped the grapnel on the back of her neck. I eased her paralysed form into a chair behind a desk, then locked the door, got cabled up and started the mind shift. Five minutes later it was my handsome former vehicle that was sitting at the desk, smiling vacantly at nothing in particular while I tried to adjust to my new physique. Not my first time in a female vehicle, but it would still take a little while to acclimatise fully to the different balance of body weight and the shorter stride.

The hair-thin transfer cable retracted into the grapnel on the back of my neck while I retrieved the other one from the shell.

"Stay here," I told it. "Do not leave the room."

The shell just nodded and continued to smile. Whatever happened next, it would shut down in just over an hour when the cortical nanoweb self-disassembled, causing brain death.

Walking in Rachel Miller's sensible flat shoes, I returned to the foyer and continued back up to the auditorium. Exchanging friendly nods with some of Thresher's meme-filled fans on the way, I was waved through the door to backstage without a hitch. Security's strengths are also its weaknesses. An ID badge is a visual meme which, in this case, denoted my official status as part of the Thresher organisation, the connotation of being part of the Big Club, that wink-and-a-warm-smile congeniality. However, once separated from the public by the filtering membrane of Security, the context changed and I became a humble personal assistant, a subordinate menial in the Thresher hierarchy.

Beyond the door was a breakout-meeting room from which radiated three corridors containing changing rooms and storage, artist prep rooms and Hospitality. I took a seat and made a pretence of scrutinising my palm-tab messages while skimming through Thresher's personnel list for the second highest rung on the ladder, and there he was—Paul Donahue, Director of Operations and about as close to a deputy as the boss was likely to allow. Donahue was originally supposed to be Mantle's target, but I had new plans for him.

I found him in a storeroom not far from the loading elevator, talking with a delivery-man standing next to a stack of boxes. I put on a nervous-informant performance, intimating that I had something vital to tell him but only in private. He frowned and concluded his business with the deliveryman, who left; then turned back to me. I anticipated a rinse-and-repeat of the first transfer but instead Donahue leered and made a grab for Ms Miller's goods. Which, of course, brought him close enough for me to hit him with the grapnel. Depatterning and overwriting the slug was an unalloyed pleasure.

In my brand new Paul Donahue meatsuit, I steered the newly empty Miller shell out of the storeroom to a deserted fire escape stairwell where I told it to head downwards and stop when it got to the bottom. With that taken care of, I tidied my appearance and walked briskly back to the breakout-meeting area. Smiles and nods flew my way, the petty currency of underlings. Not much in the way of convivial small talk, though—Donahue clearly didn't encourage it, luckily for me.

I grabbed a cup of espresso from the refreshment console and checked Donahue's skinwatch. Still about forty-five minutes until Thresher's big set-piece speech. Time enough to deal with the only real obstacles to my new plan—the rest of the Headkiller team.

I tracked down Philips, Thresher's security head, and told him that five dangerous individuals had been seen skulking around, intent on disrupting the speech, maybe even setting fire to the building! Philips frowned, asked how I knew about this; Because these terrorists had a sympathiser inside the crew, I said, none other than Rachel Miller. But her guilt and shame made her divulge the plot to me, along with the locations of these dark agents. Manly determined nod from Philips who said, We need to notify local law enforcement. Already on their way, I said, but we can't take any chances by sitting on our hands. We need to take action!

I held out a scrap of paper with the locations of the rest of the Headkiller team. With another manly nod and a steely gaze, he took the note and left.

And just like that, the clock was ticking. Standard field protocol was to avoid un-planned conflict situations. If you get into trouble just speak the trigger phrase and the cortical nanoweb would burst-cast your cognitive state to the receivers back at the Deployer, soon after updating your original quantentity sitting in one of SimHalla's suspension buffers. Faced with armed guards approaching with guns drawn, the others wouldn't waste time bailing out. I reckoned it would take about fifteen minutes, maybe twenty, for Philip's guards to reach all the locations, forcing the Headkillers to abandon the field. More than enough time to pay Dan Thresher a visit and show him the meaning of the words 'hostile takeover'!

And fuck it, when I got to the stage-prep room Thresher was deep in conversat-ion with Evans, the corporate liaison guy. For a moment I was pinned by uncertainty. Thresher wouldn't take a straight-up interruption, not even from Donahue, and I couldn't just loiter aimlessly either. So I decided to have quick private words with any of the other managers I could find, clueing them into the security situation, just the highlights, passed along with enough concern memes to persuade them of Donahue's hidden golden-heartedness. When Evans eventually emerged there were less than five of my twenty-minute estimate left, so I would have to pick up the pace.

Entering the prep room, I closed the door with my back against it, concealing my hand as it flipped the latch to locked.

"Paul!" Thresher was seated at the one-way mirror that looked out over the now-packed auditorium. Before him were a stack of speech cards and his trademark white ten-gallon hat. Dan Thresher was a big man and the ridiculous hat just enhanced the entire spectacle—he was practically a living meme. I smiled. I was going to enjoy being him.

"Dan," I said. "Can I get a moment or two of your time?"

"Not a problem, Paul, not a problem. What can I...?"

Someone began pounding at the door and even as I glanced round, there was a crash and the door flew open, splinters flying from the burst lock. A guard strode in, heading straight for me. His face was completely unknown to me but the hate in his eyes I recognised immediately. It was Mantle.

"Don't worry, *sir*," Mantle told a dumbfounded Thresher. "I just need to take care of this."

So saying, he grabbed me by the lapels of Donahue's immaculately-tailored jacket and hauled me through the door to the short passageway which led to the stage.

"Time to bring your little joyride to a close," Mantle said as he slammed me against the wall.

"Ah, c'mon, Mantle, gimme more triumphant gloating than that. Go to town, let it all out!"

He brought his face up close. "I'm glad that you screwed up, Crypto. It's going to be so much fun watching you get dissected and wiped." A pause. "Hear this: *Albedo Incarnadine!*"

There was a moment after he spoke the trigger phrase, a mere fraction of a second before the nanowebs in each of our heads responded. And in that instant my gaze locked with Mantle's and I saw a hatred so deep, dark and pure that a ripple of new doubt passed through me... closely followed by a disconnecting greyness...

I interlink my porcelain-pale, mannequin fingers, resting my arms and hands on the empty, pale-blue desktop.

"And that pretty much brings us up to date," I say to my interrogator.

Offwhite walls, a strip of mirror running all the way round. I am in SimHalla, in one of the suspension buffers, apparently. Sadly, the room service sucks.

Not getting a response, I say, "So, what happens now?"

"It's already happening."

My interrogator looks about thirty, wears a dark, high-necked uniform and has a definite military bearing. He looks like a young version of the Colonel.

"And what does that entail, exactly?"

"SimHalla's custodial systems are analysing your subpersona aspects, cross-examining them with your narrative, scanning for anomalies and inconsistencies..."

"And then? Shunt me off to the fires of data-hell? Hey, we're just happy, obedient killers, so a quick wipe and purge, then crank up version 1.0 and send them out again..."

"Everything is updated, Crypto," says my captor. "Everything, all the time. Once the custodials have finished their appraisal, the Headkiller team will be briefed on this anomalous incident before they are released to enjoy a brief spell of R&R. Your memory-sequence will be kept on file for future research."

"Waste nothing, eh?"

No response. There seems to be nothing behind those eyes but a kind of distant curiosity, the regard of something vast and pure. I wish I could run from it but I have no feet—in fact, I have no legs. I study my reflection in the mirror strip and see a perfectly alabaster, hairless mannequin figure emerging, by the waist, from the desktop.

"So when am I to be erased?"

"It's already begun."

I stare at my captor and think that actually the Colonel could be the old version of him. Then I realise that I'm sinking into the desktop, a steady uninterrupted dissolution. It's horrific, funny and bizarre all at once, yet I'm calm. Colonel Silvertop the Younger steps away from the desk. Rather than raise my arms I just lay them down on the desk and before long they are swallowed. My vision stutters slightly and it seems as if I'm seeing multiple images of the Boy-Colonel.

Everything is updated, Crypto… Everything… I want to tell him that this is wrong, that we're not just their remote instruments…but even as the words frame themselves in my mind a sickening realisation hits, cold, hard and unforgiving. Instruments, devices, gadgets, contraptions, the panoply of artifice—could there ever be a better instrument than one that thinks it's a real person? I want to tell him that I've figured it out, to laugh and damn and curse him…but my mouth is gone so all I can do track him with my eyes, my unwavering gaze, until…

The rally was over and boisterous chart hits of yesteryear were playing the audience out as they slowly filed through the exits. Under bright ceiling spots, empty styro cups, cans, plastic bottles, food boxes and spilled popcorn were being swept up by the bagging teams who worked the aisles as they were vacated.

I stood at the prep-room's one-way mirror, looking down. Thresher's speech would have been good, but my version was far better. I gave them the highs, I gave them the lows, took them on a journey full of embellished spills, thrills and chills then brought them back to the struggle's exciting threshold. I showed them anger, made them laugh, mocked their enemies and made wild promises—a word-blizzard designed to foster a meme-army. And going by the ecstatic ovations, they were fired up and ready to storm the liberal arts university campus of my choice.

"Looks like we could be in the clear." The voice behind me sounded like the guy in charge of catering & logistics.

"The city cops have been very friendly and understanding," said the corporate liaison guy.

"But can we be sure that the custodials aren't onto us?" said the PR woman.

I turned to face them, smiling as I removed the ten-gallon hat and tossed it on the table.

"If they knew the truth they would come for us," I said. "And if they were coming for us they would have been here by now. Yet here we are, which means that they know nothing about our little subterfuge…"

From the moment that I'd decided to make the break and take the leap, I knew that I'd have to be audacious. I also knew that I couldn't do it alone. That persona duplication trick, which I'd secretly perfected on previous missions, I'd put into operation as soon as I reached the VIP area. It was my Paul Donahue version who made the sacrifice, a double sacrifice—allowing us to modify his narrative memory sequence to hide all that I'd done, then setting him up to be captured by Mantle's hijacked guard.

I allowed myself a satisfied smile and let my gaze travel from face to face, knowing that five Cryptos were looking back.

"We need to play this carefully, with rigorous attention to detail. We need to know the characters of these new meatsuits, their lives, routines, weaknesses…"

"Every character will have its own peculiar set of mingled memes masquerading as a personality," the security chief added. "We must literally inhabit these roles, so our acting need only avoid failure to succeed."

I nodded, we nodded, all of me nodded. "When's the next rally?"

"Two days' time, on Saturday."

Plenty of time, then, to construct a real barnburner of a speech, and having tried it out once I was itching to get back in the saddle. That crowd…I'd felt it respond to my words, sensed intimately how it hung on my sentences, how it trembled with emotion, a crowd, a throng, a city, a nation…

And a nation is a bit like a car.

Depending on your point of view.

Crowd Control
Cameron Johnston

A handful of ghouls had already wormed their way in before I arrived, phones out, drones buzzing around the carnage, streaming visuals of burning wreckage to sate the voracious appetites of their net-viewing brethren. It didn't look like there were any survivors, but these bastards were making it hard to tell.

Comms chirped in my ear: "Warning: two minutes to viral pandemic."

"Damn. Get that Interdict up, people. We can't afford another Air Force One disaster."

The rest of my team sprinted through the portal and it collapsed behind us with a whiff of ozone. They set down their cases, slotted them together and began powering up the Interdict. I spared a moment to survey the flaming ruin of the airliner and the ground strewn with corpses and belongings. Luckily it had come down on an old and overgrown motorway before gouging a long crater through ploughed fields, hedgerows and lines of trees.

Though it hadn't crashed in an urban environment, some sort of uber-famous vlog presenters had been on board and the probability of a viral incident rocketed as the first rumours hit social media and swiftly infected friend lists and news feeds, an exponential growth of awareness rippling in ever-widening circles.

My lip curled as drones flitted eagerly from horror to horror, from splayed corpse to children's charred toys, hunting down ad-revenue clicks as viewers flocked to gaze through their glass eyes with voyeuristic fervour.

A gold sphere the size of my fist popped into being nearby—an anchor—the metallic squeal setting my teeth on-edge. It imploded, displaced air thumping me sideways as the portal opened to disgorge a cyclist in neon lycra. He hadn't even spared a moment to remove his helmet before leaping into a worming station. His expensive camera was already up to his eye, shutter chittering like a furious insect swarm while his state-of-the-art head-cam streamed the twat's-eye view. He paused to check the initial shots and his lips twisted with glee. I knew his sort of scum: semi-professional disaster-chasers making a name off the backs of the dead. They pandered to the anti-newscorp, anti-government and conspiracy theorist viewers. The 'Real-Truthers'.

Comms chirped again: "Vlogg site 'Eye on Truth' has an eye on the ground. They have just confirmed rumours to ten point nine million followers."

"Bloody ghouls," I snarled loud enough to be heard, but the cyclist ignored me. Besides, he was far from alone. Wormholes were opening all across the site as the morbidly curious arrived in person, photos and video streams not visceral enough for their desensitised tastes. Among them were the first disaster teams, trying to haul medical kits and rescue equipment through the ever-increasing crowd of gawpers. I grabbed the cyclist and shoved him aside, then stuck an arm out to block a wandering moron. A Médecins Sans Frontières team pushed through the gap I'd made, giving me a terse nod before they rushed into hell.

I clicked Comms. "Status report."

"United Kingdom, ten miles south of the city of Stirling. Local services en-route, ETA five minutes. Bi-directional worming transit station configuration, ETA ten minutes. One minute to viral pandemic."

I grunted. One minute was optimistic judging from the rapidly swelling crowd.

From behind me: "Shit!"

I spun to face Reynolds. The gaunt Canadian engineer's lined brow was furrowed deeper than ever. His fingers flickered over the Interdictor, stabbing screens. "Power regulator failure. Switching to backup."

I cursed. Thirty additional second; an age on the viral scale. "Kratz—keep these ghouls away from Reynolds. Use lethal force if you have to. Rest of you start thinning the crowd."

The big German nodded, pulled her pistol free and stood guard. The rest of my team spread out and started strafing the ghouls with shriek-guns. The crowd yelped and stumbled backwards, hands clamped over their ears. Cameras and pads got smashed underfoot. I had no sympathy.

The dispersal provided only brief respite. Newcomers were pushing in from the edges of the crowd, more and more all the time, shoving the mass back towards us whether they liked it or not, spacial displacement knocking people to the ground amongst the forest of feet. I swallowed, remembering the crowd when Airforce One came down, my own crushed fingers and broken ribs, gasping for breath in the vice of sweat-slicked bodies. And I'd been one of the lucky ones; tens of thousands had died that day.

I aimed my shriek-gun at a knot of people in danger of trampling the fallen, temporarily driving them back. It saved a few, but only made things worse elsewhere.

"Reynolds?" I screamed over the hubbub.

"Ten seconds." His voice cracked.

Flickers of gold everywhere—so many, like stars in the night sky—worming in all across the field. My heart thundered. The rescue teams that had managed to make it here were trapped in the churning belly of the beast, unable to get close to any survivors there may have been. Any moment now we would reach viral singularity, and there was no going back from that—we'd all be royally screwed.

"Establishing field encryption."

The hairs on my arms stirred with static. Panic rose, glints of gold continuing to appear: but these new portals all heralded rescue teams and U.N. military quick response units.

Then the crowd screamed in collective horror as their cameras and pads crackled and died, wailed in loss as drones dropped from the sky and their precious feeds cut off.

"Interdict field holding steady." Reynolds was barely audible over the indignation of the entitled. "Field passkey has been circulated to all official parties." He slumped in relief and wiped the sweat from his brow. "Looks like that faulty power regulator caused a field surge."

"Mein heart bleeds," Kratz shouted.

Such a shame, but it wasn't unexpected. Unlike the rescue teams, most of these amateur sightseers didn't use shielded equipment. I clapped Reynolds on the shoulder. "Good job. Don't let these brain-dead maggots anywhere near the Interdict."

Then I spotted that neon-lycra wearing cyclist. The semi-pro disaster-chaser, equipment still lit up and snapping away as he blocked a rescue team's progress in an attempt to get exclusive interviews. *Murder*, I heard. *Bomb.*

What is wrong with these people? I sighed, dropped my shriek-gun and palmed my pistol. I shouldered my way through the throng until I was right up behind the prick, and then calmly shot him in the leg. I might have shot him in the head if there wasn't a chance the bullet would pass straight through his empty skull and hit somebody else. Last thing we needed was more panic.

He went down screaming, just one more voice lost in the crowd. Nobody cared. A helpful rescue volunteer's boots made sure to crush his gear. I left him there and returned to protect the Interdict.

I sagged with relief when our backup finally wormed in en-mass, loaded with force-fences, sonic cannons and other non-lethal deterrents. I prayed they wouldn't spray the crowd with Skunk; my nose couldn't take that again. Quickly, they encircled our position before the crowd finally swamped us.

Reynolds lit a real cigarette—now illegal in fifty countries—with shaking hands. He looked every bit as sick as I felt. He offered me his hipflask. "Happy Birthday, chief."

I took a deep swig. The whisky burn helped take the edge off. "Did you get it?"

"For sure." Reynolds held up his camera. "That shitpump cycle-hoser is Meme Central already. These comments are pure gold. We're trending everywhere, and five ranks up on NaturalBornHeroes net."

Amanda
Jim Campbell

The hedge was thick, tall and overgrown. If I could find a way through it would shield me from the road. Perfect cover. There, beside a burned out farmhouse, a gap where something big had smashed the hedge flat, revealing the shell-pocked field beyond. I wanted to rush, to run now that I was so close, but I forced myself to wait, crouched down, listening for any sign of pursuit. I was sure that this was far enough from the city, but I had to be certain. What did a few more minutes matter after so long? I allowed my training to take over and, eventually, moved through the gap.

Beside a massive crater, an orbital assault tank lay burnt out, the grass already reaching half way up its ducts. Shielded from both sides then, I took one last cautious look round and pushed the trigger on the belt. Hardly able to breathe, I watched as the portal formed, a circle of light suspended in the air. I stepped through.

On the other side, the air really was cleaner, the sun brighter. *Don't get carried away, not until you know for sure.* I crouched and scanned the area. All clear, no one in sight. As the portal closed behind me, I allowed myself to acknowledge that I'd done it; I was home. Relief overwhelmed me. I stumbled and fell onto grass that was much shorter than in the place I'd left. My eyes filled and I lay sobbing, but eventually some sense returned to me and I forced myself to my feet. I was still in a daze, but soon found the road. The road that led to the city, and Amanda.

A car passed me from behind, so quiet that it had receded a distance down the road before I could react. *Get a grip,* I thought savagely. *You're too close to mess up now.* Checking that I remained unobserved, I fastened my coat over my uniform, making sure that it covered the belt and my gun. Then I flipped my collar up, hunched inside it and pressed on.

The closer I got to the outskirts, the busier the traffic became. The vehicles were subtly different from the ones I remembered, but that was to be expected. What continued to unnerve me was how quiet they were. *It's been a long time. You knew there would be differences; get used to it.*

Then I trudged round a rising bend in the road, and there it was: the city, spread out before me. From this distance, it at least looked the same. *Only a few more hours, Amanda. I'm coming.* I quickened my pace.

The midday sun was beating down on my head by the time I reached the city centre. My coat was starting to imitate a sauna bath and my mouth was desert-dry. *Idiot. Should have remembered a water bottle.* Stopping beneath a shop window canopy, I dared to take a proper look around and struggled to prevent the shock from registering on my face and betraying me. The streets were so full, there were so many people. And the shops, filled with such riches and variety that it was almost too much to take in. *I guess I forgot more than I realised.*

I turned to the shop window and stared. My reflection stared back at me, a thin man, wiry, five foot nine, brown hair cut short, grey patches at the sides drawing attention to a burn mark on a worn tired face. Below that, a thin scar curved down towards the neck. *I used to be young.*

I moved on but found the crowds, the noise and the baking heat overwhelming. I spied an oasis, a drinking fountain outside a church, and a bench behind it in the shade. I slaked my thirst, poured water over my head, and slouched thankfully down on the bench. I considered the church for a moment, but I had only one source of salvation. Reaching into an inner pocket I pulled out a faded photograph. None of these other things mattered, because one memory burned brighter than all the others.

Amanda.

I knew she'd be waiting for me, as she always had, waiting in our home. The home I'd left so long ago. We'd only been married for six months when my call up papers arrived but we'd packed more happiness and love into those six months than most people get in a lifetime. Amanda was smarter than me, pretty in a kooky sort of way, and with a smile that could stop me in my tracks. She was way out of my league, and I knew it. I thanked God every day that she disagreed.

Amanda. I'd spoken her name every night like a prayer. As the war raged, she was what had kept me alive, kept me sane. Even at Wolfshead Gate, the night the enemy broke through the orbital shield and a million men died in less than ten minutes. When survivors went mad from the horror and the last of my friends died in my arms, her name, her memory, gave me the strength to carry on. And now, after five years of hell, I was coming home to her.

I forced myself to put the photo away, reverentially slipping it back into my pocket. Then I got up and ventured back among the crowds. The water and the chance to rest had settled me, emboldened me, and for the first time I dared to gaze about me as I walked. It was like a miracle to see an unharmed city: most were just rubble now. *But not this one, not Amanda's city. Soon I'd be in her arms again. Nothing else mattered. Nothing.*

It took hours and several missteps to find the corner of her street, but that at least was exactly as I remembered. It was the trees I recognised, two leafy elms growing out of the pavement. I leaned against one and watched her door. Then reached inside my coat and took out my gun, checked that it was ready to fire, and waited. For him. The imposter who had taken my place.

Before too long, a car drew up. It wasn't one I recognised, but that meant nothing. *That's it, get out of the car you bastard. One shot and it'll all be over. And Amanda will understand, she's always been able to understand.*

With rising exultation, I aimed at the imposter's head; those features, softer, less worn, but so duplicitously similar to my own. I tightened my finger on the firing stud, and then the air shimmered. A portal opened in front of me, others to the side. A uniformed hand grabbed my gun, others gripped my arms. A stunner reached towards my face and I fell into blackness, screaming.

A pounding headache greeted me when I woke up. Instinctively, I checked my belt even as my eyes flinched from the dim light. My portal generator and my gun were gone. I was in a cell. *Where?* Then the smell hit me: death and burning. *I'm back.*

Time passed.

I hardly notice when they come for me. Two guards in full battle armour lead me into an office where my old Legion CO glares at me from behind the desk. Old habits die hard and I instinctively shuffle to a kind of attention. Out of reflex I start to salute, then remember that I'm bareheaded, so I stop myself.

He looks me up and down. For a moment I almost sense something like pity in his eyes. Then he speaks. "All right, it's over. I don't know where you got hold of a paratime portal and I don't care. Don't you know we have all the portal generators monitored? It was hopeless from the start."

As his words echo in my ears, desperation overwhelms me. *I'll explain. He'll understand. He has to understand.* "No, it's not hopeless, it can't be hopeless. She's waiting for me… She's mine."

He interrupts. "She's not yours. She never was. She's married to another you, on another world, a world that never had our war. You know that."

As I listen, I feel the last vestige of something die inside me.

"Look son," he continues wearily, "the portals won the war for us, but we can't export our troubles to other timelines. You're home now and you'll stay home. I'm sorry, but we've all lost people we loved." He nods to the guards, "Let him go."

They're gentle enough as they release me outside the bunker. One even squeezes my shoulder before they return underground.

I look out over *my* city, the outlines of ruined buildings dimmed by funeral smoke from the pyres, the gray sunlight barely illuminating the wreckage of a once proud civilisation. The smell of burning bodies chokes me, but I start to walk. It's nearly nightfall by the time I reach her street. There's no exultation this time. Just the grief I had hidden from for so long, welling up through my crumbling defences, as I slump to my knees, in front of the ruins that used to be her, no, *our* home. Where Amanda still waits for me.

The Butterflies of Dysfunction
TW Moses

Of all the worlds, Traveller, known to us now since the discovery of the Leviathan Codex, perhaps the strangest is Pilgrim Chisholm's World. It is a dull place. Its architecture is functional. Its food bland. Its people are even-tempered and do not fight, and find the laws of their world equitable. But no, Traveller, do not omit Pilgrim Chisholm from your itinerary. Visit, stay for a while. If you are fortunate, you might experience the Xhanna.

Ah, now your ears prick up. Oh, what is the Xhanna, you ask? Very well, listen. Listen and witness. Once in a generation—and give no money to anyone who tries to sell you a calendar that predicts when, for no person has ever been able to do so—during one night, across all the planet's continents, the night-blossoming flowers that the indigenes call Xha, come into bloom. During that night, the citizens each grow two pairs of shimmering wings. Beautiful, spectacular. Just like yours, Traveller. And when they wake up, they soar up, and...I believe you young people say *fuck shit up.*

You see, when they are winged, every he/she/zhe of Pilgrim Chisholm's World is free to do as they please. They make hurtful jokes. They write lewd limericks and post slanderous comments on social media. They have wanton public sex with other people's partner groups. They bully. They lie. They steal and swindle. They become inebriated and speak their minds. They brawl, burn and destroy. They murder. And their excuse for all of this? Privilege. Because they have wings.

We call them the Butterflies of Dysfunction.

How long does the carnage of Xhanna last? No one knows. Perhaps a day, maybe a week. But one morning, they wake to find the Xha wilted and their illustrious wings crumbled like paper. And so, humbled, they return to their order and their laws. It is the perfect society.

Go there, Traveller. While you are young enough to learn to appreciate your wings.

Go Cúramach
Stewart Horn

The singing followed Sarah out of the dream. She saw the music's structure and heard the interweaving melodies: the moments of harmonious beauty and the *other* bits when notes ground and screamed like scraping metal in a car crash.

She hummed the theme to herself, mentally transcribing it while trying to fit a countermelody that she could also hear clearly. She closed her eyes again and worked out some more, still humming; then stopped, and frowned.

Sarah leaped out of bed, pulled on a dressing gown and rushed through to her little living room where she pulled out a fresh manuscript pad and began to write, occasionally stopping and humming parts before attacking the score with renewed confidence. After half an hour she allowed herself a toilet break, made some tea and toast and went back to it, putting down phrases, melodies or whole sixteen-bar sections, amazed at how complete it already was in her head.

Ninety minutes after that, she sat up, let out a long breath and stared, astonished, at the last page of the score she'd just written. It was neater than her usual scrawl, with no corrections at all, as if it was a transcription rather than an original piece, and the thick final barline she had drawn at the end seemed to forbid any attempt to add or change anything. She flicked back through it—nine pages of tidy choral manuscript, all nicely aligned and legible.

"Wow," she said. "I'm a genius." She took the pad to the piano and started to play. The first eighteen bars were a slow simple tune on the alto line; it had a modal feel like an East European folk tune, exactly as it had sounded in her head. She stopped playing and wrote *solo* and *mp* under the first bar. At bar nineteen a bass entered with low pedal F, changing to F$^\sharp$ at the same time as the altos started their high staccato morse code rhythm. When the rest of the choir joined in, it became a storm of notes, with snippets of beauty emerging from the cacophony.

She worked through the score, playing bits, adding dynamic and tempo markings, effectively turning the piece into a ten-minute crescendo to a fantastically dissonant climax followed by two final minutes of quiet melody. The last section was a reprise of the first, but transformed by its experience. *Not transformed* she thought, *damaged maybe. As if it's survived a battle and emerged saddened and crippled.*

Sarah Maxwell stopped playing, sat back and smiled. "I am going to be so famous," she said.

✧   ✧   ✧

"You've finished it?" Gemma said, cradling a steaming mug and perusing the cake selection on the coffee table.

"Yep, woke up this morning with an idea in my head and had it all on paper by nine. Three months work before breakfast."

"Aren't they paying you like twenty grand or something?"

"Nearly, but they're expecting it to take me till August," Sarah said, sipping at her coffee.

"And I suppose you're still using that poem?" Gemma said, making a face.

"Totally; it's awesome. Besides, I've written the music to suit it now so it's too late to change."

"Is the music creepy too?"

"The music is *contemporary*, if you don't mind."

"Contemporary is alright if you're not actually in the choir. I don't know what's wrong with a bit of Bach. And that poem gives me the creeps."

Sarah rolled her eyes. "Yeah, whatever, Granny," she said.

"It's me that'll have to sing it. We did Mozart's *Requiem* last week—it rocked, the crowd loved it and we got every note right."

"Well if you write like Mozart these days they don't give you a degree. Are you going to offer me a cake now or what?"

"Since when were you so polite that you waited to be asked?"

"I'm accepting commissions from the BBC now. That makes me posh."

"You'd better have a cake then, your royal poshness."

"Thank you," Sarah said, selecting something large and sticky and cocking a pinky. "It's good when one can still mingle with the little people sometimes."

Back at her own flat, Sarah composed an email to Gerry Kendall, the man from the BBC who had approved the commission.

Made a breakthrough. Should be able to send you something solid in a couple of days. Sarah.

She sent it, then double clicked the *Sibelius* icon and waited for it to start.

Sarah's tutor had let Gerry hear some of her work when she had not quite finished her composition masters. Gerry liked it: a meeting was arranged; the brief was explained; a fee agreed, and Sarah had a commission for an original piece to be broadcast live from Glasgow during the Last Night of the Proms. It was the kind of thing other composers worked for decades to achieve, but the theme of the concert was to be *ancient and modern*, and Gerry had liked the idea of a very young composer setting a very old text.

The score-writing program finally produced the welcome screen and Sarah worked through the options: SATB on four clefs, 3/4, B flat, title *BBC Thing*. She selected the first bar of the alto line and started to type.

She had used the BBC like a magic talisman, gaining access to the ancient documents room of Glasgow University library, and had found The Poem in a fabulously decorated book of mediaeval manuscripts. It had caught her eye because of its strange structure: nine stanzas, each of three long lines. The geometry of it on the page was compelling. The librarian gave her physical and digital copies and sent her to the Scottish Literature department where she met the delightfully eccentric Professor McCann. In the course of an hour-long meeting he had enthusiastically delivered a phonetic version and a rough translation from the ancient Scots dialect. The Poem told the tale of a land invaded and the incumbent tribe scattered. The incomers were led by a vain woman who declared herself Queen of the Forest. A local fairie lord or forest spirit—the text was unclear— appeared and told the invaders that to own the land fully they must sing to it, but the song it taught them turned out to be a spell to summon Death.

The computer played each note as Sarah typed. It sounded even simpler than she had imagined it and she wondered if it was something she remembered and she hadn't composed it at all. It had a childish, singsong quality to it, yet she couldn't imagine with it any words other than those of The Poem.

After two hours, the transcription was complete. She scrolled back to the start and pressed play, closing her eyes to check that all the harmonies worked as she'd imagined. Yes, it sounded perfect, especially when that bass drone changed key, making the whole thing much darker.

"I am so awesome," she whispered, then jumped at a loud bang from the window. Looking out she saw the outline of a small bird imprinted in its own oil on the pane, every feather detailed in the sunlight. For a moment she admired its beauty then the bird hit the window again, making her jump. The third time the mark was streaked with red.

"Oh my God," she said, covering her mouth. The bird hit again, leaving more red, and fell from sight. Sarah rushed to the window and looked down to the street. The bird's tiny bloody body lay on the pavement, broken feathers fluttering gently in the wind. The music was at the first properly atonal section, somehow appropriate for this little death scene, and Sarah smiled sadly at the synchronicity until another bird banged into the window, making her duck and cry out. A moment later two others hit at almost the same time in a deadly flam. More hits, more blood. Bang bang BANG! Almost in time to the music.

Sarah's eyes flicked to the computer screen with its innocuous control panel.... Could something about the music be attracting them? She reached over and clicked the *stop* button but nothing happened; the music kept playing, kept building, and the birds kept coming. She pressed it again, uselessly, and in a panic reached for the reset button on the PC and the screen went blank. The bird strikes stopped and the sudden silence was eerie. Sarah edged back to the window, checked for more aggressors then nervously looked down. There were several tiny broken birds lying completely still, and another limping in a circle, unable to fly. A large crow landed at the scene, looked up at Sarah's window and cawed, then pecked the still limping bird till it no longer moved. It cawed once more, picked up the corpse and flew off. A moment later several more crows landed and squabbled over the feast.

Sarah looked back at the computer screen. It had restarted and automatically re-opened the document she'd been working on. The score looked back at her.

"Was that you?" she said. There was no reply.

Sarah checked the caller ID, smiled and clicked the green button.

"Hi Gerry."

"Sarah. I got the score."

"And is it alright?"

"Sarah, it's astonishing. I've been through it all and wouldn't ask you to change a quaver."

"Cool, thanks." She realised she'd been holding her breath and made herself relax.

"It's a completely polished and professional piece of work, and incredibly evocative, even for an oldie like me. I got shivers. The dark sections are especially effective."

"Wow."

"I'll make the call to get your next payment organised. When this is broadcast, you'll be offered commissions from all over the world, I guarantee it."

"Awesome. It just sort of came together."

"In this business nothing just comes together… it's the thought you put into it before. You were composing subconsciously without realising. It happens to all the greats. We'll be having a couple of rehearsals the week before the show. You should come along."

"Thanks," said Sarah, her grin spontaneously erupting into a little giggle.

"Well done, Sarah. You've done the work and you're going to reap the rewards. Your music's going to go round the world and touch millions of people. Bye."

"Bye," she said. The phone beeped as he hung up and Sarah's cheeks hurt from grinning so widely. *All around the world,* she thought.

"Tonight on Front Row," she said in her best BBC voice into an imaginary microphone, "we're looking at the work of Sarah Maxwell, the Glasgow-born *wunderkind* who became the greatest composer of her generation, whose music *touched millions.*" She did a little dance and giggled a bit more.

Gemma escorted Sarah to the Glasgow City Halls, showed her where to sign in and took her to Studio One on the second floor. Gerry was there, silver-haired and neatly-suited, with another dozen or so people Sarah didn't know, though several of them acknowledged Gemma.

"I'll go and join the minions," said Gemma as Gerry approached accompanied by a massively overweight man with a blond ponytail.

"Sarah," Gerry said, giving her a little showbiz hug. "I'd like you meet Bo Stigsson, the choirmaster." The fat man took her hand and shook it warmly. "Delighted," he said, his voice soft and lightly accented. "We are all very excited about your work."

"Everyone's being very kind. I'm not used to this."

"You will get used to it before long if you continue to compose pieces so good. This piece has haunted me. I have dreamed of it." He laughed, a little nervously. "I am afraid not all the dreams are nice."

Beside her, Gerry shivered. He seemed about to say something but changed his mind.

"We will have sectional rehearsals first," Bo went on, frowning. The harmonies are a little strange and will be easier if all the sections learn their own parts quite well first."

"Great," said Sarah.

There were four practice rooms, one each for the sopranos, altos, tenors and basses, and Sarah and Gerry wandered from one to the other. All the parts sounded quite simple individually, though the old Scots words were strange. The section leaders spent more time on pronunciation than they did on the music, which the choristers sight-sang with impressive ease. After an hour they broke for coffee and reassembled in Studio One for the first run through of the whole piece.

Bo got everyone in position and played on the piano first a chord, then a single note before cueing the solo alto. The tune was sweet and a little melancholy, and much more powerful in that clear voice than it had been even in Sarah's imagination. A short time later the bass chant began, and other parts entered gradually, still quiet.

The music was working just how Sarah hoped it would, conveying the story so well that it didn't matter if nobody understood the words. She felt goose pimples rise on her arms, closed her eyes, and saw:

A beautiful young woman standing proudly in a forest clearing. Resplendent in furs and jewelled crown—the epitome of regal vanity—but attended by brutish soldiers of the type that did not ask much more than to be led to battle, the music told of her shallowness, her thirst for conquest; the more cheaply bought the better. On hearing the melody, the queen and her thugs began to dance. As the tune developed, it brought to mind the smell of damp earth and ripe fruit, and the branches and stems of the surrounding forest even appeared to sway along. It was an enchanting scene, until the music took its dissonant twist and the young queen's expression changed to one of horror. The music swirled…and Sarah saw what the queen saw.

Sarah screamed. Eyes bulging, hands clasped to her temples, she screamed until her lungs were empty and her throat raw. The scream faded to silence but she kept trying to push it out, unable to inhale, until the room swirled and dimmed. She could hear for a few seconds longer and she could tell that the choir had stopped singing, but the tune and the story continued until consciousness faded to nothing.

✧   ✧   ✧

There was buzzing, which slowly coalesced into voices. Somebody said her name. Sarah opened her eyes and saw her own hand a few inches from her face. There was rough carpet under her fingers. *This will be the recovery position, then.* She considered moving, but liked lying here quietly. There was something she should be worried about but she didn't want to remember yet what it was.

"Are you with us, Sarah?" Someone took her hand and stroked it. Sarah blinked a few times and wondered why she didn't recognise the carpet.

"I'm 'kay," she slurred, but didn't move.

"Do you know where you are?" The voice was soothing, familiar. *Don't make me remember.*

"Sarah?"

"Yeah, th' 'hearsal, 'm fine. 's everyone okay?"

"Everyone except you, and maybe some poor bugger outside." Sarah finally placed the voice as Gemma's. "We must have been pretty bad. I've had some bad reviews, but never been screamed at by the composer."

"No, you were great, it was the…" Sarah stopped. *The what? Monster? Demon?* She had no image in her mind of what she had seen, but remembered the dread.

Gemma sighed. "You're too easy. Now, do you think you can sit up?" Gemma helped her to her feet and guided her to a chair. Sarah still felt weak and a little dizzy;. Nothing felt quite real.

"I feel weird. I've never fainted before," Sarah said.

"Well, you're posh now, remember? Victorian gentlewomen used to faint all the time."

Sarah gave Gemma a dirty look. "When I'm on my deathbed, you're going to be sitting beside me taking the piss, aren't you?"

Gerry appeared with a plastic cup of water. "Sorry that took so long. I had to go down to reception. Are you okay, Sarah?" Sarah took the cup gratefully and drank.

"I'm fine. What are they all looking at?" Everyone in the room apart from Sarah, Gemma and Gerry were gathered at the windows looking down at the street.

"I'm not sure," said Gemma. "There was some shouting from outside just after you had your wee turn." As if on cue, wailing sirens faded up outside.

MURDER ON ALBION STREET

Police have launched a murder inquiry after an incident in Glasgow's Merchant City area this morning. Martin Barker, thirty-five, was walking outside Glasgow's famous City Halls at around 11.30 when he was attacked by another man and repeatedly struck with what witnesses variously describe as a tree branch or a large gnarly club. The victim was rushed to the Glasgow Royal Infirmary, but died later of his injuries. A twenty-two-year-old man was arrested at the scene. Police are appealing for witnesses.

Gemma read the story again, then shut the computer down and walked to the window and looked out into the still bustling street. *Don't let it go wrong,* she thought. *I just want to be a composer. Please make this all go to plan and I'll compose nice music for the rest of my life, I promise.*

She thought about her silent prayer and wondered if it was true. Did she want to be a composer, or did she just want the fame and the money? *Whit wirth is gloir sic cheaply bought?* She wondered uneasily why that sounded familiar and then realised that it was a line from The Poem.

She sent text messages to Gerry and Gemma. *Won't make it to the rehearsal tomorrow. Let me know how it goes. See you Saturday. Sarah.*

Later, as she lay in the darkness of her bedroom, the BBC announcer's voice came back to her.

"Sarah Maxwell, whose music is so powerful that it reputedly drives people to homicidal rage. We won't be playing *that* piece tonight."

Sarah and Gerry stood on the wet grass on Glasgow Green, watching as the technicians assembled equipment on the big stage.

"Can we still go ahead?" Sarah asked without looking round.

"We can't *not* go ahead. The BBC is a behemoth; it takes time to change direction."

"Do you think it will be okay?"

"Well, with the deps we've still got enough singers. Even if we lose one or two more at the tech run."

"I mean, what if something else bad happens?"

"We've had a run of bad luck, I know. But frankly, all singers are a bit highly strung—they get a wee bad feeling and throw a strop and drop out. We've only got one performance to do. After that, you can pull it if you want and no one can perform or broadcast it without your permission till seventy years after you die. And you'll be famous."

Fame, Sarah thought, *appeared to be inevitable now and had come with unexpectedly little effort.* Her anxiety went up another notch.

They stood in silence for a while. "We'll do the gig, forget about it and get on with our lives." Sarah said nothing. There was a squeal of feedback from the stage and some swearing from the technicians.

"What if I change my mind and don't want it broadcast?"

Gerry took a deep breath and blew it out slowly. "You're allowed. We can't broadcast without your permission. But you've signed a contract, so the BBC can sue you to hell and back and your name will be dragged through the mud. In this business reputation is everything. If people think you're unstable, you might never get another commission again."

There was another minute of silence.

"It's only twelve minutes long," Gerry said. "How much harm can it do?"

The stage manager counted down. "Live in five, four, three…" He held up two fingers, then one and pointed at the plump grey-suited host on the stage, who smiled broadly and lifted the microphone.

"Hello from Glasgow!" he bellowed. The crowd cheered and clapped and waved flags.

"Welcome back. The second item from Glasgow tonight is a world premiere from a recent graduate from the Royal Conservatoire of Scotland. She is only twenty-three years old, but is already creating quite a buzz in the classical music world. And she's here with us tonight. Ladies and gentlemen, SARAH MAXWELL!" The crowd cheered again and Sarah saw her own nervous face appear forty feet tall on the screen. "Tell me, Sarah, how does it feel to be here tonight?" He thrust the microphone at her.

"Exciting, and a bit scary," she said. The audience laughed.

"Tell us about the piece we're about to hear, Sarah."

"It's called *Go Cúramach*, and it's a setting of a very old Scots poem. It's all about what a bad idea it is to make deals with the fairies." More laughter.

"So it's a folk tale?"

"Yes, and as is traditional in Scots folk tales, everybody dies at the end." More laughter.

"Well," said the host, turning back to the audience, "I heard this today at rehearsal, and I can tell you it's very beautiful and nobody died. So without further ado, please give a warm Glasgow welcome to the BBC Scottish Chorus and choirmaster Bo Stigsson!" The audience loudly obliged and Bo bowed. Then he turned to face the choir, and it began.

Sarah walked backstage and stood next to Gerry, who gave her hand a squeeze. "Twelve minutes," he said.

"I'll relax in thirteen," replied Sarah.

Through the massive PA system, the lead alto's solo was indeed beautiful, strong and clear, and when the first bass part entered Sarah felt herself relax. The choir was brilliant, really bringing out the pastoral quality that suited the outdoor venue. Then several of the stage lights went out at once, leaving the choir in darkness.

"Oh no," Sarah whispered, and Gerry gave her hand another squeeze. A commotion seemed to be starting in the audience too. The big screen went blank and rest of the lights went out, and Sarah thought she heard shouting from the crowd. Then the PA fell silent and there was no longer any doubt. Over the singing, people were screaming, as if in agony.

Gerry put a hand on her shoulder. "Wait here," he said, and walked off purposefully.

The basses began their chant and Sarah wondered for a moment how it was she could still hear it over the noise of the audience, then she could no longer stand not seeing and walked onto the stage and looked out. She felt the world fall away from beneath her feet. "Oh my God," she whispered.

In the arena, people were trying to run but seemed stuck to the grass: some looked as though they were sinking into mud; others were struggling to pull their hands away from the ground, as if they were nailed down. The screaming was deafening and there was blood everywhere.

A cameraman's head and shoulders appeared at the front of the stage as he tried to drag himself up to safety, but was snatched back. Sarah looked around as the music moved into the most atonal section, wondering again why she could hear it over the cacophony. The choir was behind her now, but the singing came from every direction at once, always audible regardless of what else was happening.

Down below, the cameraman lay on his back, eyes and mouth open wide, and looking, almost comically, like the kind of festival drug casualty you saw on the TV, until a gout of blood spouted from his mouth, followed by a green tide. *Is that grass?* A moment later one eye popped out and creepers erupted from the bloody socket. Sarah stepped back, hands over her mouth. Something grabbed her arm and she shrieked and ripped herself free. Gerry was behind her, his face white as he desperately tried to appear in control.

"Come with me," he said, hand outstretched. "I think we can get away round the back." Then he was jerked off his feet and landed on the decking with a crunch. Something that looked like a tree-root had wrapped round his ankle and it snatched him off the stage as if he weighed nothing. Sarah backed away toward the choir. *I wrote it,* she thought. *I must survive. The faerie spirit will see me as an equal, save me till last or something. That's how stories work.*

As the music continued into a rare passage of harmonic resolution, a wave of grass swept through and over the crowd, submerging many entirely. One woman started to climb a tree, but a swinging branch hit her in the face, knocking her back to the ground where the tree pulled free a root and slammed her hard enough that she burst.

Just take the crowd, leave me be. Please!

The music reached its final crescendo and Sarah felt the stage shake as the all-consuming grass swept back and forth through what had been the audience. The screaming had dwindled almost entirely now. Only the occasional human cry could be heard, that and the damp crunching sounds that came from within the grass. And as the music finally moved into its quiet coda, the ground of the arena settled, became a perfect meadow, grass standing thick and tall, and waving as if energised by a breeze. There was no evidence that there had ever been people down there. Even the control tower and camera crane were gone.

The music faded to nothing and Sarah felt tears on her cheeks.

I survived. I've been spared. A giggle burst from her mouth and she clapped a hand over her mouth. She would have to look sad for the media. *I don't know what happened,* she would say. *It's a terrible tragedy. I'm going to pull the piece and never let it be performed again, out of respect for the families of the victims.* But she would be on the news all over the world. Everyone would want to hear her music, and it would be easy to oblige. She could toss off anything now. They'd lap it up. She could see herself writing big, lush movie scores and making millions. As big breaks went, it had all worked out even better than she'd planned.

Then someone began to sing. Not Sarah's piece, but...similar. Sarah spun towards the choir, but they were still in their trance and the voice was coming from somewhere else. Panic rising again, Sarah looked around but couldn't identify the singing's source.

As the choir joined in they walked towards her, swaying, arms swinging, and with that same dead-eyed look they'd had before. The new song was very simple and the words, sounding both truly alien and almost familiar, filled her mind with images of trees bending to the wind. And there was a face, as big as the forest itself. It looked at her balefully and shook its mighty, leafy head. Sarah felt branches touch her arms, tickling at first, then stinging, and the vision vanished, leaving her at the mercy of reality.

The singers surrounded her now, swaying like the trees, arms brushing as they danced. But the arms looked wrong: they were too dark, too hard, grained like hardwood, and the fingers were spindly and studded with thorns.

"Stop," Sarah said, and tried to stand and push through, but the choir was as solid as if it was planted. Twig-fingers raked her, drawing blood. Sarah screamed as fingertips extruded roots, puncturing skin, forcing into muscle. More hands fell on her and every touch was a pinprick of agony that spread through her like fire. Someone laid a hand on her face, and it felt like a thousand tiny, burrowing needles. She felt things growing inside her, bits of her body bursting to accommodate the intrusion, but the pain was already beyond what she could bear and she could no longer breathe to cry or scream. Her mouth filled with the taste of soil and roots and grass sprouted thickly out of her nose. Her belly bloated and split like a seedpod. It felt as if a football were being forced from it, but with her fading vision she saw only a thin sapling reaching towards the sky.

As the world darkened, she heard the theme from her own piece and understood the pitiful insignificance of it. She hadn't composed anything at all, merely borrowed a small part of something much greater. A music that had always been, and would last for ever, and in which her own imminent death would be no more than a momentary cadence.

The Unusual Genitals Party
Fergus Bannon

It was only when Tim arrived and the party was well underway that I first realised I had been taken for a ride.

There was something not quite right about the man and woman supporting him, something I couldn't put my finger on, but suddenly everything began to make a terrible sense. Until then surprisingly relaxed in an environment rich with embarrassment potential, I felt the first fingers of unease tickle at my heart.

My mind fled back to the night three weeks previously in the Students' Union when Tim had had his remarkable idea. The gloomy basement bar had been full, the air heavy with the smells of damp students and crap tobacco. Cold westerlies had brought with them the ceaseless fine rain so common at this time of year and the occasional phlegmy cough was loud enough to punctuate the rock music from the video jukebox.

I remembered Tim slouching up against the jukebox, the shoulder padding of his bomber jacket piled up against the formica cladding, giving his body a comically drunken slant. Face like an angel, mind like a wolf, he kept waving his pint insouciantly as he talked, the beer almost but never quite making it over the lip and down to the grimy wood of the floor.

"Don't give up, Matt, for God's sake! Just gimme a minute and something'll come."

"But it's all been done," I whined, still churlishly unaccustomed to my good fortune. "Fancy dress parties, hat parties, mask parties. Every asshole has them! This has got to be something really special, something people'll remember for the rest of their lives."

"Yeah, it's a problem." But I saw his quick feral grin and knew it suddenly wasn't.

"Tell me!"

He opened his mouth to reply but Mona, who had been leaning ashen-faced on his free shoulder, suddenly tugged at his sleeve and moaned: "Timmy?" Her cheeks puffed out and she quickly brought her hand up to her mouth. Then she staggered away, bulldozing groups of students hunched over their drinks, punting aside bags and crash helmets, toppling piles of books and notes. I saw people open their mouths to object, catch one look at the stricken face then quickly step aside, if they could.

I followed her path of destruction with my eyes. Sickly pale and overweight though she was I still yearned for her, which I did for just about every women. Twenty-one year old male virgins always do. Trust me on this!

Tim tutted a couple of times, his wide thin lips turned down at the corners, but otherwise he didn't appear greatly moved. He blinked once as though trying to remember what he'd been saying.

"Right! So you're going to be a rich bastard. You reach twenty-one, your balls drop and you come into ten million or so. And all down to inadequately vulcanised rubber."

That last remark wasn't in the best of taste, but I didn't care.

"Yeah. Goodbye, street cred, hello, Mercedes." I raised my glass in appreciation. My very much older sister, a mega-salaried money shifter in the City, had developed a liquidity problem when her Porsche had lost traction on a tight bend.

How could I be so heartless? Because she'd been a moody, mean-spirited, self-absorbed woman who hadn't liked or been liked by anybody.

She'd died intestate. I was her only surviving relative (my family has a poor track record with big metal things that go fast). It took me maybe three-tenths of a second to suss out that I was due all her money. For m'learned friends it took another two years, intestacy being a notoriously tricky business, they said. But finally they admitted that, yes, for me twenty-one equalled dosh.

Was the sudden wealth going to change my life? Count on it! Student loans are miserably inadequate. The people who had fostered me from the age of ten were kind people but not wealthy and I had never asked them for more than they'd offered. And as for Big Sis, the best I got from her was a single measly twenty at Christmas and on my birthday, the note always mint fresh. Its newness seemed to taunt me as I sat huddled up, undernourished in my cold mildewed flat.

Tim pointed at me with his pint. "So how much you intend to spend on this party?"

I shrugged. "Outside caterers, ten grand maybe," I replied, guessing wildly.

"Make it twelve and I guarantee a party no one'll ever forget"

"For catering?"

"Naw. The extra two grand is for prize money."

"For what?"

"For the Unusual Genitals Contest."

"*The what?*"

Tim smiled broadly, clearly very pleased with himself. "People go to the trouble of making up masks and costumes and hats and so on for parties. This time they make up weird private parts. We're talking massive scope for imagination."

I rocked back a little. An Unusual Genitals Party. That *would* be new.

"And prize money's really important." Tim had come out of his slouch, his tall lean frame suddenly vibrant with enthusiasm. "People should work for it, put time and effort and thought into it. They'll need an incentive."

In my cups and stunned by the originality of the concept, I'd readily agreed to fronting the prize money. Mona had returned shame-faced but recovered and we'd drunk on into the morning. I recall little more of what was said but I do remember Tim promising again and again that it was all going to be really amazing.

And he'd been right. The party was held in my flat, a large Victorian affair I'd arranged to buy in a fit of largesse, allowing the six friends I shared with to remain rent-free. Built in more expansive times, when Glasgow was the second city of the Empire, stately, cavernous rooms had been dirtied and made threadbare by generation after generation of students. Mottled light fittings spotted by countless flies cast vapid illumination over sagging armchairs and strange, unexplained stains on the walls. The few carpets and curtains had patterns faded almost to oblivion, like hieroglyphics exposed to centuries of sun.

But that night my dingy, student-soiled dwelling came to resemble a surrealistic zoo. My guests had made their way through the cold streets huddled up within thick clothing to protect themselves from the sleeting rain of the wintery Glasgow night. Now as they crossed the threshold into the heat, they shed their coats and sweaters, emerging reborn.

My friends are not so much bohemian as off-the-wall and out-to-lunch.

They did me proud.

I had spent many sleepless nights pondering the wisdom of such an affair. There is a limit even to student sensibilities, after all. But I saw that many of my friends had come to the same dimly realised conclusion as I.

They'd understood that what would make genitals unusual wasn't size or position, though God knows there were enough outsized plaster-of-Paris pudenda stuck on foreheads and chests, or sprouting from ears and armpits. What genitals needed to make them unusual, they realised, was beauty.

Some of the transformations and creations were marvellous. I saw glistening ruby-lipped vulvas made from sugar candy, with clitoral tongue licking cheekily out of one corner, or with labia themselves parted in a 'O' of surprise. I saw penises painted like animals, grey and sadly drooping in the form of an elephant's trunk, or rampant and arching as an anteater's nose.

Among the women, Gina's design was perhaps the most sublime. Displaced slightly up her abdomen with wings tailing down between her thighs, expanded versions of labia and clitoris had been transformed into the wings and thorax of a huge butterfly. Flesh-coloured but with delicate traceries of vasculature making them seem alive, the wings flexed as Gina moved, sometimes revealing the inner lips as smaller dorsal wings fluttering against the larger ones.

Simon had concentrated on colour. His penis had been painted a shiny aquamarine and dotted with tiny yellow rings enclosing white centres. On either side of the head a round unblinking fish eye was depicted and the rest of his groin had been painted coral grey but for multi-coloured sea urchins and snails nestling amongst pubic hairs dyed sea-frond green.

Yes, it was absurd but, if you just looked with your eyes and not your mind, there were occasional hints of real beauty.

Many had chosen to cross their own anatomies with those of flowers, producing a profusion of orchids with genitalia variously included as fulsome petals and leaves, or slender, languid stamens and anthers. And all in such striking colours!

There were other marvels amongst the shyer guests. Some had baked huge exuberant confections. Cakes and pastries, shaped into mouth-wateringly bizarre organs of reproduction and covered with surreal icing designs, like the tattooed genitalia of some long-lost and determinedly primitive tribe. Others had brought succulent fruit salads: plums and figs, bananas and peaches, arranged in lustful, orgy like profusion.

I was happily regarding a breathtaking mechanical penis, its smooth curved steel warping and reflecting all the crazy colours around it, when Mandy, a fellow medical student and another object of my relentless desire, suddenly stuck her tongue in my ear. Had I seen it coming I would have relished it, instead I flinched gauchely. She gave me a big broad smile and struck a pose, hands on hips and legs slightly parted so I could admire her handiwork.

It was the fifth *vagina dentata* I'd seen that evening, but I wasn't complaining. I guessed it had been a rabbit trap, the hinged jaws having had some convexity beaten out of them then polished to the gleaming steel. The contraption had been attached to her flesh coloured tights to fit snugly over her *mons venus*.

Her mischievous eyes met mine. "Don't worry," she breathed, "I won't bite."

I glanced furtively over her full figure. *Thanks, Sis,* I thought. Only Tim and Mona had known the real scale of my windfall beforehand but I'd casually mentioned my good fortune to someone a few hours earlier and let rumour do the rest. In the last couple of hours women had been paying me more attention than in all my twenty-one years put together.

As we talked, she with assurance beyond her years, me with my usual gaucheness, the gaily coloured throng eddied noisily around us.

The food and drink were going down very well. The money had bought more than I could possibly have imagined. I was no gourmet then but even I could appreciate the fineness of the brandy, the dry bite of the champagne, the succulent meats swimming in rich sauces, the heavenly creaminess of the gateau, the pungency of the cheeses.

The high ceiling echoed with the roar of the guests as each champagne cork popped, the sound little diminishing as they continued to laugh and shout. Daringly for a student party I had selected light classical music. There'd been a few moans at first, cries for the usual brutish percussion and tortured guitars, but they'd diminished as we'd slipped into a mood of easy celebration.

And what about my own genitals, you may ask? Ever the technofreak, I'd modelled them on Concorde, no less. A long elegant neck, coning down to a sharpened tip on one end and flaring slightly towards the stern, with chrome testicles like underslung engines, streamlined to minimise air resistance.

Eighteen inches from tip to tail, it made turning hazardous and the supporting strap played merry hell with my perineum. But my pudenda, for once, looked great.

I'd carefully turned up the heat in the apartment to accommodate the more daring. The flat had become a jungle full of bizarre plants and animals, somehow co-existing in peace and, dare I say it, joy. Admittedly I was drunk but for one instant I thought of Eden, before people became somehow ashamed of their most vital parts, before they made them taboo.

Being male and heterosexual I can only speak about the beauty of women, though I can dimly appreciate it in other men. Women's faces and bodies can be so beautiful they make you want to cry. There's the wonder of eyes and lips and hair, the delicacy and smoothness of necks and shoulders, the glories of the breasts and hips and legs. But the human genitals, though at times infinitely attractive, can hardly be said to possess beauty.

The purple-veined penis, whether engorged or flaccid, the wrinkled skin beneath holding the soft-toy floppiness and asymmetry of the testicles, are rarely pretty sights. And the female genitalia, so carefully hidden, with their mottled and variegated nubbins, their fleshy grooves encroached on by crabgrass hair, seem similarly ill-starred.

Light and shade and the skill of the artist or photographer *can* make silk purses out of these sows' ears, but not easily. With subjects so naturally grotesque and infinitely risible, how else could it be?

Why are genitals so aesthetically unpleasing? Aside from the Eden myth I've found no explanation. But, at least that night, at my party, I felt perhaps we'd briefly recaptured the time in the Garden before our perception of beauty had changed to exclude them. In our hearts I think we were celebrating what might have been.

But, like I say, I'd been drinking.

Then Tim arrived with his friends and my heart sank. With such prize money on offer, my party had become the talk of the University. We'd expected gatecrashers to be a major problem and so Tim and some of his friends had agreed to guard the tenement entrance. Tim's shift had finished half an hour previously and he'd presumably spent the time since readying his 'costume', details of which he had kept secret.

There was a single premonitory bang on the lounge door then it flew open to smash against the wall. The three entered sideways on a slope, the thin man holding Tim up with a hand round his waist from one side, whilst a petite woman tried to support him under his other arm. After they had filed carefully through the door the threesome swung round to face the room. The reason for Tim's unsteadiness, aside from his evident drunkenness, was revealed. Bow-legged and naked from the waist down, his penis was unadorned and dwarfed by the huge udder-like papier-mâché testicles which hung below it.

"How's it goin', Matt?" Even those simple words were slurred. He winked down. "Doan get many a these t'the pound."

En masse we shrunk away. My eyes quickly flicked back to the thin man at his side and I thought about the prize money that had been Tim's suggestion. I thought of his seedy, desperate friends and remembered that even Mona, a graduate of Roedean no less, had had her clitoris pierced.

Would that be Tim's scam? Had he trawled the internet looking for mutilated genitals, with a fifty-fifty split between Tim and the mutilee? Even as I thought this I realised Tim would've had his own willy pierced for that kind of dosh.

Just then the man, having propped Tim up against a wall, stepped confidently forward.

He positioned himself proudly, almost professionally, in the light cast by the one spotlight in the ceiling. The light glistened off beads of sweat already dripping down his cheeks. His vivid green eyes, white showing round the irises, stared fixedly at a point in space while his mouth widened into a huge lascivious grin. No words were spoken as his long fingers worked at the buttons of his coat. Somehow I knew he would be naked underneath.

He pulled the coat open with a flourish, an impresario for his own malformed body.

There were gasps all round. I saw immediately that these genitals were no constructs, no artefacts of Styrofoam or paper.

Diphallia is a one in five million condition in men. As a medical student I'd seen a photo of a case amongst a galaxy of other appalling genital malformations in one of my textbooks. I knew that others at the party would be less prepared and the sense of horror in the room was almost palpable. Having two cocks might not by itself have been too appalling but the condition was almost always associated with other congenital anomalies. This poor guy had a tumourous growth the colour of a clown's nose above them.

Tim had made his way to a low divan and was viewing the reactions with a triumphant smirk. His legs were spread wide to accommodate his huge sacs. I joined him just as he began to clap. Looking back I saw the man strutting and looking immensely pleased with the agitation he'd caused. I guess he had to take his pleasures where he could.

"You bastard!" I yelled at Tim's smug face. "You've spoiled everything!"

"Don't be such a wanker, Matt." He roared with laughter.

"You're not getting the money. I decide the winner, remember?"

He sobered up quickly. "Oh no you don't. This is an unusual genitals contest and there is nothing…" he pointed across at the guy who was striking bodybuilders' poses, "… more unusual than that. Because it's real, not plasticene or cakemix. You're not sleazing your way out of this." Colour had come to his cheeks and I saw his hands become fists.

I can be as hard as nails sometimes but only when I'm safely alone in my room. And, anyway, he was right.

Not wanting to lose too much face I tried to shift the focus.

"What about her?" I indicated the petite woman in the grey dufflecoat, the other one who had carried Tim in. She was staring without expression at the man with two cocks. "How many sets of genitals has *she* got?"

Tim muzzily followed the direction I was pointing,

"Dunno, met her on the stairs." He held his hands up quickly. "Yeah I know, invites only. But she was really desperate to come," he leered, "so we made a deal…if you know what I mean."

The rising noise of the crowd, now electric with witch-burning fervour, seemed to shake the small woman out of her contemplation. Blinking once, she stepped forward. Gently but firmly she pushed the diphallic out of the spotlight. The man looked startled but didn't resist.

Turning back towards us the woman, her mousy hair looking lifeless in the penetrating light, undid her coat and let it fall to the floor. At first I thought she was wearing a body stocking or some other tight garment that smoothed out her sexual features. There were no nipples and only the faintest mounds for breasts. Then, checking downwards, my stomach turned to vacuum. Midway between crotch and bellybutton hung a large pendulous object, still swaying slightly from the coat being removed.

Never in textbook or morbid anatomy museum had I seen anything like this. This was no hernia or neurofibromatous mass, no aneurysm or cyst. The shape of the huge fleshy pod that surrounds a coconut, though a little smaller, it was smooth and featureless.

Then three long furrows appeared along its length like someone trailing fingers through sand. The end of the pod pulsed once, the tip engorging into a fist-like shape.

On the second pulse the skin split, peeling back silently, pushed open by the expanding mass beneath. Revealed was something multifaceted, almost transparent with ghost hints of structures and interfaces within. As we watched it underwent a rapid unfolding, two huge planes uncoiling, puffing out and filling with gas, becoming transparent wings shaped by fine skeletal restraints.

The wings shuddered once and rose out of the flaccid pod skin. As it did so the woman leaned back on her arms, forming a platform with her body. As I backed away I caught a glimpse of a hardening glass-like rod, ascending in a gentle arc to the join in the wings.

Thrusting out and down from the front of the wings was a thin pellucid bone holding a bud. As we watched, this burst open into a delicate mass of red-purple flesh, like a brain coloured by a madman.

The wings pulsed once in a spastic, almost yearning movement. Instantly a fine mist puffed out of the mass, suffusing the room with a heavy, musky scent.

Everyone fell silent. It was as though all the air in the room had disappeared, isolating us. Then the wings began to beat with an irregular pattern, bathing us in coy, teasing, seductive zephyrs.

Thus began its first calming overtures to us.

The lights were extinguished, I did not see by whom or what, and the room became filled with the flickering pastel glows from a second crucible-like organ unfolding below the wings, suspended by a skein of blood-red chords. Azure sparks from chemical fires flickered in amongst its interior intricacies.

The gusts and eddies from the wing beats had become hotter now, more urgent, more demanding. It was an invitation and we all accepted it, stripping naked without fear and allowing ourselves willingly to be led. I lay down with the others and looked up at the phantom hovering above us. There was beauty in it, even in its ungainliness, and as I thought this I had a fleeting sensation of ages of darkness and loneliness and profound, urgent need. I tried to focus my thoughts, tried to touch it again with my mind, but...

The fingers of the wind caressing my body were harder now, massaging the blood through me. I felt my desire as a single note rising to a wracking pitch.

Suddenly the room was chaotic with dancing fireflies. They flew hither and thither, twisting and untwisting the filaments that tethered them to the crucible.

As I watched I felt my chest grow heavier as my breathing became more laboured. My hands and feet clenched and I heard my teeth grate. My body had become a spring, growing tighter with each eddy of the hot, woman-scented air.

The fireflies danced to our gasps and moans, sometimes flickering close. I saw tiny iridescent eyes set above funnel-like mouths with transparent hollow bodies behind. The little creatures' wings moved so fast that they were crescent shaped blurs around their smooth sides.

My lust had become an agony and blackness was beginning to claim me. But then, as consciousness threatened to leave, and the room became rent with moans of masculine despair, a firefly lightly touched my swollen flesh. Relief was instant and I pushed my seed out in wave after wave of blissful release.

Through my tears I saw the fireflies return to the cauldron, entering through tiny ports from which their tethers hung. I saw them dimly moving within the flashing radiance of the interior.

The wings beat again and I felt the heavy perfume of sleep. Unable to speak, barely able to breathe, I fought the darkness. The beat became gentle and caressing, but suddenly the eldritch fire from the cauldron became whiter, more terribly intense. Through its walls I saw the fireflies changing their shape as though warped by terrible forces.

I don't know how long it took. It seemed like only minutes before the fireflies began to retreat, manoeuvring their elongated probosces with difficulty through the crucible's labyrinthine tangle of transparencies.

I almost drifted away then but at the last moment managed to scrape a sharp fingernail painfully across my palm. I felt hot liquid pool there. As I did so, through the deep reverberations of masculine snoring, I heard the women's first cries of arousal.

Now the fireflies hung in a wavering line radiating from a tiny tube protruding from the cauldron. The strange chemistry must at last have been completed because the cauldron's internal fires were suddenly diminished as the walls lost their transparency. Only the tube remained illuminated, its sides glowing with bright blue phosphorescence.

The first firefly's proboscis poked unerringly into the tube and a thick opaque fluid was drawn slowly up into its abdominal cavity. Then it fell away in a gliding arc and I saw another take its place.

I saw the first firefly's hummingbird beak descend between the thighs of a woman then blackness finally claimed me.

✧   ✧   ✧

How, you may wonder, does a group of intelligent, articulate people cope with such a profoundly bizarre experience?

The answer is easy: they pretend it never happened.

There was a lot of pretending it never happened the morning after. We woke more or less simultaneously, bathed in sunbeams pouring in through holes in the curtains. The petite woman had gone. We glanced uneasily at the other naked bodies piled about us, then shuffled quickly into our clothes, eyes carefully averted.

A few feeble smiles and muffled farewells then I was left with only Tim and a mortally shocked diphallic for company. Tim clearly wasn't himself, his eyes kept darting around the room and his hand would occasionally touch his groin, as though checking everything was still there.

I tried to talk to him as I started to sack up the mountains of spoiled food. His replies, whenever the conversation threatened to encroach on the evening before, were uncharacteristically evasive.

"Wow, that was really strong grass," he kept saying. "Fuck knows what they marinated it in. PCP minimum!" I knew he was starting to construct a fiction, an alternative version of events, one infinitely more acceptable than what had really happened.

I would've perhaps begun to doubt my own sanity then, supposing that I had hallucinated everything, and that all we'd been recovering from was your typical, though probably mythical, clusterfuck. Except that even when he found the strength to leave, thankfully taking the thin man with him, Tim didn't once mention the prize money.

I guessed deep down inside he knew who the real winner was. And he didn't want to talk about that. Not ever.

Six months have passed since the Unusual Genitals Party. My friends rapidly lost touch with me and, I later found out, with everyone else but their immediate partners. That's easy to do in a socially active city like Glasgow. If you set your mind to it.

Only Mandy keeps in touch, indeed we find great comfort in each other's company though we never mention you-know-what.

And, of course, she's pregnant. We'd become lovers during the nights of desperate, silent clinging that'd followed the party. It's our fiction that the child is mine. About twenty parts fiction to one part truth, I suspect.

What was the real winner of the Unusual Genitals Contest. A sexual opportunist? Certainly. A sexual parasite? No. A symbiote? Perhaps. In simple evolutionary terms it doesn't fit. Perhaps that's an indication of how far it must have come from. On Earth sexual selfishness is *de rigeur*.

After all, it could simply have inseminated the women without taking the men's seed. Instead it mixed our essence with its own, merging with us, creating a unity from two disparate species.

Why had we all surrendered ourselves like that? Why had we let ourselves be seduced? Perhaps, at a deeper, less conscious, level we had sensed there was something so much greater at stake.

I've seen Mandy's ultrasound scans, non-invasive peeks into her swelling belly. There's something there on the foetus, something not much bigger than a grape. I saw the frown on the gynaecologist's face, before he dismissed the thing as a loop of umbilicus.

He was wrong but I didn't tell him.

For whose sake did I remain silent? Mandy's? The child's?

For all our sakes, I think.

Ascending
Hal Duncan

Westbound on the road less travelled, take a left and left and left again, another left, a hard left now, by roads and side-streets, out of New Sodom, out of the intersticed metropolis of gay villages built by cuckoo-in-the-nest queer hatchlings in exile from a homeland in Canaan, out of the city rebuilt internationally, rebuilt in skin and salt as much as stone, out of this heterotopia, into Ginsberg's nightmare of automaton apartments and ossuaries of lucre, by a turn and a turn and a turn into Moloch City, into the breathless constriction of a back-alley canyon sliced straight and narrow, black with decades of smog, emphysema in brownstone of a dumpsters-and-fire-escapes dead end, a cramped courtyard for cars and garbage, hatchwork of iron wrought to zigzag stairs and balconies and bars on blind windows closing in all round, the patch of grey sky overhead only an oubliette's *outside*. Beyond.

Park your car now, shut the engine off, step out and orient yourself: knife-thin alley dark at your back, you face the blunt termination of your path where arse-ends of buildings slice as walls of: brick ahead; concrete to your left; red sandstone to the right. Innards of a city hotchpotching its materials, no facades here to integrate aesthetics of rival centuries, no porticos for the fire exits, no lintels for bricked windows, no edifices except: dead in one corner—the far-right or near-left? You decide—the marquee of a flophouse curves a corner, as the once-grand back entrance to some wannabe Savoy or Ritz, shading double doors with glass panels boarded, graffitied, spelling the old name out in dirt outlines where the letters once were: HOTEL HAVEN.

There's fuck all to hint the new identity of a dosser's palace now gutted of its transients, but Pascal was right: just knock and ask if it's where the game is played, and they'll let you in. Yes, madamonsieur, the doorman in gold-brocaded crimson coat will say, green eyes gazing blank from a white plaster mask. Welcome to the House of Heavenly Rewards.

Don't worry. It's not what *anyone* expects.

And if you go for it, past the receptionist's cubbyhole, plush carpeted stairs leading up to muted moans and thumps, down a scarlet corridor and through a door, you'll have been ushered in, to sit in a bar fitted out in fine bordello drag. The whole place has been reamed and rebuilt, you could tell the moment you walked in. The arch where a wall's been knocked through to a back room, *that* looked shoddy enough to be a remnant of past inglories, but all else is new even where it's antiqued: wallpaper in tobacco-stained tan; wooden floors tinted and polished; Persian rugs which look worn but which lack the musty smell of service; black and white prints on the walls; red velvet armchairs and drapes (closed.) All the fauxthenticity of an Irish pub, you might have muttered under your breath as you took your seat.

The barman brings a tray of fresh drinks now as you fidget, gathers the empties. White shirt, tuxedo vest and bow-tie, kidskin gloves and plaster mask, he seems a silver service android designed by Saville Row and Silicon Valley. An iRobot playing the Commedia dell'arte in Weimar Germany. You gaze at the wood-framed clock on the mantelpiece. You're waiting now, waiting to win elysium. Pascal beside you lifts his JD and Coke.

To borrowed time, you say.

You met Pascal at the support group that you found a refuge from your loving family, this cornfed erstwhile high school quarterback out of Iowa and San Diego gay porn looking as far from a terminal patient as you could imagine, sunlight easy in his grin. "Blaze" was his nickname on the team, like some jock out of Archie comics. Came to New Sodom by way of New York's Chelsea in the 1970s and a leatherman lover who fucked him out of the closet and out of time, side-stepping the AIDS epidemic you were born into and blinking awake in 2016. (Even time is queer in New Sodom.) From barefoot in rural idyll to bareback in urban Arcadia, carefree and invulnerable until he wasn't, and still carefree then. So it seemed.

Wasn't even sure why he was there, he shrugged, as you chatted outside the community centre after the meeting, as he leaned against the rainbow mural and sparked up this monster joint that would bond you quietly, instantly, into a pact, the high wasters of the group. Even if he hadn't ended up coming to you for weed all through chemo, you'd have ended up hanging out, you reckon, simpatico, synched even; you went through the treatment at the same time, went into remission together… even got the word within three weeks of each other when the cancer came back more ravaging than ever. You'd shared so many taxis, you said, might as well share the hearse.

And you laughed, the two of you, and if there was a sharp edge to the humour, that just made it all the funnier, and cut some of the cords that stitch your throats shut when you call each other at three am, so you can say… well, something at least *close* to what can't be said, say *enough*, at least, even when you don't really say anything at all. Pascal sneaking out onto the porch so he won't wake the hubby. You slumping back on the sofa, staring at the ceiling, cellphone crooked between ear and shoulder as you roll, spark up.

What's up?

What isn't? You got an hour to spare?

Sure, I can spot you a couple if you want.

And then the one being called will do all the talking, answering what can't be said. After a while of this, those spare hours became… an in-joke? A code? That *borrowed time* you're living on has become your debts to each other, debts so deep it surely all cancels out to a decade of compound interest each. Right?

Hey, you.

111

Hey, you.

Got time to talk?

How does a week sound?

I don't need all that.

If you don't use it… whatever. You can pay me back.

Saturday after you got the all-clear, you were celebrating on Boulevard Rimbaud, in this queer hipster bar called Rebellion, when Pascal turned it into a toast. Elysium was on the news, a TV in the corner splitscreened between a photograph of Dr Gregor Z___ on the right and, on the left, the plastic sincerity of an anchor performing that inimitable blend of solemnity and shock—muted in favour of The Pixies' *Velouria* on the jukebox, for sure, but visible in her face. And, as Pascal laid the drinks down on the graffitied table, slipped into his seat in the booth, bullet-pointed in the panel of text that replaced the photograph of Z___:

• *performed assisted suicides over a three year period;*

• *thirty seven cases confirmed;*

• *used designer drug in the tryptamine family.*

Neither of you were paying it any mind as Pascal slid your drink across the scarred and scribbled wood; Doctor Eternity was old news three months on from his own death, just another Kevorkian or Nitschke if you didn't buy into the crazy around Sandra Goulding, his thirty-eighth patient, the one who came back. Who dictated a five hundred page tome in the week before she slipped into a coma, claiming it was a testament she'd written and rehearsed over aeons inside her head. Claiming she'd lived forever in an instant.

To borrowed time, said Pascal.

Sandra Goulding's photograph replaced the factoids and quotes on the TV, but you were leaning forward to pick up your drink, oblivious of the face.

(Wait, you're thinking, how do I know this? Don't worry. I wasn't watching you. It's just… this is how the wager works, how the game begins for any given you. Or thereabouts. Truth be told, the truth itself is queer in New Sodom, so I can't *guarantee* you'll remember any of this now. Just run with it: you had other things on your mind on the day the Goulding story became the story of the House of Heavenly Rewards…)

By then, the initial buzz was dead. By then, the quacks and cranks had all come out of the woodwork with their decodings of the Goulding Text to a Unified Field Theory, a Hard AI solution, secrets of reality itself; and they'd all been bugsprayed back to the fringe by experts answering credulous pundits with wearied reiterations of reason—apophenia and word salad, subjective perceptions of time distortion, drug-induced schizophrenia. By then, the story had moved on—as the TV news moved on over your shoulder—to feed the audience's appetite for sensation with rumours of suicide clubs. On the TV, an MCPD spokesman listened with obvious restraint, shook his head, answered with a frown. Whatever he was saying, it might as well have been, *Oh, for fuck's sake.* You paid it no mind, this tattle of elysium and an Overdose Hotel.

But now, since you both got the bad news a month ago last Tuesday, here you are, to gamble for eternity:

To borrowed time, you say.

You joked a couple of times about it, you or Pascal, and then one night on the phone it wasn't quite a joke; instead you were both sounding each other out, you realised, talking yourselves round to it: the House of Heavenly Rewards. Road trips to Moloch City followed, to snoop in the shittiest clubs of Baltimore or Blackpool, putting out feelers for the chance that *borrowed time* might be more than a flippant jest; you found someone who knew someone who knew someone, got hooked up to a hustler in a pork-pie hat who told you... maybe. The House of Heavenly Rewards turns their offer of elysium on a coin toss, so you might walk in and get nothing; but if you don't go in at all, of course... nothing ventured, nothing gained. You came away with directions and a dilemma: faith or doubt. You came away with Pascal and a wager.

In the House of Heavenly Rewards, the door to the outside is locked now. You've been waiting here for half an hour, just emptied your second rum and apple juice, and the waiter has disappeared somewhere, so you've set the glass down on the wee table between your armchair and Pascal's, and wandered up from your seat and around, noseyed the prints on the walls, gave the handle of the door that you came in a jiggle: locked.

The first twelve hours on elysium, so you're told, seem like twenty four. The next six feel like another twenty four, and in the next three hours, time halves its speed again. The hour and a half after that stretches to seem another day, likewise the forty-five minutes after. And so it goes, time's shift slowing until you lie there frozen, each exponentially more infinitesimal moment lived as a day, eternity in your skull. That's what you're gambling on. Why wouldn't you when you've got forever to win and nothing to lose? Think of it: all the borrowed time in the world.

Pascal wonders aloud if he has, on some level, always been in the hotel. Raised in a family, a folk, a world of faith, maybe the real choice for him was not whether to enter but whether to leave. Raised in another world entirely, you're not altogether sure you belong here even now. But it's too late, it seems.

The concierge appears at last. At last, the concierge appears. White tunic buttoned to the collar like some military dress uniform, white plaster mask as with the waiter, she carries a little steel dish of coins—though the drinks are free, in canniest Las Vegas lure, so it's nowt to do with change for the bar bill, rather a selection of silver dollars, pounds and guineas and euros, talents and drachma and yen, a choice for the coin toss to decide if God is or is not. She offers the dish between you—to you, to Pascal, back to the middle. You nod to Pascal—it seems his territory somehow—and he picks out a silver dollar, flips it high. If the coin falls tails-up, God is only a word, but you lose nothing, just walk out the unlocked door back to your death. If it lands heads-up though, if it lands heads-up, you stand to gain faith's infinite reward.

A snatch, a slap on the back of a hand, a slow unpeeling: heads. Today there is a God.

There is also a catch.

If there is a God, drones Pascal in a trance of glazed eyes, (seems those JD and Cokes have hit him hard, or something, or something else,) He is infinitely incomprehensible, since, having neither parts nor limits, He has no affinity to us. We are then incapable of knowing either what He is or *whether* He is.

You have wagered and won on *whether* He is, but not yet on *what* He is.

Or what *it* is, you think. No. Don't think that.

The concierge snaps her fingers, and now a crowd of valets files in through that arch—were they hidden in the shadows of the backroom? you don't remember them—all silent in their animal-head masks and white tuxedos: ass; bull; camel; dog; elephant; fox; goat; horse; iguana; jackal; kingfisher; lion; moth; nightingale; owl; pig; quail; rat; snake; tiger; unicorn; vulture; wolf; xiphias; yak; zebra; and... something you can't make sense of. If it has a name, you think, it must begin with some forgotten letter of the alphabet coming after *Z*.

Choose your deity, says the concierge.

She leans in close to whisper:

Don't worry. Whichever one you choose, it will be right.

A deity has aspects, faces, masks. Three gambles in one move here, you are to pick one of the god's three aspects by picking one of the three faces of that aspect, by picking one of the three masks of that face; and in so doing you will decide which floor, which wing, which corridor is your path. The House of Heavenly Rewards has infinite rooms—triple infinity, really, all the odd numbers on the first floor, all the even numbers on the second, and a selection of the in-betweens on floor three; whichever level you take the elevator to, whichever of the three wings you set out for, whichever of three corridors you arrive at, each corridor stretches out to forever with rooms beyond your capacity to imagine. A deity has a triple infinity of avatars.

You have already picked. Or Pascal has already picked. Either way, you are following now the valet in the mask of a beast that has no name you know, following the Twenty-Seventh Mask on the Ninth Face of God, through the backroom and through the tile-floored entryway between a front door and storm door, into a tenement stairwell, where an old cage elevator waits to take you to your fate. The valet rattles the iron grill open for you, follows you in, and clatters it shut behind. They grasp a black knob atop a fat brass control disc and crank it forward, the elevator rising with a clunk and a hum of ancient engine.

You might have chosen the first floor. You might have chosen the mercy of kind Che Zeus, who rewards sycophants and sceptics alike, cocks head like a quizzical dog at such a quaint conceit as punishment. In each of the wings, in each corridor of the wings, every room on this floor is empty of all but a door leading back out into the world, somewhere and somewhen entirely unpredictable. A lover greater than which none can be imagined, Che cannot be sought; Che comes to you, in the world of flesh and fuckery Che is evermade a part of, the best fuck of your life, someday in New

Sodom. For that moment of bliss stretched broad, sideways in time, to infinite span, you would have been as well to live your life out where you could be found. You might have chosen the first floor, but the result would have been no different than had you never come to the House of Heavenly Rewards. So, the elevator ascends, up past a tableau of carpet and marble landing that quickly disappears at your feet.

You might have chosen the second floor. You might have chosen the wisdom of blind Ann Soph, who scorns all bribery and extortion, wields neither carrot nor stick to lead or drive a person to the enrichments that she offers as freely as Che offers communion. Not to the faithful though. Wisdom, the mellowing of nimble wits into agency's callisthenic grace, is for the free, for the sovereign of stance. Here each room has countless secret doors to many other rooms, each door activated, in time-honoured fashion, by the sliding of a book from its place in the shelves that line the walls. And this is to say nothing of the marvel sat waiting for you in a glass museum case in the centre of each room. (In case of existence, break glass.) To describe the marvels to be lived in this infinitude would take forever, and would do no justice to, as you navigate the maze, the ever-deepening joy of ever-deepening skills: magnanimity; esteem; courage; poise; prudence; gusto; ardour. But. Every door in the world leads directly into this labyrinth of attention if only it's opened right, so were you in search of *this*... there would be little point in having come by way of a gamble. So, the elevator carries on ascending, and that chance too disappears at your feet, where you notice now the linoleum beneath your high-top Vans tessellated in Escher's design of crows and doves. Where you notice now the yellowing of the doves.

At the third floor, the elevator stops. The cage door is opened. Pascal steps out. You step out after him. And you stand now, the two of you, on the floor of the Mad God, who threatens eternal torture for the scorned, promises unbound euphoria for the select. You follow the valet down the bland beige-carpeted hallway of some Travel Lodge, into the Western Wing, to the junction of the three branch corridors, indistinguishable in their banality of buff walls and uplighters and framed prints of watercolour seaside scenes punctuating the walls between doors. In the subdued light and leaden air, you might be a mile underground, you think, or a million miles out in space, in some air-tight simulacrum of the everyday.

The valet flourishes a hand in Harlequin bow, beckoning you down the endless hallway of closed doors, the hallway receding to a vanishing point that ought to be beyond the far horizon, each door plated in brass with an irrational number to design-ate the avatar of the Mad God who waits to scorn you or select you. Knowing what happens now, you cannot remember why you have come. You cannot remember why. There is no—

Reason can decide nothing here, says Pascal.

The Mad God requires faith but scorns most piety and prayers as hubris and hag-gling, all but the most exquisitely abject. The Mad God graves its rules in stone, then sets above them all a law to question every rule, scorns those who forfeited fealty to integrity,

115

scorns those who forfeited integrity to fealty. The Mad God sets a measure of its rules in contradiction, ranks crimes in loops, A trumping B trumping C trumping A, the lesser of two evils always greater by another reckoning. The Mad God redefines and scorns: magnanimity as pride; esteem as envy; courage as wrath; poise as sloth; prudence as greed; gusto as gluttony; and ardour as lust. That infinitesimal pinprick of a vanishing point as far away as a singularity at the centre of the cosmos falling ever inward inward inward leaving in its wake a space that only seems to be expanding? That is the chance you have of meeting the Mad God's ineffable criteria for selection. Given a greater chance of Hell than of Heaven, it would seem better never to have wagered perhaps, but it's too late for that now.

What did you expect? What did you fucking expect? A god who'd punish a heathen of healthy stance solely for the absence of obeisance is a cruel extorter of tribute. A god who'd hide his truth away in a mansion of many rooms is a torturer willing to forego the paeans for sweeter treats. A god who'd strip you of your ethics and make piety a ritual acrobatics through a minefield is a predator toying with his food.

Still, time is not so queer in Moloch City, no, but rather clockwork mechanical ticking tocking from each certain cause to each inexorable effect, so as I tell you here of how the gamble plays for any given you, let me put your mind at ease if you are thinking now the game is rigged and you've already lost. This is not written for the scorned but the select. Rejoice, sing hallelujah then: *you* have already won.

So, it hardly matters how Pascal rolls dice, and how you pick a playing card, how you both draw straws, both spin the bottle and pick stones out of a bag. How you play rock, paper, scissors, eeny, meeny, miny, mo, and by a complex rite of combination and calculation chart your way to the chosen door. You need not worry.

You will enter the room of the irrationally numbered avatar of the nameless beast that is the last mask of the Mad God, and the creature that waits within will bid you kneel. It will gather you gently into its embrace even as it grips Pascal by wrists and ankles, throat and balls. It will snuggle you to its bosom, little spoon, caress with a hand laid soft across your heart, kiss your neck to a tingling chill of numbness so you will not even feel the prick of the syringe injecting elysium to slow time's shift for you into forever, injecting also the cocktail of scopolamine and MDMA to make eternity a guiltless bliss as you watch it strip Pascal to naked wretch, scour the hair from his flesh, suck fat and muscle from his bone, sup youth from his skin, and sink its stings into his softest places, pumping elysium and lysergic acid and box jellyfish venom into every inch of him. You will come up in the most exhilarating rush you've ever felt as his screams begin, and you will keep coming up, keep coming up, fuck yeah, you keep coming up as he is riven into an infinity of selves to suffer every agony the Mad God begs you to imagine for him.

Naked in a throne of fuckery, sunk back into the thick of tendrils toying with every erogenous inch of flesh, you will have won eternal ecstasy in the House of Heavenly Rewards, the Mad God fondling your frenulum, kneading your perineum, easing a smooth and pliant appendage in through your relaxing sphincter to massage the prostrate, worming its mycelia in via ears and nostrils and moaning mouth, into the tender tissues of your brain, stimulating hedonic hotspots in the nucleus accumbens shell, the ventral pallidum, and the parabrachial nucleus of the pons, and oh, as the fibres of it pervade your frontal, temporal and parietal lobes, how you giggle with the innocence of a newborn to see Pascal's perdition of

scaphism, waterboarding, garrotting, asphyxiation,

the breaking of his bones on Catherine Wheel and rack,

the branding, burning, boiling alive,

the whipping, flaying, tarring and feathering,

the strappado and bastinado,

crucifixion and impalement,

all the slow mutilation,

genital and facial,

wrought by screws and drills and razors,

oh the divine disembowelment and dis-memberment of Pascal,

and your rapture in its righteousness,

your spirit ascending,

ever ascending,

beyond mere orgasm and euphoria,

ascending into beatitude,

into sainted grace ascending,

yes, ascending,

ascending.

Enjoy.

5AM Saint
Elaine Gallagher

The rain streaks Sally's mascara. She huddles in the back door of the club, clutching her coat around her, waiting for her lover to finish work. She's uneasy here, down this alley choked with dustbins and piles of rotting rubbish, brown bags torn by rats. The rain splashes on puddles that she doesn't want to know about, ripples scattering rainbow sheens, yellow sodium sparkles from the street light beyond the alley's mouth.

The club door opens behind her and she stumbles off the step.

"Sally?"

She sighs, relieved, and folds into Catherine's arms. She feels a wave of tension leave her, and she sighs again, catching a sob before it escapes.

"What's the matter, love?" Catherine gives her a tissue from her bag.

"Bad trick. I'll be all right."

Catherine eases herself away and regards Sally in the light of the alley door's dim bulb. Taking her chin, she turns her face this way and that, scrutinizing.

Catherine has been looking after her since the Fall, since the Angel of Theneu withdrew from the city and all grace and beauty and worth left with her. A time of grief and death and black desolation.

"Did he hit you?"

"Not to leave a mark, but I'll be sore in the morning."

Catherine scowls. "Bastard. I'm telling you, love…"

"But you know fine well there's nothing else." She gathers Catherine's hands, holds them in her own. "We need the money and no-one will employ someone like me. They fired Charlie from your place just for doing a drag act."

"You still shouldn't be out on the street alone." Catherine looks in her eyes, pleading. "Not around here. It's not safe any more."

"I'm keeping my head down. I'm being careful. Please."

Catherine pulls her into an embrace again, squeezes her, making her hiss as her bruised ribs complain. "Come on. Let's get you home."

The main road is light and bustle, streetlights gleaming on paving stones and cobbles polished by traffic, shining sickly yellow. Neon strips emblazon the facades of the theatres and cinemas, the bars and restaurants, picked out in flowing lines of radiator vanes, of zooming perspectives, buildings at once speeding while standing still. But bulbs flicker and buzz in the frontages, leaving spaces in the streamlines like gaps in a smile. A sedan rattles past, skirting too close to the tram coming the other way ringing its bell, the tram driver shaking his fist out the window. They pass shuttered shop windows below peeling signs and skirt filthy puddles in the cracked flagstones.

They walk through the crowds towards a tram stop. An ashes cart trundles along the roadside, the dray horse old and skeleton-thin in its harness, tarnished brasses black under the lights. The people hustle, hunched against the rain or under umbrellas; workers heading home from late shift or going to back shift, restaurant-goers going on to other entertainments, each in their own world. Sally and Catherine do the same, arm in arm, Catherine insisting over Sally's caution. They hold their coats closed, heads down, ignoring the press of their fellow commuters, the jostles and curses.

She feels Catherine stiffen, looks up. There is a knot ahead; she can see placards above the heads of the pedestrians. *Redeemers.* Mobs raised by demagogues, scouring the city for whatever might have displeased the Angel. Vanity, profanity, hedonism; apportioning guilt and meting out retribution. Because *someone* has to take the blame.

A tram further along the street, the one that they want to catch, is stalled, bell ringing. Catherine's arm slips from hers, a prudent abandonment. They walk on, a couple of feet apart now, just two women trying to get home in the rough weather, nothing to see here.

The crowd noise swells as they approach, chants spelling out the slogans of sin and redemption scrawled on the placards, messages rendered hellish by the mix of yellow street light and fire brand flicker. Sally and Catherine are committed now. It's too late to turn around and take another route without drawing attention. The Redeemers will give chase to anything that runs; hounding any sign of weakness, anything they can interpret as deviance, as sin, as *difference.* Better to keep their heads down and try to get past.

They try to edge their way around the angry assembly, squeezing between the bodies and the shuttered store fronts. Elbows and backs jostle them. Coarse shouts clamour in their ears, denouncing the sins of the city; the corruption that caused its guardian Angel to abandon them, to withdraw its grace and leave them fallen.

Catherine takes the lead, murmuring, "Excuse me"; demure, modest. Sally follows, eyes down, desperately hoping not to meet the gaze of any of the agitators.

Someone barges between them, shoving Sally into the wall. She can't help but gasp as her shoulder slams into the stonework. She staggers upright again, tries to move on, but the damage is done. Heads turn at her traitor voice, a hand slams her back against the wall. Immediately, she is the focus of a widening semicircle of hostility. She looks up, desperate, at the glowering faces, sees Catherine's between two of them, just as despairing.

"What are you?"

"It's a man! In a dress!"

"Look at it, filthy pervert!"

Sally is shoved again, this time to the ground. Catherine manages to slip through the wall of bodies, to crouch over her.

They huddle together as the crowd's anger builds. Then the leaders of the mob make their way to the front, to see what their followers have found to be outraged against, placards and sticks and fire brands at their backs. Cries of *Slut, Lesbian*, and *Pervert; Filth, Corrupt*, and *Damned*. Faces twisted, hating, frame a man who has come forward, the mob parting for him, a channel through the sea of rage.

He shouts to the crowd, making some speech that Sally doesn't hear. It hardly matters, she's heard it, knows that it ends in blood and fire. He doesn't even look at the women as he denounces them as sin, corruption, the cause of the fall, but the one beside him can't take his eyes off them. Sally meets that one's stare, hungry, gleaming; an attack dog among hounds.

The leader steps back and the mob leaps forward. First among them is the eager one, raising his placard, ready to drive its butt-end at Sally's face. Catherine surges up, her arm warding both of them, and the blow smashes her down. She struggles up again, and a second blow strikes her in the temple, fells her.

Sally catches her lover as she falls, tries to cradle her to the ground, protect her from the blows that are raining now around them, indiscriminate as a hailstorm. She can't protect her own head, can't let go and fight back. She curls up, kicks landing on her back, her sides, explosions of pain flowering, sun-bright.

Then the storm abates, the blows falter and quickly stop. Sally cowers closer about her Catherine, not trusting in the lull. She can hear a voice cutting through the mob's, which has muted to a sullen rumble, but cannot make out what it says. The leader replies, his voice clear to her for the first time.

"Prophet! What are you doing? Why are you in our way?"

"This is not the way! It is not the way of Thanet."

Another voice, younger, "What would you know, you daft old bastard?" This one is hushed quickly by the others.

"Why do you need to hurt these people? What have they done to you?" It is the voice again, an old man, this 'prophet'. She can barely hear him over her own gasping for breath, the roar of pain, the fear for Catherine.

"Why don't you see it, man? We have to show the Angel that we're clean, so that He'll bring the light back."

"What I see is a lynch mob. Jack McGoogan, you're old enough to remember the light, you lived in Her grace for thirty years. Do you remember Her ever being delighted by murder?"

"This isn't murder, this is the justice of the Angel. We are His…" The voice trails off. The crowd, which had fallen quiet, begins to murmur again, uncertain now.

"Murder it would be if I hadn't stopped you, an abomination in Her eyes. It might be, yet. The polis will be here soon enough." His voice rises to engulf the mob, "You don't need to be here. Move!" The last word is a roar that scatters the people before it, tumbling them away like timbers before a gale.

Silence.

✧   ✧   ✧

Time passes, no knowing how long. Sally knows only that she has her Catherine in her arms and the beating has stopped. Things happen around her, she is dimly aware of shouts, whistles. A rising hubbub. Is it the mob returned? A hand on her shoulder, gentle. She flinches, curls closer around Catherine. *Not her, take me instead.*

A voice, insistent, "Miss? You need to let her go. Please? Let me look at her. An ambulance is coming." Firm hands on hers, cradling Catherine, easing her away. *No!* The voice murmurs nonsense, repeated phrases to gentle a wounded animal, to soothe panic. She holds on.

Another voice, instructing the new crowd to disperse. A blanket around Sally's shoulders, covering her and Catherine; the light touch on her back flares pain. She is trembling, drenched, numbed. She can't tell if the runnels on her face are blood or rainwater, if her shivering is from shock or chill. She clutches the blanket around them both, gasps as the movement shoots further bright fireworks across her back, through her vision. Her head swims. She holds on.

A bell ringing, approaching, calls her from her delirium. More voices, more gentle hands. Soft swearing, the state of them both. The hands lift up Catherine's head, place a folded blanket on the ground to cushion her.

"Miss? The ambulance is here. You need to let go now. We need to get you both on stretchers."

Please. Take care of her.

She dreams of the journey from the toll cross and up the high street, past the merchant's city of graceful manses and townhouses. She had visited them in happier times, when her art and craft was still valued even after the Fall. When courtesans could be entertainers, before the Redeemers' power rose, before the fires. She dreams of the golden stone, the graceful ballrooms and bedrooms, the beautiful dresses that Catherine made for her. She dreams that they decay, black rain leaving sooty runnels carved into the gold, tracks of bitter tears after the Angel left.

She struggles to get up. She can't see Catherine.

"Where do you think you're going?" He is all authority in his white coat and stethoscope, his shirt and tie that look like he's been wearing them for the last sixteen hours straight.

"I have to be with her." She falls back, struggles up again.

"You're going nowhere except Accident and Emergency." He turns away.

She is too weak to protest as a porter and a nurse bundle her into a wheelchair and wheel her inside. She tries to ask them, *where is she?* But she can't put the words together and they ignore her. They leave her in a cubicle, surrounded by curtains.

She drifts in and out of awareness as a nurse comes in to clean her up and bandage scrapes and cuts. A doctor comes to examine her, shines lights in her eyes, gently presses on various places on her arms, legs, torso. Flaring agony in her ribs jolts her into the present. Cold swab, prick of a needle, a wall settles down between her and all of the pain.

She is a passenger in her body as they wheel her to be X-rayed, and then back in the curtained cubicles where a nurse takes off her clothes and holds her sitting up as another winds her around with bandages. Something is wrong, missing, it beats against the swaddling of the drug with the strength of a butterfly. *Catherine…*

She tries to get up, fails, moans as her body won't obey her.

A hand on her shoulder, "Are you all right?" It's another nurse, one who looks like she's in charge, with a junior hovering at her shoulder.

Struggle again to sit up, to look up, "I want to see my, my…" *my girlfriend, my partner, my love,* "…Catherine. I need to be with her." She doesn't recognise her voice, thick, slurring.

The nurse's eyes are warm, understanding, although her face is professionally stony. "Yes, I see. Wait here."

Muffled argument from beyond the curtains, "But the doctor said—" "I don't care what he told you, I'm telling you now." "But…" "Who is staff nurse here?" "Yes, Staff."

The same beefy porter comes to lift her into a wheelchair and take her past the curtains. He wheels her down corridors lit with dim bulbs, past curtained wards, past closed and shuttered rooms that might have once housed patients. Smells assault her, of disinfectant and illness, soap and corrupt wounds. The hospital is quiet, patients supposed to be sleeping, the only noise whispered conversations at the nurses' stations, the quiet emphasised by the occasional groan, by someone's muffled sobbing. He wheels her into a half-lit room; without a word he parks her in a corner and leaves.

She struggles to get up out of the chair, stumbling as it slips away from behind her, the brakes not set. The room is crowded with equipment, surrounding a single bed with a figure lying in it. She steadies herself against the wall, then slowly, fearfully, approaches.

Catherine is so pale and still, a bandage around her head, hair tangled across the pillow, her hands at her sides above the sheets. There is a mask over her face, a hose leading to a gas bottle behind her. A cloth band around her elbow holds in place a fine rubber hose that leads to a device with dials whose needles twitch in time with her heartbeat; too slow. Too slow.

Sally moves her wheelchair to where she can see Catherine's closed eyes and hold her hand. A nurse comes in and checks Catherine's pulse, holding her other wrist and checking her watch against the tick of the dials. Dimly, Sally sees the nurse look over at her, sitting by the bed half asleep. The nurse purses her lips and walks out again.

Sally drifts in a haze. She starts awake, tightens her grip in Catherine's hand, drifts away again…

… She finds Catherine, Catherine finds her in the orphanage after the Fall. Their parents died somewhere in the rioting and the fires, she knows. She doesn't remember. Neither of them remember anything from before.

… In the orphanage, Catherine holds Sally as she cries, appalled at the sound of her broken voice; holds her back from fights, pulling her away from the jeers of boys that she can never back down from no matter how often she gets beaten; holds her hand with the knife away from her wrist.

… Their room together in the hostel, runaways from the orphanage that insists that Sally has to wear trousers and sleep in the boys' dormitory, use the boys' showers and toilets, ashamed; Catherine waitresses and works in a tailor's shop while Sally dogs school to sit on steps outside the salons, staring at the beautiful hosts and hostesses and their clients and dreaming of how wonderful it must have been in the city before the Fall.

… Catherine working three jobs, eighteen-hour days to keep them both, while Sally can't get work. In the time of the Angel, maybe Her grace would have meant that people wouldn't look sideways at her, sneer at a girlish boy, make crude suggestions as to where and how she could make cash.

… Catherine finds her drugs; herbal preparations, potions distilled from mares' urine, medicines that stop her from growing out of her stripling slimness, shape her body to a more comfortable femininity; makes clothes for her, tailoring fashionable dresses and suits to make her pretty, to hide her masculinity.

… Quarrels into the night over money, Sally passionate with a sixteen-year-old's sense that she knows what she is doing, that she should go into the salons, work as a hostess; Catherine stubbornly insists that it would not be safe for her, that the clients have become brutal since the time of the Angel. Neither giving ground, both near tears, Catherine ends the argument by taking her face in both hands and kissing her, hard. Sex that night for the first time, exploring their love, the only beautiful thing in the world.

… In the salon, Sally holds Catherine's hand as they talk to the Madam about apprenticeship. Her ethereal slimness appeals to men and women both, and the living is still good. Catherine's own pleasure is in creating costumes and her joy in wearing them and performing. Tailoring shops and bar work quickly make way for the stage, singing show tunes and torch songs for jaded restaurant diners and dance hall patrons. Wherever she goes, there is a little of the grace that had been before the Fall.

For a while.

… Running from shouts and jeers, fires behind her as a gang of Redeemers burn out the salon; forced into the alleys to scrape a living, working on the streets, hiding and running scared, one step up from begging.

Sally comes to. Catherine hasn't moved. She is so pale; she barely breathes.

"What do I do now?"

"What do you want to do?"

Sally starts, gasps as her ribs flare with sudden pain. Someone else is there, has been for some time; a dark shape in the corner of her eye. She rouses herself, tears her view away from Catherine. It's a man, thin and careworn with grey hair. The lines on his face are drawn deep around his mouth, but also at the corners of his eyes, as if he used to smile all the time. She recognises him, the one they called 'Prophet'. He has brought another chair with him, sat in a corner of the room, watching her and Catherine.

"You came too late."

"I'm sorry. I did what I could."

"They called you Prophet." She scowls. "Are you one of them?"

"No. My name is Thomas."

"Thomas. They did what you told them."

"They're afraid of me." He looks sad rather than proud.

"Why do they call you Prophet?"

"I have the sight. A gift She left me before She… left."

She can hear the emphasis on the word, "She? The Angel?"

"Yes."

"The Redeemers call him He."

"How can an Angel be tied to He, She or anything else? They remember what suits them if they remember at all."

"And you knew Her." In the time before, when everything was wonderful. Sally can't imagine what that must have been like.

"I was in Her presence from time to time."

"And She gave you a gift. You can see the future?"

"At times I see what is *likely*."

Sally slumps and turns back to Catherine, "What good did that do her?"

"I saw *you* die. You died and there was nothing I could do about it. But your friend? She has given me the chance to save you."

"I'd rather have died."

"You will, in time. But right now at least you have a choice. Will you make her sacrifice for nothing?"

Sally reaches for Catherine's hand, holds it tight. "What are you talking about?"

"I can help you."

"Why are you here?"

"Do you trust me?"

"… Yes."

"Why?"

"You knew the Angel. I have faith in you."

"Then you're an idiot. Trust is based on something, but faith is wishful thinking bullshit. If you trust me, tell me why, or we're done."

"All right. You didn't have to do it, and I don't know what you did, but *she* tried to stop them and look at her. You should have ended up the same way. You didn't have to take that risk. So thank you. I trust you. Do whatever you're going to do."

"Fair enough." He drags his chair around Catherine's bed. Sits and holds out his hands to her. "Here."

Sally puts her hands in his.

"Close your eyes."

She looks over to where Catherine is lying still, so still. Tears her gaze away again, bows her head. Closes her eyes.

Falling. Panic. She tries to flail her arms, but his hands are strong. It's dark, then a light glimmers. A street light. *The* street. The blow falls, Catherine falls, she falls. She's lying there, the mob is scattering, Catherine is bleeding. Sally tries to reach her but hands hold her back.

Impressions, as in a dream, it's a procession of scenes and meanings. She rides inside her body as the vision passes. The hospital. Catherine is dead. *No!* His hands tighten on hers. Funeral, terrible grief, too terrible to bear. Loss, distilling to uncontainable fury.

Two passions, two lives:

…She finds the man,
    confronts him in an alley…

            …She swallows her grief,
                    puts her scant energies
                    into looking for work
                    like Catherine wanted…

…She kills him,
    half-brick in her hand,
    swings with all the leverage of
    her despised shoulders and muscles,
    stoves in his temple…

            …She leaves the city,
                    never settles,
                    never finds another love,
                    never forgets or forgives…

…She stays on the street,
    taking punters for rent money, drugs,
    false joy covering the desolation
    that never leaves her…

            …She dies old,
                    regretful, far away,
                    never resolved…

…She dies in a year,
    a heroin skank in an alley,
    battered to death
    by another violent punter…

The Prophet releases her hands. Sally heaves a deep, shuddering breath and the tears come, finally. Just as when the Angel left, she loses herself in blackness.

She comes back to herself and scrubs her face with the back of her hand. He is still here, a companionable presence, no judgement or disapproval. The light through the curtain is dim, pre-dawn. He stands, pours a glass of water from the jug on the stand beside Catherine's bed. Holds it steady as her hands shake and she sips.

"So that's it? My future? Futures." She stretches, arching her back and neck, staring at the ceiling as she speaks. Then back down to Catherine, so still.

"Choices. The most likely ones, and the most likely outcomes."

"Why bother? There's no future where she'll live, is there?"

"Maybe what I showed you can make a difference. Once, when She lived here, people lived without hatred. Lived in tolerance and forgiveness of one another. If I can bring those times back, then perhaps she'll return."

"So what do I do now?"

"It's up to you. I showed you the most likely paths from here. If you don't like them, do something else."

It has been a week since Catherine died. The world has cruelly refused to end. Nothing has changed. Everything is different. The streets are meaner, more shabby, the people walking them more beaten down.

Everything is different. Nothing has changed. She still has to make the rent, now without Catherine's help. She stands on an alley corner in the banking district. There are plenty of young brokers here, arrogant and flush and with an itch to scratch. In their world of transactions this is just another, unencumbered even by the meaning and manners that attend a visit to a pleasure house. It is a popular area for women and boys who need the money.

She sees him before he sees her.

Prophet's vision had showed him to her as he had struck Catherine down, had showed his face and everything in it; the fear fuelled by desire, fear of the mob, of being found out, being shunned, one of the sinners, another potential victim. His malice borne not of rage but of shame, driving him constantly to purge the filth from the city because he cannot purge it from himself.

He is furtive, looking sidelong at the street walkers as he passes them. He hesitates at one, a slim boy in a slip dress, then hurries on, muttering to himself. She reads his lips, *sinners, whores, filth.*

Is it a remnant of Prophet's gift? She sees it in his face, the need, the fear. He is a Redeemer; he knows that what he desires is a sin, the people he would go to are sinners. He is—they are—the reason why the Angel left and why he has to feel his shame. She sees other victims, other streetwalkers in the past, in his future. He is brutal in his denial, the tension between his beliefs and his needs expressed in blows. No-one else has died. Yet.

He passes her unknowing and she steps up behind him, "Business?"

He starts and turns, fist raised, lowers it. He meets her eyes.

She sees confirmation in them, nods to the alley behind her and smiles. She turns her back on him and sashays into the shadows.

She hears him follow.

She leads him down the alley, to a recessed doorway that cannot be seen from the street. Gently pushes him against the door, caressing his chest, slipping her hand up and around his neck. She is actually taller than he is, but she sinks down, leans against his body, hip tilted, thigh against his, feeling his cock rise against her, seeing his lips twist in disgust.

"It's all right," she whispers. She kisses him gently, sweetly.

He shakes his head. She kisses him again and holds it, feeling him respond his lips soften against hers. His arms reach around her, one hand on her arse, the other on the small of her back. She runs her free hand down the front of his belly, past his belt, caresses his cock.

...He pulls her close.

    Her hand slips to her side,
    into her bag, grasps what she needs.
    She runs her closed hand up between his legs.
    Thumb flick, soft snick of the straight razor.
    The blade that caressed her cheek this morning
    bites inside his thigh...

        ...He pulls her close.
           One arm about her shoulders,
           the other grasps her throat
           and he spins her and
           slams her into a wall...

...He gasps,

    jerks, tries to shove her away,
    strength failing by the second as he struggles,
    blood gushing from his artery.
    She lets him sag, holds him
    as he sinks to the alley floor,
    body away from his,
    away from the gouting blood...

        ...He beats her head repeatedly
           against the bricks, drops her,
           bleeding, into the alley filth.
           Kicks her, crotch, ribs, face...

Do something else..."

Paths open up into the future, unfolding around her like the wings of the Angel. She leans back, stands tall, kisses his forehead.

"I forgive you," she says.

The Witch at the End of the World
Peter Morrison

"Like the generations of leaves, the lives of mortal man.
Now the wind scatters the old leaves across the earth,
now the living timber bursts with the new buds
and spring comes round again.
And so with men: as one generation comes to life,
another dies away."

"The Iliad"—Homer.

1. Wild Hunt

Sheil anDoull is the last of my children to come ashore, though first that the Witch Hunter General, Papa Oki Din, parleyed with. She looks back across the water, thinking of safety left behind to come here. I stand with her brother Angu, who offers his hand. Taking it, she steps ashore. Snow, crushed beneath her foot fall, the way the land is crushed beneath this tainted, endless winter.

"No turning back now," Angu grunts, looking over her shoulder.

"No, here we are, entering the land of the dead." She frowns as she speaks. "We may be tempted to bury hope by this shore, though we must carry it with us all the way." Angu touches her face, smiles.

Papa Oki Din, a pale, one-eyed man, with salted hair, watches the pair of towering highlanders trudge their way up the embankment to complete the dozen witches who have travelled here to form my coven. Sheil and Angu have travelled from The Land Lost In The Mists Up High. Dressed in beat up leather jackets, kilts of their clan's hunting tartan and great big kickety boots. I walk with them, matching them step for every crunching step, though we leave only two sets of prints.

"A real pretty flag you've got there," Angu shouts. The remains of Papa Oki Din's army gather within the arches of a leviathan's rib cage, bone struts like the ruins of a church dedicated to a dead god. Driven into the ground there is a spear, tattered cloth fluttering from the end, depicting a black tree on green. The witches of the wild hunt and their dogs mill around laughing, ignoring the army's nervous mutters of discontent. While Angu is amused by his joke, Sheil's face shows distress as she caresses the base of the arching bone.

"A pennant you glaikit bastard!" Junna Soldottir of The Land of Northern Ice tells Angu, punching his arm affectionately, her brass knuckles leave a glancing print on his jacket's leather.

"Fine, a pretty pennant you've got." Angu shrugs. "If I'd known we were going to hang pretty things I'd have brought some bunting."

"Smart arse," Chloe Lunadottir snorts, standing by Junna's side, the two as pale as the snow.

Papa Oki Din claps his hands together, watches the puff of his breath. "It was here before us. The flag of Iggy da Drasil." He carefully avoids the eyes of my children, this dirty dozen ostensibly gathered to do his bidding. These soldiers know him as a ferocious fighter, with enough of the trickster spirit to make his plotting unpredictable. The son of a queen of a slaughtered tribe, rumours of a father not entirely human. In a conflict torn world, the soldiers who survive regard him with awe and perhaps a degree of fear. Who else would journey into the mountains in search of the hidden folk? But my people and their arcane ways scare *him* shitless. "This is a bad omen," Sheil whispers to herself. "It can only be a warning that nothing is certain. Failure is a likely outcome."

"Well, hunter, we came," Jo Sun Lin address Papa Oki Din. She is the speaker for the three from the Eastern Islands Bathed in Sun. Lanky, dark haired women: Jo Sun Lin dressed in orange silk, red leather, Go Low Rhi dressed in yellow silk, orange leather, and Co Fan Tui in red silk, yellow leather. "What now?"

"You are the children of the tree, I have brought you from far afield, to come together at this time. The stars tell us now is the time to act. Only the goddess of the one tree can invoke the healing that is needed. You must lead us to Iggy da Drasil that we may petition her." For all his doubt he has the patter, my children would not be here if they had no confidence in this man.

"The stars don't lie when they suggest this is a malleable moment in time. But we caution you, the outcome is not foreordained. The weaknesses providing us this opportunity may instead wipe any trace of us from reality." Jo Sun glances from the stars to the forlorn pennant. "If we do *not* have Her blessing then this is a fool's journey."

"You don't feel her?" Lakshmi Monkey King of the Silver Mountain tribes asks. "She stalks our footprints."

It is true, I walk among them unseen.

Jo Sun sniffs the air, licks Lakshmi's face from chin to brow, savours the taste. "Yes. She is here and we are sacred in her company. We may proceed."

Capin Song, a lanky brown-skinned woman to whom Papa Oki Din appears to answer, blanches as she watches these exchanges. "Who are these people?" she asks him. "You advise us that they are our hope?"

"Stand fast mistress, stay strong," Papa's voice is pitched so only Song can hear. "These are the cunning folk. Care must be taken neither to offend, nor to trust too far."

Lakshmi steps away, lips pouted, holding back a slight shudder. Her dark hair pinned atop her head with chopsticks, the mountain woman stands hunched in a coat made from the skin of a feral animal, her hands buried in pockets. Despite the cold, it remains unbuttoned, the bare brown skin of her mid-riff exposed, a figure hugging crop top—the slogan SUCK MY COCK across her breasts, written in the font of a soft drinks company long forgotten by the passage of time. Music fills the air as if by magic and Lakshmi fishes a device from one of her pockets; looks at it with confusion. Poking at the screen till the music stops, she lifts it to her ear and bellows. "ALLO? WHAT? NO, I'M IN THE WASTED LAND." A pause. "NO IT'S SHIT. IT'S COLD AND SOME BITCH JUST LICKED MY FACE!" A pause. "THIS IS A FOOL'S MISSION AND WE'RE ALL GOING TO DIE? AWESOME, THANKS FOR CALLING!" Ending the call, Lakshmi slips the phone back into her pocket and resumes staring at Papa Oki Din as though nothing has happened. Capin Song motions to quell the mutterings of black magic amongst the guard.

"End of The World Song—nice ring tone." The red-mohawk-sporting Chow Urltin, representative of the Sky Valley Dragons, grins.

"Ahem," Papa Oki Din clears his throat, pulls back his sleeve miming looking at his watch. "We're on a schedule here!"

"Well you did go out of your way to recruit wretched, scummy villains," Vishmal River Snake of Silver Mountains offers. "You got what you asked for: the mad, the bad, and the wicked…"

"Indeed. Thank you for your contribution…"

"…hunters, nutters, bawbags of all kinds…"

"…if you are quite done? Now we are all here, if one of you can pick a ley path and guide us to where the lines cross, then we will be off to see the witch, the wonderful witch da Drasil." Papa Oki Din blurts this out, afraid that the group will find some other way to interrupt him and delay their journey.

"Good, good, let the gathered noctambulant herlapers come to order. For it is witch season, and we ur hunting witch!" Hope Sunrise from The City of The Burning Sun calls out, turning to an imaginary onlooker and raising a single sarcastic eyebrow. Her call is met with a cheer from her fellow witches.

Capin Song brings a horse forward for Papa Oki Din, passing him the reins, while the soldiers mount up. Song watches the strangers and shakes her head. She has staked everything on this garish crew touted by Oki Din as the secret weapon that'll save the world. In a world of desolate, never ending, tribal war nothing else has worked but Capin Song struggles to believe.

2. Spook Riders

The group rides out, trailing after Avid Unkin of the sunken continent, Amurca Fuyeh. It wears body armour that hides every inch of flesh. Some amongst my children speculate as to what lies behind the expressionless mask, but none ken. The Unkin is closer to the dead, can more readily discern the spookwegen; the ghost paths threaded through this collapsed civilization. As they ride, Sheil explains to Papa Oki Din that there are dead cities beneath the snow, one wrong step and they will all fall, lost to the depths below.

The soldiers spread out into a defensive formation. In this desolate world all that is left is war. Any party they encounter will attack, the only options are kill or starve. As they move they glance at the witches amongst them, who ride strange hobby horses. At first they took them for toys, till the witches straddled the broom sticks with horse's heads and began to hover above the ground. There is something comical about the sight, the soldiers feel, but the blatant display of witchcraft unsettles them. Even worse, they catch sight of titanic figures out of the corner of their eyes. Some of the soldiers suspect the witches are more than they appear to be, hushed whispers exchanging theories. The horses trudge, their passage laboured, the only sound in the still darkness.

"Boom, bo-bo-bom. Bom-bo-bo-bom." Angu starts to sing. The sudden sound startles everyone. On the other side of the train of riders, Sheil adds to Angu's voice, with a "ti-tch-ti-tch." As the two voices work together another is added to the mix, Lakshmi working through a "ba, dadaba, ba, dadaba." The others join in till the whole group is singing a version of the folk song, Spook Rider. Riding on, they amuse themselves with other songs handed down through generations—Off To See The Witch, 500 Mile and the like—but the jovial *a cappella* witch choir does little to reassure their companions.

After the first attack from a rival group the singing stops, the soldiers focus on killing, surviving. Progress in these harsh lands is exhausting, they lose people and victory is hard fought. But there are other things out there. Things which are not human, though at times they may appear to be wearing human guise. Corrupted things, product of this polluted land, who would prevent them from reaching their goal. A little girl stands atop a hill ahead. She has been regarding their advance for a long time. Her face hidden by a red hoodie, she is wearing brown boots and a tartan skirt. A trio of soldiers break from the group to investigate. One of them a young woman, clambering up the slope ahead of her fellows. The child makes a peculiar sound, in response the woman's head explodes, a pop and a floral spatter of blood. Her companions stop, one glances back at the group, they are unsure what to do next. But before they can be offered guidance they both die as suddenly. The girl's giggling carries across the distance till Avid Unkin, dismounting, draws a wicked short sword. The Unkin throws the blade, spinning through the air towards the child. The child gestures and the blade slows, but it does not stop. She spits, draws a finger cross her throat in a slashing motion, running off into darkness before the blade reaches where she was.

The ride continues for days; though, with no sunrise or set, tracking time is difficult. While trying to steer clear of the danger of cities as well as they can, it isn't always possible. One time they ride slowly through empty streets, cadaverous buildings lining their way. They debate which city it is—Aris perhaps? No, totally Urik! Ospensilke, another insists. But they agree it makes no difference, as sounds of a battle drift through the artificial canyons, reminding them that caution is paramount.

Silence returning, they pick a spot to rest, sheltering behind a bus long buried in a snowdrift. Clearly converted at some point, there are tables and chairs inside, "Noodle Bar" painted along the side. All these things are strange to the soldiers, who Papa Oki Din and Capin Song continually have to assure that there is hope, that this is not a fool's journey. During these rest breaks not all find that relief comes readily. Lakshmi and Chloe console Sheil, racked with grief at how bad things have become outside of the refuges. Papa Oki Din wakes from disturbed dreams of an old woman sitting on his chest—the explanation that I am offering him my protection seems to do little to reassure.

One occasion, Sheil calls for everyone to stay still, stay quiet. A vast behemoth in the dark, its cries deep and reverbatory, haunting and wrong. The beast appears to come closer: the scent of panic staining the air, the sound of huge feet crunching through snow, coming fast. Passing close, passing fast, a hideous thing that, miraculously, seems never to notice them huddling in the dark. A monstrosity of such terrifying proportions it is some time before they are able to continue.

The deeper they travel, the stranger things become. Capin Song asks Papa Oki Din whether they have been drugged. Surely they are hallucinating? The sounds in the distance can't be real? The smell of chemical burning that saturates the land isn't natural, the reek of dead cultures impregnates these reclaimed lands. Sometimes they can even see the paths the Unkin leads them along; glowing, uncanny against the luminescent snow. None here can be sure anymore as to what is real and I keep my answers to myself as they come ever closer to me.

"There it is, the World Tree, our destination." Hope Sunrise draws alongside Papa Oki Din as they ride, points to the distance. There the one tree has become visible. Huge, gnarled, skeletal. Ancient.

"My god!" Papa Oki Din is stunned by its size. "It's a monster!"

"There is nothing like it left in the world," Go Low Rhi calls from where she rides. "This is the last of the deep magic."

Papa Oki Din looks again, judges that it will yet be some hours before they reach the tree. But perhaps at last everything *is* coming together. Maybe they are right and there is still some hope in the world. I smile listening to the way of his thoughts.

Here now waits my physical form. My spirit leaves them as they draw close. No further need for projection, I return to ancient flesh.

3. World Tree

First to arrive at the tree, Chow Urltin bellows, "Allo lil ole lady!" His fellows gather round him smiling and laughing at his greeting, the traditional ancestral call between the dragon tribes and old witches. The dogs run round them, yipping and full of energy.

"So, we meet her here?" Papa Oki Din asks, sidling up beside Chloe Lunadottir.

"She is here, you see?" Chloe points to where I sit nestled in the sparse branches. Her fingers are blue, glitter glinting like stars, tattooed planetary symbols visible through the dye. White blonde hair, dreaded and hanging past her shoulders, an orange flower tucked in behind her ear. "This is a sacred place where everything is possible."

"OK." Papa Oki Din nods. He glances back at his men, pulls in on himself, looks out into the darkness. "So, uh, with Iggy we will be able save the world?"

"Ha!" Hope Sunrise barks with laughter, contrasting Chloe by being the darkest skinned, even more than those of the silver mountains. Her clothing is as bright as the silks of the Eastern Island ladies. Her eyes meet Chloe's and together they turn to look upon Papa Oki Din, grinning with too many teeth. "With Iggy da Drasil, everything will change!"

"Uh, great." Sighing, Papa Oki Din turns his horse and his voice shakes. "Make camp. See if you can make a fire." Looking over his shoulder he watches the twelve dismount, their rides reverting to their idle toy like forms. He has brought these strangers together, persuaded them with hard bargaining to leave their refuges and travel all this way, because he had faith in the old ways, but his resolve is crumbling. Perhaps all of this is proving too strange, or perhaps he's finally admitting that his faith was really little more than desperate, childish hope. But these are my children, Papa. The mark of my tree upon their flesh, a potential flows between them.

"Create first circle," Angu shouts. Sheil, Chloe and Hope join him in stepping out a circle, sprinkling powders as they go, enclosing the entire expanse of the tree and the camp forming now beneath the expanse of these great spreading branches. Chanting yelps and whispers, they put the first line of a defence system into place while Chow and Lakshmi pull out their pouches and get a brew on.

The soldiers drink calming tea round the fire while the witches complete the ritual. During this time I have descended slowly from the tree. My children greet me: with embraces, pecks on the cheek, whispered words of power, each taking their turn with great solemn pride.

Each of these night programmers has brought a gift. In turn they present to me holy chalices, skulls of old friends, sacred tarot decks worn from use, an apple from the tree of the fallen, and the like. Then it is the turn of the representative of the drowned nation. Carefully Avid Unkin removes its mask, loosing the straps and cradling the false face in its hands. Carefully we do not look into the emptiness, though all see the fish that swims out into my hands, the final offering. Hungrily, I eat it.

Chloe and Hope take my hands and help me stand. This body is frail and needs help. Some change in the air attracts the attention of the soldiers. Capin Song ambles over, standing beside Oki Din who crouches, entranced, nearby. They watch, bemused, as my children strip the rags from my withered flesh, exposing me to the elements. Chloe in turn strips to her underclothes, child of the ice, wire-reinforced muscles. The group starts to sing. This, the most ancient of our songs. It makes the soldiers whine with a primal unease. Chloe kneels before me in supplication before kissing my forehead, my cheeks, my mouth. She presses her head against mine.

"Do it," I croon. Hands grasp my head. The movement quick. A twist to break my neck. Her teeth sink in. Tear deep. Drag me to the ground. Pinning me as big cats of legend were once said to do. Gasps are heard by those inclined to listen. Soldiers hardened by battle, shocked by the sight.

"What have you done?" Oki Din cries out, struggling to find his voice. But my children are busy dismembering me, devouring my flesh. Chloe stands first, her face slick with blood, her eyes staring and feral. The soldiers back away, drawing weapons. She ignores them. Dragging a thigh bone, she makes her way towards the limits of the circle. There she draws sigils with my blood, harnessing new knowledge consumed. Each of the witches follow suit, taking up position. Bloodied, they draw, adding new layers and complexities to the marks; building protection. Plugging into the depths of the world's operating structures in preparation for what comes next.

"What have you done?" Oki Din cries once more. Chloe turns to him, her part complete, and the soldiers under his command wince as he flinches from her. "This wasn't the plan! You were supposed to save the world!"

"We use her flesh to carry out deep rituals, big magic." Chloe half-whispers. It is unclear whether her response is directed to Papa Oki Din or those gathered within the circle in general. She drags herself back to where my remains lie and starts to vomit.

"What we do here is the start of the planetary decontamination," Chow adds, before joining Chloe. Purging themselves they collapse together on the ground, exhausted.

"Disco nap," Lakshmi shouts, half-hearted, before dragging a blood-stained hand across her blood-stained mouth. They each drift back to the viscera of my corpse, dragging back my bones, returning the essence of me to the earth. Lying down in the snow together.

Papa Oki Din grabs hold of Shiel's arm. "You better have good fucking plan! Cause it looks like a bag of shite from here," hissing to balance anger with some level of discretion. "You're lucky I don't get these bastards to stab you in your sleep after pulling a stunt like that!"

Shiel glances at him, shrugs. "It'll be fine; everything is going exactly as planned. Trust me."

Shiel lifts his hand from her arm, walking to where her fellows are already asleep, as she clambers into the pile she is followed by the hunting dogs. The pile issues animal whimpers of contentment, followed by snoring.

"Everything is awesome!" Papa Oki Din claps his hands together and turns to the soldiers. "We're just about sorted, keep doing your job—set up watch, stand watch—all that good stuff. This will all be over soon." The soldiers return to their posts, glancing back as they go. "Fucking tickety-boo," Oki Din mutters to himself.

✧   ✧   ✧

4. One For Sorrow

"The last time I slept, I had a troubling dream," Capin Song says to Papa Oki Din as the pair stare into the flames and drink tea. "You advise that you have had many troubling dreams on this journey. I dreamt of the last battle, where we all died, I the last of all. I was a queen, but I died just the same as everyone else. As I lay waiting to expel my last breath, I watched a black and white bird, hopping from corpse to corpse. Lying there, I believed I heard the bird singing, repeating the same phrase over and over: *one for sorrow, one for sorrow*. Then I realised it wasn't the bird that was singing; it was Death, as she piled the skulls of those already departed into a pyramid."

Oki Din sighs, rubs a hand across his face. "You dreamt our possible fate, one that may still come to pass. But on this journey we seek to find a better outcome, one where we all get to live. I dreamt you were our queen, I dreamt the same dream." They lapse into silence, lost in their own thoughts about what lies ahead.

"Papa?" Capin Song's voice brings him back to the present. Slowly she stands, points at the little girl who has emerged from the drifts of freezing fog. It is the girl who slaughtered the soldiers so horribly on the journey here. Papa Oki Din rises and together they watch the figure advance determinedly, stopping at the outer circle. An inhuman face peers at them from within the hood. Skin a viscous fluid, writhing and shifting, glimpses of teeth and eyes. Then the contaminated child thing reaches out and touches an unseen something that separates those within the circle from the world outside. Lowering herself to the ground, maintaining contact the entire time, leaving a momentary smear on the air with the motion, she rests her head against the barrier and starts to sing.

"We appear to be safe." The intervals and intonations of the song make Papa Oki Din uncomfortable, but he doesn't believe that she poses a threat.

"There are more of them." Song indicates other figures emerging from the night, each joining in with the song of the first. They keep coming, these children of a polluted world, absorbed in their alien ritual. Soon the camp is surrounded by song, under siege.

A hideously familiar bellow is heard from far away. Frantic soldiers wake, tugging on sword belts, recalling the fear they felt with their previous brush with the behemoth. The creatures seem unperturbed as the beast grumbles into view. Still more of the tiny figures ride it, guiding the monster with spears driven deep into its back. A terrible sound rends the night, like the sound of cities collapsing.

"In the name of Iggy," Angu growls from the pile-up beneath the tree, "give us five more minutes!"

The soldiers within the circle brace for the charge, weapons held hopelessly, few believing they'll make a difference. Yawning Angu stands and, one by one, the other sleepers awaken too, bleary eyed, stretching. "Och, bugger," he mutters. "We're right in the shite now!"

"Sir?" One of the soldiers tugs at Capin Song's sleeve and points. She and Papa turn to find that, where there were twelve who went to sleep, there are now thirteen, for I sit among them, reborn, naked and radiant. Slowly each soldier turns, to see what has caught the attention of their fellows and is awed by my wonder. My planetary scientists come to me, taking my hand and kissing it. Chloe and Hope help me stand, though in my new flesh I do not need their aid. The women of the Eastern Islands Bathed In Sun produce a final gift; in layered silken robes they dress me in all the colours of the sun. Around the circumference, straddling the binding sigils, the coven takes up position for the final ritual. Twisting hand gestures. Grasping air. Letting it go. Turning in place. A humming builds with each motion. Then there is a *click,* the planetary gestural interface is aligned. We are ready to experiment with reality. "Prepare the root code," I say. "In...three, two, *one.*"

The behemoth crashes against the witch barrier. It claws at our invisible shell, huge paws scrabbling. The dogs that came with the hunt howl and snarl as the beast crashes into it again. Sigils flicker, ours and theirs, as damage is done. Encouraged, the child things sing louder.

"For fuck's sake are you going to do something?" Papa Oki Din shouts.

A roar and a crash. Everything becomes confused. People are screaming. There is blood. I take a deep breath into my new lungs, and say, "Now."

∞. Possible Worlds

Blink.
There is nothing.
A bubble floating in nothing.
In the heart of the bubble a tree.
A world tree.

In front of the tree sits:
A nymph.
A witch.
A goddess.
She who gives life.
And death.
She who bore the world.
Fruited children.

In the nothingness
other bubbles
drifting.
From the nothingness titans emerge.

They form a circle.
Huge figures floating in nothing.
Focused on this one particular bubble.
Dragon, wolf, fox; avatars of the lost tribes.
The invisible people
Carriers of imagination.
Those who serve the mother.
Deep programmers of place.
Highland minotaur of Sheil and Angu.
Lakshmi my monkey king.
Something aquatic and unknowable.

Stepping through sequences.
Celestial programming.
Primordial debugging.
My children continue to work.
To reach out into the expanse of everything.
Caressing the fabrics of possibility.
Sliding new pieces into place.

0. Sun Arise

Blink. The light has gone. The bubble has gone. Take a breath, any breath. Now close your eyes. *Blink.* Light returns. For a moment it is blinding. The passage from relentless darkness, oppressive winter, to the nothing of white potential, to this... what is it? World's end?

No. A beginning. The start of a new day. Capin Song wakes to a sun rise, to the start of a new day. A vast and ancient being sits in front of her. *Blink.* No, it is Iggy, looking into her eyes. Over them the tree is erupting, vibrant with life. The memory of the skeleton that stood there before is already fading. Beneath Song's hand there is grass. She looks around in confusion.

Round the line of the circle, the titans sit. Flesh form, transcendent, The Recalled. Between the blinks of nothing and everything the enemy is vanished. The behemoth is gone. Instead, sat facing the circle are the new people: the tribes of dragon and snake, of monkey and bull, of fox and wolf, of the imagined and magical. Between the titans and the ground where Iggy and Song sit, Papa Oki Din and their guard stand dazed.

Song's gaze returns to meet Iggy's. Iggy leans forward, grabbing the layered rags that Song wears and tears them aside, revealing naked flesh, Song is surprised to find what appears to be a tattoo of an acorn on her ribs. Iggy pushes a hand, too warm, too hard, against Song's chest, covering the acorn and pushing, pushing. Song fears she will push through her skin or perhaps that she will burn up. Instead, branches emerge and spread up towards Song's collar bones. Iggy removes her hand to reveal now the image of a strong, healthy tree.

"You are mine now. I name you Song Rebuilder," Iggy says. "Remember, you have to plant the seed, to grow the tree." Iggy stands, walks by Song, returning to her tree. As she heaves herself into the branches, a bird alights. Its feathers are black and white. A moment later, a second joins it.

Song hears Iggy's last words drift down to her "Two for joy."

What Bliss It Was
Louise Welsh

Part One

Madoc woke to the sound of screaming. He was lying on his back in the mess hall, half under one of the tables that were bolted to the floor, to prevent them from floating should there be a sudden loss of atmosphere, a departure of gravity. Madoc pulled himself up onto a bench. He rapped his forehead with his knuckles and the screams stopped abruptly, as if someone had flicked a switch and shut them off.

Madoc felt as if his soul had been ripped from his body. He saw the blood smeared across the white surface of the table and then saw that he was missing the third finger of his left hand.

MADOC

He watched the blood pooling beneath the nub of flesh where his finger should have been and wondered why his heart hurt, when his hand did not.

MADOC

Someone leaned over his shoulder. Madoc saw familiar features reflected in the crimson shine of the table. He whirled around, but no one was there, only Nevis lying face down by the door.

MADOC

He could hear the rush and boom of the ventilation system. They had been six months in space. Every breath Madoc took had already filled the lungs of his fellow crewmembers many times.

"I can smell your filthy tubes." He muttered to Nevis. Nevis said nothing. A man stood over the prostrate body, dressed in ship's overalls. "Who are you?" Madoc whispered.

The man held up his hand and Madoc saw the bloody stub where his finger should have been. The stranger opened the door and vanished.

Part Two

The screaming started again. Madoc had been staring at his wounded hand. If he could remember how his finger had been severed, he would remember everything—where the rest of the crew had gone, why Nevis was lying face down by the door, who the stranger was. Madoc rapped his knuckles against his skull, but the screams continued. He slammed his forehead against the table and they stopped.

MADOC

The voice was familiar.

MADOC

He whirled around. "Go away."

No one was there.

Something slammed against the mess room door. Madoc got to his feet. His white overall was grubby and bloodstained. He remembered the weight of the cleaver in his hand and wondered if *he* had chopped his finger off. It was a strange notion. It made him smile.

MADOC

The ventilation system whooshed and roared and the metal door to the mess hall rattled as if something was desperate to get in. Madoc felt dizzy. The floor seemed to tip beneath him. The ship was thousands of miles above the atmosphere, deep in the starry blackness of space. Madoc felt an urge to go to the viewing deck and look down on his home planet, that small blue disc, smaller than his thumbnail.

A man stood beside Nevis's body. He raised his mutilated hand, then stepped over Nevis and reached for the door. Madoc looked at his own hand, the bloody stump where his finger should be. He got to his feet and followed the stranger.

Part Three

The other side of the door was a confusion of sound and darkness. Air rushed around him, stabbing his face with saltwater and the deck tipped and rolled beneath his feet.

MADOC

"Shut up!" he shouted. "Shut up, shut up, shut up!"

The moon was full and round-faced, high in the black of the night sky. What had cut the strings that had held the ship level with the moon and cast it down into this roaring sea? The boat hit a swell. Madoc lost his footing and only just managed to grab the railings. A froth of brine washed over him.

MADOC

He pushed his hair from his eyes and blinked away salt water. His vision was adjusting to the dark. He could make out the long deck, the containers stacked high as a house along the centre of the vessel. He remembered the weight of the cleaver in his hand.

MADOC

The stranger stood at the opposite end of the ship. The door to the mess flew open illuminating the deck. The cleaver gleamed silver beside Nevis's body on the mess room floor. Madoc leant in and lifted it in his right hand. It fitted his grip.

MADOC the stranger whispered in a voice that was Madoc's own. The man lifted his head and Madoc saw his own features, his own eyes staring into him.

"Aye," Madoc answered. "Fear no more. I'm coming for you."

Part Four

A wave crashed over the ship. It reached for Madoc, caught him in its grip and tried to pull him down into the Death-Sea. Madoc grabbed the railings. He spat blood and salt water, tightened his hold on the cleaver and lumbered towards the waiting figure.

MADOC

The scream was in his head again, louder than the rage of the sea. The stranger had cut the cords that had held the ship in outer space. It had cast them down into the ocean and then murdered the rest of the crew, picking them off one by one. The monster had severed Madoc's finger and would not rest until it had cut him to pieces.

MADOC

The stranger that had stolen his face raised a hand in the air and a weapon glinted miraculous against the night.

"I'll chop *you* up." Madoc ran towards his double. He cut the air with his cleaver, slicing the blade through a froth of spray and raised his voice in a scream that swelled the screams in his head. Madoc's feet slipped from beneath him. The ship tipped and rolled and he rolled with it, tumbling towards the plunging depths.

MADOC

The sea sucked at his legs but the cleaver snagged the ship's railings and Madoc hauled himself on board.

MADOC

The figure was at his shoulder, a blade striking towards him. Madoc sank his strength into his cleaver. He hacked and slashed. The screaming grew and then, there was only the sound of the waves.

Run
Kenneth Kelly

—to run, so I run, but who can outrun the heat from the heart of a blast that strips electrons from their shells, flash fries human flesh exposing skeletons for a nanosecond, then the shockwave, a daemon of destruction, that howls them out of existence and obliterates everything—trees, buildings, people—as it radiates like a ripple, its force lessening as I continue to run away from the epicenter, but that is... *impossible*... unless I absorbed energy from the blast, transformed it somehow into a huge influx of kinetic energy, allowing me to run at this impossible speed, moving so fast that I run out of land, and now I'm running on the ocean, moving so fast I deny the laws of physics and if I can deny the laws of physics maybe I have a chance to stop this madness before it begins, now it's me versus Einstein, who said to travel in time you would need to move faster than the speed of light and that is impossible, right now I'm doing the impossible so I focus and the landscape changes, blurs gives way to streaks, reality shreds, I focus and focus—BOOM—I circumnavigate the world in a minute, a second, point one three two of a second and then I'm running through time, events happening backwards around me, I pass myself running from the explosion, I see the bomb imploding, coalescing, flying back into the sky, I exit the time stream and head for the White House moving so fast that anything I come into contact with disintegrates, barriers, buildings, Presidents; it takes me seconds to cross to Russia and the Kremlin, I wipe out the Chinese, Israeli, Indian, French and UK Governments, then the landscape is no longer a blur and I'm slowing down, running out of energy and I stop and I hear it, the air raid siren, secondary protocol, with the Governments wiped out the Military let the missiles fly... I've failed, a missile bears down on me, my instinct tells me—

I Believe That This Nation Should Commit Itself
Duncan Lunan

Elliot See and Charles Bassett died in a plane crash in February 1966 while training for the Gemini IX mission, so changing the order of the flight assignments for the later ones and for Apollo. Virgil Grissom was killed with Ed White and Roger Chaffee in the Apollo fire of January 1967. Vladimir Komarov died in Soyuz 1 in April 1967, after a possible rendezvous with Soyuz 2 had been aborted. Yuri Gagarin died on what should have been a routine practise flight in March 1968; and but for the altered mission of Apollo 8 in December that year, Pete Conrad would have commanded Apollo 11 and been first man on the Moon. It didn't happen—but maybe it could all have been different...

We beat the Russians to the Moon by ten minutes.

We still can't go public with the story, and the official line is that none of it ever happened. There are layers upon layers of secrecy and misdirection piled over the existence of our project, and still more over this incident. We were acting completely without authorisation, and looking back on it, we did go a little crazy with the excitement of it all. Whether we deserved to be shut down for it—well, you can be the judge of that once you've read this.

We were part of the CIA's Remote Viewing Programme, in a discreet building on the edge of the Johnson Space Centre in Houston. Believe me, there are such buildings, occupied by the USAF Space Command and other less public agencies. I know, NASA is a civilian agency, but there's a lot of interaction between their programmes, the military and Intelligence, and there was a lot more then, at the height of the Cold War. It was an old building, predating the Space Centre, and at one time it had been a courthouse. We took down the insignia in what became our main viewing room: you don't want a big American eagle and the Stars and Stripes staring you in the face when you're trying to think in Russian.

Our specific briefs were to gather information, by psychical means, about conditions on the lunar surface and about Soviet progress in the Moon Race. Everything that was going badly for us was going well for them. Our Gemini programme had been an initial success, with Armstrong and Scott achieving the first docking in space on Gemini VIII, but they had to abort the mission with a jammed thruster and from then on we hit problems. Meanwhile Komarov successfully docked with Soyuz 2 on the first such flight of their programme, and by 1969 crew transfers between their spacecraft were routine. Grumman was struggling to fit our Lunar Module on to the Saturn V because we were stuck with the Block 1 Apollo, which was too heavy, and Nixon wouldn't give NASA the money for the Block 2, while the Soviets had flown their *Lunniy Korabl* unmanned on Proton boosters in Earth orbit, and their lunar variant of Soyuz, the Zond, had flown manned around the Moon. They were waiting only for the successful flight test of their super-booster, the Lenin, and that was achieved in January 1969. They were ready, and we were among the few who knew just how confident they were.

In later years Remote Viewing was derided as worthless or even a hoax, but the Soviets took psychical research very seriously and the CIA had no option but to follow suit. Our part of the programme was marginalised, partly because it wasn't specifically to gather military intelligence, but also because our teacher was even less reputable than some of the ones who were subsequently made public. He was a Native American who claimed to be the hereditary chief of a tribe which no longer existed, and also to have inherited the knowledge of its shamans. Apparently his name translated as 'Chief Two Horns', which he didn't care for because of its implications in English, so we just called him 'The Chief'. There was no proof of his origins but frankly we didn't care, because he was the one who persuaded us to stop staring at goats, and the techniques he taught us really worked. But he was additionally unpopular with our superiors because he had early involvement with the Soviet psychic programme, and was believed still to have contacts there.

He didn't confirm that until that July morning when the Soviets re-launched Gagarin. Khrushchev had promised that he would be the first man on the Moon and although the Premier was long out of favour, Korolev had honoured that 1961 promise. Gagarin and Komarov, the best they had, were bound together for the Moon— Komarov to stay in the Zond while Gagarin landed, solo. There had been no public announcement but our watchers knew it for a fact. Jodrell Bank and Kettering were tracking the spacecraft and our Deep Space Network would soon pick it up.

"They asked me to be there, you know," he said, as the reports piled up on my desk. "If I'd accepted, I could be in Star City right now, as a witness to this."

"Why didn't you go, then?" I snapped. On the TV in the corner Walter Cronkite was speculating about the launch, but he didn't know what I knew—so far as the USA was concerned, the Moon Race was lost.

"I didn't like their attitude," he replied. "They're very big on how all men are equal, but there's prejudice just like there is here. Even when I was over there before, and I'd showed them enough of what I knew to be convincing, to some people I was just the poor Indian and they were doing me the favour by recognising my existence. They call themselves Red, but that doesn't mean the red man is their equal. They wanted me there as a symbol, a victim of Western oppression, so they could show that their mission in space wasn't colonialism, not imperialistic—no, just to bring Marxist-Leninism to a poor benighted Universe. Just like all the things you brought us for our own good."

I couldn't say much in reply to that, except that I was glad he was on our side nonetheless. On the TV Cronkite was demonstrating with models how the lunar orbit rendezvous might be performed. It wasn't completely right, but it was close. "This means a lot to you, doesn't it?" said the Chief.

"I believe it's important," I said. "If they succeed, it will seem to the rest of the world as if their way is the right way, the one that gets results. And I've spent years trying to get that importance across, knowing they were ahead of us, with my hands tied because of the secrecy."

He seemed to withdraw into himself, weighing that up, before he came to a decision. "We could still do it," he said. "Not just *view* the landing, but reach it before them, once we can see where they're going to touch down."

I'd had to swallow a lot of unlikely things when I took charge of the Department, but you can imagine my reaction to that. "You're telling me that you can send someone to the Moon?" I exclaimed.

"Not send them, no, but I can *take* someone," he replied. "I've never done it, but I know people who have."

"And why wouldn't you tell us that before, when we're spending all that money on Saturn Fives?"

"Partly because of that," he said. "A lot of powerful organisations have a lot of money tied up in the space programme, and a lot of jobs depend on it. If I give you an alternative, there will be a lot of unemployment and big economic disruption. And what will you do with the power to teleport, once you have it? Just because I didn't share it with the Russians doesn't mean I trust the US military, or the White House. My people have plenty of reason not to—but if I'm going to do it, we need to get it done. The Soviets will be on the Moon in four days."

He had a deal of preparation to go through—not much compared with counting down a Saturn, but a lot for a few days. The rest was remarkably simple: we even had a pair of spacesuits in the building, which we sometimes put people in when they were monitoring Soviet spacewalks, to give them a better rapport. And I knew just the astronaut to ask—no, not Mitchell, he might have taken it too seriously! The one I chose was Pete Conrad, a great guy, a pilot's pilot. He'd flown on Gemini V and been a backup twice, but the word was that he was too fond of practical jokes and wisecracks to suit the NASA management, and that was the attitude we needed for this wild idea. He might even have commanded Apollo 11 and been first on the Moon, if things had turned out differently, but with that mission on indefinite hold, this way he was still the first to walk on the Moon—him and the Chief—and nobody can take that away from him.

Like NASA, later, we nearly forgot about the flag, but somebody remembered that we'd better take one. The only one available was the big wooden plaque from the old courtroom, but that proved to be just what we needed (and if ever the pictures are released, nobody will be able to say that one is flapping in a non-existent breeze). We didn't know then how destructive the dust flying out from a rocket landing on the Moon could be—that was supposedly found out in the eventual Apollo landing by Surveyor 3—but as Gagarin came in, and Conrad and the Chief found themselves being sandblasted, they had a shield right there to hold up. So the rumours about Gagarin's first and supposedly last words are true. As he pitched up the *Lunniy Korabl* for landing, his words in his native Russian were, "This is [a] ******* Tranquillity Base! The ******* Eagle has landed!" There's a burst of static over the 'a', so we're not sure he actually said it. Gagarin's call-sign was 'Cedar', 'Eagle' was Titov's, and Gagarin's garbled transmission was supposed to be evidence that he'd become disoriented. But what actually happened was that when their Mission Control saw two guys on the Moon holding up an American flag, they immediately cut the signal.

The Johnson Centre had a number of lunar shelters on test for future use, and we had enough priority to obtain one. Conrad and the Chief inflated it and stood by, in a clear invitation to Gagarin to come and join them. He had no English and Conrad had no Russian, but the Chief had picked up some Russian during his time there and once they had their helmets off, they were able to talk, to some extent. We'd provided them with vodka and whiskey to celebrate; we knew they wouldn't overdo it, their natural exuberance was enough for the situation. And as they were toasting their success, we were sending TV to both sides telling the bosses what we had done.

Perhaps it was inevitable that the reaction would be to put a complete security lid on it. We expected the Russians to do the same, and indeed they had broken contact with Gagarin, as Houston would have done with the Apollo landers if they had been stranded. What we didn't anticipate was that the Soviets would be so determined to conceal failure—*any* failure—that they would place a nuclear device in their descent stage. If they lost their cosmonaut, they didn't want any future American astronaut paying tribute at the site the way James Caan does in *Countdown*. They didn't know how we had got there ahead of them, but what the Kremlin ordered was that the whole business had to be stopped dead, now.

When we found that out—when our remote viewers *saw* it—of course Gagarin wanted to save his ship, but there was no time for that. The Chief had to bring them all back. They had to leave their spacesuits behind, and everything else except the one roll of film to prove they were there. Even so, the effort burned out his powers—his gifts were gone, and that was another reason why our Department was so quickly dismantled afterwards. Those financial interests that the Chief had mentioned had a lot to do with it, as well.

So there you have it. The official version is that Gagarin was the first man to reach the Moon, but he died a hero. His braking system failed on approach and his lander was destroyed on impact. If Komarov knew differently, he never talked, and the evidence on the Moon itself was vaporised. Back here, Gagarin and Conrad went into Witness Protection, started a specialist aviation business under new names, and lived long and happy lives. The rest of us were sworn permanently to secrecy, and indeed, who would believe us if we told it? This record is going to be sealed with the film in a vault somewhere, and who knows when it will surface, if ever.

So we put Americans first on the Moon, and nobody knows it. Was it a good or a bad thing that we did? Grissom certainly thought so, when NASA finally got the money for the Block 2 Apollo. "If we'd gone on with Block 1," he said to me, "sooner or later we'd have killed somebody." Also, once the pressure of the race was off, the Command and Service Module was redesigned, putting in the SIM bay for scientific research and repositioning the oxygen and hydrogen tanks in case of an explosion. Maybe that prevented some bad things from happening. Also, the people at Star City had seen a Russian and Americans celebrating together; maybe that helped to bring on the Apollo-Soyuz Rendezvous and our subsequent cooperation on space stations. Maybe, but for that, our nations wouldn't be together on Mars now. I can't say, but I can tell you this: by God, we had some fun with it at the time.

The Crock of Shet
Jim Steel

Many stories start like this, with two *disreputable* heroes: a big, tough one and a shorter, smarter one. Unfortunately there have been so many stories of this ilk that all the better heroes have long since been used up, and we will have to make do with barrel scrapings. But lots of interesting things have been found at the bottom of a barrel.

Bobo Getz could have been one of them, if there had been a big enough barrel. He was massive, but not in a muscle-bound barbarian way. Oh, there were muscles aplenty under those rolls of fat, but Bobo was not built for speed. You could only fail to see him coming if you were blind. If you were blind, then the sound of swarming bluebottles would alert you. If you were also deaf, then it would be the stench. If all of those senses failed you, then you would eventually be made aware of his presence through your sense of taste. Bobo had a most peculiar sense of humour.

Sly Slavren was not particularly smart and there was a theory that his first name was an ironic nickname. That was wrong; he was merely the latest in a long line of Slys. However, nobody could call him stupid as long as he stood next to Bobo. Bobo did not know many things, but one of the things that he *did* know was that Sly was cleverer than him, and therefore if someone was calling Sly a fool, then they were also implying…

Anyway, we take up the story of our two heroes in a dusty, southern land as they approached, from the civilised side, the last victualler's before the south-winding road entered rocky desert. The establishment had rooms but, as it rarely rained and never snowed in that barren country, most passers-by slept outside to save what little money they possessed. The likelihood of stumbling across anyone with a surfeit of cash in that area would be, you would imagine, slim. Ordinarily, anyway. Sly had heard otherwise.

The sign said: *Beer and Clothing.* "This is the place," Sly said. "Keep your mouth shut and *no fighting.*"

"Okay," said Bobo. "Busy, in't it?" He licked the palm of his hand and used it to brush his monobrow up over his low forehead. From below, it gave the impression that he wasn't bald as an egg. Most people viewed Bobo's head from below.

"No, Bobo, it's not busy. There's less than twenty people here. However, it's not always quantity that counts… Let's get a beer and see who's about."

"Waurrr, Sly… Look etta big tits on that!" said Bobo, slapping his foot repeatedly on the ground for emphasis.

"That, Bobo, is a camel."

A sneaky smile crept across Bobo's face. "Think Bobo should… buy it a drink?"

"No, Bobo," said Sly, wearily. "A camel is a beast of burden; like a horse. You ever ridden a horse?"

"Tried once, but it kept trying to kick Bobo's shins. What 'bout that one over there? That's people."

"That, Bobo, is a statue."

"Oooooh. It's very good."

"No, it's not. It looks like it was carved by a furious drunk, and the head's missing. Look, you're not going to fit through this door, so I'll get the beers. You stay out here."

Sly entered a low, wide room filled with dark shadows buttressed by beams of dusty light. Even in this remoteness, several of the tables were occupied by solitary drinkers but Sly soon spotted a group huddled around a table in a snug. These must be his men. They had the desperate, wary look of questers. And none of them looked like muscle, which was to Sly's advantage because that was what he was here to offer them. Noticing his scrutiny, the group's conversation stopped and they attempted to stare nonchalantly in his direction.

Smiling to himself, Sly approached the bar.

The barman stopped dirtying glasses with a rag that looked like it had been on latrine duty. "Yus?"

"What ales you got?"

The barman looked puzzled. "My name's not Got."

Sly could feel a small headache starting between his eyes. "No. What different kinds of ales do you have for sale?"

"We only have ale," said the barman, still looking confused.

"No…" said Sly. "Okay… I'll take two ales. One in a pint pot and one in a four-pint pot. And could you half fill the four-pint pot with water first?"

The barman pursed his lips. "It'll cost you."

Sly drummed his fingers on the bar before asking, "For what?"

"The water," said the barman. "You're in the desert now, lad."

Sly sighed. "Okay. Just fill both of them up with ale, then."

Eventually, he was able to pick up the pots and head for the door. As he passed the adventurers' table, however, he swerved and squeezed himself onto one of their benches. He took a long draft from his pint, then slammed both pots down on the table. "Gentlemen."

Silence.

"I hear you're looking for swordsmen."

"No, we're not," said a man in a pointy hat.

"Yes, you are," said Sly. "Are you aware of what awaits you on the other side of that desert? You'll need swordsmen."

"We've already got a swordsman," replied another.

"Oh! Just the one?" asked Sly with a laugh, "And has *he* served with the Royal Regiment in battle?"

"Yes."

"Ah... when, exactly?"

"He's a twenty-year man. He's taken a six-month leave to join our expedition," said Pointy Hat.

"Ah..." said Sly. "Then he'll know us, of course. Outside, is he?"

"Yes. He's putting in some weapon practise. That's what real swordsmen do."

"Okay," said Sly, touching his skullcap to them. "He's the man to speak to, then. I'll go outside and, uh... reintroduce myself to him. I'll see you gentlemen later."

Bobo, sitting on his arse in the shade of a gable end with his legs splayed out in front of him, was picking his nose with a contented expression. Sly squatted down next to him and handed him his pot of ale. Bobo downed half of it instantly.

"Hold on, Bobo—I'm going to need to borrow some of that back. Seen a soldier about here?"

"Yeah. Over in dose bushes, choppin' 'em to pieces. Hey, dis is good beer! Bobo told you, dose last four pubs, they wos watering der beer. You shoulda let Bobo say sometin."

"Well, too late now, Bobo," said Sly, prising the pot out of his big, sweaty fingers. Sly refilled his own pot from it and then checked the inside pockets of his jerkin. He pulled out several powders wrapped in paper and selected one. "*Mister Scrumpy's Surprise Attack*, I think." He unwrapped the powder and poured it into the beer.

"You gonna fuck someone tonight, Sly?" asked Bobo, watching the procedure.

"In a manner of speaking, Bobo. In a manner of speaking."

Sly quickly detected the sound of thrashing shrubbery and followed it until he came to a very recently cleared clearing occupied by a short, wiry man with either a tonsure or a poor choice in ancestors. The man was leaping from foot to foot and hacking at bushes with a broadsword. He was also shouting, "Hi! Ha! Ah-ha!", and so forth.

Sly cleared his throat.

The man leapt three feet into the air and spun around, the point of the sword quivering. He had bulbous eyes and a tiny waxed moustache. Naturally, he was dressed entirely in black.

"Sir! Sir!" he spluttered. "Don't you know that it is dangerous to sneak up on a man—especially a trained killer such as myself? You're lucky my highly efficient reflexes held me back from striking you down where you stand!"

"Lucky me," said Sly, bowing slightly. "Anyway, your party have had me bring this out to you with their compliments. They are drinking one final toast to the success of the quest, and knew that you wouldn't want to be missed out. The bond of the fellowship, and all of that."

"Quite," said the swordsman, taking the pint from Sly. Then: "Who told you about the quest? It's supposed to be a secret."

"Oh, I've been asked to join," said Sly. "But I still haven't made up my mind, so they told me to talk it over with you."

"Really? Anyway, here's to..." he looked at Sly warily as he raised the pot to his lips, "the... success of the quest!"

He glugged the entire pint down, burped long and loud, and passed out where he stood.

"Shit," said Sly.

The next morning saw Sly and Bobo up with the sun, shaking the sand from their blankets. The swordsman's pockets had surrendered enough brass to have kept Sly in ale for the rest of the day, but that had only equated to another round when Bobo was factored in, so there was no hangover to test their willpower. Unlike the questers, it seemed.

Six of the party surfaced at noon, staggering under the weight of the heat as they made ready to depart. Occasionally, one of them vomitted discreetly into a bush or waved an angry fist at the sun. The seventh, whose name according to his underwear label was Hach, Sly and Bobo led over to them slung over the back of his black military thoroughbred of a horse, still unconscious. "Old Hach never could hold his drink," Sly said. "I bet you're glad that me and Bobo agreed to join you now, eh? Well, we're ready to ride if you are." As he'd hoped, none of the party had the heart to argue.

While they rode, Sly explained the 'arrangement' he'd made with the soldier. "Hach said he thought the expedition was a bit light on muscle," he told them. "He'll split his share fifty-fifty with us, seeing as we go way back, half to him, quarter each to me 'n' Bobo. Assuming we're successful, of course, otherwise..." He shrugged fatalistically.

They made reasonable time. The slowest creatures with the fellowship were the three oxen carrying the supplies, the camel at their head to encourage them. Sly rode Hach's horse, with Hach draped across its rump held in place by a rope tied underneath. Occasionally he came around enough to treat the fellowship to a verse of *The Sausage Man Gets Up In The Morn So The Housewives Can Get His Meat*. Mister Scrumpy could always be relied on, but its effect would wear off sooner or later. That was the real reason for the rope. Sly had considered a gag too, but hadn't been able to think of a plausible excuse.

The rest of the troupe comprised Adolphus, the magician in the pointy hat, and four merchants who looked as if they had never been beyond the city walls before, riding a variety of horses and mules. The final member claimed to be a dwarf, but Sly was dubious. Seated on his donkey, his toes dragged in the dust. His name was Robert.

"I don't like the way that your man is looking at my camel," said Robert as Sly came up beside him.

"He's not 'my' man," said Sly.

"Okay. I don't like the way your *thing* is looking at my camel," said Robert.

"Ah... fair enough." Sly looked round at Bobo. "You might have a point there. I think it'd be a good idea to get his mind onto other things. Why don't you go and try and tell him what the objectives of the quest are? Grok knows, I've tried. It'll keep him confused for the rest of the day."

"Why don't you do it?"

"It's not my camel."

Robert swore and, digging his heel into the dust, neatly swung his donkey around to walk alongside Bobo instead.

"Bobo, you know of what we seek?" asked Robert.

"Eh?"

"Do you know what we are looking for?"

"Yeah. Treasure!"

"That's right. Do you know what sort of treasure?

"Eh?"

"Ye gods!" said Robert. "Okay, look... We're crossing the Great Southern Desert. That'll bring us to the jungle land of Patata. The people there were very primitive and worshiped three barbarous gods called Shet, Ashet and Bashet. Shet was the god of agriculture, Ashet was the god of fishing and Bashet was the god of hunting. Now the three groups of worshippers lived amongst each other in a complimentary manner until one day Shet refused to share his produce with his two brothers, and in the resulting war both he and his followers were crushed. That's why Patata is all jungle now. We are seeking the legendry produce that Shet refused to share. It is a copper cornucopia that contains everything that his worshippers ever desired. Recently, Amod over there received explicit directions in lieu of a bad debt, and so here we are..."

There was a pause while Bobo scratched his flaky scalp. Then he asked, "Dat your camel?"

That night, during his spell on guard duty, Sly was woken by something pressing into his bedroll.

"Bobo! What are you doing?" he hissed.

"Oh, Bobo can't sleep on des rocks, Sly. Bobo miss his li'l bear."

"Well, you shouldn't have eaten him, then. Now fuck off! I'm trying to sleep. I've got to get up in two hours to wake up my relief."

Bobo snuffled and rolled away.

Then Sly remembered something. "Wait! Since you're awake, Bobo, there's something that needs doing..."

Whump!

✧   ✧   ✧

Sly was awoken the following morning by a commotion. Climbing out of his bedroll, he wandered over and saw that Hach was now no more than three inches thick at any one point. "Oh, that's terrible," said Sly. "This kind of tragedy happens all the time in the army. Drunk man gets up in the night for a piss, and an ox—which, as you all know, can fall asleep on its feet—topples on him. What a senseless waste."

"He's still lying where you threw him down last night," said Adolphus, glaring at Sly with suspicion.

"You don't say," said Sly. "Do any of your oxen sleepwalk?"

They were two days out when Sly made his move. He and Bobo gradually dropped to the back of the column, then he gave a loud whistle and waited for the others to turn around.

The six questers were shocked to find themselves facing two loaded crossbows.

"Get down off your mounts," said Sly, "and place your weapons and any valuables that you are carrying on the ground in front of you."

No one moved.

"Okay, Bobo. Shoot one of them."

Bobo pulled the trigger of his crossbow and had another bolt loaded with the bowstring cocked before the first bolt had hit its target; a feat of strength that intimidated people at least as much as killing someone did. Nobody was likely to rush them after that.

"Nice shot, Bobo," said Sly. "Right between the eyes."

"Hanks, Sly!"

"Just one question. You were supposed to shoot the most dangerous one. Why did you kill the camel?"

"It wos givin' Bobo a stiffy, Sly!"

Sly raised his eyebrows. That was, he had to admit, a dangerous situation.

"Okay, people," said Sly. "I'm now going to move amongst you, retrieving your valuables and patting you down for anything that you happen to have forgotten to lay out. I would strongly advise that you *not* try anything stupid."

Robert, hands on head, glared across at Adolphus and said, "You're a magician. Can't you cast a spell on them or something?"

"I'm a magician," growled Adolphus, "Not a bloody miracle worker. What do you want me to do? Challenge them to a game of cards, winner takes all?"

One of the merchants started to sob.

"Now, now, gentlemen," said Sly. "All is not lost. Remember that large, dirty puddle we passed about five miles back? That, I believe, was an oasis. All you have to do is head back there and wait for the next expedition to pass this way. Shouldn't be longer than a week or two at most."

There followed much blaspheming and shaking of fists as Sly and Bobo sped off into the distance at a shimmering three miles an hour.

"Sly?"

"Yes, Bobo?"

"Bobo still gotta stiffy!"

They stopped when evening fell. The rocky terrain made night travel impossible and, besides, they were in no great rush. Sly removed the packs from the animals and now was going through them, tossing stuff about with increasing frustration.

"Stupid, stupid bastards!" he shouted. "I don't believe it! How could... who let these idiots out on an expedition on their own?"

"Is sumpin' wrong, Sly?" asked Bobo.

"Yes!" screamed Sly. "Against all established practise, these fools have loaded all of their water skins onto the one animal. And you shot it!"

"So we goin' back fur it?"

Sly pinched the bridge of his nose. "Well, *they've* got the water now, haven't they? They'll be well on their way back to that *Beer and Clothing* dive."

"Wot 'bout that oasis...sis...sis?"

"Think you can find it again? Because I don't think I could. Deserts aren't noted for their distinguishing features. I don't know if you've noticed, but we've been moving in a big curve. The plan was to end up back where we set off, sell this gear to the next expedition stupid enough to be heading out here and clear off with a profit in our pockets."

He gestured at the stuff lying around him. "Look at this stuff! Dried rice, dried oats, salt... anal butter? Who takes anal butter on a quest?"

"Bobo'll eat dat!" said Bobo with a toothy grin.

Sly tossed him the packet and continued to go through their gains. "Books... soap... don't even know what *this* is... jar of large pebbles with a sling wrapped around it—they took stones into a stony desert! Ah! A map." He picked up a sheet of parchment and scrutinised it before snorting in derision. "This is a copy of a fake—one of *my* fakes at that."

"We leaving all dis stuff, Sly?"

"Not until we have to, Bobo. However we do need to find water. We'll head to Patata after all, dump some of these useless goods, fill up the empty containers and get back to civilisation. and first for the chop is that bloody jar of stones."

✧   ✧   ✧

"Hey, Sly, are jungles green?"

"Yes, Bobo."

"Hey, Sly, Bobo can see da jungle!"

Sly stood up on his saddle. There did seem to be a green smudge on the horizon, separating the brown of the desert from the deep purple of the sky.

"Why, Bobo, I do believe you're right. However, we're not going to get there by this evening, and I do not like the look of that sky. In fact, I'm beginning to think that we may not even have to go as far as cannibal country. Smell that air? That's rain coming." As if on cue, a low, distant rumble punctuated his words. "In fact I think it would be a very good idea to get ourselves some sort of shelter."

Sly jumped down from his mount. He had noticed that many of the rocks lying around them had been dressed, remnants of some long obliterated civilisation. Enough to build a couple of shelters sufficient to keep the goods and themselves dry. Stone walls, he thought, with groundsheets stretched to make sloping roofs. Leave these newly emptied amphorae out to catch the rain. Simple…providing they started right away.

"Right, Bobo, start gathering all the square stones like this one—yes, the ones with corners—and bring them over here. I'll start building shelters."

Soon the supply of building stones was outstripping Sly's ability to use them up.

"Hey, Sly, you want Bobo t'build sometin'? Please? Bobo wanna go!"

"Um… Fancy a go at building your own shelter? These big blocks are too heavy for me, but you could manage them. While you do that, I'll finish packing the—ah—important gear."

Sly quickly stowed everything, then he crawled into one of the shelters where he had stashed a bottle of fortified wine that he had come across. It would have been madness to drink it earlier but, now that they were going to be awash with water, there was no good reason for holding back.

"Hey, Sly—come 'n' look at wot Bobo builded!"

Sly roused himself. For a moment he feared that he had gone blind but then he heard the patter of heavy raindrops and remembered the storm. His tongue was stuck to the roof of his mouth, but mercifully he was still drunk and not yet hung-over. He pushed the empty bottle aside and crawled out of the shelter. The rain splashed sensuously onto his forehead and he closed his eyes and opened his mouth. It tasted even better than the wine.

"Sly!"

Sly opened his eyes. At first he thought that there were two Bobos until an explosion of sheet lightening revealed that Bobo was standing next to a crude, blasphemous parody of a man. Its head was half of its total height, with black hollows for eyes and a slot for a mouth. Its arms dropped straight down from its shoulders, its balled fists resting on the ground next to its oversized feet. There was a hole in its paunch that Sly hoped was intended as a navel. It also had legs, but they were not one of its more impressive features.

"Bobo make statue!"

Sly was briefly speechless until the sky opened upon them.

"Ye gods, just get under cover!" Sly tossed a groundsheet to Bobo and ducked back into his own shelter.

"Hey, Sly," shouted Bobo, hunkering down at the entrance, "You like it?"

"It's very good," Sly shouted back. It was a remarkable feat for Bobo. He normally couldn't build a fire without committing arson. "Did you really build it all by yourself?"

"Yeah. Well, all Bobo do wos put da bits together. Arms wos over der, head wos over *der*, feets was..."

"Yes, yes. Very good. Now get some sleep."

Sly awoke the next day stiff and cold, but essentially dry. He stuck his head outside and was amazed. Everywhere was green and flowering.

He prodded the huge bundle at the mouth of his shelter. Bobo muttered a few obscenities as he awoke and pulled the groundsheet off his head. He looked around and growled, "Why'd ya move Bobo's statue?"

"What?" Sly looked at the statue. It did look as if it was in a different place, but everything looked so different today that he couldn't truthfully have sworn to it. "Don't be silly. How could *I* move that thing? C'mon, let's check on the animals and get out of here. We'll have enough water to get back now."

There was no doubting that the animals had moved. Or most of them had. Bits were still where they had been tethered, but that was probably just by chance. It looked as if they had been turned inside out and emptied over a wide area.

"Shitshitshit! This is *not* good. We've got to get out of here now!"

Briskly, they sealed their now brimming amphorae, packed up their food and weapons and were just about to leave when Bobo looked across at his statue.

"Aw, Bobo has to leave 'is statue. Look at way da eyes follows us 'bout."

Sly looked up at the sound of grinding rock and saw that the statue's head had turned towards him.

"Worship me, mortal." A voice of blood-drenched earth boomed around them. "Worship the great god Shet, or die!"

"Fuck!" screamed Sly. "Run!"

The two adventurers ran. When Sly looked over his shoulder, he saw that the god was following, its massive feet pounding the rocks to dust, its head and torso swaying violently. But on its short legs, it was slow; even slower than Bobo. Sly began to relax. They had water, and they were easily leaving Shet behind. They had been in tighter spots before.

It was the next morning that they discovered the true horror of their situation. They were woken by the shaking of the ground, and found Shet barely a hundred yards away. Gods do not sleep.

Onwards they fled, panic and fear piling exhaustion upon their backs.

"We been here before," announced Bobo, nodding wisely on one occasion when Shet was sufficiently out of sight to stop for water.

"And how do you work that out?" asked Sly, wiping the sweat from his forehead.

"Dead camel behind you," said Bobo, pointing.

Sly spun round and saw the expedition's camel, still lying where the bolt between its eyes had ended its life. Putrefaction and desiccation had already turned it into skin and bones. Sly went over to have a look anyway.

"Well, they took the water, like I said, but they left a couple of other saddlebags." He went through their contents. A couple of pouches in particular caught his attention. "Well, well, well… See this black stuff? It's magician's powder. And it might just save our lives."

Sly and Bobo were crouching behind a huge boulder, but Bobo couldn't help looking over the top every few seconds and giggling. They had propped the camel up in a very rough approximation of life and had stuffed it with the magic black powder. Bobo had insisted that he do that part because Sly had bagsied the job of throwing the lighted torch.

"Don't get too excited, Bobo," said Sly. "This probably won't work and we'll have to run for it again."

"He comin' Sly. Bobo see 'im!"

Sure enough, Sly heard the now familiar sound of stone grinding on stone and then, as Shet saw the camel, the low, inhuman voice, bellowing, "Be gone, abominable creature of the hunt. I will send you back to the soil!"

Sly sprang up and threw the torch. The flame hit the cascading powder just as Shet tore the camel in half, and the blast threw Sly backwards for several feet. Afterwards Sly was never entirely certain if he'd blacked out or not, but his first clear memory was of Bobo trying to reassemble the statue.

"Dat was fun, Sly. Let's do dat again!"

"No, Bobo! Stop!" Sly managed to persuade Bobo to disassemble the pieces that he had already put back together. As they hauled the torso away from the head, he noticed something glinting in the stomach cavity. A copper jar.

"What have we here?" mused Sly, unscrewing the top. "Could this be the fabled treasure of Shet?"

Sly lifted off the cap and nearly passed out again from the stench. He swiftly screwed the lid back on tight, then dropped the copper jar on the ground and wiped his hands on his jerkin.

"Bobo," he said, "When you were putting that… that thing together, you didn't happen to take a dump in that copper jar, did you? I'm just asking."

Sly woke when somebody slapped his face with the flat side of a sword blade. He opened his eyes and reached for his dagger. It was gone. He looked up. Robert the dwarf stood above him. The rest of the quest party were also present, new weapons in their hands and fresh mounts in the background. Bobo stood to the side, his arms tied to his sides.

"Erm…" said Sly, "Would it do any good to say that we found Shet for you?"

Adolphus walked over to the others holding the copper jar. "Found it. Let's mount up and get back." He looked at Sly. "You'd better hope that this is the genuine article. It's the only reason that we're keeping you alive."

Ah, thought Sly.

The landlord of *Beer and Clothing*, who had bankrolled the hapless questers' second expedition for a half share of the rewards, was a lucky fool, Sly thought. If it hadn't been for the explosion, then he would never have seen his horses again. If Sly and Bobo hadn't decided to sleep where they were, drunk with exhaustion and relief, then he would never have seen his weapons again.

Now, as they all gathered around this dead bush at the back of the inn, the landlord wore an expression of bemused smugness as he watched Adolphus prepare to empty the contents of the copper jar onto the roots. Sly tensed, waiting for the jar to be opened, for the confusion and recriminations that would follow. For the chance to escape.

Adolphus removed the lid and a green miasma drifted out. The magician turned white, fell to his knees and dropped the jar, allowing the brown contents to ooze out over the ground.

"Run, Bobo, ru…" Sly took a couple of steps and then stopped in amazement. A musical tinkling filled the air and, by some miracle, the stench transformed into the scent of honeysuckle. The withered bush first turned green, then white flowers blossom-ed on it. Soon green fruits appeared and grew swiftly to become golden apples that fell to the ground with a *clank*.

"Ha ha! We're rich!" cried Robert, dancing around the bush.

Adolphus got back up off his knees and picked up the copper jar. "Here's your cut," he said, laughing, as he tossed the empty jar at Sly.

✧   ✧   ✧

"At least de give us de jar."

"Shut up, Bobo. We're selling it in the first town we hit."

"And de let you pick some food from da store."

"Shut up, Bobo, and keep eating."

"Sure, Sly. Hey, wot is dis stuff you picked?"

"Prunes, Bobo. *Keep eating.*"

Hot Breath
Matthew Horsley

I elegantly landed on the overlook, a sheer cliff at the top of a hill steep enough to put off anyone idiotic enough to consider bothering me at short notice, but somehow managed to dislodge a few rocks. Perched there, I watched them tumble down onto the dirt road below and roll across it before coming to rest against the fence of one of the farms they have around here. At least, most of them rested against the fence. One of the bigger ones crashed through, missing a peasant's hovel, to my disappointment, but still flattening a few of the crops before coming to a standstill.

As though that's the worst damage I'm going to do around here.

Oh, they love me in this kingdom, they really do.

It was getting dark. It usually is when I decide to come out and play around with the locals. I can sometimes be seen when the sun is still high in the sky, but it really is very rare and I'm not convinced it has the same dramatic impact. There are those who will tell you we look more intimidating during the day because there's no darkness to hide our size but, frankly, the idiots who say that have forgotten that we breathe fire. You can't beat the cloak of night when it comes to that. I like to think I look suitably impressive silhouetted against the moon, flying high and wreathed in flame. The same thing really doesn't work with the sun.

We like to parcel ourselves out, mark our territory. One kingdom for each of us, or maybe a county if the kingdoms are especially large, like the ones they have if you point yourself east and keep going for a month or two. This kingdom, my kingdom, is called Addolan, the name of the ruling family, or so I gather. A dozen or so towns, one city, innumerable farms, farming villages and farmland. This is it, my scorching ground.

Aren't I worried about their horse-riding "champions" looking to kill me? Frankly, no. The men they send against me are generally deluded, egotistical and in a few cases actually suicidal. What sort of chance does someone in metal armour have against something that breaths fire? Think about that for a moment. And there's the small matter of our being able to fly as well; that one is hugely entertaining if they get close, especially if they've spent hours or even days climbing a mountain first. I'll admit that a lance with the power of a charging warhorse could do us serious damage were it to catch our softer underbelly—and it's clearly that which their champions are aiming for—but all we have to do is flap the old wings well in advance of them reaching us and we're out of harm's way. One day men will find a flying animal that'll take their weight (they used to have pegasi, centuries ago, but of course they managed to hunt and cage them to extinction; for an intelligent race humans can be so stupid) and then they might be some kind of a challenge one on one, but until then they're just wasting our time trying to deal with us using horses, bravado and a long pointy stick.

None of that, of course, stops them from trying. Over and over again.

So why don't I just lay fiery waste to the whole kingdom? Multiple reasons. First of all, I'm not invulnerable. I can deal with a hot-headed young idiot on a horse without too much trouble. Barrages of catapults and ballistae are a whole different story, and even arrows can be extremely painful, especially if they catch me in... certain areas. A few of our more arrogant number have fallen foul of trying to fight a whole army; in that situation it's best to flee, even before they pay out for the services of one of those damned wizards. Because believe you me, magic—done properly—is something that causes us no end of problems when it's backed by the power of an army of little men and their war machines.

If you fly just west of the Great Salt Lake, along the road leading to the Sun Kingdoms you'll find a huge skeleton, bleached bones, half buried in the sand and soil of ages. That was Great Grazorr who thought he could take on an army backed by two wizards. Not so Great in the end. Now grubby little peasants travel from miles around to perch on his bony snout and coo at his ribs, sticking out of the ground like so many dead pillars. I'm not going to end up like that. I'm clever.

The other reason for avoiding all-out war with the humans is that people, especially the ones that live out here in the country, are very, very good at raising fat delicious livestock and we need to eat something. When did you last hear of one of us going into farming? Difficult work and not really practical for one of us, from what I've seen.

In fact, if you were to look at our place in the ecosystem objectively, we're not so much the evil nemesis of the world of men as troublesome but not terminally-destructive fire-breathing minor parasites who give the stupid and the macho something to be killed by. We steal mankind's tasty sheep and cattle, we terrorise the occasional village, we land on castle walls and roar at the sentries, gleefully watching them leap into the moat in terror, and we swoop low over trading ships when the weather's nice and the sea's not too stormy and the sea serpents have gone south for the summer. Sea serpents are absolute buggers, by the way; they have no class, all muscle and teeth and salty breath and they jump out of the depths with barely a warning and can give us a nasty nip. I've had a few nips in my time and still have the scars on my left leg. They eat sharks as well, and what the hell sort of species sees a shark and thinks that that looks like an easy meal?

Anyway, my point is that like sea serpents, I suppose we're just a nuisance. We steal livestock, we burn crops, we roast stupid young men in armour alive and we lurk menacingly but dashingly on mountaintops. But we could be worse. We could be hydras, like they have down past the southern sea. Have you seen what happens when you cut one of their heads off? How is that kind of thing is even fair? It could even be argued that it's only our presence in these lands that keeps monsters like that from spreading. In that regard, I suppose the humans owe us.

It's getting darker and the stars are starting to come out. It's a full moon tonight and the landscape is picked out in silver and shades of grey. In the distance are the twinkling torch lights of the farming village, somewhere where they have some of that delicious fat livestock I was telling you about, and where the biggest threat will come from a farm-boy's bow and arrow.

I spread my wings and prepare to take flight.

It is a good night to make a nuisance of myself.

Danny Dyer Is
Professor Stiles Langstrom!
Ian Hunter

Following their success with *Scary Woman Behind You* and *Scary Woman at the Window*, starring lesser-known cast members from the Harry Potter movies, British horror studio, Toffee Hammer, decided to emulate the success of American movies such as *Mega Python vs. Gatoroid*, which starred former pop starlets Debbie Gibson and Tiffany.

Released in 2010, *Mega-Pike vs. Flesh Eating Mutant Tadpoles* has 1980s pop star, Sonia, a student of Molecular Biophysics, noticing strange goings following a chemical spill at a local lake. She consults Professor of Molecular Biochemistry, Stiles Langstrom, played by Danny Dyer and together they defeat the monster menace.

Dyer's character—actually, Nobby Stiles Langstrom, though he detests the name, Nobby—returned to help two vets played by Hazell Dean and Carol Decker in *Manic Moles vs. Giant Badgers* (2011) when illegal fracking releases an underground gas that causes animals to grow at an alarming rate.

The last film in the series was *Mega-Budgie vs. Killer Pigeons* (2012), in which Langstrom and his assistant, Tiffany Smoulders, played by Kym Wilde, uncover a secret programme to turn birds into killers. The film ends with the indelible tableau of Dyer wielding two wormhole plasma guns that he has invented to send the giant birds into another dimension, standing bare-chested on top of the Shard building in London and bellowing the immortal line: "Die, you feathered filth!"

Sadly, this was the last outing for the heroic academic, Professor Langstrom, memorable for his grey highlights, tweed jacket, pipe, and peripatetic eye-patch, and his habit for keeping a gun down one sock and a knife down the other because: "you can never be too careful invigilating exams".

Perhaps, when Dyer is finished with *Eastenders*, the professor might return. One can only hope so.

The Marquis of Alcatraz
Richard Mosses

"Here. I thought you might like this," Catherine said. "It's a first edition."

I tore through the tissue paper. The book had a worn, green cloth cover on board and the binding was sound. The gold leaf lettering was almost gone on the spine. "Dumas? You're giving me a Dumas?"

"I needed to make some room in the library."

Usually I was trying to get Catherine to stay while she danced away just out of my grasp. This time I wasn't so sad to see her go. As soon as the door closed I opened the book. *The Baron of the Bastille*, by Alexandre Dumas. Printed by George Routledge and Co. in 1857. That I'd never heard of it was astounding, but there was more: on the title page was a round stamp.

U.S. PENITENTIARY, ALCATRAZ, CALIF., LIBRARY

I got a mug of coffee and sat down at my desk. The layer of dust showed not only my poor housekeeping, but how little I now used it. I switched on the lamp and pored over every surface of the book, noting every detail. I opened my laptop and did a quick search. The printers had published earlier Dumas works, but there was no record of *The Baron of the Bastille*. I recalled reading that some expert had recently found and reconstructed another lost Dumas. This was either a very good fake or something completely unique. And, while Catherine's father had been many things, easily fooled was not amongst them.

I settled into my reading chair.

Thomas de Belleme, the son of a merchant, lives by a philosophy of complete freedom. He seduces a woman who accuses him and his manservant of unnatural treatment. They barely escape Northern Italy ahead of the authorities. Returning to pre-Revolution France, de Belleme preaches his ideas to the young and seduces women from their husbands. Before long the forces of the establishment catch up with them.

Their horses had failed them a league before and now a river raged at their backs. De Belleme loosened his blade, anticipating it may shortly be put to good use.

"If you were a gentleman you would throw down your sword," cried the lieutenant, the avant garde of the mob that pursued them.

"You underestimate me, Sir," de Belleme replied, unsheathing. "I am no gentleman."

Baudin, with the practicality of a Picard, joined his master. Better to breathe your last breath a fighting man than to hang from a gibbet for a crime you did not commit. Side by side they faced the forces arraigned against them.

De Belleme parried the lieutenant's testing thrusts. "Why do you hound us so?" de Belleme asked, as it was his manner to engage his foe with words the better to distract him. "What is it that drives you like the devil that you would follow us back to hell?"

"The lady whose drink you laced with deadly spirits is my sister," the lieutenant replied, trying again to breach de Belleme's defences.

"And my wife, whom you defiled," declared a red-faced rogue who pulled up short, white foam at his horse's mouth.

"I only sought to lift the scales from her eyes. I still have some of that tincture if you would care to join me?" De Belleme scratched the lieutenant's arm and leg.

"If there is one here with the whiff of sulphur about them then it is you. You're more sorcerer than man. I would see you burn but I should run you through than see you tried and twist the court with your honeyed tongue."

De Belleme, expert swordsman that he was, saw no point in playing and wounded the lieutenant gravely. "Please forgive me, Sir. It should not have come to this." The cuckolded husband withdrew a pistol from his saddle. He discharged it towards de Belleme. Baudin, brave lackey that he was, stepped between the pistol and his master. The ball entered Baudin's breast. What man could ask for a finer lackey than one who gave his life for him?

De Belleme is crushed. Captured, tried and sent to the Bastille while in a catatonic state. When de Belleme comes around he is convinced he is a Norman Baron and the Bastille is his demesne. A wooden bowl is placed on his head as a coronet by the guards. De Belleme endures the mockery and sarcasm of the prisoners and jailors with such dignity that the situation is turned around. Originally acting their parts ironically, they don't notice that they start treating him like royalty.

De Belleme held court in his damp cell on a rough wooden chair with a straw-stuffed velvet pillow. All the sorrows of his subjects were poured into his ear.

Number seventy-nine came forward and bended his knee. "I was not served a full breakfast, my liege," he said.

De Belleme pondered this for a moment. "Who amongst my staff served this subject so poorly? It should never be said this Baron ill-treated his guests. Let my food not be taken from the hungry but given to them. Here is my plate, eat your fill. Rest assured that the parsimonious servant who short-changed your stomach will repay me in full from his pocket."

> *The guards stood to attention when Monsieur Jourdan walked in. "My dear friend, Monsieur Harlequin," said de Belleme. "You've come to brighten up this dreary day. What do you have for us? A clever verse, or perhaps a dance?"*
>
> *The warden smiled. He had discovered he had a hidden talent for satirical poetry that he would never have exercised outside the prison.*

De Belleme's influence spreads outside the walls of his castle into Paris beyond. After many years everyone is so used to playing their role that de Belleme is allowed to leave the prison to survey his lands. He acquires thousands of livres in taxation and many of the prisoners and guards occupy positions of power in and around the Bastille. One night de Belleme vanishes. The prison collapses into chaos with no one running it and, fearing the consequences, many guards and prisoners escape. Dumas doesn't reveal what happened to de Belleme, instead he closes, incongruously, on a ship heading West for Louisiana.

The book was everything I wished I could write, though my joy in it was bittersweet. Since I'd met Catherine, my own career had stalled, my mind as blank as the page. Nevertheless, it was a great story, full of duels, double-crosses, tragic romance and dark but noble characters. It was also subversive, sexually liberated and mocked power and society—no wonder *The Baron of the Bastille* was little known. It should have been infamous, but I suspected it was either suppressed or Dumas lost his nerve. If so, how had it come be printed in English at all? Once more I came back to the idea that this was some elaborate fake. But Catherine's father would have been more proud of owning an extravagant forgery than the real thing. We all would have heard about it before now.

Did Catherine know? She wasn't answering her phone.

I didn't sleep well that night. My dreams kept waking me, leaving me irritable and restless. I got up hoping that a dose of pure Dumas would have inspired me; instead my words felt clumsy and lifeless, and I could hear Catherine's sardonic commentary like she was in the room with me. In the morning, she was still unreachable.

I took the book to the closest thing I had to an expert. Alexander never seemed to move from his seat by the window in Voltaire's World. While the walls slowly accreted more books, he merely smoked his pipe and was occasionally interrupted by his cat or a stray customer wanting to buy something.

"I was hoping you could give me some confidential advice," I said, laying the Dumas and a pouch of his favourite cherry tobacco on top of the newspaper. It was too early for browsers, but I looked around, just in case. Alexander stopped clearing out the bowl of his pipe. The gilt must have caught his eye. "What have we got here?" He ruffled the book's pages, holding them to his ear. He drew in a long deep breath with the spine near his nose. He knocked the boards, front and back. Only then did he read the spine. I saw an eyebrow rise and he examined the title page. "Dumas," he said. "And yet it doesn't… *shouldn't*… exist, right?" I nodded. Alexander smiled. "I know. It seems too good to be true. But it looks legit to me. If I were you, I'd take it to the big boys and cash it in for whatever you can get. It'll be more hassle than it's worth to hang on to. Believe you me."

This wasn't what I wanted to hear. I was in no mood to go round the auction houses. I had no proof of ownership for a start. "What about the Alcatraz stamp?" More than anything else about the remarkable book, this had been puzzling me the most.

"Alcatraz had a library like any other prison. How else do you reform the atavistic tendencies other than with Kant, Berkeley and the Classics?"

I've been to Alcatraz. Taken the ferry across the cold waters of the bay, alighted at the small dock. After a quick orientation by a Park Ranger, I walked up the steep hill to the main prison building, passing the family homes and the officers' social club. Inside, I snaked through the shower room, with its industrial heads and bars of carbolic soap, before locating the cells. The standard ones were tiny, and in solitary there was hardly room to turn or stand. With the door shut you'd have been in total darkness. If he was lucky, all a prisoner would have had to occupy his time between work shifts was look back at the city; or to read, to lose himself in a story.

The prison shut its doors in '63, the prisoners relocated throughout America. Who knew what happened to the library's books? Perhaps some of the prisoners took them with them. I looked through lists of known inmates of the penitentiary at that time. One of them was John Bellamy. Catherine had the same surname. Her father had called himself Jack, but they'd used his Sunday name at his funeral.

Catherine still wasn't answering her phone. Worried, I went across town to her apartment but no one was in. When I got back home, my door was open.

"Catherine?" I felt like an idiot, announcing myself to any burglar. There was neither a response nor any sound of movement. I went from room to room. Nothing seemed disturbed.

I jumped. A man sat in my reading chair. Without the lamp on, his features were obscured by shadow, yet his presence felt familiar. "Who are you?" I demanded.

"You've read my book?"

"I didn't steal it—it was a gift."

His laugh was loud and brazen. It reminded me of another's laugh. Catherine's father. "No one accused you of being a thief. The book you read is about me."

What he was saying was impossible. "Here, take it. This is all too weird."

"I don't want it back. You can find its secrets out for yourself. Think of it as a down payment."

"For what?"

"Catherine tells me you haven't written in years. Blocked she said. It's been some time since my story was updated. I want you to write the next chapter." It felt like a deal with the devil. "No. I can't," I said.

"Surely you want to know about my adventures since I came to America? About what took me to Alcatraz, perhaps; about what I got up to afterwards…and what happens next?"

I should have seen it coming since Catherine handed the book to me, expected the twist at the end of the story. He had me hooked from the start and now he pulled me in. I had no choice in the matter. Every day he came, we talked, and I took the notes. I've worked them into this book, in which art reflects a reality inspired by art. I don't know if he really is a centuries-old libertine or a sixties jailbird inspired to raise hell by a book he read, but it's quite a story.

Welcome, dear reader, to the Marquis of Alcatraz.

Kikinasai
Eliza Chan

A fly banged erratically into the light bulb, looking for a way into that enticing honey-dew elixir, unaware that it was nothing more than white hot filament. Its drone was the melody of a gypsy song, the percussion supplied by the instrument buzzing in the tattoo artist's hand.

The artist thrust a worn photocopy into his face. She pointed. "This one?"

Kazuya nodded, pulling his hat down over his eyes. He had not really looked. It didn't matter which one he chose. Dark roses and laughing skulls tacked to the walls blurred together. The tones of skin and ink swirled like an oil slick. He winced as the needle cut under the skin of his back. It had been nearly two years since his first tattoo. A tattoo he had not even wanted, but had needed.

The noise pounded through the walls of the tiny venue; clapping and stamping. The crowd was going to go home happy. Their crowds always did.

"Did you see the two in the front? I'd take either of them home," Taichi said.

Kazuya shook his head, caressing his guitar and adjusting one string until it sounded just right. "Don't give a shit about girls. Were any of the journalists we invited here? I gave guest passes to half a dozen bloggers as well."

Yosuke offered Kazuya the joint. "We can't rush these things, Kazu. It was a good gig. We nearly sold the place out."

"To teenagers who know nothing about music!" Kazuya argued, shaking his head to the weed.

Taichi had dropped out of the conversation, crooning the opening chords to their encore song, a background track to the discussion.

"It pays the bills." Yosuke shrugged. "Maybe think about lowering those expectations a bit."

"Fuck off," Kazuya said. "*I'm* going to be someone. We all are."

Yosuke smiled and took a drag from the joint. Kazuya looked down at his guitar, picking his frustrations out in the encore's chords, matching Taichi's melody. Something ran through his head like a forgotten promise, pressing at his attention until he acknowledged it. There, *there*; he caught it. If he changed the key on that chord it sounded like something familiar, an old song his father had taught him on the biwa perhaps. He strummed it on his guitar and it was changing, his fingers altering the melody into something else. It flew from his hands without conscious thought, mutating in the space between his nails and the steel strings.

"Kazu, time!" Taichi yelled him back into reality as they stood to go. Kazuya nodded but still his hands were at his guitar, finger-picking the haunting melody. He didn't want to stop. It was like muscle memory of a tune he knew, its name just catching in his throat. If he kept playing, he would remember it. But now the band would force him back on stage to go through the motions, play the worn covers that would predictably get a bigger reaction than their own material, and the tune would be gone. He'd be the same nobody he'd always been. Mediocre as he had always feared. Kazuya looked up, knowing he had to refuse and yet not knowing what words could suffice.

He used his foot to kick open the door that was closing in their wake. "Guys, I—" Kazuya stopped. An empty white corridor greeted him. Silence. The smell of cigarettes and sweat had gone. And where were the cables, the precarious boxes of toilet rolls and mop bucket that reeked of stale beer, the staff rotas stuffed in dog-eared plastic wallets, the crowd, the people, the band? The corridor wasn't just silent, it was still. A reverential art gallery air. He realized that his fingers were still strumming, but they made no noise; not even the unplugged metallic twang.

He sensed movement and saw that a figure had appeared in the corridor, although he was certain no door had opened. In the white *jōe* robes of a Shinto priest, it moved like a sheet of paper drifting in the wake of a gust, slip-sliding until it was almost upon him.

"Master musician, Kazuya Hoichi! We have heard of your skills! Your talent. We want to hear you play." The voice possessed neither gender nor accent. Its words, Kazuya noted, were ancient Japanese, stiff-backed as the cherry wood baton the figure pointed at him.

Kazuya looked at his hands and saw he no longer held his guitar, but a stunning carved shamisen with tiger claw tuning pegs. His fingers held a fat fan-shaped plectrum carved like a diving fish with ivory teeth. The figure turned and walked quickly, so fast that it was soon a speck far along the white hall and Kazuya had neither the time nor voice to call out.

He followed on, feeling the firm ground beneath each step but losing the sense of where the walls met ceiling and floor. The robed figure bobbed at the limit of his vision. Or was that just a twitch of his eye? Kazuya couldn't tell. He blinked and he couldn't see. He dare not reach out to touch the corridor walls for fear that the contact would make him lose that song that now played beneath his skin; silent to his ears but within his fingers and inside his head, a rhythm more than a melody, a series of erratic numbers and movements. He walked on, blind. Bodiless voices, blaring, screeching, droning like musical instruments, spoke to him from all around, blowing air around his ears and brushing past his face like an itch, buffering him playfully with their sounds.

Play, play, wonderful music, rare and precious, the voices whispered, pushing at his hands with their cajoling words, caressing his ego and clamouring round him until he stopped walking. The shamisen, so silent up until now, started mid-refrain. Music flamed unbidden from his fingers and changed. The muscles in his arms tightened. Sound flew from taut strings. He felt the strain across his range and his fingertips grew inflamed and then numb as the music swept through him.

Chords poured out of him instinctively, as effortless as drawing breath. The song was forceful, waves of sound spilling from the strings. Two countermelodies twisted together in a duel. One engulfed the other, gaining tempo and reaching a crescendo as it twisted bodily around its opponent.

The song crashed to a close like waves battering their heads against a rocky shore. The last note reverberated and there wasn't even an exhale as the adrenaline drained rapidly from Kazuya's body. He was devastated. Slowly, he crumpled to the floor, his eyes squeezed as he sought the comfort of darkness.

"I knew," he said. "I always knew I had the talent."

"Beautiful music," a voice said with sincerity. "Our ancient arts live through masters such as you. Play for us. Stay and entertain us for a week. Everywhere you go, music will follow. You will receive the acclaim you have always coveted. And then, your reward."

"Yes," Kazuya said, his voice soaring as his eyes flashed open. "I want it." *I deserve it.* He let the unspoken words sink in.

"Then tomorrow, we will meet again tomorrow…"

Kazuya clutched the shamisen until his knuckles shook. He had the drive, the ability. His mind filled with the rich possibilities. The light drained from the corridor as he contemplated, turning the world to dusk and then on to night.

A pinprick of colour reached Kazuya's eyes as if from the end of a telescope. It grew suddenly, a riot of shades spilling over him; sound and smells, too, overpowering his senses. Then, flashes of movement and hundreds of faces were screaming at him. Awareness came back with the sound of the bass and drums, the people in the front row and the lights blinding him.

Someone was jamming out an insane guitar solo. Intense finger-picking staccatoed with body-slapping rolls and taps. It wasn't the band's normal style but it was sending feedback through the sound system and the crowd into frenzy. Kazuya looked down. It was him. His hands were making those delirious sounds. His fingers were like claws at the strings and the rest of the band were struggling to keep up. Yosuke had just stopped playing and stared.

With an abrupt off-key slide, Kazuya's hands slipped off the guitar strings and fell limp to his sides. It didn't matter. The crowd were in a dazed state and the drummer had the sense to wrap it up nicely in a flourish of cymbals and rolls.

Kazuya's hands ached like he'd been clenching his fists for years. He examined his fingers; the calluses, hardened since he was a teenager, were bleeding. The music rang through the noise. No, the music was the noise: the applause, the shouts and whistles,

Taichi's under-the-breath swearing, the buzz of the amp behind him and the erratic dripping of sweat down the back of his neck. It was his. All his.

That night, the music flowed through him even as he slept. Tossed between the buffers of melody and rhythm, he woke to find his toes twitching out the beat and his voice crooning softly to itself. He grabbed handfuls of sheet music and let his pencil fall over them, salting the pages with notes and then lines, guitar chords and vocal melodies.

They came for him that night, and every night after. He opened his bedroom door and found the same white corridor, the same robed figure beckoning him. The questions he had prepared dissipated into the blinding silence. He played again, played songs he had never even learnt. He played the koto zither, the biwa lute and even drew a bow across the kokyu. He played to fill in the gaps when he was not speaking or eating because the hunger would never be sated. Only once did he dare pause, to ask if he could play the guitar for them instead. But the voices hissed in the harmony of sho pipes. Nothing new.

It was like being possessed, he thought as he headed for the Shibuya subway. It started to rain and all he could hear were those rain drops falling on car roofs, a thousand tempered taps on a taiko drum. A woman shook her closed umbrella free of rain and the scattered water trickled through bamboo flutes in a forest.

On the subway the hiss of the doors opening made his hand roll and slap against his leg. He clicked his tongue in time as sat down next to a sleeping salary man.

"Is that him?" he heard someone whisper in excitement. A group of high school kids peered over a phone screen then looked up at Kazuya. The one with the phone grinned, brandishing his screen in Kazuya's direction. "It is you, isn't it?"

Kazuya had seen the first video clip from the gig already. It had half a million hits when he last checked. He had not seen this clip though. It was him alright, the day before at a ramen stand with Taichi, making percussions sounds on his beer glass and rim of the noodle bowl as they argued about their set list. As he watched, the viewing number increased by another one.

"Yes, that's me."

His neighbour was startled awake as everyone reached for their phones in bags and pockets, sending a rustle of anticipation down the length of the carriage. Kazuya laughed as he cracked his fingers and stood up. His audience awaited.

Near the end of the week, he was in the coffee shop where they had already nicknamed him Drummer Boy. They had taken a selfie with him to put on the wall, and his drinks were constantly being paid for by other customers. The waitress brought him an empty glass and plate with his coffee and loitered by the table with a grin on her face. Kazuya grabbed chopsticks from the container on the table and played a percussion sequence on the crockery, alternating beats with the table top and the back of a metal chair. The beat slid him to the counter top, the improvised drumsticks travelling down its long edge and onto to leather sofas at the end. He played on the tray of change, making the coins dance. He tapped on the teapot and sent the forks rattling towards each other. Drum-rolling on a plastic tray, Kazuya rang the service bell as he spun and let the chopsticks fall to the floor in a flourish. Someone was already uploading the video on the internet. Which reminded him, he hadn't had time to respond the emails for interviews yet. Or return Yosuke's call about record labels. A young woman sitting with her boyfriend caught his eye and blushed. Kazuya held her gaze and stood up a bit taller. This was it. The cover songs, the shitty day jobs, the lacklustre applause and crowds that talked through their sets. They would stand up and listen now. Others clapped as he swaggered back to his booth, grin broad across his face.

"You, are very loud."

Kazuya winced at the grating edge of the voice. There was someone sat at his table. One tattooed hand circled Kazuya's coffee cup, the other hand, the whole left arm, was missing entirely. A baseball cap and beard obscured the stranger's face. "Makes it really easy to find you." Kazuya sucked in air through his teeth, the discordant music emanating from the stranger like sweat, pulsing feedback off a loudspeaker. He looked around but the other people seemed oblivious.

"Sorry, do I know you?" Kazuya said.

"No. But tell me, do you know *Heike Monogatari*?"

"Children know what *monogatari* means: a story, a tale. What the heck is the *Heike* and why should I care?"

"It's classic literature! You know it, you've been chanting it under your breath the whole time I've been watching you." The man's voice cracked and slipped off-key.

Heike Monogatari was the song, the unknown song he had performed for *them*, Kazuya realised. He knew the story. A tale of warring clans that had traditionally been recited by travelling monks. The balance. The proud fell and the humble rose. "What do you want?"

The stranger took off his cap and Kazuya found himself slipping from the seat in fright. The cacophony grew with his alarm. "I always get that reaction," the other man said with a wry smile. "You've played for them, haven't you? You have the look of a blind man enjoying the music of a truck horn as it careers towards him. They liked my drumming, so they took my arm as a souvenir." He waved his stumped left arm across his chest. "But you! Your smug sense of self-worth is loud and brash. They can hear you a mile off. You can't hold onto what you have forever. Everything is in decay."

Kazuya couldn't take his eyes off the man's skin. Every inch of exposed skin was inked. Tattooed. Faces winked at him from the stranger's cheeks. And the beautiful melodies which had followed him around jarred in broken strings and mistimed beats. Kazuya could not bear it any longer. He pressed his fingers against his ears.

"I, need to go…" Kazuya said as he edged towards the door.

"You need to hide. A fool wants everything now and pays for it all in one sharp fall of the katana. I learnt the hard way. Before I hid they took my arm. So I ran. And never stopped running. Until five days ago, when it all stopped. They stopped haunting me because they found you."

The tattoo artist passed him a hand-mirror so thick in fingerprints that it had acquired an opaque quality. Kazuya shook his head and pushed it away as he had done the day before. He never looked.

The music still ran through him. But he ran ahead of it. It always came back, assailing Kazuya and begging to be heard. Weakness made him give in. Scratch out the song on a busker's guitar or write down chords on the back of receipts before the itch consumed all of his concentration. At other times it simply simmered, low level elevator music or someone else's headphones on the train. But always it came back.

He would get to a new town, seek out a tattoo parlour and pay, beg or lie to get this strange manuscript, his camouflage, painted one square at a time across the canvas of his skin. He had started on his chest and radiated outwards in ripples towards his neck and down his limbs by the end of his first year. Then, like a carefully wrapped parcel, it started to envelope him, tattooing around his sides and back inwards so that the last space of clear skin was at the centre. His back. This was the final piece.

The tattoo artist was clearing up her accessories. The fan whirled behind them, sending the posters of tattoos fluttering briefly in its wake. It was quiet. Kazuya slipped his hand into his jeans' pocket and felt the smooth surface of the one-way train ticket he had bought the day before. That would take him to the next town in two days' time. Reverently he pushed it further down into his pocket.

"There's a live night over at Zepp tonight," the woman said, leaning back in her chair to tear a flyer from the corkboard behind. She handed it to Kazuya as he tucked his ears carefully beneath his beanie hat. "Up and coming bands. Reckon it's your scene."

Scanning the line-up, Kazuya was struck by the name of the third band. He remembered his old band with fond nostalgia. He could still strum their familiar set list. But none of it poured music into his ears. None of it sent him on a percussion trip across the room. The music simmered quietly in whispered breaths.

For the first time in almost two years, Kazuya smiled.

At the door, the guy collecting money did a double-take. Kazuya was used to it. Used to the stares, the nervous laughter and slowly retreating feet. Most people took at least a minute before they even thought to feign indifference. But it wasn't just the tattoos this time. Kazuya found himself man-handled from his place slouching against the wall near the bar. Taiko drums rumbled gently as he was marched backstage and thrown into a back room. The music died and before he could see the occupants, someone had spat in his face. Kazuya blinked through the wet phlegm. Taichi was glaring at him.

"Well look who returns! If it isn't Jack White himself!"

Taichi's hair had grown in the last two years. Age had sketched lines over his face but he still wore the same glam rock leather jacket. Just a little more worn now, as they all were.

"Shit man, did you get mixed up with the yakuza?" Yosuke asked, throwing Kazuya a hand towel to wipe down his face.

Kazuya took a moment before he answered, noticing the other two in the room, new band members who looked bewildered. "Something like that."

"Well, it had better be something like that, Kazu," Taichi said. "For fuck's sake, we were in talks with a record label on the back of that night! And then, you bastard, you just walked out!"

"You seem to be doing alright," Kazuya commented.

"This is not alright! We've been playing in tiny bars against high school bands who only know four chords. The Tokyo Budokan! That's where we should be right now. That's where we were headed!"

Yosuke moved between them, his hands held out placatingly. Taichi groaned and sat down, a scowl lingering on his brow. He pulled out a cigarette.

"Kazu, just, tell us what happened," Yosuke said. "Nerves? We all get it. But an email, a message you know, would've been nice." He patted Kazuya on his shoulder awkwardly. The noise reminded Kazuya of the wooden naruko clappers that dancers raised in the air during festival performances. Kazuya pushed it back, zipping the music beneath his jacket. It quietened.

"It, it wasn't safe. I need protection," he said. Fans. Colourful fans waved across his vision, twisting to the rhythm of the drumming. Kazuya rubbed his eyes and the colours faded. The sound subsided to a dull headache.

"How does this shit protect you? Can't believe my cousin even recognised you under all this crap," Taichi said, grabbing his hand and turning it over and over like he was looking for a secret door. Kazuya rolled down the sleeves of his shirt rather than answering.

"2D barcodes," the new drummer said, "like the ones you can scan on your mobile phone to get to a website."

"A website?"

"You don't know what a website is, Tai?" Kazuya said.

"Fuck off, I know what a website is."

"Hey, it works!" Yosuke mused, his phone aligned with a QR code on Kazuya's neck. "Japanese Medical Association Journal?"

"This one is the BBC website," the drummer commented. In mutual agreement they all had their phones out now, checking the exposed squares of Kazuya's skin.

"National Geographic."

"The Human Genome Project."

"University of Tokyo…what are you, a university research project?"

"It's, hard to explain," Kazuya said quietly. The smiling tattoos of celebrities and politicians all across that man's face and neck still gave Kazuya nightmares to this day. But he heeded the warning. He had to. It wasn't merely his words, it was the noise that wafted from the one-armed stranger: the antithesis of harmony. At the first tattoo parlour, Kazuya had grabbed his phone, looking for something that was modern, something they would dislike. He had blanked. His mind so filled with musicality that everything else was being pushed to the very edges. Finally he had tapped the phone itself, told the man to tattoo it across his chest, for want of inspiration. The music had engulfed him, leaving his senseless to anything until the tattoo artist had shaken his shoulder and pointed down. A 2D barcode the size of a CD cover centred on Kazuya's sternum. The image had been on his phone's screen, a link to a news article his sister had sent him. It had evolved from there.

Yosuke yanked the knitted hat from Kazuya's head. "You idiot, you missed out your ears," he said, flicking Kazuya's right lobe with a finger.

Kazuya ducked and batted his friend's hand away. Grabbing the hat back, he pulled it firmly over his head. "I didn't forget; no-one is getting near my fucking ears with a needle! My life wouldn't be worth shit without my hearing."

"But you let them ink your dick? Then you are a fucking idiot!" Yosuke said.

"Piss off," Kazuya said.

"So where've you been then? The last couple of years?" Taichi cut in.

"I couldn't stay anywhere for a week. I just had to keep moving," Kazuya said.

"And now?" Taichi asked. He had lost his anger, always as quick to forget as he was to get pissed off.

"Now things have changed," Kazuya said, rubbing the dressing on his back. "I can… well, I can do anything."

"*We* can do anything," Yosuke said. He looked at Taichi who nodded. "We'll do the circuits, get our name back out there, make a demo, send it out. Busk in Yayogi Park if we need to."

"Screw that," Taichi said. "Kazuya here was an internet sensation. All we need is to upload a couple of new videos and the record labels will be phoning us. We deserve a break!"

Yosuke, Taichi, even the other two were looking at him expectantly. Kazuya listened. The music remained tranquil. Kazuya nodded, slowly.

Yosuke handed him a glass and poured out a large measure of whiskey. The golden liquid trickled and flowed, swirling around the glass's surfaces and swaying from side to side as Kazuya looked. It was him that was moving, not the glass. His hand was shaking. The squares of black that covered his skin blurred together in a dark mass.

"Kazu?" Yosuke asked. The band had all raised their drinks. They were waiting.

Kazuya forced himself to be still. He listened. It was still quiet. So what if he felt sick tomorrow, he could sleep in, take his time. He was safe, cloaked from them. The possibilities unfurled before him: rejoin the band, make a new one, sell the scribbles he had written over the past two years, get what he deserved. He felt cheek muscles tighten and a smile breaking across his mouth.

"To new beginnings," he said.

Taichi's floor smelt like weed and stale beer. Opening his eyes, Kazuya found his head next to a pile of mildewed music magazines and half a bottle of shochu. He didn't dare sit up, knowing the inevitable headache was looming. Music played in another room and he could hear the bass line rattling low and unobtrusive. It was a warm towel pressed against the throbbing of his temples. He had been catching up with Taichi and Yosuke for days now. And catching up mostly meant drinking.

Kazuya used the toilet and went to wash his face, startled to see his own reflection. For once, he forced himself to look. It was as if a child had drawn across his face with black markers, rendering his features indistinct. The code was a chequerboard of squares within squares. His eyes stared back at him, wide and bloodshot.

Reverently he peeled off his shirt and twisted to see his back. The tattoo still looked shiny, the skin an angry red around the pixelated squares. Peering over his shoulder his eyes roved the mirror, looking for gaps. It was seamless. The joins from tattoo to tattoo were unperceivable. A patchwork quilt made by over a hundred artists.

His mobile vibrated from his back pocket and he answered the call, still staring into the mirror.

"Yeah?"

"Even Taichi showed up on time. You were supposed to be here twenty minutes ago," Yosuke said.

"Chill, I just woke up. You can't rush talent."

"We've been waiting for two years already."

"Then thirty more minutes won't hurt."

"Just get here already," Yosuke said, his voice tense with annoyance. "I can't keep stalling. And put on a clean shirt or something. They are going to freak out as it is with your face, throw us out as yakuza."

"Not when they hear me play."

"Well you have to be here for that," Yosuke said as he hung up the phone.

Kazuya smiled at his reflection, put his shirt back on, looking for his hat before he headed out. He thought about taking a shower, breezing in an hour late and blowing those industry snobs off their feet. But he pitied Yosuke. The bass player needed a break and Kazuya was feeling generous enough to share his.

The music, barely registering on his conscience up until now, had grown louder. Like a glitching track on a loop, the same few bars played over and over. It was a peculiar song, ethereal and full of choral voices singing dazzling upward spirals against a lacka-daisical beat. Kazuya didn't recognise it. Probably a local DJ. He walked back through to the main room and saw a stereo-shape under half empty bottles of green tea. The black box was retro, the buttons markings completely worn off. But it wasn't on. It wasn't even plugged in. Through in Taichi's bedroom there was a mixing deck, currently an expensive clothes horse, hooked up to a laptop. It was on standby.

He opened the window, letting the cool air sweep around him and listened, straining his ears to identify the source of the music. It wasn't out on street level. His bare feet padding on the tatami mat flooring like additional bass beats to the crescendo of sound.

The music grew louder still, waves emanating, ripples so loud they were almost visible as they poured over him. It was coming from the front door. Kazuya walked towards it, fumbling for the spare key hanging on the same hook as a dog-eared calendar. He didn't have to look. It had been a week and he had not run.

Kazuya threw open the front door and the music stopped. Voices muted. The silence was so sudden that he found himself clutching onto the door handle for support. The robed figure walked in slow measured steps of certainty down the corridor. Kazuya didn't dare breathe. He stood as still as his panicking mind would let him.

"Hoichi! Kazuya Hoichi!" the voice rumbled.

He didn't reply. Kazuya shut his eyes so tight that they began to twitch. He covered his ears with his hands, trying to block out the voices.

"How terrible, the great musician Hoichi has gone. Gone and left only his ears behind? We gave him the gift and he must pay for it."

Kazuya's eyes snapped open. The robed figure reached. Fingers of ice sank through Kazuya's hands, through his hat, to pinch at both ear lobes.

"He will receive his reward," the voice said. The flat tone of the clipped words gave him warning. But not enough.

The hands ripped and twisted with equal force. Kazuya felt his ears being pulled, stretched around tightening tuning pegs. With an audible tear, the strings broke. Pain speared through his skull. His eyes closed again, trying to deny the pain, contain the scream that ripped through him and demanded to be voiced. He would not let them rip out his tongue also. The liquid warmth of his own blood trickled down his neck and dripped from his forearms, a steady rhythm at odds with the pulse at his temples. But he couldn't hear it.

It was just noise.

Foreign Bodies
Neil Williamson

Darryl rides a wave up to Calton to confront a ghost. They call them waves for the graceful curl that sweeps up and over to form the cabin. Grown from the ubiquitous substrate of Uide, the vehicle is a sandstoneish ripple that flows as it moves, rushing him through the streets towards his nominated destination. *Just like a taxi.* That's what he and Lai and the other community volunteers tell people.

They call them ghosts because, well…

Darryl leans back, tries to look relaxed. The ride is not exactly enjoyable. In addition to the grinding vibration as the substrate works the nano-magic that allows this extruded city-stuff to move around at such speed, there are jolts and swerves as the vehicle shoots along the avenues, traverses the junctions, climbs the tightly spiralling wynds, avoiding buildings and statuary, stalls and handcarts and glowering pedestrians. Darryl smiles wide for them. *See? The waves are perfectly safe.* In all his time here there have been no accidents, yet grisly rumours persist. It is true that people *have* died after being caught by a speeding wave, but those fatalities are not the result of accidents. You have to time it to the second, and there are easier ways to commit suicide in Uide.

The wave grinds to a halt outside the ghost's apartment block. Darryl climbs out and the vehicle collapses with a whisper of sand, the smell of hot glass. On his pad he reviews the woman's details. Name's Karen Massie. She arrived on the last spin, a month ago. No companions. Singletons are always the most likely to cut themselves off, slip into solipsism—what they call *turning ghost*—despite the efforts of community volunteers to integrate them. Sharing experiences gives everyone a much better chance of accepting the reality of being here and the longer a ghost is alone, the harder they are to persuade. Not for the first time, Darryl wonders how the Uideans failed to predict this when they provide everything else for those who choose to accept their invitation to leave the Earth before the planet is remade. But then the aliens do not seem to have any notion of *community.* Among humankind, individuals are not strong. Everybody needs help.

Best get this over with. Second arm of the starfish, his pad says. Third floor. His boots scuff as he climbs the stairs and he's soon out of breath. He repeats faithfully to newcomers what the doctors say about the oxygen levels in the planet's atmosphere being slightly lower than Earth's, but it's hard to resist the feeling that he's got out of condition.

Massie's apartment is at the end of the arm. As Darryl walks the long balcony, he is pleased to see how many of the residents have made some sort of effort at personalising their new homes, blending colour and pattern into their walls, making designs out of the shimmering glow strips. Some of them have really gone to town, emblazoning the likenesses of popstars and the emblems of football teams on their walls. For others, it's just a name and a number, but any effort to pin their personalities to their homes is a good sign. Massie's is entirely inert. Grey and dark. A month is a long time to be left alone, but it looks like Lai's been putting it off. Darryl doesn't really blame his friend. You never know what you'll find when you go looking for a ghost. If you find anything at all. These apartments recycle their contents with extreme efficiency when they determine that they are functionally empty.

People who drop out can, literally, vanish.

Darryl pushes with his palm, feels the vibration of the doorbell, and then turns to the balcony and enjoys the view while he hopes for an answer. Calton is a new district, extruded only six months ago to meet the continuing flow of incomers, grown in a night to fill one high reach of the geological bowl that the city already fills. He gazes down across the expanse of interconnected star-shaped buildings and the streets that whorl and knot them together between this vantage and the glittering sea. Nodes of gentle brightness that get more intense at the clustered centre where there are bars and music venues, community halls and sports grounds. Where little Lai, always so full of light, of hope, has used every trick she's been able to think of to get people to come and congregate—concerts and festivals, markets, tournaments. And some do, but she has high expectations. It's exhausting her, diminishing her. Uide gets to everyone sooner or later. When you received your visit from the caring, paternal aliens, when you made your choice and lined-up for your seat in the spinship, your one-way ride to a new world, the last thing you expected was to be left to just get on with it on your own.

Darryl knows that the ghost is probably observing him, willing him to leave, wondering why he doesn't, and he tries to effect a friendly posture that tells her he's happy to wait here, marvelling at the miracle of the city and the entire world waiting to be wondered-at beyond its limits. The unfamiliar stars studding the moonless sky. The darkling mystery of the sea.

It's a full minute before his patience is rewarded by the hourglass hiss of the opening door. "All right, man. What do you want?" She's not a ghost yet, then.

Darryl dials his grin of relief down into a friendly smile and turns. "Karen, is it?" She's framed by the doorway, but stands well back from the actual threshold where five seconds earlier a solid wall had been. She's tight, hunched, hands in the pockets of a puffy jacket. Her face is pinched, her hair a shag of messy plaits, mousey roots reclaiming blonde dye. "My name's Darryl. I'm one of the Integration volunteers. We were wondering how you're settling in."

She flinches at his approach. "I'm all right."

"It's not easy, is it? Being here." Darryl mirrors her, slips his hands into his own pockets. "Do you mind if I come in?"

Massie wants to refuse but hesitates, which means there's something left, a splinter of hope. Then she ducks back, leaving the arch clear for him to enter.

Massie's apartment conforms to the standard model—low ceiling, glow strips illuminating the organic corners and easy edges—but it is a bare space. In the corner, where a comfortable couch or chair or bed could in seconds be raised from the floor, dirty thermal sheets are gathered into a nest. Among the spillage from an overturned owl-print shoulder bag are clothes, a zipped make-up purse, a tube of wet wipes, a useless iPhone and charger. Opposite, a neat pile of food tins, peeled back lids bearing dried out baked beans or the yellowing residue of creamed rice. Other discarded packets that had held cereal bars, biscuits, fizzy sweets. Plastic water bottles. Once-familiar brand labels that belong to another world.

"I see you came prepared," he says. "When did your supplies run out?"

Massie is surprised by his directness, but matches it. "The food, two days ago. The water lasted till yesterday."

"Oh, dear." He tries again to not lay blame at Lai's door. "If you'd only come for your induction you'd have been saved a lot of discomfort, Karen. We'd have demonstrated the kitchen for a start." Her blank look suggests that she's discovered none of the features that make these rooms remotely habitable. Then he notices the boxy recess below the wall panel and he sees that it's not discovery that's that problem. It contains a dollop of mealy sludge which is skinning over.

"Yeah, man." Massie's braids shiver when she shakes her head. "No way am I eating that."

Darryl sighs. Sometimes he wonders if it wouldn't be better if the authorities were to take over Uide, impose rule, but of course the Uideans do not recognise governments. As Darryl has heard it, they appeal only to individuals, giving people the choice, one at a time. Trust them and leave, or stay and accept the fate of all those who will not take personal responsibility—the erasure of all life on Earth, including humanity.

As far as Darryl knows every government on Earth is still entrenched, guarding their little scraps of territory with bristling military, calling the Uidean Declaration an enemy ruse, although few agree who the enemy in question is. They try to stop people leaving of course, destroying the ships even as the people queue to board, but the Uidean imperative is strong. Strong enough that, despite all the obstacles put in their way, many people still make the leap of faith and find their way to Uide. They arrive here completely unprepared for what they'll encounter, but at least they are safe.

"The food takes some getting used to." Darryl always tries not to sound patronising but can't quite shake it from his tone. "But with a little learning this thing can make just about anything you want. He dips his finger into the crusty glue, sucks it, makes a face. "Tastes shit, but if we had to we could survive on this and water. Fortunately, we don't have to." He presses on the wall and the apartment's ubiquitous pad pops out into his hand. He taps out a sequence and characters begin to scroll, words in English. A menu. Massie's eyes widen.

"There's quite a choice," Darryl says. "Since we discovered that the kitchens can synthesise anything we can give them a sample of or formula for, people have been filling them up with recipes. It's like the best home-delivery service you can imagine. Of course, we have all the essentials too—coffee, tea, sugar, a hundred forms of alcohol. Oh, and chocolate." The chocolate gets a smile, of sorts. If he's done this spiel once, he's done it a hundred times and, once his new arrivals know they can eat pretty much like they always used to, they almost always soften. "Now, you need to eat. What can I get you?"

"No," she says.

Darryl scrutinises her. That tight little smile pinning down a deliberately neutral expression. The eyes, though, are quick with something.

"You can go now. If you want."

"I'd be happier to see you eat," he says. "I'm half wondering if I should take you to the infirmary."

"You've showed me how it works. I can manage myself." She tries to usher him towards the exit, but the way she stands, fingers digging into the soft skin of her arms, the stern clench of her jaw, the rapid, shallow flaring of her nostrils—these things tell him this is a serious case.

"Karen?" Darryl moves towards her in the confined space.

She stumbles to get away. "Don't touch me. Just…don't. You can't touch me and you can't make me eat, and, yes, I know I'm going to die if I don't eat the food here, but it's better than the way I'll die if I do. Do you think I'm mental? Every breath I take in this godawful shitehole of a place is killing me. Thanks for caring, mate. But all I want is to go home and I guess you can't fix that for me can you?"

Darryl shakes his head silently, knowing that she has to get over this. That it's better to let her vent everything she'd been holding in.

"Do you know where we are? Do you really? We're on an *alien planet*, Darryl." Massie approaches the pile of tins, face twisting with disgust. "An alien planet full of alien fucking germs." She tumbles the little pyramid with the toe of her Converse. Those on the bottom are furred over with striated red and orange. Massie rubs her arms vigorously. "Fuck's sake, man. Alien *fucking* germs." She's even paler now, pink spots in her cheeks. Hyperventilating in rapid pants like a puppy on a hot day.

"Karen, slow down. Breathe."

But she's shaking her head, eyes wide, imploring as the panic finally surfaces. "I can't. I can't." Tears now too. Chest heaving as she hitches and gasps. "Can't breathe. *Mustn't.*"

Hard thing to do, sit with your back to a wall, empty of comfort to offer while another human being weeps out their terrors. Darryl has done it on numerous occasions, although Lai's always the best at dealing with the really difficult ones, with her gentle patience, her sweet stories that bring everything into perspective. He thinks about calling her now, but she's not been answering calls lately. So Darryl waits until Massie exhausts herself, and waits while she sleeps. He watches over her and when she wakes he is still there. Waiting. With as close to a story as he can muster.

"My parents moved around a lot when I was younger," Darryl tells her. "I was born on a seven-forty-seven over the Indian Ocean. Grew up somewhere between Bali, Boston and Bruges. School in California, first job in Cambridge—the English one. Last ten years took me progressively north from there. My four years in Glasgow were practically the longest I've stayed anywhere. So, yeah. I don't really subscribe to the concept of home."

Karen blinks, rubs her hands so hard it looks painful.

"What I'm trying to say is I know what it's like. Moving around, settling somewhere new. Really, it's amazing how quickly you get used to your new surroundings—"

With Lai's stories they often nod and smile, sometimes even look for a hug. Massie gives a short moan, shakes her head, squeezes her fingers until they're white.

"Karen. *Karen*. Look at me. I've been eating the food here for months and...see?" He lays a hand on his belly, wobbles it. "I've put on weight." Her eyes track down for a second. When her attention returns he thinks, thank goodness, that there might be the tiniest connection. "In the twenty two months since people started coming here, Karen, not one person has died of anything like food poisoning, or of any disease that we didn't bring with us. I promise you. The Uideans wouldn't let that happen."

Lai, never a fan of offering unfounded hope, wouldn't have said that last thing, but it's out now.

Massie huddles in her nest, the conflict in her palpable. When she speaks, it is plaintively, childlike. "When you go to Lanzarote and Tunisia and Turkey, they tell you to always drink bottled water and not eat the salad..." Her voice dwindles as she realises that what she knows, her Brit-abroad surety, doesn't apply here. What terrifies her is what she doesn't know, and that is *everything*. She holds out her sore hands. "There's nowhere to wash."

Darryl uses her pad to make the kitchen produce a stream of water, a pearl of soap, but Massie shakes her head again. "How do you know what those are?"

That's the dichotomy right there. The promise and the fear. Darryl never had that promise, at least not placed directly into his heart by a gentle, buttery, smoky finger. He never needed to be persuaded. He was mentally all packed and ready to go long before the Uideans made their global appeal, and every single thing they said chimed with him as obvious: the planet was fucked and human society was too far up its own greedy arse to ever redeem it. He'd jumped at the chance to be on one of the first Govan spins, and instantly adored the place that they only called Uide because no-one had been here to tell them its real name, if it even had a name. No-one had been here to help them at all.

Or so it seemed. He has never quite believed that these benefactors, who have the power to remake worlds and have gone to such pains as to try to persuade Earth's inhabitants to flee their planet and provide them with somewhere safe to go, would simply leave their fragile charges to it. He has always had faith that they're around, watching, guiding. Even if, increasingly, it feels like that faith is being tested.

A few weeks ago he told Lai what he suspected, what he hoped. He'd meant it as a gift, hoped it would help, but he has never seen such desolation, such fury in another human face. He hasn't spoken to her since that night.

Darryl looks at Massie and sees only a middle-aged Glaswegian woman, who has been persuaded in her heart to leave her home forever and is now attempting to deal with the mind-bending enormity of that decision. Bringing her into the fold on his own is as stern a test as Darryl has faced so far. What would Lai do?

"I have something to show you," he says. "It might help." He offers a hand to help her up. She looks at it, then at his face, her teeth fretting her lip; then, coming to some conclusion—perhaps simply that she has nothing to lose—she reaches up. Her hand is uncommonly hot as she lets him lever her up off the floor. Darryl ponders that.

"Bring your coat," he says. "We're going down to the sea."

They leave the city by the south port and follow the path through a wild meadow that smells of pepper. Tall grasses, seed heads knocking in the sea breeze. A lightening of the horizon signals that dawn is close. Darryl quickens his pace. Karen trudges at his shoulder, hands stuffed into her pockets.

"I suppose this isn't actually, you know, where *they* come from," she says out of the blue.

Darryl smiles inwardly. "You mean Uide itself? Truth is we don't know. We've mapped the neighbourhood pretty good, but so far no sign that we have any neighbours here. You want my theory?"

They're halfway across the meadow already and, beginning to feel the pace, he eases up a little. "We know the Uideans are this real caring bunch of guys, right? My guess is they've set themselves up as wardens of all the planets that are potentially good homes for intelligent species. Perhaps they're a lot scarcer than we imagine. Maybe, on the galactic scale, the human race and our dear old planet Earth, are something special after all. I don't know where they come from, but I think they've been watching over us. More closely than we know. I like to believe they still are."

They leave the grasses behind. The wind has stiffened, now carrying a stinging, briny tang. "Do we get to go back?" Massie's voice is snatched, ethereal.

"I think so, yes. Not you and me, though. It will be generations before the Earth is ready to take humanity back. Until then, it's up to us to get on with getting on. Maybe more than that. Maybe we'll build something beautiful here and not want to go home."

He stops where the land crumbles away. Below, the sea thunders against the base of the cliff. Lai comes here, on her lonely sabbaticals. Darryl finds himself peering down at where the rocks meet the dark water.

"It's like Fife," Massie says at last.

"Sorry?"

"This place, it's like the coast of Fife, but without—"

"Without the people?"

"Is this what you wanted to show me? How this place isn't really much different to home?"

"Don't you think that's significant?"

Her face is unreadable. He waits her out, silently imploring her to say she gets it. Looks down again until he is certain there is no unwarranted colour among the rocks; no red scarf, no sodden sun-yellow shawl.

"Come on," Darryl says. "It's nearly time."

Awkward at its best, tonight the path is treacherous with mud. Parts of it have slid away and have to be traversed using the roots of bushes as handholds. They go down the cliff face in one direction and then cut back along the other before arriving at the hidden cove.

"Now what?" Massie's voice has a new calmness, a genuine curiosity.

"Now we wait." They make themselves comfortable, partly concealed behind a thorny bush that smells like spearmint. They watch the horizon bloom. They watch the waves roll into the cove, reach up the beach and retreat leaving a line of foam and black-blue weed. Nature going about its business. Darryl imagines this is how Earth might have been if evolution hadn't worked its magic down the mammalian line— how it might be again once the Uideans have finished their work there. Fixed the planet. Reset it.

Then, at last the limb of what he tells everyone to think of as the sun breaks the horizon, turning sea and sky the colour of cooling shipyard steel and, as if waiting for that signal, a shape rises out of the surf and pulls itself up the beach. He hears Massie catch her breath as she spots the animal. The closest analogue he can think of from Earth is that of the manatee. The creature has to weigh at least a ton and it hauls its bulk up the sand on two powerful flipper-like forelimbs. But, unlike the manatee, this is sleek, a long neck ending in a tapered head, an elegant tail sweeping arcs in the sand behind it. Its stippled hide is deep blue in colour and is veined throughout with vibrant red and pink. When the creature is high enough up the beach it flops down, begins to dig. As it does this, a further two creatures emerge from the waves and join it. Across the distance Darryl makes out the occasional huff of effort.

"What are they doing?

"Shh, just watch."

Within minutes the powerful animals have excavated a pit. As they lie recuperating from their exertions, sandy flanks heaving, a fourth creature rises from the surf. This one, heavier than the rest, labours up the beach and settles itself in the pit. The others cluster around it, and start to sing. Three voices—a rumbling bass from the largest of the diggers, joined by two tenor notes. As each of the attendants sing its own steady, achromatic melody, creating a complex weft of sound that, while never in harmony, is always strangely, beautifully, in accord, the one at their centre begins to heave and strain in the pit.

Darryl hears Karen breathe, "Oh my God—"

The birth doesn't take long. A slippery sac is suddenly evident in the pit beside the mother, who slumps for a moment. Then she begins to peel gummy strips from the newborn, nudging it to take its first breath and, when at last the baby wriggles and coughs, the mother lets out a single pure, threnodic note.

Darryl and Karen watch the group for another half an hour or so. There is little activity save for the mother's tender ministrations to its offspring. Then she noses the baby toward the sea, helping patiently when its limbs fail and it flops in the sand, encouraging at its first baffling encounter with the water, at last following it in as it slips under the waves and is gone. The remaining three creatures carefully fill the pit, burying the remains of the birth material and then follow, leaving the beach as they had come to it. This is the third time Darryl has witnessed this, and still his chest aches with wonder. Massie wears a glassy smile. "So these are the locals?"

He could say *yes*. He could keep secret the conversations he and Lai have had, the long-houred, insomniac conjectures about the extent of the Uidean remit, about Earth's cetaceans, its apex mammals, its clever birds. Conjectures to which he would so dearly love an answer. But what if he *is* being tested? What if, for all the colony's tentative fragility, this a chance to prove they have the maturity and insight to be treated as equals? Not even the whole community. Just him. Just a glimpse.

"You heard the despair in their music, didn't you?" He rushes the words. "The displacement?" Massie doesn't answer, just stares out to sea, screwing her eyes against the sun. But he's started now, and the words come tumbling out. Seeking—*needing*—confirmation. "Do I think these creatures are native to this planet? No, I don't, and I believe that if the Uideans brought them here, to a place where the biosphere is benign enough for them to birth live young, then it absolutely must be safe for us too."

"But you don't know for sure," Massie says quietly.

"In the end, doesn't it all come down to faith?" And that is as plain as he dares to make it.

"Faith?" She looks at him then with such unexpected depth that his heart skips. "You know, when the Uideans first came on the TV, I didn't believe it wasn't just another science fiction show. How could it be real? Even when they started building the ships down on the river, even when I went to watch them take off with my own eyes, it wasn't real. It wasn't *real* until I met one."

"Where?" he whispers.

Karen leans forward earnestly. "The housewares department of Watt Brothers. Next to the towels and bath mats. It just appeared, and it was beautiful. It moved so slowly and the smoky stuff they're made of followed after it like aeroplane trails. It spoke to me, a few seconds and then it was gone. But they were *my* few seconds. I just stood there. My body was fizzing, like Christmas morning when you're five and like horniness when you're fifteen, both at once. After that I just had to come here. Is that how it was for you?"

Darryl stares at her. Is it the light from the sun that lends her skin that buttery glow, the movement of her braids that gave the impression of blurring when she moves her head?

"Close," he croaks.

"It was only when I stepped off the ship that it really sank in that I was on an alien planet," she says. "I'm afraid I sort of lost it for a bit, didn't I? But if I'm not dead already and you're not dead, and those things in the sea aren't dead, I suppose we're going to be all right, aren't we? Like you say, it's all in our own hands now. I guess that's what you mean by having faith, isn't it? Faith in ourselves."

He senses such a stillness in her now. Exactly the way he imagines them to be. Still and wise. He looks, and thinks, maybe—but there is nothing. No ghosts in this girl. Only a simple kind of optimism. He hopes she'll hang on to it as long as she can.

It starts to rain. Large drops booming out of the cloudscape that has gathered above them in the dawn sky. "Ah, shit." Massie starts to pick her way back along the path. "Just like home sweet home, eh?"

They head for home.

Up the cliff, entering the meadow, Karen asks if he'll show her how to programme the kitchen for chocolate. He only half hears, but watches the bob and sway of her back closely.

He tries to have faith, but he's running out of reasons.

The New Ways
Amal El-Mohtar

The old ways were lost on a dusty road between
Orion and Abora, sewn with the splintered skins of stars,
tracked in spirals, where once a small boy
fit Jupiter in his eye. It became a habit with him, the vast—an ocean fell
out of his mouth, and in it he rolled
the planets up with small green snakes,
made cormorants of his mistakes,
until his blood ran cold.
> *Three centaurs wearing bowls of glass*
> *in a vision once I saw*
> *they were a mesh of light and shade*
> *and through the vastness whole they neighed*
> *singing of bright Carina.*

The new ways were found tucked inside a nautilus shell,
spat up from the swell—a missive white and tiger—striped,
a particle from waves. Cradled against the ear it spoke
old names in careful sequence, hummed
a path to walk in spirals, drummed
the silence 'til it broke—and hatched
uncanny creatures mixed and matched
to thunder through the air, ablaze,
to toss their fractal hair, to raise
a thousand voices in a song
of praise, of wonder, loud and long—
> *the new ways will cost*
> they sang as they flew
> but they flew so high.

The Glaswegian Chalk Dust Circle
(Or, My Dinner with Alan Dean Foster)
Michael Mooney

For Crazy Al, and Fergus, For Jade and Da Boss, for One-Legged Dave, and most of all for a Saturnine High Priest of the Damnoni, without whom our futures would have been much poorer.

"Have you seen this?" Aidan shoved a copy of Glasgow's world-renowned broadsheet in my face. I recoiled, partly because as a card-carrying member of Militant I was above reading such bourgeois manifestations of the middle classes, and partly because it had spent the last week in the cludgie, hanging on a hook.

At first sight, it was just another telling indictment of 1980s Scotland.

"164 Arrested after Subdued Old Firm Match, 'No Fatalities' Says Surprised Police Chief?"

"Naw, under that."

"PM Visit to Glasgow Cancelled after 'Die Margaret Thatcher, Die, Die, Die!' Threats Received?"

"Under that, idiot." He reinforced the point by clobbering me with a pillow.

"Hmm. Glasgow Herald Science Fiction Competition?"

"Yes, that. You're always reading that SF crap. Your side of the bed is piled up with militaristic wank fantasy. And you did win those prizes for composition at school. Why don't you enter?"

"Robert E Heinlein does not write militaristic wank fantasy. It's just that guns and spaceships make better covers than existential dilemmas..."

I read the little article. Sure enough, it was a call for short stories. The winner to be published in the Herald. Runners up, a meal at the Central Hotel with the Convention Guest of Honour. Length such and such, judges so and so, closing date...

"Aw shit, the closing date is tomorrow. How the hell am I supposed to write a story in..." I rolled up my sleeve and pressed the button on my watch; the little red numbers told me I wasn't wrong "...twelve hours?"

"What's the problem? I've seen you taking notes in lectures, you can write at least that fast."

"Only two things, constant companion. One, it needs to be typed, not handwritten, and two, I have no idea what to write about."

"Who cast me as Watson to your Holmes? Oh, I know, one is totally useless in the real world, and the other one is always bailing him out with his trusty service revolver." He waggled his eyebrows in a not totally unappealing way.

"My sister is doing seccy studies at Glasgow Tech—they've got typewriters there,

189

we can sneak in. And you know what we need for inspiration, don't you?"

I reached out for him, drew him onto the bed.

"I do, but afterwards we're going for a beer."

Our tenement flat has two great advantages. The first, and best, is that it lets Aidan and I sleep together without anyone else knowing—it would be a lot cheaper to get a one-bedroom place, of course, but God knows how we'd get that one past our parents, or anyone else for that matter. The other advantage, lesser but not to be despised, is that it's a five-minute walk from the best real-ale pub in Glasgow.

An hour later, I fought my way through the smoke to the bar of the Bon Accord. Aidan had left fifteen minutes before me to leave a safe time between the two of us arriving.

I slapped him on the back as if I hadn't seen him for a week, careful not to let my hand linger there too long, and waved the barman over.

"A pint of Virus, please, and my friend will pay."

"That's a pound, please."

"A quid for a drink!" Aidan protested, "What a rip off..."

"Look, this is genuine real ale. It has bits in it." I called it Virus, since more than one pint inevitably led to a call to work the next morning. *No, I can't make it in today, it must be that virus that's going around...*

We looked around for seats, and found a table back in one of the dark corners of the bar. I scanned the crowd, furtively: nope, no one who knew us, nobody who knew we were together.

"Right. Ideas. What have you got?"

I squinted through watering eyes. The cigarette fug was strong tonight.

"I have absolutely no idea."

"You said that already. Look, this is simple. You need to think about the target market."

"Six months working in an ad agency and you think you're Charles fucking Saatchi."

"Well you're not working at all, are you? Listen, the competition is for Science Fiction. That's all about the future, right?"

"Well not necessarily. Some SF can be set in the past—"

"Blade Runner is the best SF movie ever. Was it set in the past?"

"No..."

"Was Star Wars set in the past?"

"Well, that's an interesting question because—"

"No, it fucking wisnae. It's set in the future. And the competition is in the Glasgow Herald. The GLASGOW Herald. The readers are from Glasgow, the judges are probably from Glasgow, they want to hear about Glasgow. You are going to write a story set in Glasgow in the future."

"Actually, that's not the stupidest thing I've ever heard. How far in the future?"

"Well let's face it, the way the Cold War is hotting up, and the amount of nukes at Faslane, maybe it shouldn't be too far in the future?"

"Thirty years?"

"That's the ticket. You can call it: *Jock Rogers In The Year 2016.*"

"I'll do the SF jokes, Twiki."

"All you need to do is write a few hundred words about Glasgow thirty years from now, and you'll be having dinner with, what's his name again?"

"Never you mind. He wrote the book for Star Wars, that's all you need to know."

"Excellent. Whatever. The meal is free, right?"

"Yup."

"Any chance of a plus one?"

"Well the small print says you can bring your wife or girlfriend."

"I'll take that as a no, then." He shook his head, but it was more in sorrow than anger. "Right. Next up, extrapolation of existing trends."

I looked up. This was my territory. And my pint was finished.

"My round."

"Damn right. Get me a packet of fags, will you?"

I lurched to the bar, and just as I got there the phone started to ring. The barman held his hand out to me to wait, and picked it up.

"Who? You want to speak to who?" He held the receiver to his ear. "Oh aye, Duncan? Naw, he's no here. I think he's up at the Halt for their folk night. Aye, he'll be in about ten o'clock, in time for last orders."

I got the pints in, and twenty Marlboro Light, and carried them back to the table, marshalling my thoughts like beer mats. I let myself brush against Aidan as I sat down, catching a furtive trace of his smell over the beer and cigarettes.

"Okay, we'll start with politics. How's about this: Scotland takes the Oil Money and goes Independent."

"Don't be daft, the SNP are a busted flush. What did they get last time, one MP?"

"Naw, listen, Labour get Thatcher out, and John Smith follows through on setting up a Scottish Parliament. They get to run it a bit, cock it up, and the SNP get in. Referendum in 2005, Independent Scotland by 2007, breaking up the Union three hundred years too late."

"Aw right, no chance of that happening, but run with it. Can't be too provincial, though—what about world politics?"

"Well there's only two ways to go. Radioactive wastelands have limited potential for comedy..."

"Yup, we both saw the Bed Sitting Room. Not even Spike Milligan could get a laugh out of that. Then again, there were a lot of comedy moments in Mad Max Beyond Thunderdome."

"Yes, but they weren't supposed to be funny. So the obvious alternative is that the USSR expands as the USA calls back the troops. So Scotland independent, all right, but not for long."

"The Independent Scottish Socialist Republic!"

"Exactly. All black market whisky and Tupolev bombers based in Machrihanish."

"Brilliant. I'm telling you, this real ale is good stuff."

"Enjoy it while you can—thirty years from now there will only be one beer, and Tennants will be making it."

"So it's a Dystopia then?"

"Not necessarily. Because by then we'll all be working fifteen hour weeks!"

"How come?"

"Computers, that's how come. No more typing away in wee offices. Put a big stack of punch cards in one end, fire up they big tapes, and there's your five year economic plan."

"Brilliant. And what about robots? You could have them in factories, building cars and, hey, building more robots!"

"Steady. That way lies the Robot Apocalypse! Besides, getting them to walk and talk will be too hard. And building the brains to make them intelligent enough to learn? Nah, fifty years out at least for that."

"Transport, then, how will we be getting around? I fancy conveyor belts."

"Your sexual perversion for giant rubber bands isn't the point. And don't say jet-packs. It'll be something like it is today, only fewer buses on the road, and more electric bikes and cars. The place will be silent at rush hour."

I was taking notes furiously—this was good stuff, and it was all going in the story. I could feel it coming together. Transport would lead to space, and the Mars Base, and great algae factories for food, and a cure for AIDS... Maybe, hopefully, with a following wind... It was going to be good.

I looked across the table, and winked.

"Have I told you how much you inspire me? How great things have been since we got together? You've changed my life, you know." I reached across, and our hands came together.

I hadn't seen the barman come over, didn't know he was there until he cleared his throat. I pulled back my hand, guiltily but too late.

It could have been worse, a lot worse. It had been worse before.

He didn't shout, seemed almost embarrassed for us, didn't want to cause a big scene by throwing us out.

"C'mon, you need to take it outside. This isn't that sort of place, you know that."

The old guy next to us tutted. Shook his head. A tableful of girls giggled and stared. One of the guys at another table started to get up, a hard look on his face. His mate pulled him down, though. I recognised his face from a club night somewhere, but he wouldn't meet my eyes.

We finished our pints, blushing, shamed. I was the one who wanted to make a scene. I wanted to shout, to say that we were as good as anyone else, that why couldn't we just behave naturally?

But I didn't say any of that. The two of us just got up, avoiding anyone's eyes, and we left, quietly.

The rain was hammering down on Berkley Street, but it was dark, dark enough, I thought, to hide my angry tears. Dark enough, so that maybe the arm slipped through mine wouldn't be seen.

"Don't worry, Gordon, we'll finish the story at home."

I smiled, tried to lift the mood.

"Aye we will, and I'll enter it for the competition, and it will win. Or get close, anyway. I'll have my dinner with Alan Dean Foster, and he'll have read the story and he'll tell me how good it is.

"And I haven't finished the story yet, but I'll tell you one thing. In my story. In Glasgow, in 2016, I'll walk down any street holding your hand. More than that, I'll make an honest man of you, Aidan. You and I will be husband and husband some day."

"Ach. We're that already, no matter what the bigots say." He laughed, squeezed my arm, recovering already, unafraid, the trace of a Gallus swagger coming into his walk. "Remember, my boy, this story of yours has to be Science Fiction. Not Fantasy."

We walked off into the rain, arms linked, laughing. Laughing quietly, mind, but laughing all the same.

The Circle
Phil Raines

At every stop of the tour I tell them, this is where the real magic is—not out there, not in the worlds between the pages, but between us, storyteller and audience, our little secret. A temporary community maybe, a little shelter for an hour or two.

And at every stop of the tour they lap it up—standing room only, everyone hanging off every word, and even though I only give them a taste, the full story blooms in their heads. Then afterwards, queues at the counter, spilling over to the pub where they ask me questions and I give them the illusion of a private view. I indulge it for a while, and eventually I turn the conversations around, get them to talk about themselves, and listen out for little nuggets, hooks for future books that I note down in the taxi. The great circle of writing, stories begetting stories, and I never have to buy a round, and if I'm in the mood, I never have to go home alone.

Only tonight the circle is broken.

I spot her in the crowd at Waterstones. I don't recognize her at first—her hair is completely grey now, and she wears it longer—but when I do, I jump several paragraphs and nearly topple my glass of wine. I can just about get through the local journalist's questions afterwards, blanking out the ones about my next book or how it feels to be back in Scotland. No way am I going to open it up to the floor, but having a reputation for legendary rudeness has its advantages, so no one protests too much when I cut it short. I still have to dodge the autograph-baggers and the wannabes, ducking and swerving around the tables piled high with my latest, keeping my eye out for her but, as soon as I get out the door, I brick it all the way back to the hotel.

I was tempting fate to bring the tour north. But it's okay. I wasn't followed. I survived Going Home, and I celebrate by emptying the minibar. But the next day, Antonia phones to say that a single Scottish stop isn't going to be quite enough and couldn't I just squeeze in that extra night in Glasgow we talked about? *Oh, couldn't I just?* I imagine her holding the receiver a foot from her face as I let rip—no surprise, I'm sure, she's bound to have spoken to my former publicists. But Antonia is patient and waits until I've run out of abuse before she places her shot, saying how much Chesney and the senior team *appreciate* me going the extra mile for the book—and after that, the steam peters out quickly. There's a reason why I picked Aberdeen rather than Glasgow for the tour, but I'm not going to give Amberline Publishing any more aggro just as Walter is negotiating the next deal without an actual proposal on the table. I give in.

And so the Lord tracks me down.

She makes sure she's last in line and, of course, she doesn't want the new book signed. "You never did send a complimentary copy." She drops a copy of my first book, *Time's Pyre*, on the table with a bang. "Don't worry, I paid for this one."

I smile at her because I'm damned if I'm not going to be a good sport. I take off my sunglasses for the first time that evening, hell, I even stand to hug her. She pecks my cheek, though she has an arm between us to stop me getting too close.

"You look good," I lie.

She ignores that, taps the book on the table. "I'm serious about the signature."

"Sure"—and I laugh, so that Antonia and the bookstore owner will think that it's old friends sharing a joke. "Where—"

"Acknowledgements page."

Right—so it's going to be like that. Of all of them, I'd never have figured the Lord would be the one to harbour resentment after twenty years. "And I'll write it out to my dearest—"

"To Mog," the Lord says.

I have trouble holding onto the pen. "Well, I guess that pre-empts my first question—"

"Yes, we're still together. No kids, no dogs." That edge to her voice—I really think for a moment Susan Monica Lord's going to forget an upbringing of private school training and generations of good manners from both mama's and papa's lines and scream me out there and then.

I'm used to scenes—well, it's expected of me at these things. But I really do want to see her. The hoops around her eyes are old mineworks, her skin webbed like an abandoned family home. Yet she's still got that tilt of the head, that intense regard, *You can't hide, I see you in there*, but lifted by a smile, *maybe I'll stick around if you come out*.

I could stand to be publicly humiliated to see that look. "So come on—your second question, Liddy."

Liddy. No one calls me that anymore. "Sure—and why not a second, maybe a third or fourth over a drink? The Griffin's still round here, isn't—"

"And the answer is—yes, I'm fine. I'm doing fine enough." She touches my hand. "Now ask me about Mog."

"Okay. How's—"

"He's ill. Really ill."

"Ah. I'm sorry."

"Sure. You need to come."

"I've got a free few days in—"

"Now. Let's go."

Of course. I copy her number down, apologizing when she says it hasn't changed and I have to get her to repeat it. I explain I have to make nice with my crowd a while longer, an hour tops, and with perfect timing, a gang of fans swoop in when they see me looking around. The Lord is going to say something else, but the moment's snatched, and after several minutes, she retreats from the bookstore. I think she might be hanging around outside, but when I turn down the drink with Antonia and the organizer, the coast looks clear all the way back to where I'm staying. I nearly get lost, relying on a knowledge of streets that changed years ago, but I make up the time at the hotel. No minibar jubilee this time. Ten minutes, packing, settling the bill, and down the hill to the station, throwing away the paper with her number on it.

Central is swirling with commuters. This is more like it, surrounded by people who have better places to be. I scan the faces. Stop it, I tell myself. The Lord isn't going to stalk me.

Except—there, in Costa's, waiting to get a coffee.

Is it really her? I can't be sure at this distance, but I don't want to chance getting closer. How did she do that? What am I going to do?

What would Lexter Manson do? Lexter Manson would flick away the sweat. He wanders over and tell her to fuck off. He would have a word with the station police about that woman with the suspicious bag. He would wave as he strolled off to his platform. But in Glasgow, Lexter Manson is Liddy, and Liddy wants to run.

Tell a story. Just tell a story. *Calmly, quickly, he let his training kick in and he hurried out of the station. On the way over to Buchanan Street, he had the hint of a plan, and by the time he was crossing Red Square, he knew how to ditch his pursuer. Trains ran south from Edinburgh as well, and a connection from Queen Street would only add an hour.*

Safe now. I let out a long breath and pop into WH Smith at Queen Street. Out of habit, I check the bestsellers. There's a new one there I don't recognize—*Traitors Fall*—and I read the back of it. *When Lester Manning betrayed his fellow spies all those years ago, Sarah Madison Link was determined to hunt him down and bring him to justice. When she saw him years later at Quantrain Street station, she knew fate had given her—*

Lester Manning, Sarah—LM, SML, Q Street—

Everyone's staring as I throw the book away and bolt out of the shop. Out of the station, up the back past what used to be Avalanche Records, finding my way around a new shopping centre to the bus depot. Chill. I can break the journey in Manchester or somewhere.

There's a bus leaving in ten minutes, I can get my ticket on board—but no, I remind myself: Lexter Manson style. Make it your story. *He went up to the ticket office. She wasn't there. She wasn't anywhere in the station.*

Lexter Manson recounts his daring escape from Glasgow. A few minutes left, and Lexter Manson would know there was plenty of time to get a beer for the journey. In the café, I joke with the girl at the counter. I'm still looking around out of habit, and I tell myself to relax when I notice the till receipt has something written on the back.

A number.

I remember it this time.

I get into the taxi—nearly jump out again when the driver turns around, but it isn't, it isn't. I have enough cash for Edinburgh.

But I give the address instead. The address is something I've never forgotten.

The body can remember a dance years later if you start off with the right moves. Just a step to the left, then a turn to the right, the hands find the hips and it all comes back. But change one part, break the rhythm, everything trips. Staring out of the taxi window, glimpsing a shop front or a pub from my past, I start tapping on the door handle, but there are mystery blocks of concrete and time erupting at corners and I've no idea where I am until the driver snorts and repeats, "This is it."

When I knock, I almost feel like I should be asking for help, directions on how to get back to the world I know. The Lord seems genuinely surprised when she opens the door. For a second, I almost believe this really isn't some weird trap they've concocted, and I nearly spit out, *What, you really didn't expect me to come?*

But instead, I say, "Okay, you win. I won't leave until I see Mog."

She frowns, but steps aside, and I enter into 45 Foxglove Terrace for the first time since 1997. The tiny tunnel of a hallway still cramps sound and vision, coats and shoes crowd from the walls just as they've always done. My body remembers this, shrivelling into itself, careful where I step. And my head remembers every single time I've walked this hallway, maybe because it radiated such a feeling of being a home and I've always felt anything but in need of a home, maybe because I was afraid if I touched anything here, something deeper would have touched and claimed me—or maybe it was all just bullshit casting backwards.

The Lord takes me into the front room. It's their house now—I sense that immediately—but there's something familiar about the sudden feeling of space, exploding up and out. Lexter reminds me. *The shadows of the untrimmed ivy outside, like flames across the wallpaper on summer days, the shadows of bottles and books rising higher than the ceiling could possibly allow on winter nights. Things had changed: framed pictures where there used to be posters, nicer sofas. But there were still the overlapping Persian rugs and quilted blankets, coating everything with exotic possibility. Out of the corner of his memory, he saw Tim sliding off the settee with the giggles as he couldn't quite reach the spliff Liddy was holding, Cass talking about another bad date, teary to start with but quickly falling in love with the telling of it. And of course, the scripts in their hands—Cass's embroidered with doodles and love hearts, Tim's with just a single word here and there in faded pencil, the Lord's crabbed with analysis and pointers, and Liddy's underlined with the phrases he could nick.*

Mog never did bring his own copies of the stories.

"Seven weeks now." I must have asked a question because the Lord is explaining this to me. "That's from the diagnosis, but Christ knows how long before that. You can't tell with Mog. You remember that, right? You can't tell."

I nod because it's what she needs, and I put my hand on her elbow, because I think it's what I need. "We talked about chemo—not really to stop it, just to make it easier on—well, chemo wasn't going to make anything easier."

"What kind of—I mean, is it spreading?"

"Liver. I know—doesn't drink, doesn't smoke. It's in his lymph nodes now."

"Jesus. So—months? Or—"

The Lord shrugs, and then gives me a good hard look. "Not long enough for you to duck out of this one, Liddy."

And right on cue, there's a rap on the floor above us, twice, a proper summoning sound. And the Lord grabs my hand, grips it just short of a death squeeze and drags me upstairs. And before I can gather myself she throws me straight into Mog's room.

The one big change in the house—the bedroom and boxroom on the top floor have been knocked together. At first, it looks like nothing else has changed—bed still below the window, and I remember reaching up to pull the curtains closed while someone— I'd like to think the Lord, but probably Cass—was murmuring beside me. There's murmuring now, but not one voice—hives of them, televisions, radios and tablets lining the chests of drawers and tables. I nearly trip over the medusa cabling, reaching out to, then almost toppling, a pillar of colour supplements and free magazines by the door. All around: soaps, documentaries, phone-in shows. All across the bed: celebrity profiles, blogs, true tales. I only pick out Mog when the Lord goes to the bedside and finds a human hand in this mess.

God, he's looking dapper—the Lord's obviously grooming him. Good hair—some white, but just as cheeky curly as way back, like the accidental explosion from a kid's prank gone wrong. But the skin is shiny, sucked in at the cheekbones, and he's lost in the black cable-knit sweater. His eyes are closed, but he smiles the same idiot smile he did the last time I saw him. The Lord bends her head down to him: she's whispering, he's whispering. There's a routine in their tenderness. I really don't want to be here.

Perspective feels wonkier the longer I stand. There's a slow tipping and I reach behind me to find something to hang onto. Crazy, this vertigo—I'm terrified I'll leap straight into this. I make a pathetic wave—*not a good time, maybe?*—but the Lord breaks their privacy, signals me over. I tiptoe.

"Christ, Mog. This is a thing." Then to the Lord: "Think we should turn it down here? Can he hear me?"

"He hears everything."

"Yeah, but he can't be listening—"

Mog's hand takes mine—it's dry and gentle, but still I cry out and have to sit down in a chair by him. He whispers to me, too low to make out. "So Don Corleone," I joke. "Are you going to make me an offer I can't refuse?"

He doesn't laugh but his lips twitch and the eyes almost open. That last time in this room, I was panicking so much I could smell how scared I was, and now I want to gag again.

Memory lane, but not the path I'm used to travelling when I make my occasional trip to the past. This isn't the one where I outgrew the Circle and shed the past in a one-er, realizing that there were no half-measures and transitions, and fuck them if they didn't understand the importance of a clean break. This is the one with a dark secret, the guilt raddling away at me, the little poison that keeps me away from Glasgow but curdles my dreams. Flashbacks of the women who got close enough to ask and me snarling, of avoiding interviews and when I finally acquiesce, losing it at a misheard question by some blogger before I went off on one and smashed stuff. *But you are back here, really here, and Mog's ready at the confessional, waiting with absolution. And all you have to do is—*

That's not how it happens. Don't listen, I tell myself. He's whispering—

Take his hand, and listen to what he—

This is bullshit. And aloud: "This is bullshit."

"Liddy, what are—"

I just about jump up. He's still whispering, my head is swirling—but I shake that damned voice away. "Look, man, I'm sorry about the cancer, but that's no fucking excuse. Leave me alone."

My dramatic exit, but my head's fucked with the Mog Effect, and I trip over the vines underfoot. I can hear the hounds in the distance. *You pick up the hem of your skirt. Horses now, not so distant. The estate boundary can't be far. Keep running—*

Galloping across one of the screens. Some old movie. "No is no," I tell him.

I steady myself on the doorframe, cool stone, looking down to the rocks below. *Whistles, then sirens. Or is that the wind across the cliff face? Is it forward, or back to the cells? You can't face solitary again. But no one's ever climbed down—*

"Fuck this," and I leave the room, staggering down the steps as the Mog Effect and the Lord's shouts recede. I'll escape on my own terms, just like I did before. My head won't stop throbbing, but it's not the first time I've had to negotiate this staircase under the influence. Once, Tim stood at the bottom, me suddenly petrified by heights, but he still coached me down the stairs like an amateur landing a jumbo jet. Independently, we both used that scene in stories for the Circle, and while his was shit, it was way better than what I'd done with it, so I cut his scene out for my clippings file. The Lord had been forensic in her analysis of the differences between them—*now I don't want to confuse the writer with the narrator here, but one of you appears to be a sharp observer of human foibles and the other comes across as a twat.* Cass hated them both because we hadn't invited her over the night in question while Mog was just cryptic and tangential in his remarks as usual. I put my hands behind my head and smirked, until the Lord kicked me and someone said, *Recreate the scene now,* and I said, *We aren't drunk enough,* so Tim broke out the cider. We never made it to the staircase and I dozed off on the couch, only waking when Cass prods me hard enough to ask for a light.

"Liddy, I bet you've you been sleeping here secretly all this time." I reach in my jacket pocket for matches that aren't there, haven't been for years. "Cass?"

"As if there could be any question. I'm almost insulted, Liddy."

I rub my eyes. Here and now. How long's it been?

Cass is real. She's puffed out a lot—her face, round the waist—but she still looks like a cherub. The dramatic vampire-black hair is now rainbow dreads and ribbons, but her face is just as corpse-white and the eyebrows plucked to keep her gaze intense.

"So the band's getting back together." I push myself up on the couch. "Tim too?"

"He's around somewhere." Cass waves an arm to a corner of the room—new tattoos I see, some kind of flower-vine-skull thing trailing up her wrist. "You look different from the jacket photos."

"Older, right?"

"Younger. But geekier."

"Localized effect, I reckon."

"Localized—ah, Mog. Yeah, the place is pretty thick with the good old days. But there are limits to what Mog can do." Cass pats her belly. "He can shed the years, but not the pounds."

"How long you been here?"

Cass laughs, and the sound triggers a wave of flashbacks. The first time we met, I found the sound so annoying, I almost decided not to come back, wouldn't have if I hadn't been intrigued by the Lord's iciness. A time later, arm in arm after the reading by that hack bestseller writer—what was her name now?—and each time she laughed, I laughed too. Then, the aftermath of that Christmas party, snogging, and the laugh becoming all breathy and muttering.

"Earth to Liddy." I blink at Cass. Does it feel lighter outside? How long was I out this time? "Don't worry—it's happening to all of us. Nostalgia's haywire in here."

My body is fossilized from sleeping wrong. "Did Susan bring you here too?"

"Sure, she emailed about Mog." For a moment, I'm embarrassed I had to be hunted down in person. "Now he won't let us go. Every time I head for the front door I get lost in another memory. If I stay in this room, I can just about stick to the present."

"Really? How? It's like trying to surf. The waves keep knocking me over."

"Oh, just a trick I've learnt over the years." A knowing grin. "I'll show you."

Cass leans over to kiss my forehead. Her perfume is a Doc Martin kick. When I regather, I'm remembering the night we slept together in the bed upstairs. I reached up to pull the curtains closed, and Cass snuggled under the hook of my arm. We stayed there for hours, and ignored the what-the-fuck looks from the others in the kitchen. What do you want to do today? Whatever it was, we held hands through it, and the days after. Two amazing weeks—until one Tuesday, Cass sat me down in Kelvingrove Park and with practiced kindness, explained that she didn't want to ruin our friendship. We both tried to stay cool about it, but after the *ritual* and the business with Mog, then the Lord seeing that proof copy of *Time's Byre* and it all coming out, the book deal, the notes I'd been taking of their stories—Cass just erupted, a fury that scared the others and sent me fleeing from Glasgow. But she followed me, waiting in my dreams, sneaking into any significant female character in my books, haunting me until I came back here, and here she was, at last, after all these years, my love, my heart made whole at last—

Whoa, whoa, whoa. "Bloody hell!" I bend over, trying to retch.

I'm shaking from the loss of control. *So that's what it feels like to be told*, I think ruefully. It would be Cass who suckers me where Mog failed.

I can barely speak. "Christ, you're as bad as Mog."

She giggles, amused by my outrage. "You should talk. *One of the most exciting storytellers of this generation*—that's how it goes, right? Looks like he can dish it out but he can't take it."

"Yeah, and it looks like you've had practice."

"Not my fault you don't like girls that take charge."

"That what you've told the boys all these years?"

Cass doesn't answer. Her lips crunch to a dangerous line. *One of the most exciting storytellers of this generation* can recall her vampire romances, how she always cast herself as the star-crossed heroine forced to choose which doomed love to follow. Lexter Manson fills in the gaps. *Over the years, the story got stronger, putting down deeper roots, until its fully-leafed crown blotted out the sky. Imagine her at any point, and she had not changed. She probably had her own table in her favourite restaurant, a wink from the owner as she took another mesmerized boy back home and a shrug when she returned a few weeks later, bragging how none of them were ever enough as the owner poured the first glass and left the bottle at the table.*

I look at my watch. Six-thirty in the morning or six-thirty in the evening? Friday or Saturday? I'm starving. Sunday?

"Come on, Cass, this is nuts. How long's he going to keep us here? What's this about? Mog just missed us?"

No. That's not it at all.

Both our heads turn at the same time, facing different points in the room. Not quite a voice—but the words are there, low in the world's mix, piggy-backing the clicks and shushes of the room.

"*Tim?*"

Maybe in the shadows over there. Maybe if I look away just far enough to let him flicker at the edge of my eye.

"Are you here, Tim?"

A thickening of focus. Of course Tim's here. He's been here all the time, and we just haven't noticed.

"How you been, mate?"

A haze of images, cards flicked quickly, the magician only letting you see the ones he wants you to see. Lexter picks up the story: *sitting in corners, eating the food that's left or finishing pints, slipping into hotels, sleeping and washing in empty rooms, taking clothes to the changing rooms, no one stopping him as leaves the shop. Yeah, don't mind him.*

"Ah, Jesus, Tim. What happened?"

The deck is withdrawn. The magician pulls his cloak tight. A long moment that bleaches what came before. "Sorry, what were you saying, Cass?"

She snaps back too. "What?"

"I—ah. Asked about Mog?"

"Did you?"

And the Lord comes into the room at just that moment, because timing was always her thing. She sits in the chair that was her throne back in the day, and it's silent for a while, as if we're waiting for someone to volunteer their story for crit first.

"Sorry," she says. "I didn't mean to be so long. Mog doesn't appreciate time the way the rest of us do."

She looks tired, like she hasn't a good night's sleep in decades. I want Lexter to tell her story as well, but that would mean telling *their story*, and I'm not ready to hear about the Lord-and-Mog. "So what's going on?" I ask.

"He's dying."

"Normally the wake happens after the funeral."

She swallows what she was going to say first. "We have to decide now."

"Decide what?"

This is dragging it out of the Lord, and I can see that all she wants is to be left in peace. She always hated spelling out everything.

What she means is decide which one should take his place.

Another voice, but ever so faint. He's beside me, and if I reach out I can touch Tim's shoulder. There's a trace smell of fresh earth and rushed cologne. *How does he do that?* I think, then, of course, *How can I stop him?* I reach into my pocket, find the scrap paper I always have with me.

"The Story Whisperer," Cass says.

I put away my pencil. "Story what?"

"What I call him." A very Cass name, and the Cass Effect must still be working because now I can't think of Mog as anything but the Story Whisperer.

"Look, he made the choice."

"And the rest of us reaped the benefits," the Lord says. "It's someone else's turn now."

"Well, maybe it doesn't have to be anyone's turn."

You know that can't happen. There has to be a Story Whisperer.

"I know nothing of the sort, Tim! Mog chose. Fine. Thank you, really, thank you, but I'm sure he had his reasons. He dies, well then, I'm sorry, but it's been a good run for all of us."

"You don't mean that, Liddy." Cass puts her hand in my jacket pocket, just like she did at the Christmas party.

"Stop it, Cass. All of you. So there won't be a Story Whisperer. We'll live."

"He won't let us go," the Lord says, barely able to stay awake in the chair. "He can't. Until someone agrees."

"Then you do it," I snarl. "In sickness and in health, right?"

Her face—it changes so quickly. The years have scraped away the camouflage, making it easy for her emotions to fly straight out of her. "You really think I wanted all of this, you, everything back? Mog is going to die. If I could, if there was any way I could have done it myself—"

But she won't let herself cry—never before, not now. "Our stories are too—tangled. I can't. I'm sorry."

She stands, sways for a few seconds on her feet, and heads back up to the bedroom. I can just about imagine her going up those stairs, with trays of food, with clean diaper pads, with a daily catechism of why she's doing this and why she will always do this, knowing that every thought started with *we* now, never *I*.

That sets off Cass, and then it's back and forth, back and forth between us, just like that last time we were together—*Mog didn't sacrifice himself for* you *to steal our stories* and *You never really gave a shit about the Circle, or any of us, did you?* and all of it. It rages on and on until the Lord shouts from the top of the stairs, "Stop! For God's sake, just stop!" Cass leaves me to scavenge spare sheets and blankets.

I want to keep on shouting, but I'm exhausted too. I make one attempt on the front door, and it opened to let in the Lord's parents, goggling at me as I stood there with the joint in my hand and me thinking, This is the shittiest farce in the world, and I retreat from the door, and after a few more steps, the memory. My phone doesn't have a signal, of course. I think about taking a knife from the kitchen and showing them who they're messing with, but Lexter can't convince me with that story, with any story right now, and before I can catch up with what I'm doing, there's a nice little nest of blankets and cushions on the couch and I don't remember my head hitting the sheet.

My best stories come at the edge of sleep. I want to leap out of consciousness, but my brain nags me, *Just one more, you'll really want to hear this one.* No wonder my eyes are cave-set with circles. No wonder I don't like to spend the night alone.

I knew this one was coming, ever since I stepped into the house. As soon as the door opened, a whisper, *Do you remember the first time that door opened?* We'd all responded separately: Mog and Cass from the invite going around the University's creative writing course, Tim through word of mouth at a con, me, the local boy, from a flyer in a comics shop in town. The Lord was nervous when she greeted us in the house her parents had bought for her, trying to be matter-of-fact about being serious about stories, but still apologizing for how there was no tutor for this, it would all be self-crit. Cass jumped on the barricades first—*We'll teach ourselves!*—and Mog said, *How about next week? I've got a story ready,* and the Lord said, *Me too,* and didn't the two of them lock eyes there and then.

Lexter picks up the memory, works it. *Mog's first story was too unusual for them, and no one got their footing in it—but it didn't matter, it wasn't boring. The Lord brought a rambling ghost story, but they were all convinced there was a better one trying to get out. That was how it was for the first few months: they all had better stories trying to get out. That might have been the same story over and over for Cass, depending on what part of the cycle she was in her latest romance, or Tim doing his damnedest to hide what were obviously autobiographical tales, or the Lord stumbling her way to something that wanted to be a novel, or Mog with his what-the-fuck head-scratchers—but they all had that urge to tell stories.*

Liddy was the quickest to learn—zero to sixty with his first sale to Interzone *before the end of that first year. When he got the acceptance letter, they all went out to celebrate at the pub that Friday, then back to the Lord's with a carry-out, and after that, they were sharing stories every week, whether there was a formal meeting or not, whether it was typed out and photocopied for everyone or they just recounted stories from what had happened to them that week or what they had seen on TV.*

Two years. Stuff happened—a little soap opera, who slept with who broke up with who, all remembered in insistent detail as I try to sleep, but I know where this is going. I can skip ahead.

It was his suggestion. They all knew others who had tried it. They had gone to workshops at cons, grilled writers about it at readings, so no one needed persuading. But he was the one to say it was time to spin the Circle a little faster, and because everyone could feel that they were just short of that place where storytelling was effortless, where the stories just poured out, no one questioned his motivation. But his novel had stalled, a quilt of stolen parts, and he knew it needed something else, something he could not get on his own, but through the group; something the group could not get itself, but through magic.

The only magic Liddy had ever found was through stories, so he did what he had always done, and told himself a story about magic. Wouldn't it be great if there was a guy? He told it to himself night after night, letting the details shift and the structure warp until finally he found a version that worked. The day after the last time he told it, he got the name of someone in Coventry who had succeeded, a comic writer he knew from the shop, and he went down one weekend on the bus and got the writer to tell him how he and his friends had done it while Liddy kept the chasers coming.

Hey, I know how to do it now, *he told them when he got back.* We can do it next month.

The moment was so big it was crushing them. Did they really want to do this?

No, *Mog said, grasping the Lord's hand.* We do it tonight.

Shouting upstairs knocks me this side of waking. I'm out on the landing, standing in a pool of streetlight from the window, craning to hear. One sound, and I'll rush up, adrenaline blazing, but there's nothing, just a silence I could fall into.

I'm not alone.

We stare at each other for nearly a minute, before Cass says, "This is just like that time."

Yeah, I remember. "We crashed after the party, and we heard that banging—"

"Tim had left the kitchen door open when he went for a smoke. Next door's cat managed to knock over the stack of dirty dishes."

"And we all stood still for ages. And we all stared—"

"At Mog, naked. I swear, his cock was erect. Do you remember Susan?"

"She screamed."

We listen for another minute. Standing there makes me feel like I'm peeking between the curtains of someone's window, so I let the yawn sweep through me.

"I can't sleep."

"Still have insomnia, Cass?"

"If I'd known Mog wasn't going to take no for an answer, I'd have brought my pills. And a toothbrush. But—" Cass slips back through her open door, shadows ruffling until I make out her arm beckoning me and the clink of a bottle. "Always prepared."

She's found every lamp in the house and plugged them in, pointing the cones upward so the ceiling is ablaze and the floor is shrouded. Cass curls up in a den of duvets, pillows and four novels that she seems to be reading simultaneously. She takes a swig and passes it to me—a bottle of Jack—and I hover outside the entrance to the den, part of me still fuming at what she did earlier, part not sure what invitation is on offer and whether I want to accept it.

"Do you remember your first story, Liddy? Not an idea for a story, not something you had to work at for weeks. I mean, a story that came to you total and complete, every bit of it, like you were a vessel and it was just flowing through you."

Sure: *Time's Pyre*. I was reading the Lord's revised outline for her novel and it hit me there in the café off Sauchiehall Street, and by the time I surfaced, my pizza was stone cold. "Sure. You?"

"Oh yeah."

She settles into it, a subtle tightening of the muscles that doesn't come over as tension, but relaxing with total focus. "It was my afternoon shift in the bookshop. I saw this fellow over by the science textbooks—I'd met him at a party, but didn't know him well. I'd clocked him as some stoner artist—cute, but after Desmo—you remember Desmo?—I wasn't looking for another landlocked surfer. But he wasn't what I was expecting. He was checking out the astronomy set reading, comparing the indices of the different books, and he looked pretty sharp with a button-down shirt. What's your story? I thought."

Cass pulls her knees up to her chin. "So I went over and talked to him. And we talked all night. His name was Bennett. He wanted to look at stars and had brought a telescope from home to university. His parents were artists living the hippy dream and he lived in a squat and smoked dope because he didn't want to let them down, but he really just wanted to get the marks and work in an observatory.

"And while we were talking, it came to me. All of it. What his story could be, if only he had a little—help. I kinda took him in. I nudged. He moved out of the squat, he found a decent distance from his parents and went hell for leather for astronomy. And he was happy, really happy. He had a story. And I saw it all in that night in a flash."

She makes shadows on the wall, animals, I think, but they loom like monsters. "I really wished the story would have included me. Even now, some days, I still wish that. But that wouldn't have been part of his story. It wouldn't have been true."

She smiles, I think, but I can't tell in the gloom. "I felt lonely after Bennett, but that didn't stop me finding other stories to tell. I guess that's what I loved about all of you. No matter how many Bennetts came after, I never felt lonely with you. You all understood what it was like."

I remember conversations like this years back. Uncorking hearts, no rush to drain the confession. Then and now are smeared together by Jack and the unmoored night and the magic stinking up this house. A pillow rolls away like the rock before a cave and I accept the invitation at last. Butterfly kisses, darting like stitching, every other one a nip, and we're binding ourselves into something bigger. My hand tugs down her tracksuit, it's all sighs. Her breath, mine, there's a rhythm between them, words where there shouldn't be words.

This isn't fair.

It's not fair on any of us, Cass.

So when's it going to be fair?

She cries in tiny gasps, small suffocations. I coo. Lexter's smooth tones.

Love isn't fair, Cass. The sacrifices of love aren't fair. But we embrace them freely.

I'm tired of sacrifices.

It's who you are, Cass. You weren't telling Bennett's story. You were telling your own.

But when does it stop? I want it to stop!

When the story's over, my love. You can finish it anytime you want, but you have to follow it to the end.

And so she kissed his forehead, rose, straightened up. She knew this walk had been done by others before her—Joan of Arc, Anne Boleyn. Her decision limned her with grace. The sacrifices of love made all who could gaze upon her ache, and Liddy's heart was as hard and thin and doomed as church glass before a bomb blast.

She glided up the stairs, while he tripped on every step, helplessly behind her all the way. He pined for her touch, so she blew him a final kiss before she entered the bedroom.

When he got there, she was holding Mog's hand, sitting on the side of the bed. Her head was bent towards his, and he was still grinning away, looking somewhere beyond her, still whispering. Finally, she stood. "I don't understand. Don't you want my sacrifice?"

Then Cass looks at me, and the spell is broken. The understanding on her face is the last seconds before the explosion. "You fucking player."

It didn't work. What the hell was wrong with Mog? "You were *telling* me!"

I can't help it. "Come on, Cass. Drop the outrage. Single, middle-aged Ms Kettle seeks like-minded Mr Pot for home truths—you'd have done the same."

"Fuck you!"

I steel myself: I've seen what happens when her witch switch is flicked. "I'd have offered anyway! *I'd have offered!*"

Beside Mog, the Lord stirs—first time I noticed her there, my brain filtering out images of *them*. She turns on the bedside lamp and in a barely-there voice, "Why do you two always shout in the middle of the night?"

"Don't be cute, Susan," I tell her, tell all of them though Mog is still oblivious. "Let me guess: you all got together a few days ago and planned how you could pin this on me? Payback for *Time's Pyre*? What is this—*A Christmas Carol*? What next, Tim with a pair of crutches and a cheeky urchin's grin and an appeal to my conscience? Well, I'm not going to be the Story Whisperer, okay?"

I look around: what's wrong with this picture? "That's right—*Tim*."

I reach in my jeans pocket: the note's still there. *Once upon a time there was Tim.* "Think I'd forgotten about you?" I knew if I wrote it down, he couldn't get me to forget forever.

But he really doesn't want to be found. Concentrating is hard with Cass screaming and the Lord not far behind and the radios turned down low like locusts feeding, but I close my eyes, and I could be in Walter's office, or on the conference call to Chesney and his team, or just sitting in my studio flat overlooking the English Channel, doesn't matter, they're all the same place behind my eyes, and Lexter takes over.

Once upon a time—the man wanted to disappear—not completely, but to get below the radar, find the cellar in the life of the world and run around unnoticed. His story—

Tim, our Tim, what can I remember? A sister who died. Tim found the body. He suddenly wouldn't speak about her if the conversation was getting too delicate for him, and it feels right, so I follow the groove of that narrative.

He never spoke about her suicide, or the promise he had made to himself. The others never did understand the depression that descended on him, crushing out days and nights at a time, so they never understood why he was so desperate to tell stories. If you knew how they were told, you knew how to escape them, the way his sister could not escape hers. The night after the ritual, while they slept, he kissed each of them lightly on the forehead, even Liddy, and he slipped away from the house, from their lives, from himself.

But he could not slip away from his sister. Her final words clung to him: remember family. *And after years of holding it all at bay, when Susan found a way to track him down, he could not deny that voice any longer. He could not run away from his family—Cass, Susan, all of them—not when they needed him.*

Okay. I'm here.

And while they could never ask him, would not even think of asking him, his sister could: why don't you do it, Timmy?

Stop it.

That insistent voice that badgered him all through childhood, please please please, and just as he had never said no to her then, he could not say no now. He would go to Mog—

"Enough!"

Here, flesh, not ghost. Cass and the Lord stare open-mouthed. He's not looking half bad for a wandering spirit. Hair tied back in a long ponytail, but he's got his Van Dyck nicely trimmed and his acne scarring has gone.

But the gaze is as brutal as ever, and he's fixing me with it. "Seriously, Liddy, you think those tricks will work on me?"

I slap him on the back, make the point that he's solid like the rest of us. "There's got to be a Story Whisperer apparently. You said it, not me."

"Rock, paper, scissors?"

"Well, I was kinda hoping you might just offer. You know, maybe for Cass." And doesn't Tim just blush in front of everyone. "Seeing how you haven't got much else on."

"Good to see you haven't changed, Liddy." His fists clench. We scrapped once: I can't remember who came out of it better. But he lets them go. "There's not much point. Not *now.*"

Cass gives him a look, she's twigged something, but I don't care. "You're right, Tim. Two minutes as the Story Whisperer and we'd all forget there ever was one."

"Yep, that's pretty much it," he says. Sadly, I realize.

"Is that what Mog told you?" Cass says. She's holding Tim's hand as he nods. The penny finally drops. Shit, two steps behind everyone again. Tim has already gone to Mog.

"I'm too far gone, I guess," and the room goes a little hurdy-gurdy. I'm sorry. I tried.

"I know you did, Tim."

I would have done it for you, Cass.

"I know—I—" She's about to say something, but it's lost. She looks around the room, but can't find it.

"My fucking head," I say. What's hit me? "Sorry, Cass, where were we?"

Cass sits on one side of the bed, the Lord the other, Mog between them, whispering, coughing. "I guess that's it."

"Mog dies. No one takes his place. We go back to being the way we were. So it goes." I hate being the bad guy, but if no one else is going to show sense here. "Stories didn't make us happy, did they?"

"No." Cass pulls the pillows around her, protection against the blows to come. "But telling them did."

Do you remember your first story?

Not really. There never was a first story. Not *Time's Pyre,* which only showed I was a crafty thief. No, just that one long slide of my life, unfinished, drifting or careening but never gliding or striding, and if I felt a moment's control by spinning a perfect story inside it, captivating the group in the Lord's front room with another awful tale from growing up on the farm or seducing the world one bestseller at a time, then that was enough for me. A feeling that I knew where this was going—a feeling that fades quicker each time now.

But I remember *our* first story together.

No, *Mog said.* We do it tonight.

They all sat down in their seats. Cass asked if they should move the chairs closer together and hold hands. Yeah, and then we sing folk songs, *Liddy said, and he talked them through the ritual. Like all genuine rituals, there were things that were there to make it feel like something special was happening, the mood-lighting, the framing, and then there was the thing that really did make it special. Everyone was raring, so he cut to the chase.*

I'll start off.

He began with the first time he knocked on the door downstairs. He said he knew he wanted to stay when he saw how cute Susan was in that professional typist's sweater, and he glanced over at her as he said this, but the Lord just nodded. Liddy continued: but as soon as he saw Cass and Tim and Mog, he had second thoughts, such nerds, and Liddy looked over at them as well, but they were Okay. They understood: stories had to be true. And he would have made his excuses that first time and left, but he thought, Look, just give it an evening. And while he sat there, something happened, something between and under what they all were saying in awkward small talk, something about how they really loved writing, how terrified they were they'd never be any good, how they couldn't face the idea that stories would never visit them. It could have been Tim or Mog or any of them saying whatever they were saying, but the same translated sub-titles hung under each one of them. Okay, he thought, give it another week.

And then he handed over to Tim, who picked up the story with the first few weeks of the Circle. He was much funnier than Liddy, a nice dry wit they had not expected in him, dovetailing nicely into the Lord's unexpectedly raunchy accounts of life when the soap opera kicked in after a few months. And on and on, to Mog to Cass back to Liddy, the Circle kept going, letting the story take shape through them, growing larger and lighter, until it was floating beyond them, and they were floating inside of it, all that crazy shit that guy in Coventry had said suddenly making sense to Liddy as they all realized at the same time just how big, how infinite it was in here.

Someone had to open the door. They were just waiting there, the story slowing down as the Lord brought it up to that very evening, all of them scared to speak the next bit. That was how the ritual worked: they wanted the power, they had to make a sacrifice. Liddy hadn't explained that to the others, he was too frightened to, but they all knew it because the story knew it, and everyone knew it should be Liddy, it was his idea, he should open that door. But he stalled, just long enough, and while he waited, Mog might have thought, Well, why not me?

Cass is waiting. The Lord, too, Tim, frozen in the snapshot of a moment. They all would have taken my place. I can't hide from that anymore.

"Ah, shit." Light pins and streaks my vision, like decades of night sky spinning to catch up with me. "Shit, shit. This isn't me. I'm not the hero."

But why not? And while part of me is paralyzed with dread, Lexter is relieved to have a story to tell. I take both of Mog's hands, and in a single jerk, pull him to his feet. The Lord protests but I cradle him there, and damn, doesn't Mog just smirk like he knows that it was always going to end up this way.

"Let's get this over with. What do I have to do? Shit, do we really have to hold hands?"

Fucking Peter Pan and Wendy. Well, I guess after this I get to be Peter, but that's all I get to think as the light and sound go nauseous and Mog takes me to this other place. Instinctively, I let Lexter take over.

He looked down—sand—then up—beach—then out—sea.

Mog was kneeling down at the waterline, waves sweeping past him, pulling at his shoes with the undertow. It was a prayerful pose before a sun that was setting, always setting, a permanent fix of evening. The sky was all repose. As the waves crashed, he could just catch the chitter of words, radio static but not so harsh or insistent, inviting instead, waiting for him to plunge in, dive deep and see what he might find.

He had swum in the sea—well, never this sea, never swimming as such, but the feeling was the same—and so had Cass and Tim and the Lord and the guy in Coventry and all the circles that had discovered this magic. Each took their cupful, pursed themselves against its salt, and were always surprised when the second or third sip turned sweet. They took their share of the sea, and came back for another cupful, and another.

But the sea only seemed infinite. And while a cupful was not much, there were cupfuls and cupfuls, and at some point, the tide did not reach as high, and at some point, there were salt licks and a pan that was emptied and cracked, and at some point, there were no more cups. Or would have been—if not for the Story Whisperers.

Someone had to give back. Someone had to replenish the sea. Those new stories had to come from somewhere.

How did Mog—who had never lived away from his mother's in Cumbernauld before uni, who did not have a passport, whose own writing did not travel to fantastic places—find all the stories to pour back into the sea? But that was not how it worked— the sea knew what to do. It could fill itself, but it needed a pipe, a vessel. All the Whisperer had to do was to renounce and let go. That was how the exchange, the ecology worked.

"I'm not kneeling," he told Mog. "And does it have to be a sea? That just seems to— I mean, what about space? Stars? These are the voyages et cetera."

Mog was so intent on his whispering that Liddy was not sure he could hear. "So what do you need me to do?" And then, out to the sea, shouting, "Come on, what do I do?"

He walked out into the water, up to his calves. It was colder than he expected. He held his arms out, Take me.

Heroes may only get a single moment to choose. He was ready. His life rushed past but it tugged no more strongly than the waves around him. Everything must have been leading to this moment. Do it.

"Come on!"

And he held there for a minute, the waves going back and forth. The air chilled but the sun was not any lower.

And then the story faltered.

Shit. What if—maybe we got this wrong. What if *none of us* can be the Whisperer?

My arms collapse to my side. "I don't get it," I whisper. "It was always meant to be me, right? I took *Time's Pyre* from them, now it's my turn to give back. That's the way this is supposed to go?"

But the sea isn't listening. "Hey! I'm not asking. *I'm not asking!*"

I'm crazy now. Right out of nowhere, the way I used to get on those tick-tock afternoons on my step-dad's farm, I'm blind with this anger, and when I see again, it's someone else looking out, someone that my long run of assistants and ex-girlfriends put up with until I made a stupid joke about Jekyll and Hyde and my face was slapped and the door slammed. I run into the water, chasing God knows what, but I'll know it when I find the fucker, and when it's deep enough, I dive, come back up and slurp air, and I dive, go deeper and deeper, following the slope of the bottom down, deep, deep, deep, won't get away from me, uh uh.

I open my mouth, and gulp. *He stood up from the bed, put his hand over Mog's mouth and started speaking. No more whispering. He would give the sea a story to reckon with. But the Lord woke up and started clawing at his hand, and Cass was behind him, and someone else at his arm, and they pulled him off Mog.*

I gag on the brine spit it out. Swim deeper then. Breathe in. *They waited Mog's dying out. They paced the house until it got worse, and it got worse quicker than anyone expected. Soon they were all gathered around him, and Liddy started talking about the first time he met him, and then he was* telling *them about Mog, and they chipped in. The story of Mog took hold, and they were a Circle again, only this time, when the moment came, Liddy would step forward—but the circuit broke suddenly, the Lord shook off his hand. Who are you to tell his story? she yelled, and her grief swept away the magic.*

I'm coughing now. No, drowning. Stupid. I've done this a thousand times. I'll find the story that works. This time: *He abandoned them. He picked a new group, acolytes eager to spend time with THE Lexter Manson, and he bided his time, until they were ready to make a Circle. He was on the verge of stepping forward—but one of the kids beat him to it, having innocuously taken notes all this time, studying Liddy's moves, and so the other sacrifice was accepted instead.*

And so on. Each version, fucked and fucked and I'm sinking in all the stories that I can't get to work. Drowning is losing oneself. I stop being the protagonist, I give in and decide meat is meat and let the bottom-feeders feed on my hubris. One last gulp for the weight I need—

Only I'm rising. A hand on my scruff. I kick feebly in protest, but he's got stronger strokes.

He. *Mog*. I can't look up from the sand—all those stories are coming out of me, vomiting up from deep in my gut—but I know it's him.

"The. Others. Won't. Thank. You." That's all I can manage before I'm spewing again. "Did you get it?"

His voice is weird, but only because it's so normal. He looks weird too because he's just standing there, like an ordinary guy. I do look up now and I almost cry when I see him. Mog—it's really him, and I realize how much I've missed him.

"What? What was I—" I breathe again. "What was I supposed to do?"

"There you go," he says, and he takes a little whisky tumbler he's palmed in his hand, squeezes my hair so it runs into it, enough for a sip.

I push his hand away. "Knock yourself out."

"I can't drink this," he says cheerily, and we are full-blown Alice In Wonderland now. "This is yours."

He hands me back the tumbler, and I'm so weak, I do what the man who's saved my life tells me. The water is that yuck between green and brown, but when I hold it up to the everlasting light, for a moment, doesn't it just sparkle.

So I take a final cupful.

When I wake, Cass is curled on the floor alongside. The light coming through the curtains is unequivocally morning. I teeter downstairs to where the Lord is making toast and coffee, but before I go into the kitchen, I try the front door handle. No electric shocks. It turns, the door opens and I can walk out and away anytime I want. But that's not how this one goes, of course.

The Lord frowns when she sees me, but passes a mug. Black with sugar: I feel strangely delighted she remembers. We both carry the coffee and toast upstairs, where Cass is yawning behind a curtain of tangled hair. I remember I've got something in my pocket, and when I feel the folded paper, I realize that Tim is still around, somewhere. We drink and munch in silence.

"Hey," I finally say, "want to hear a story?"

The Lord allows a smile—a small one, but it makes Cass giggle.

I wait for Lexter to start—but his voice is silent. Wow. I'm going to have to do this one raw. So I recount how the Lord came to me at a reading in Waterstones to let me know about Mog and how I was convinced that it was part of a trap to get me to take over as the Story Whisperer and how I did everything I could to avoid the inevitable until I gave in the only way I knew how, being the bloody hero. Only to find out that this wasn't what was supposed to happen.

"I never did understand your stories." Tim shuffles in his seat, uncomfortable at visibility. "Just spit it out: which one of us is going to be the Story Whisperer?"

"Not one of us," I say, but I don't grin the way I usually would to annoy people. Then, to the Lord: "Was that the cunning plan? That I would find a solution?"

She shook her head. "I'm not sure. Maybe Mog did think you'd be the one to come up with a way out of this. You just needed a little persuading."

"And you? Did you think I could do it?"

She doesn't say, and my heart's a little more dented. But hey—we're here, we're drinking coffee together, and there's no one else from twenty years ago, hell, not even from five years ago, I can say that about.

"Okay," Cass says slowly. "So who becomes the Story Whisperer?"

"Let me tell you."

Only five minutes late this time.

I feel my hand being squeezed gently—so gently, I let my attention take him in. I don't look at Tim until I know he's all there. He's looking squarely at me, not noticing or caring that others in the coffee shop are glancing at him, aware he's there. That's a change. That's a nice change.

We don't talk about what we've been up to. I quickly learnt that's not what you do with Tim, but you find out what's been happening to him sideways. This time, it's the number of posters around town for the next Avengers movie, which means that he's been going to movies, which means he's doing more than just thinking about places to eat and places to sleep. Baby steps, but he's trying.

And, of course, the fact he's here. "We got a few hours," he says, "if you want to see it. I checked the times."

"That's alright. It'll be out on video when I'm back."

"We can do a night of it. Iron Man, Captain America, Avengers. The others will be up for it."

"Just like old times."

Both of us know that we never stayed up late watching movies, but it's accepted shorthand. "You organise it then, Tim. It'll take you all that time to pin Liddy down."

"He has to come?"

I pout: *be nice*. "Are you ready then?" he asks me.

"Are you? You don't have to do this."

"I want to do this."

He says this and he isn't embarrassed—so I take a chance. I reach over and kiss him on the lips. He stays put. No one forgets anything.

Who'd have guessed?

We take our time going to the house, walking in the unexpected sunshine. We get there in the late afternoon, and see the changeover of the carers Liddy has hired. Tim thinks it's pretty shabby that Liddy's not there full-time, but I'm relieved none of us have to worry about what could happen to him cooped up in there. Anyway, Mrs McNiven, the evening shift, is lovely and insists on fixing bolognese for us. Tim says yes, but I have to turn her down—best to do this on an empty stomach, I'm told.

Upstairs, Susan is starting to surface. Tim said she stopped whispering yesterday and was starting to mumble words that could be made out: *Mog* mainly, but she didn't seemed distressed. I haven't seen her since the evening of the funeral, and I'm surprised at how well she's looking despite everything. I never thought this could be as kind to a body as sleeping, but thinking about the last few years for her, heck, the last few decades, maybe this isn't such a hardship after all.

"Ready?"

I nod at Tim. "Susan, it's Cass."

She groans at first, but then makes a sound that could be a sleepy *hi*. I formally summon her: "It's time. Alright? Time to come back."

I remember that night of the funeral, six months ago, downstairs in the front room. Liddy was up here, in the bed next door. He insisted on taking the first shift as Story Whisperer, and for a minute, it went through everyone's head that maybe we could just leave him. It was tempting—but then Susan said, "Of course not, that's not what the Circle does," and she ignored Tim's suggestion of drawing straws and put herself down next.

We discovered the hard way between Liddy and Susan that it's not good to leave a gap, so I kiss Susan's forehead and go and get into my pyjamas. Everthing's set up in the room next door. "Wait for me?"

"Lifetime habit," he says. I know how hard it will be for him to stay here, tethered to me. I know he'll run off for periods, and we won't talk about it afterwards. But that's alright. The world is full of secret stories, and Tim deserves his own. We've got ours, unearthed from the bottom of the trunk of our lives, and there are so many more down there.

When I lie down, it's not like sleep. It's like losing focus on one thing. It's finding out there's so many other things to notice—

—it's gradually winnowing down all the things that needed to be noticed, spoken, given to the sea, to the one thing. The smell of pasta. Bolognese.

"Welcome home, Susan."

The carer feeds me slowly while Tim brings me up to speed on people and the world and movies he's seen. I don't take it in. I must seem rude, and despite how tired I feel, that bothers me—but it's a nice kind of being bothered. It means I care. Giving a shit means I'm home again.

They leave me alone and I lie awake, trying to remember what it was like. I can't. I can only remember blocks of stuff that must have passed through me. An old refugee's fight to get her daughter citizenship. The roller-coaster season of an unlikely championship club. Wow, my dreams are going to be something fierce for weeks. Then another two years before I get to find out what it's like again. The thought exhausts me, but it doesn't sadden me.

But I don't fall asleep. The weight of the bed feels all wrong. Ah—he's not beside me.

"Sweet Mog," I say aloud, but I don't cry. Quite suddenly, the walls that were there aren't there, and I can hear wind in the distance. "What will I do without your story?"

I don't know. But I don't cry, and I don't grieve. What will I make of myself? I don't know. But it will be something new—

And that's a story for another day.

Contributing Authors

Fergus Bannon writes fast paced thrillers which take a jaded and heretical view of what we think we know of science and technology. His latest is *Leviathan's Fall*. Following graduation, he ran away to sea, his merchant shipping line taking him to some of the choicer trouble spots around the world. Rich though the seafaring life was, it could also be rather dangerous. After having a run-in with a death squad in South America (the basis of a key scene in his thriller *Heretic*), and then nearly getting his throat slit in Jamaica, he began to harbour doubts about his long term prospects. A hurricane in the Atlantic, and a major fire on board ship in the Pacific, only reinforced this concern. Nursing an ambition to live until the age of forty, he therefore came ashore and eventually became a professor of clinical physics. Fergus Bannon is a pen name for his fiction, but he has also recently published a non-fiction book called *Science for Heretics* under his real world name of Barrie Condon.

TJ Berg is a molecular and cellular biologist working and writing in Sweden. She is a graduate of the Odyssey Writing Workshop. She spent two years in Glasgow, where she was a member of the Glasgow SF Writer's Circle. She still misses Glasgow, especially when she smells fresh cut, wet grass. She can be found on the web at www.infinity-press.com.

Ruth EJ Booth is a BSFA Award winning writer and lapsed northerner living in Glasgow. She is a regular columnist for Shoreline of Infinity, and her non-fiction has appeared in The Independent and Kerrang! magazine. Her stories and poetry appeared in anthologies from NewCon Press and Fox Spirit Books, Far Horizons magazine, The Speculative Book and more. She has variously been a science historian and a shopgirl, a nun and a bartender, and she used to photograph musicians talking for a living. Sometimes she likes to point her BSFA award at the cats, make pew-pew noises, and dream of her next life as a librarian space outlaw. This poem is for C, inspired by A, and written in remembrance of light.

Jim Campbell wrote comic scripts for 2000AD and taught scripting at Duncan Lunan's SF writing course. He used to dress in clothes which were up to a thousand years out of fashion and run around muddy fields, hitting people with bits of iron. He called this historical re-enactment. He now hides in his flat, cackling to himself and clutching weapons while waiting for the zombie apocalypse. He calls this research for his next novel.

Eliza Chan tried to join the GSFWC in high school but it was full of bearded men talking about Doctor Who and her dad thought it was a cult. In university she rejoined the cult of geekdom and regularly attended meetings to have her work justifiable savaged. She has since lived in Japan, Vietnam and England, improved a little in her writing and joined writing groups wherever she goes. Eliza writes about modernised folklore, dark fantasy and mad women in the attic. Her work has been published in *Fantasy Magazine*, *Lontar*, *Holdfast* and *Winter Tales* (Fox Spirit). Follow her @elizawchan or www.elizawchan.wordpress.com.

Michael Cobley, SF writer—half-Scottish, half-English, quarter-Irish, and all maverick! Author of proto-grimdark fantasy epic, the *Shadowkings* trilogy, who then retooled his brain for the chill wildernesses of deep space in order to produce the *Humanity's Fire* trilogy, an epic space opera involving Scots, Russians and Scandinavians, as well as a concatenation of strange aliens and stranger AIs. Now awaiting the paperback publication of *Ancestral Machines*, a senses-shattering saga centred on the Warcage, a megastructure built on a frankly mind-meltingly vast scale!

Training in maths and physics may explain **Elsie WK Donald**'s pathological fixation on the internal logic of stories, while a career in nuclear medicine technology has introduced her to people at their best and bravest. Elsie has been a member of the GSFWC since its inception and won the Glasgow Herald science fiction short story competition in 1989. She writes science fiction and fantasy—and the occasional psychological horror—if putting it on paper is the only way to get it out of her head.

Hal Duncan is the author of *Vellum* and *Ink*, more recently *Testament*, and numerous short stories, poems, essays, even a few musicals. Homophobic hatemail once dubbed him "THE.... Sodomite Hal Duncan!!" (sic), and you can find him online at www.halduncan.com or at his Patreon for readings, revelling in that role.

Amal El-Mohtar has received the Locus Award and been a Nebula Award finalist for her short fiction, and won the Rhysling Award for poetry three times. She is the author of *The Honey Month*, a collection of poetry and prose written to the taste of twenty-eight different kinds of honey, and contributes reviews to the *LA Times*, *NPR Books* and *Tor.com*. Her fiction has appeared most recently in *Lightspeed*, *Uncanny Magazine*, and is forthcoming in *The Starlit Wood* anthology from Saga Press. She divides her time and heart between Ottawa and Glasgow. Find her at amalelmohtar.com or on Twitter @tithenai.

Elaine Gallagher has been a member of GSFWC for over ten years, and her stories have appeared in *The Speculative Book* anthology and *The Queen's Head* and *Freak Circus* magazines. She writes reviews, interviews and recently an editorial for Interzone magazine. Elaine also writes poetry and performs in spoken word events in Glasgow and Edinburgh, and her short film *High Heels Aren't Compulsory* won Best Scottish Short at the Scottish Queer International Film Festival.

Gary Gibson was born. He breathes, eats, walks, sleeps, and engages in a variety of culturally acceptable social activities. On occasion he has written books, which have been published. He has publicly stated he hates vampire stories, and was thereby cursed to write one.

Stewart Horn is a professional musician and amateur author, poet, photographer and film-maker based on the West coast of Scotland. His work has appeared in various online and print publications and has been podcast in *Lovecraft Ezine podcast, Tales to Terrify* and *Pseudopod*. He is a member of the Glasgow Science Fiction Writers' Circle and the British Fantasy Society, for whom he also writes reviews. He blogs infrequently at stewartguitar.wordpress.com.

Matthew Horsley has been writing since his teens, but only got published last year at the grand old age of 38. This is his second published story, if you are very persuasive he might even agree that it's his best. He lives in Glasgow with a number of entirely imagined creatures including a manticore, a three-legged dire wolf, and an over-friendly basilisk.

Ian Hunter is a children's novelist, short story writer, and poet as well as being a Director of the Scottish writer's collective, Read Raw, and poetry editor for the British Fantasy Society.

Cameron Johnston's fiction has appeared in *The Lovecraft eZine, Buzzymag*, and several other magazines and anthologies. He is a student of Historical European Martial Arts, and when not reading far too much he can be found swinging swords, exploring ancient stone circles and ruined castles, and eyeing dragon-shaped hills with great suspicion. His musings can be found on Twitter at @CamJohnston.

Kenneth Kelly once lived in Dublin and worked at the Gate Theatre but now lives in Glasgow where he studied creative writing at Glasgow University before graduating in 2016.

William King lives in Prague, Czech Republic with his lovely wife Radka and his sons Dan and William Karel. He has been a professional author and games developer for over a quarter of a century. He is the creator of Gotrek and Felix for Black Library. He is also the author of the World of Warcraft novel *Illidan*. Over a million of his books are in print in English. He has been nominated for the David Gemmell Legend Award. His short fiction has appeared in *Year's Best SF* and *Best of Interzone*. He has twice won the Origins Awards For Game Design. His hobbies include role-playing games and MMOs as well as travel.

Duncan Lunan is a full-time author and speaker with emphasis on astronomy, spaceflight and science fiction. His earlier books are *Man and the Stars, New Worlds for Old, Man and the Planets, Starfield, Science Fiction by Scottish Writers* (edited), and since 2012, *Children from the Sky, The Stones and the Stars,* and *Incoming Asteroid! With Time Comes Concord and Other Stories* was published in 2012 and an enlarged, illustrated edition will be published in September 2016 by Shoreline of Infinity as *The Elements of Time*. A contributor to 31 other books, he's published over 1230 articles and 37 stories, including ten for the comic strip *Lance McLane* in the Daily Record in the 1980s. He was SF critic of the Glasgow Herald, 1971-85, and ran the paper's SF short story competition, 1986-92. Currently he reviews for *Interzone, Shoreline of Infinity* and *Concatenation*; his regular astronomy column, The Sky Above You, appears in various magazines including *Jeff Hawke's Cosmos*, for which he writes notes on the classic Jeff Hawke strip cartoon as it's being reprinted. After 30 years in Glasgow he returned in 2012 to his home town of Troon, Ayrshire, where he lives with his wife Linda and chairs Troon Writers as well as the Astronomers of the Future Club, an astronomy society for beginners.

Brian M Milton is a short, rumpled, writer of short, rumpled, fiction who is constantly at war with his sense of whimsy. He would like to apologise for its breakout into this story and assures the world that he is working hard to keep it contained in the future. He has had slightly more sensible stories published in *KZine, Caledonia Dreamin', The Speculative Book* and *Sein und Werden*, amongst others. He can be found, rarely any more sensible, on the Twitters @munchkinstein.

Michael Mooney was born in Glasgow, in 1964, graduated in Law from that University in 1985, and lived a fairly blameless life before attending Duncan Lunan's "Science Fiction and Writing" night class. From there he joined the GSFWC, and contributed many stories to the merciless dissection of his fellows. He left the circle in 1994 when he re-located to Newcastle, and kept in touch with many of the members who had become fast friends. He works in IT Consultancy, writes intermittently, and this is his first SF short story in almost 20 years.

Peter Morrison has always written. For many years he wrote about music and culture for *re:mote induction*. This led to the role of promoter and DJ for in:duced, which included monthly events at Glasgow's CCA and the blink and you miss it re:mote core records. Peter has previously been published in *Mythaxis, Weaponizer, Jack Move* and *Giant Chicken Stories*, along with the *Telling of Tales* and *Dark Fiction* podcasts. You can find him at www.remotevoices.co.uk and @remotevoices

Theodore W Moses was a GSFWC regular in the mid-1990s, during which time he was central to a nefarious plan to game the New British Space Opera market. He now resides in legend and fond memory.

Word shaman, lapsed scientist, research business manager, **Richard Mosses**, has had a number of short stories published in magazines and anthologies like this one, but this one is his favourite. You can find him at www.khaibit.com.

Anya Penfold was a brief attending member of the GSFWC but ran away due to a combination of social anxiety and the inability to offer insightful critiques, which makes this whole thing both humbling and acutely embarrassing, really. As you can tell from that, she is very British, despite being a Scot. She has short stories in a couple of other anthologies out this year, namely *Outliers of Speculative Fiction* and *Women in Practical Armour*, and plans to self-publish a novel in the autumn of 2016, this being the fourth time she's felt she's written one good enough, and quite possibly the fourth time she bottles it at the last minute instead. When not writing speculative fiction, fantasy or horror, Anya is an artist, subsistence gardener and wine-maker, housekeeper / landlady, secretary, and sometimes sleeps.

Phil Raines lives in Linlithgow, Scotland and has been a proud member of the Glasgow Science Fiction Writers Circle for 26 years.

Jim Steel is the book reviews editor for *Interzone*. He also reviews for *Vector* and has been a columnist for *SF Eye*, the *Scotsman's* science fiction critic, and a juror for the British Fantasy Awards. His complexly-structured literary metafictions frequently receive honourable mentions in Year's Best anthologies and occasionally win awards. "The Crock of Shet" is not one of his complexly-structured literary metafictions.

Heather Valentine is a graduate from the University of Glasgow's Creative Writing MLitt. While on this programme she was co-editor of the *Mnemosyne Anthology*, a collection of genre fiction short stories. She is currently working on her first novel.

Louise Welsh is the author of seven novels, most recently in 2015 *Death is a Welcome Guest*. She has written many short stories and articles and is a regular radio broadcaster. Louise has also written libretti for opera including *Ghost Patrol*, which won a Southbank Sky Arts Award and *The Devil Inside*, which toured to critical acclaim in 2016. Louise has received several awards and international fellowships, including an honorary doctorate from Edinburgh Napier University and an honorary fellowship on the University of Iowa's International Writing Program. She is Professor of Creative Writing at the University of Glasgow.

Neil Williamson's debut novel, The Moon King, was nominated for the BSFA Award and the British Fantasy Society Award. His short fiction has been collected in *The Ephemera* (2006) and *Secret Language* (2016). "Foreign Bodies" is based on a story abandoned in 1999 and recently unearthed on an obsolete ZIP drive. Truly, time passes in mysterious ways.